CRAVING CECILIA

The Aces' Sons

By Nicole Jacquelyn

Craving Cecilia
Copyright © ©2020 by Nicole Jacquelyn
Print Edition
All Rights Reserved

No part of this book may be reproduced or transmitted in any form or by any means, electronic or mechanical, including photocopying, recording, or by any information storage and retrieval system without the written permission of the author, except for the use of brief quotations in a book review.

This is a work of fiction. Names, characters, businesses, places, events, and incidents are either the products of the author's imagination or used in a fictitious manner. Any resemblance to actual persons, living or dead, or actual events is purely coincidental. The author acknowledges the trademarked status and trademark owners of various products referenced in this work of fiction, which have been used without permission. The publication/use of these trademarks is not authorized, associated with, or sponsored by the trademark owners.

Dedication

To my kids,
who make everything in life worth doing.
Mom loves you.

Chapter 1

CECILIA

I'D BEEN TERRIFIED before, the kind of fear that paralyzes your thought processes so completely that your body moves with pure muscle memory to keep you safe. So, I guess I was more prepared than most for the moment that gunshots erupted downstairs.

It still took me a moment to comprehend what was happening, drawn out seconds where I sat there in disbelief, a million memories running through my head and my heartbeat pounding in my ears. It was only seconds, though, and then I was silently standing from the rocker, putting my hand on the arm to stop any movement, and racing toward the closet.

The sound of my best friend Liv screaming made me pause in my mad dash, but only for a split second, when the scream was cut off with another gunshot. I couldn't help her anymore, not that I could've in the first place. I had no idea how many people were shooting. Growing up in the company of outlaw bikers had taught me a lot of lessons, but one of the most important ones was, if you weren't sure of your odds, lay low until you were. I looked down at the baby sleeping against my chest. I'd also been taught that protecting children always came first.

Grabbing my purse and bag off the dresser, I glanced around the room, making sure that I hadn't left any sign of my presence. I wasn't even supposed to be there. I'd planned on staying home with a TV dinner and uninterrupted episodes of my favorite shows for Thanksgiving. I grit my teeth as the sound of more gunshots filtered up the stairs.

I needed to get moving.

I'd given Liv so much shit for using this closet as overflow for her main closet, but I was thankful as hell as I stepped inside and saw the rows and rows of clothing. Finding a particularly full rack, I pressed in between a large wool cape-looking thing and a floor length fur coat. Who wore fur anymore? Jesus. As soon as I'd put everything down along the wall, I turned off the light and climbed into the space, pulling the coats in front of me.

It didn't take long for someone to come into the bedroom. I'd known it wouldn't. I'd assume that if you shot someone, you'd want to make sure you hadn't left any witnesses. The person was trying to be quiet, but houses had a way of spilling their secrets, if you knew what to listen for. The soft squeak of the door hinges and the swish of steps on carpet made the hair on the back of my neck stand on end. Then, the closet door was open.

I took a slow, steady breath and rested my hand on the pistol I kept in my purse. One second passed. Then another. The light came on and I stopped breathing.

Then, with a click of the switch, the light was off again and the door shut.

I closed my eyes and kissed the tiny head tucked beneath my chin. Thank God, she'd stayed asleep.

We stayed curled in that closet for a while, but I knew at some point, I'd need to get us out of there. I couldn't hear anyone in the house, but there was a good chance they were still around. We were secluded up here, and whoever had done the shooting probably thought they had plenty of time to do whatever it was they'd come to do.

Pulling out my phone, I scrolled through the contacts. Most of the time, I loved that there was some distance between me and my family. This was not one of those times. I turned the volume on my phone down as low as it could go and listened to it ring and ring, finally going to voicemail.

"Shit," I breathed. Of course my mom didn't have her phone with her. It was Thanksgiving. She was probably already half drunk and had set it down somewhere. She wouldn't even notice I'd called until tomorrow when the cleanup started, and she found it sitting on the edge of the stove or something.

Scrolling past my dad's number—I was pretty sure he wasn't using that throw-away anymore – I pressed send again.

After one ring, my brother answered. Dependable Cam.

"Who's this?" he barked.

"It's me," I replied, relief making the words come out a little shaky. Just hearing his voice bolstered me, even though I knew he was a thousand miles away, and no help whatsoever.

"CeeCee?"

"Yeah, is Mom with you?"

"Everything okay?" he asked. I could hear the noise changing in the background as he moved.

"Not even a little," I replied quietly.

"Fuck," he muttered, his voice lower than it had been before.

Then, my mom's voice filled the line. "Cecilia, what's wrong?"

"I've got a bit of a situation," I said, downplaying it. I don't know why I still did that. Habit, I guess. A lifetime of hiding my true thoughts and feelings, especially those that would worry my parents, didn't disappear in one phone call.

"What kind of a situation?" my mom asked worriedly.

"Dad with you?"

"He's right here, hold on." The sound changed when she put the phone on speaker.

"I'm here," my dad said. "What's going on?"

"I'm at a friend's house," I replied, rocking a little as the baby started to stir. "And I'm pretty sure they're dead."

"Say what?" he snapped.

"I was up in their daughter's room, rocking her to sleep, and I heard gunshots downstairs," I whispered. "Then my friend was screaming, more gunshots, then quiet."

"Oh, shit," my mom mumbled.

"Where are you now?" my dad asked, his tone changing to the unnatural calm that always presented itself when one of us was in danger or hurt. I'd heard it countless times growing up, but it had never comforted me as much as it did right then.

"I'm hiding in the closet."

"You think it's a good spot to stay?"

"Well, I'm behind a massive fur coat," I said, pushing it back from my face a little. "And they've already come in here looking and didn't find me."

"Christ," he hissed.

"But I've got a week-old baby with me," I said, trying to keep the panic out of my voice. "So, this isn't a long-term solution."

"Yeah, no shit."

"Holy hell," my mom said. "That poor baby."

"Yeah, I know," I replied, rubbing my cheek over the top of her head. Her world had changed in an instant. I swallowed back the bile rising in my throat.

"I'll send someone to get you," my dad said, ignoring the side conversation between my mom and I. "Text me the address."

"I don't know the address. I'll drop a pin and send it."

"I've got no fuckin' clue what that means," he snapped.

"Cam can help you," I said with a sigh. "Please don't tell anyone else about this, okay?"

"What?" my mom asked. "Why?"

"Because I don't need everyone all up in my shit," I replied, trying to keep my voice low and calm. It was a familiar argument, even though the circumstances were far from normal. I'd escaped from that life for a lot of reasons, but leaving behind the people who'd talked shit about me both to my face and behind my back was one of the main factors.

Did I think the whole club would come down, guns blazing? Absolutely. I was one of theirs. A club member's kid, who'd grown up before their eyes. Did I want them to come down here with their snide comments and dirty looks? Not even a little bit.

"Do you have someone close that can come?" I asked my dad, leaning against the wool coat behind me, then jerking back upright when the hanger squeaked along the rod it was hanging on. "Because I'm not sure how long I'll be able to stay in here."

"Yeah," he replied. "I've got some people that owe me favors. You got a piece on you?"

"Always," I replied. "But I have no idea how many people are in the house."

"You know of a safer place you can hide?"

"I could probably find one," I said, reaching up to wipe at the sweat on my face. Jesus, it was warm in there. "But this house has cameras everywhere. If they're in the office, they'd see me moving around."

"They got cameras, they can go back through them and see that you're in the motherfucking house," my dad replied. "Fuck."

I closed my eyes in defeat. He was right. After a couple silent seconds, he spoke again.

"We're gonna assume that they aren't doin' that because they haven't found you yet," he said, his voice grim. "They decide to do that, you stay put. Take 'em out one by one as they come through the door. Don't fuckin' miss, Cecilia."

"I won't," I replied around the frog in my throat. I was so fucked.

"Your mom's got our shit packed and we'll be on the road as soon as I can line up someone to come get you out. I'll keep this shit quiet for now because there's nothin' the boys can do at this point, but if I have to pull the others in, I'll do it. Don't care if that pisses you off."

"Okay," I said through gritted teeth, trying hard not to cry. Crying wouldn't help the situation. Crying would only upset my mom more than she already was. Crying would make me lose focus. It would make noise. And frankly, it was a waste of fucking time.

"We're coming, baby," my mom said, her voice firm. "You stay safe until we get there."

"Send me those coordinates," my dad ordered. "I love you."

"Love you, too," I whispered.

"Love you more than your dad does!" my mom called right before the call disconnected.

I rolled my eyes and sniffed as quietly as I could as I sent location pin to my brother Cameron's phone. After he replied with a thumbs up, I set it down next to my thigh and shifted, trying to get comfortable. It wasn't easy in the confined space.

There weren't any cameras in this closet, I knew that much, but I still couldn't move anything to make the space more accommodating. If the gunman came back, I couldn't take the chance that they'd notice if something was out of place. God, how did I get myself into messes like this?

I was a barber. I owned a condo. I liked to eat white cheddar popcorn and binge watch entire seasons of television shows on my time off. I hadn't been laid in… longer than I wanted to contemplate. I paid my taxes and drove like an old lady. So, how in the hell did I end up hiding from a fucking shooter in the closet of a house that I could never in a million years afford, or even want to live in?

Liv was the one who wanted more, who liked exciting shit and was always reaching. She's the one who had grabbed the attention of the guy who owned this place and somehow married him. And, yeah, Cane seemed like an okay guy. He was into some shady shit, I was sure, because he never seemed to work, but always seemed to have endless supplies of cash, but he was good to Liv. He freaking worshipped her, and because of that, he'd always treated me like family. So, even if he wasn't my favorite person and something about him always rubbed me the wrong way—who was I to judge? I lived the straight and narrow myself, but I hadn't grown up that way. My entire family, who I loved and respected, lived a life that kept them perpetually on the FBI's radar.

As the baby started to stir, I pulled a little green pacifier out of the bag next to me and popped it in her mouth. She was wet, I could tell by how squishy her diaper was, but changing her was going to be a problem. She hated being undressed and made that known in a variety of ways, not the least of which was screaming at the top of her lungs. I laid her on the floor between my legs and ran my finger over my bottom lip, a nervous habit that I'd never been able to break. If I left her in the wet diaper, she was going to scream anyway.

I was just going to have to move as fast as humanly possible and hope I could have her dressed again before she got loud. Pressing the button on my phone screen, I used the little bit of light to see what I was doing. Even with everything happening around us, I couldn't help the way my lips twitched when her little hands shot up to her face to hold the pacifier in her mouth, her fists completely uncoordinated and awkward as they pushed at her chin and nose. She was going to be hungry soon.

Grabbing a diaper out of the bag, I unfolded it and pressed the tabs out so they'd be ready when I needed them. It was kind of funny. When I'd first seen the newborn diapers, I hadn't been able to imagine them actually fitting on a baby, but she practically swam in the things. If the tabs didn't overlap at her belly, her legs were so skinny that she'd pee right out of the leg holes.

"Let's do this," I whispered as I unwrapped her.

Thankfully, the little gown she was wearing meant easy access to her diaper, and I shoved it up and put the clean diaper under her quickly.

Then, as fast as I could, I unwrapped the wet diaper, slid it out from under her and closed the clean diaper around her. Before she could let out a whimper, I pulled the gown back down and rewrapped her blanket.

I let out a long breath while I wrapped the dirty diaper into a little ball and stashed it behind me. I'd conquered one small mountain, at least. The phone screen went dark again as I picked her up and snuggled her back against my chest, turning so that my back was against the wall. It was hot in there, but at least we had a little space to move, and I'd remembered to grab her bag off the dresser. It could've been worse. We could've been trying to hide outside in the cold. That really would've sucked. Or we could've been stuck in a crawlspace, like my aunt when my grandparents were killed when she was a teenager, waiting for a man she'd just met to come rescue her. I felt a new respect for her as I curled my legs under me. The waiting was excruciating, and I wasn't sixteen years old like she had been.

"We'll be okay," I whispered as she jerked her legs inside the blanket. "My dad is taking care of things, and he's a good guy to have on our side."

My phone lit up beside me and I opened it to a text message from an unknown number.

It's me, Bumblebee. Got someone headed your way. Stay put until they get there.

I will, I texted back.

I leaned my head back against the wall and closed my eyes, relief hitting me hard. My dad was the only person in the world who'd ever called me that, and it had been years since he had. He'd sent in the cavalry and I just had to wait it out. God, I hoped they got here before things went to hell.

It was pretty telling that I'd called my dad and not the police. I grimaced. I'd left the club behind, but I guess the lessons I'd learned hadn't been so easy to forget. It was instinctive to take care of things in-house, to keep the government—and more importantly, the police—in the dark. Maybe if I'd been at home, or a public place, I would've called 911. But I knew in my gut that Cane was into some shit that I didn't want any part of, and calling in the police would put me right in the middle of it. In the eyes of the law, I'd be tied to him, and so would the tiny human that was currently scratching her razor sharp nails against my collarbone.

No, it was better if I could just get the fuck out of there before anyone knew what had happened. If we could disappear without anyone the wiser, we'd be in the clear. We could leave all of this shit behind us.

I hated the idea of starting over somewhere new, but I'd do it. I could work anywhere. Most of my business was military, but I could find a different place to set up shop. The east coast had a ton of bases, and I could probably find somewhere cheaper to live than San Diego anyway. North Carolina was on the coast, and I was pretty sure that I could find a place there for a lot less than I was spending to live here. I had plenty of cash, and I could easily sell my condo.

I let myself fall down that rabbit hole, planning long-term instead of thinking about the fact that we were stuck in a closet, and I had no idea when help would come or if they'd be there before we were found. Dying inside that closet was not an option. I wouldn't even let myself think about it.

Eventually, my mind traveled back to what I'd need to do if someone came in that door looking for us. My .38 had six rounds in the magazine and one in the chamber. Assuming that I hit what I was aiming at, I'd have a good chance if there were less than four men in the house. Ideally, I could take another weapon off of someone, but I couldn't count on that. I'd be working one-handed, because there was no way I could leave the baby behind.

My plans were interrupted when a small, hungry mouth started rooting around against my neck. She'd held out longer than I'd thought she would, but she was impatient as hell as I tried to get us situated. Making shushing noises, I bounced her as I searched the bag for supplies. If she started screaming, we were fucked.

Just as she started to eat, I heard a sound in the bedroom outside the closet. I strained, trying to figure out what it was as I slid my hand into my purse and grabbed my pistol.

By the time the closet door opened and the light came on, I was ready. Through the small gap in the coats, I stared at the spot in front of us, lifted the .38, and waited.

Chapter 2

MARK

I DIDN'T SLEEP well. Years in the military and working as a private contractor afterward meant I'd seen more than my fair share of shit that liked to replay behind my eyelids when I closed them. I'd gotten used to it for the most part, figured out ways to shut my mind down enough that I could get the rest I needed. On the worst nights, I found myself replaying memories of long blonde hair, tanned limbs, breathy sighs and hoarse groans, using good memories to replace the bad. Most of the time, I didn't even feel guilty about it. I hadn't been able to use any of my tricks when I'd climbed into bed that night, though, so I'd gotten dressed and headed out to the garage. Something was churning in my gut and I had no idea why, but I'd learned not to ignore the feeling, not even for fantasies of a lover I hadn't seen in nearly a decade.

I set my phone face up next to me on the bench as I got to work polishing an old bike frame. I'd probably sell this particular piece, since I had no interest in completely rebuilding the bike, but I still got satisfaction out of restoring it. Working with my hands centered me and cleared my head in a way nothing else did. I just wished I had more time for it.

When my phone finally rang, I wasn't even surprised. What did surprise me was the unknown number that scrolled across the screen. Normally, I wouldn't have answered it, telemarketers irritated the hell out of me, but there was no way I was going to miss that call.

"Eastwood," I answered, tucking the phone between my shoulder and face so I could wipe off my hands.

"Woody," the caller replied. It had been a long fucking time since I'd heard that familiar rasp.

I hadn't left Oregon on good terms with Casper's family, especially his older daughter Cecilia, but we'd crossed paths a few times when I'd been out to visit. It was impossible to avoid each other at the clubhouse, and while I'd left that life behind, I hadn't lost the respect I had for the men who'd stepped in and helped raise me after my father died. Whenever I was in Oregon, I tried to stop by and say hello. They deserved that much. I hadn't actually spoken to Casper in years, though, and as soon as I heard his voice, I knew there was only one reason he'd be calling.

"Is she okay?" I asked, getting up from the bench. Ignoring the frame I'd been working on, I went straight to the house, locking the garage behind me as he started to speak.

"Won't ask how you know I'm calling about Cecilia," he replied drolly. "She called me a couple hours ago, said she's hidin' in a house that just got shot up. Doesn't know how many men are there, doesn't know if they've left, doesn't know shit, just that she's in a fuckin' closet scared outta her mind."

"She told you she was scared?" I asked as nausea burned in my stomach.

"Hell, no," he said grimly. "But I know my kid. We're on our way down—"

"Everyone?" I asked as I jogged down the hallway to my bedroom, where I kept the gun safe.

"Just me, Farrah and Cam," Casper replied. "CeeCee didn't want everyone knowin', so we've kept it between us. We need the boys, I'll let them know. Far as I can tell, any of the heavy liftin' will have to be done by someone else because we won't get there until tomorrow." He didn't sound happy about that fact, and I couldn't blame him. Urgency thrummed under my skin and she wasn't my kid.

"That's where I come in," I said as I started pulling gear out of the safe.

"That's where you come in," he confirmed. "You in town?"

"Just got in two days ago," I replied. "Good timing."

"Yeah, no shit," he said with a huff. "And thank fuck for that. I tried my other contacts—one's in the wind and the other is vacationing in fuckin' Tahoe."

"I got this," I muttered. "Where's she at?"

"She dropped a fuckin' dot on her phone. You know what that means?"

"A pin?" I asked, surprised that I could feel amused and fucking frantic at the same time.

"Yeah. That. Sent it to Cam's phone. He'll send it to you."

"That works," I said as I stripped out of my jeans and flannel.

"You got back up?" he asked. "If you don't, I can probably scramble some boys—just none that I'd be willing to lead the pack, if you know what I mean."

I knew exactly what he meant, and I had no interest in having shit-bird dumbfucks at my back.

"I've got a team," I replied.

"Figures."

"Anything else I should know?"

"She's gonna be trigger-happy and ridin' the edge," he warned. "I let her know someone's on the way, but you better fuckin' announce yourself so she doesn't shoot you." He paused before muttering, "No promises that she doesn't shoot anyway."

"I'll take my chances," I replied, silently acknowledging the truth in his words. "I'll let you know when we're headed that way. Should take less than an hour."

"Hurry, but don't hurry so much that you're stupid," he said.

"You forget what I do for a living?" I asked, pausing in annoyance with my pants half-buttoned.

"Didn't forget, that's why I called you," he replied. "But I also know how different shit is when it's someone you care about."

"I'm good," I lied. "I'll text you when it's done. Send that pin."

"It's already sent," he said before hanging up.

I checked my messages and found the pin that Cam sent, cursing when I realized it would take forty minutes to get there. San Diego County was fucking huge and the traffic sucked.

Scrolling through my contacts, I found the number I was looking for and pressed send.

"Just cause you don't sleep, doesn't mean I don't," Forrest answered groggily.

"Need your help," I replied grimly.

His voice was immediately alert when he spoke again. "Talk to me."

TEN MINUTES LATER, I'd reached out to each member of my team and Forrest was knocking on my front door.

"Josiah and Ephraim just pulled up behind me," he said as he strode in the front door.

"Wilson and Eli should be here shortly," I replied as I repacked the duffle bag on my kitchen table. "Lu said she was going to run over, should be walking in—"

I didn't finish my sentence before the only woman on our team, Lu, was opening the sliding glass door that led to my back yard.

"Decided to just jump the fences," she said, swinging her backpack off her shoulder. "Boys almost here?"

"Yep," Forrest confirmed.

Within minutes, our entire team was crowded around my kitchen table, a seven-person unit that worked like a well-oiled machine.

"I don't know much," I said as I looked around the group. "Old friend called me tonight and said that his daughter is in trouble. She heard gunshots and hid in a closet of some house in La Jolla. Fair warning, I have no fucking clue what we're walking into."

"How old is this daughter?" Wilson asked.

"My age," I replied, meeting his eyes.

"And you know her in the biblical sense?" he asked, his head tilting a little to the side. He must have read something in my tone or body language, but I couldn't take the time to figure out what my tell had been.

"When we were teenagers," I said with a short nod.

"I'm takin' point," Forrest said firmly.

I opened my mouth to argue then closed it again. He was right. It galled me to realize that I was too close to the situation to be objective.

"Vests, paint, and night vision," Eli ordered. "Masks at the ready for when we get close enough for the cameras."

"You know for sure if they have eyes?" Siah asked.

"It's a house in La Jolla," Eli replied. "They've definitely got cameras. We'll avoid them if we can, but if we miss one, I don't want any of our mugs on the six o'clock news."

We geared up and climbed into Forrest's black SUV and Ephraim's Jeep. As soon as I was sitting, anxiety hit me so hard and fast that my knee started to bounce up and down. I didn't even recognize the emotion for a second, because it had been so long since I'd felt it. I got nervous, sure. I felt fear. You didn't put yourself into high risk situations and never feel those things—those instincts kept you alive. But I hadn't felt this pure, helpless fear in years, not since I was seventeen years old, beat to shit, and laying on my back in the shade of an old white house while gunfire erupted all around me.

"You good?" Lu asked, reaching forward from the back seat to pat my shoulders.

"Yeah," I replied. "Hate not knowing what we're walking into."

"We're in the US of A," she said, slapping me once more on my shoulder. "This is gonna be a piece of cake compared to anywhere we've been overseas."

"Gonna be nice drivin' away without havin' to watch for shit in the road," Forrest said, thumping his hand against the steering wheel.

"Exactly," Lu said, leaning back in her seat with a sigh. "No IED's, no ambushes, just a quick snatch and grab and then we're gone. Poof."

I didn't vocalize the crap swirling around in my head. I knew they were trying to downplay it all, even if they were telling the truth, but that didn't mean shit, not really. Because if we didn't reach her in time, I wouldn't give a fuck how easy it was to get out of there. My only concern was getting to her, making sure she was safe, and extracting her from the house. Getting away clean was the least of my worries.

It took less time than I'd planned for to get to the end of the long, gated driveway, which was a plus, but the gate was locked up tight, which meant we were going to have to get to the house on foot. We drove a quarter of a mile past the gate and spun around before parking further down the hill on the side of the road. Thankfully, both the rigs were dark, because parked cars were definitely out of the ordinary on that stretch of road. They'd be noticed, but hopefully, the color would make it harder for any other drivers to remember them later.

"We'll hop the fence down here," Forrest said. "Looks like the owners like trees, thank fuck, so we should have some cover until we get closer to the house. Assume that there's an alarm system and move forward accordingly."

"Got it," Wilson said. "Should take me about forty seconds to disable it once I'm within ten feet of the house."

"Me, Eli and Lu will stick to the front with Wilson," Forrest said. "Eph, Siah and Chief around the back. Don't breach until you get my say-so." He locked eyes with me. "Everyone's comms working?"

"Yep."

"Yep."

"Mine's good."

"Ay-oh."

"Yep."

"All good," I replied with a nod.

"Let's—" Forrest paused. "Christ. What's her name, man? We show up in there, we're going to scare the hell out of her."

"Cecilia," I replied. I shook my head. Fuck, I needed to get my shit together. "And she's armed."

Eli jerked his head forward in surprise and widened his eyes at me. "Probably a good thing to know," he spat.

"And this is why I took point," Forrest muttered. "Try not to get yourselves shot."

I didn't bother to apologize, because I already looked like a fucking moron. Jesus Christ, I was always on top of my shit. We had to grab a couple of preschoolers out of a house somewhere on the other side of the world? I was the one who had candy in my pocket for the inevitable freak out. Stuck inside a busted-up school with no conceivable way out? Hey, I'd packed fucking water for this eventuality, it looked like we wouldn't die of dehydration before we could get extracted. You're welcome.

"Cecilia," Wilson mused over the comm. "Now, where have I seen that name before?"

Lu chuckled.

"Was it a tattoo, maybe?" Ephraim joked. "I swear I've seen a bad tattoo of that name."

"Enough," Forrest snapped quietly.

"Don't make me take you down," Siah said to me as we cleared the fence and moved swiftly through the trees. "You start bein' stupid and I'll drop your ass."

"I won't," I said through my teeth. Fuck, we were so close. I was hyper focused as the house came into view, the driveway and front porch lit up like a fucking Christmas tree.

There was a car out front, and everyone dropped to the ground as a man came out the front door, closing it behind him. He didn't rush as he walked to the car and put a box of shit on the front seat. My head jerked in surprise when I realized he was whistling as he rounded the hood and climbed inside.

"It can't be that fuckin' easy," Forrest breathed into the mic. "Once he's out the gate, move in. Slowly."

It felt like it took an hour for the car to drive off the property, but it had to be only minutes. Then we were on the move. Slow and steady, watching for any movement, keeping out of camera range, pausing as Wilson checked for an alarm system and then muttered that it wasn't armed. Breaching the back door quietly with Siah's unparalleled lockpicking skill. Moving into the mud room, then the kitchen, then the hallway. Meeting up with the rest of the team in the foyer, ignoring the opulence of the house as the sight of a woman's bare feet came into view from a room opposite the stairs. Forrest and Wilson checked on the woman as the rest of us cleared the bottom floor of the house. The place was empty.

We moved up the stairs slowly, waiting and watching.

"Cameras are down," Wilson said into the comm. "Got two cold ones down here. Man and a woman."

We moved faster once we didn't have to be careful of the cameras, but the house was fucking enormous. I had no idea what people did with so much space. All the rooms were furnished and came with a walk-in closet and private bathroom, and we cleared every single one. Each time I opened the door to a closet, I braced myself, but most of them were empty. The few that held anything were still so bare that no one could hide in them.

The master bedroom took the longest to search because it had so much shit in it. This was the bedroom that was actually lived in. Instead of a perfectly made bed and tastefully arranged furniture, there were clothes thrown over a chair back and shoes nearly covering the floor of the closet. Books were stacked on one nightstand and a laptop on the other. The bed was sloppily made, as if they'd just thrown the comforter over everything and called it good. Apparently, these people didn't have a live-in maid, because the living spaces hadn't been straightened up for a few days. At least we knew that there wasn't some other innocent hiding or dead somewhere in the house.

My patience grew thin as we went through the room, because I knew she wasn't in there. If she had been, she would've identified it to Casper so we'd know where to look. Still, we had to make sure that the house was empty, every inch of it.

When we hit the fifth bedroom, the one directly next to the master, something clicked into place. It was a nursery, painted a pale yellow, and like the rest of the guest bedrooms, it looked unused, but something niggled at the back of my mind. Something was off. I held up my hand to stop the men behind me, and looked over the room. A crib was in the corner with a blanket tastefully thrown over the edge. On the opposite wall was a changing table, diapers and wipes and bath supplies perfectly aligned on the shelves, like they hadn't been used yet. A rocking chair sat in the middle of a fuzzy area rug. Next to that was a baby swing that hadn't even been plugged in.

My gaze snapped back to the rocking chair. Something—yeah, someone had been sitting on the cushions of that chair. The rest of the room looked untouched, but that chair had been used. There was a slight depression in the light gray cushion, not where their ass had been, but oddly, where they'd rested their head.

"She's in here," I said, inaudible beyond the comm in my ear.

I checked the bathroom first, just to be sure, but I knew it would be empty. Then, as if they knew to wait and let me go in first, I met Josiah and Ephraim at the door to the closet.

Taking a deep breath, I swung open the door and reached for the switch. The closet was full of shit, racks and racks of women's clothes from one end of the space to the other. A damn near perfect place to hide. I stepped forward, but instinct made me pause and pull the mask up to the top of my head. Holding my weapon at the ready, I turned my gaze toward the side that was thickest with coats.

"Cec?"

I barely breathed as a long fur coat twitched and then was slowly pushed to the side.

Then there she was, blinking against the bright lights of the closet, pointing a .38 directly at my crotch, with a baby nursing at her breast.

"Mark?" she asked, her eyes widening with shock.

I tried to reply, but couldn't. It felt like my tongue was stuck to the roof of my mouth.

"We've got two in here," Eph murmured into the comm as he looked over my shoulder. "Cecilia and a newborn baby."

"I'm gonna fuckin' kill you," Forrest growled. He didn't have to specify who he was speaking to.

"I didn't know," I rasped, still staring at Cecilia. "Jesus Christ."

Chapter 3

CECILIA

IT FELT LIKE I was staring at a ghost. His face had greasepaint all over the skin not covered by a full beard, and he was about a thousand times broader than when we were kids—but I'd know his blue eyes, the nose that slanted slightly to the left from being broken by a right cross when we were fourteen, and the wide mouth that had gotten him teased—anywhere. I'd know him anywhere.

"Time to move," the man behind him said. When Mark didn't even shift his weight, too busy staring right back at me, the man shoved his way into the closet and extended his hand. "I'm Ephraim. Let me help you up."

I shook my head, trying to make sense of things, and lowered my weapon. "Sorry," I murmured as I pressed the safety and stashed it back in my purse. "Give me a second."

Reaching around the baby, who was still nursing drowsily, I grabbed first the bag and then my purse, slinging them over my shoulder.

"I can get those for you," Ephraim said, reaching for my stuff.

"No, thanks, I got it." I used my free hand to brace myself as I rolled to my knees, barely holding back a groan. I was stiff and sore from sitting on the floor for so long, but I wasn't about to complain. As soon as I was on my feet, Mark snapped out of his daze.

"Let me help you," he said, taking the bags from me without waiting for a response. "Come on."

Holding the baby snug against my body, I followed Mark out of the closet.

"Wait," I said, jerking to a stop. "I left a dirty diaper in there on the floor."

"Don't think they're gonna mind," Mark said.

"Nice save," Ephraim said at the same time. "Better to leave no trace you were here."

"You better get it the fuck together," a new man muttered to Mark, taking a couple steps forward. He looked at me. "I'm Josiah. Glad you're okay."

"Got it," Ephraim said, holding the diaper. "Let's go."

The house was eerily quiet as we moved through the hallway and down the stairs. It reminded me of when windstorms would knock out the power back home. Sometimes it would take hours for the electric company to get the lines fixed, and the house would be so quiet while we waited, like a tomb.

"Takin' her out the back," Mark murmured too quiet for anyone but me to hear.

"Who are you talking to?" I asked quietly.

Turning to me, he lifted a finger to his lips. I nodded.

As we made our way through the kitchen, Mark stuffed his hand inside my bag and rummaged around for a minute. When he didn't find what he was looking for, he stopped. Setting the bag and purse down on the floor, he unzipped his hoodie and quickly pulled it off.

"It's cool out," he said, his mouth so close to my ear I could feel his breath. "Put this on."

I didn't stop to question him. Letting him hold the sweatshirt for me, I carefully shifted the baby from one arm to the other so I could get the sleeves on. When I was done, he gently zipped us both inside.

"All good," a woman whispered from the doorway, motioning for us to follow her out.

I had no idea who these people were or how the hell Mark Eastwood fit into it all, but I followed them blindly anyway. What did they say about the devil you knew? Leave it to my father to send a savior in the form of the last person in the world I'd ever want to see.

I didn't question it when they ushered me toward the trees to the side of the house instead of the driveway, and I didn't say a word as I ducked and weaved through branches and leaves, but when we came to a six foot high fence I balked.

"There's no way I'm going over that thing," I said seriously. Inside my sweater, the baby's mouth went lax as she fell fully asleep.

"Piece of cake," Ephraim said. When he smiled, his teeth were startlingly white against the dark of the greasepaint.

"No, really," I replied, looking at the fence again as I reached inside the sweatshirt and pulled my sports bra back over my boob and my t-shirt down. "Not happening."

"This ain't our first rodeo," Josiah said. "The wall is about ten inches thick at the top. We'll lift you up to straddle it, someone else will help you on the other side."

"This is insane," I sputtered.

"It'll be fine," Josiah reassured me.

Just as I started to take a step backward, because no fucking way was I going to attempt that wall while carrying a baby, a hand on my lower back made me freeze.

"Can't use the front gate," Mark said in my ear. "This is the only way out of here."

I stared at the wall. Okay, logically, I knew I was going over it. I wanted to get the fuck out of there, and if this was how it had to be, then this was how it had to be. However, I honestly didn't know how in the world I was going to actually do it.

"I'll hold—" Ephraim came toward me and I jerked backward, instinctively pressing my back against Mark.

"The fuck you will," I snapped. "She stays with me."

"Hey," Josiah said soothingly. "It's all good, yeah? We're here to help you."

"This is takin' too fuckin' long," Mark said shortly.

Before I knew what was happening, I'd taken about five steps forward and I was suddenly turned and lifted into the air. My ass hit the wall with a thump as I yelped.

"Get your balance," Mark ordered, his hands still bracing my waist. He waited until I was steady before letting me go. Then, in one smooth movement, he hopped the fence. Just seconds later, I was being tugged backward and lowered to the ground.

It was over in less than a minute.

"Told you," Ephraim said teasingly after he'd cleared the fence. "Piece of cake."

"Let's go," a southern accented voice rumbled from somewhere in the trees.

Four shadows emerged out of the darkness, and I damn near tripped over my own feet.

"Jesus," I whispered, tugging the baby even closer.

"Load up," the same voice ordered. "We'll meet at Chief's. Different routes. Catch you on the flip side."

I was ushered into a dark SUV as the two groups split up, and before I knew it, we'd made it out of Liv's neighborhood and were flying down the freeway.

"Call your pop," Mark ordered, his voice startling in the silent car. "Let him know you're safe."

I nodded and reached for my purse that was stashed near his feet. Without another word, he lifted it up and set it on the seat between us.

The phone rang and rang with no answer, but I hadn't expected one. If my parents were on the road, they wouldn't be able to answer until they'd found somewhere to stop.

"Thank you," I rasped before clearing my throat. "Thank you for coming to get us. I don't understand how—"

"Casper called me," Mark said. Yeah, I'd figured that much out already.

"But why?" I prodded. "Who are these people? What the hell?"

"This is what we do," the southern guy said from the driver's seat. "Get people out of sticky situations."

I looked at Mark for clarification, but he ignored me.

"You're some kind of *commando*?" I asked dubiously.

The woman who'd ushered us out of the house earlier laughed and turned to the side so she could see me from the passenger seat. "Oh, yeah, he's a regular Rambo."

"Shut it, Lu," Mark muttered.

"What the fuck is happening right now?" I said under my breath, shaking my head. The whole situation was surreal. It felt like one of the vivid nightmares I'd had when I was pregnant.

"Who were those people?" Mark asked, as I pinched my leg just to be sure I was awake. "How the fuck did you get caught up in that shit?"

It wasn't necessarily the words he'd used, but his tone that made my back snap straight. "I wasn't caught up in anything," I shot back. "I was in the wrong place at the wrong fucking time."

"Understatement, Cecilia."

"Liv's a friend—" I caught myself. "*Was* a friend. A good one."

Mark didn't say a word as he glanced down at where I'd unzipped the hoodie so baby girl had room to get some air. I could tell he wanted to ask more questions, but he didn't, so I didn't offer up any more information. The SUV was quiet as we weaved our way through the county toward Mark's house.

Dammit, I really didn't want to go to his place. Dread mixed with the relief of escaping the closet.

I didn't want to see where he lived, whether he had a bachelor pad or his place felt like a home. I didn't want to know what kind of life he lived. I knew he kept in touch with people back home because I'd heard his name mentioned in passing more than once, but I never, ever stayed around long enough to hear more than that. I couldn't. I'd survived and thrived to that point because I *didn't* know those things, because I'd completely distanced myself from him.

The whole night had been one horrendous horror show, and I knew the full weight of it hadn't hit me yet. I was still running on pure adrenalin. I recognized the feeling—the racing heartbeat and hypervigilance. While logically I understood that we were no longer in danger, nothing felt safe yet. We were still, for all intents and purposes, on the run. As I stared out the window, I wondered if I'd ever feel settled again.

"Home sweet home," the driver said as he pulled into the driveway of an older, ranch style house. "I'll grab the gear out of the back."

"Thank fuck we didn't have to use any of it," the woman said as she threw open her door. "Easiest night we've had in a while."

I grit my teeth and refused to reply to her comment. It was an easy night for her? Congratu-fucking-lations. So glad that one of the worst nights of my life had been a piece of cake for her.

I clenched my jaw and grabbed my purse off the seat. Climbing out of the SUV to stand awkwardly beside it, I stared at Mark's house like it was going to bite me. God, I didn't want to go in there. I was so grateful for everything they'd done, so relieved that we were okay and they'd come to save us, but what I wanted more than anything was to get as far away from Mark Eastwood as I could, before the weight of the past was thrown on top of the weight of the present and I suffocated.

"Come on," Mark ordered. I drug my feet as he led me to a door between the detached garage and the house.

The door opened into a kitchen, and I catalogued it without conscious thought. While it wasn't a complete bachelor pad, it wasn't exactly homey, either. The dining room table was covered in newspaper, and on top of that was some sort of rusty car part, but the kitchen counters were clean and there was even a half-burned candle sitting between the burners on the stove. I couldn't imagine Mark actually buying a candle at the store. Did he sniff a bunch of them before he decided which one he wanted? Did his *girlfriend* buy it for him? Did he have a girlfriend? Dammit, why was I even thinking about that?

"I've got a guest room," he said, catching me checking out his place. "You can stay in there tonight."

"Thanks," I mumbled as I followed him down a short hallway.

He stopped in the doorway of the furthest room down the hall and flipped on the light, gesturing me inside. The room wasn't decorated, but the furniture he had was definitely not of the discount variety. Another surprise. I would have guessed I'd be sleeping on a futon.

"I'll grab the bedding," Mark said, nodding toward the bed. "It gets dusty if I leave it made, so it's just easier to keep it in the closet."

He left the room and I took a minute to just breathe. We were safe. We were unhurt. We had a place to stay until my parents got there. Everything was going to be okay.

I glanced down at the baby as she started to stir, making little noises and rolling her head around. Maybe *okay* was an overstatement. We were going to get through it. She chose that moment to make a sucking noise that sounded a whole lot like she was trying to blow me a kiss.

Fuck it. I'd *make* things okay.

"It's you and me kid," I whispered, kissing the top of her head. "And we should probably figure out the name situation."

"Got 'em," Mark announced as he strode back into the room. "I don't think this mattress has ever even been slept on, so I have no idea if it's comfortable or not."

"I can pretty much sleep anywhere," I lied. The truth was that I had a hard time sleeping anywhere, but I figured the point was the same—it didn't matter how comfortable the mattress was or wasn't—I'd get the same amount of sleep either way.

"Everyone's gonna be here for a while," he said as he put the sheets on the bed, tucking them neatly at the corners. "So, if you wanna get settled and then come out, feel free."

"Okay," I replied, standing there like a lazy ass while he made my bed. I knew I should offer to help, but Jesus, I was tired. My arms ached from holding the baby all night, the lower half of my body was still stiff and sore from sitting on the floor of that closet for so long, and I was trying to ignore the incessant throbbing of my downstairs. I felt about a million years old.

"Or," he said as he threw a quilt over the sheets, "you can stay in here and get some rest and get her settled. Up to you."

"Yeah, she probably needs her diaper changed," I said to his back. "I don't know about her, but I was definitely shitting my pants back there."

I have no idea what possessed me to make the joke. None of it was funny. Not one bit. It was absolutely terrifying, and claw at my chest, scream until my voice was raw, devastating. But I'd never said the right thing, and that moment wasn't any different.

"Right," he said before turning to face me. "I'll be in the kitchen if you need anything."

"Mark—"

"You know, Cecilia, tonight wasn't a fuckin' lark for me," he said, pausing in the doorway to look back at me. He paused and thumped the side of his fist against the doorframe. "So keep your bullshit comments to yourself, alright? I don't want to fuckin' hear 'em."

I stood dumbly, staring at the door long after he'd left. Once upon a time, he'd been the only person who hadn't gotten offended by the shit that spilled out of my mouth. When we were together, I hadn't had to censor myself at all. I sighed. Or maybe he'd just pretended he didn't care what I said because he'd been nineteen and getting regular blowjobs. Whatever. I'd be gone tomorrow and he could think whatever he wanted about me. What did it matter, really?

"Let's get you changed, huh?" I finally said to baby girl as she began to squirm in earnest. After laying her on the bed, I grabbed our bag off the floor and started pulling everything out of it. Four diapers, a half empty package of wipes, two little shirts that snapped at the crotch, another baby gown, a pair of footie pajamas, a blue and pink hat from the hospital, my toiletry bag, a set of dirty clothes I'd rolled up into a ball, my hairbrush, a sample size bottle of baby soap, two pacifiers, two nipple shields that I hadn't had to use after the first day, and a plastic bag with two pads left.

"Damn, girl," I cooed even though my stomach churned. "We don't have much."

I upended my purse next. Two more pads, a couple of very old tampons, keys, wallet, two medical bracelets, a pair of fuzzy socks with grippers on the bottom, a tube of lanolin, my .38, an envelope of paperwork, two pens, my phone, a phone charger, and a tube of lipstick.

There was no getting around it—we needed supplies. I had a single blanket to wrap her in and I cursed as I realized I'd left her car seat in the back of Cane's car. It had felt weird as hell, unnatural, holding her as we'd driven to Mark's house, but I hadn't even thought about the fact that I'd left the expensive ass car seat Liv had picked out behind.

Taking a deep breath, I shook out my hands. There was nothing I could do about it now. What was done, was done. When my parents got there tomorrow, we could figure out logistics. Get her a new car seat and other shit she'd need. There was no reason to panic, not about this. It was only one night and then we could go back to my place, pack up, and hit the road.

I'd feel stronger then. I'd be ready to get things done and make things happen. I just needed one night.

"Okay, sweetheart," I said as I leaned over her. "Diaper time."

As I changed her, I kept up a stream of conversation that she probably couldn't understand, but it made me feel better.

"My dad is cool. You'll like him. I'm not sure what he looks like right now. Last time I saw him, he had a beard and his hair was getting pretty long, but he likes to change it up. My mom says it keeps things spicy when she never knows who she's coming home to, but we just ignore her when she says things like that because it's gross. So, just pretend you don't hear her, that's what I do."

Once her diaper was changed, I lifted her into my arms, leaving her little hospital blanket on the bed. I still couldn't believe how tiny she was, especially when the added bulk of the blanket was gone. She was so light, and she naturally curled into a ball, making her seem even smaller.

"Oh, come on," I chuckled as I felt her fill the brand new diaper. "We've only got a couple of these left, dude."

She stretched, arching her back, and I felt my chest get tight with a surge of protectiveness and love. That feeling still caught me by surprise every time it happened. I hadn't expected it. When I'd first felt her start moving around in my belly, I'd tried to just ignore it. I'd went about my days, refusing to even acknowledge to myself that there was a tiny human taking up space in my body, growing and saying hello with little taps of her fists and elbows and feet and knees. It was safer that way. I thought it would make things easier.

It hadn't.

"Okay, this one is going to piss you off," I murmured, grabbing for the wipes.

I was right. The cold wipes meant an end to our quiet diaper changes, and by the time I was done and picked her back up, she was so loud that I was sure the people in the kitchen thought I was torturing her.

Popping one of the pacifiers in her mouth and bouncing from side to side, I calmed her down. Biting the inside of my cheek, I slowly let out a breath through my nose, trying to calm the anxiety and tension that thrummed under my skin. She was fine and I was fine.

But Liv wasn't.

I cleared my throat and straightened my shoulders, trying to ignore the way Liv's scream seemed to echo in my ears. The sound hadn't been one of fury or surprise, it had been pure fear. I swallowed hard, trying to make myself think of literally anything else. She'd been so happy, practically floating out of the nursery when Cane had called her downstairs to help him with their sound system. I huffed out a frustrated breath. They'd wanted to listen to Christmas music. It was the only reason she'd been downstairs.

Maybe, if she hadn't gone down there—no. I shook my head as if to clear it. No maybes. No what-ifs. I knew where that led, and it was nowhere good. Logically, I knew that if Liv would've been upstairs with us, all of us would have died. I wasn't supposed to even be there tonight—but Liv was—and whoever killed her and Cane would have searched until they'd found her.

Sucking in a sharp breath and then blowing it out through my lips as if blowing out a birthday candle, I tucked my phone into the waistband of my yoga pants, grabbed the dirty diapers off the bed and ventured out of the room. I couldn't just stand there in the silence with my thoughts, even if I felt weird walking through Mark's house.

I didn't belong with the people in the kitchen. I didn't know them. Yet, they'd saved my life. I didn't know if there had been anyone in the house by the time they'd arrived, I'd ask for the details later, but in the end, it didn't really matter. They'd come for me. For us. It was a debt I'd never be able to repay.

My stomach churned with anxiety as I made my way down the hallway.

"Come on, man," a guy's voice said. "You know you were fucking out of it tonight."

"Subpar work at best," a different voice stated.

"Cut him some slack," Ephraim said. At least I thought it was him. "Have you seen her? Jesus."

"Watch it," Mark barked.

Ephraim laughed.

"We get it," the southern guy drawled. "There's history. But you were about as useless as tits on a boar tonight."

"Won't happen again," Mark said flatly.

"Hey," the woman said in surprise as she came around the corner almost running into me. "Everything okay?"

"Peachy," I muttered. "Just tossing these in the garbage." I lifted up the dirty diapers.

"Go on in, they're just giving Chief shit." She gestured with her head toward the kitchen. "I'm Lu, by the way."

"Cecilia," I replied.

"They're a rowdy bunch, but they're all softies. Don't let them intimidate you."

I laughed. "They don't scare me."

Lu smiled before sliding past me. She strode down the hall like she knew exactly where she was going, and I felt a small twinge of something. Jealousy? Sadness? I couldn't decide, but whatever it was needed to disappear.

"Hey," I said as I rounded the corner.

Ephraim, Josiah, Mark and the southern guy were sitting around the table, beers in hand. A man I didn't recognize was sitting on the island between the cooking area and the table. Another unfamiliar man was sitting on a bar stool, pointed toward the table with his elbows on the island.

"Everything alright?" Mark asked, leaning forward to rest his elbows on the table.

"We're good," I said with a nod. I lifted the diapers and cocked my head to the side.

"Under the kitchen sink."

I nodded again and moved to throw them away.

"That's Wilson sitting on my counter," Mark said. "Eli's the one sitting on a stool like a normal person, and Grizzly Adams here is Forrest."

Looking at the group, I wanted to explain to them how scared I'd been, how I still felt shaky, how I was trying to think of anything else except the fact that my best friend was dead on the floor of the house she'd dreamed about her entire life and it all felt like such a gigantic waste. I wanted to tell them that I didn't know what I would've done if they hadn't showed up when they did. That even though I had talked myself into believing that I'd do whatever I had to in order to get me and the baby girl out of there safely, history had shown that fear paralyzed me and I probably would've stayed in that closet forever.

Instead, when I opened my mouth, the only thing that came out was, "Nice to meet you guys. Thank you so much for tonight."

"Our pleasure," Eli said.

"While I wouldn't say it was pleasurable, per se," Wilson countered, "I would say that it was satisfying. You're welcome."

I stared at him for a second. He looked like a normal guy. In his twenties. Short hair. Dressed in black like everyone else. But his speech was almost formal, and I couldn't detect an accent.

"Glad we got you two out safe," Forrest said in his southern drawl. "Unfortunate that we got there too late for the party, though."

"What do you mean?" I asked.

"Only one man there when we showed," he explained, leaning back in his seat. "And he was already on his way out with a box of shit."

"It was a robbery?" My mind swirled with confusion. Had I hid upstairs while some random druggy killed my friends? If there was only one person, I could've done something. I could have stopped him. Familiar guilt and shame rolled over me like a wave.

"No," Mark said, shaking his head. "The box wasn't filled with shit he could hock or sell."

"Your friends had expensive taste," Wilson added. "But nothing of any value was touched. Her engagement ring and earrings were still on."

"Husband's Rolex and cufflinks were, too," Eli said.

"We're real sorry about your friends," Forrest said gently. "By the time we got there, they were gone."

Raising my fingers to my forehead, I rubbed at the headache forming above my eyes. I didn't want to think about it anymore. The memory of Liv's scream replayed over and over.

"Has your pop called?" Mark asked, watching me closely.

"I don't think so," I replied, reaching down to check my phone. "Shit. It was still on silent and I missed it."

"He'll call again," he said.

"Yeah." Just as the silence grew long enough to be uncomfortable, my phone rang. "Speak of the devil," I said.

I turned toward the living room as I answered.

"Hey, Dad."

"You're okay?" he asked.

"I'm okay. We're at Woody's house now."

"Thank Christ."

"How far away are you?" I asked, anxious for them to arrive.

"We won't be there until early afternoon," he replied. "But we're making good time. Might be able to shave a little time off."

"Be careful and don't rush," I said quickly.

"Don't worry about us," he murmured. He sounded tired. "We'll be there as soon as we can, Bumblebee."

"Okay," I whispered, my throat tight. God, I just wanted them to get there. It had been years since I'd been so homesick for my parents.

"Your mom says she loves you," he said. "I'd put her on the phone, but then we'd never get out of here."

"It's okay."

"We'll see you soon, baby."

"Okay. Love you."

"Love you, too," he said before the line went dead.

I took a minute to compose myself before turning around to face the men again. Shaking my phone side to side, I attempted to smile, but I was pretty sure it was wobbly as hell. I walked back toward the kitchen, but when I met Mark's eyes, my footsteps faltered.

I couldn't interpret the look on his face.

"It's been a long time since I've heard you call me Woody," he said quietly. His lips tipped up at the corners, and suddenly, it was as if we were the only two people in the room. I knew that look. I'd seen it a million times. I used to crave it like a drug addict. A Mark Eastwood addict. My belly swooped, like I was on the downward slide of a roller coaster.

Oh, shit.

Chapter 4

MARK

"I'M UNCOMFORTABLE WITH the amount of emotion in this room right now," Wilson muttered seriously to Eli, making him laugh.

"We only have two diapers left," Cecilia said suddenly, glancing at Wilson as she readjusted the baby in her arms. "And almost out of wipes."

"Make a list, and one of the boys'll go pick some up for you," Forrest replied easily.

"Why us?" Eli asked.

"I have no fuckin' clue what to buy a newborn. Send Lu," Siah muttered, pointing at her as she came back into the room.

"Why would I know what to get?" she asked, rolling her eyes. "What? Because I'm a woman?"

"You have a niece," Siah argued.

"That doesn't mean I know what to get."

"I'll go," I cut in before they really started arguing. The two of them could happily argue about the color of the sky for hours. They got off on that shit, but it irritated the hell out of the rest of us. "Uh, make a list like Forrest said. I'll grab you some paper and a pen."

"I can just go myself," Cecilia argued, lifting her hand to wave me off. "Do you have a Target or something around here?"

"You gonna walk?" I asked, getting up from the table.

"Well, if it's close enough, sure," she said slowly.

"I was bein' sarcastic," I muttered as I searched through the junk drawer by the back door. "You're not walking to the store in the middle of the night."

"There a reason the two of you can't go together?" Forrest asked dryly, amusement lacing his words.

I paused, bracing my hands on the countertop. Jesus, I needed to get my shit together. Never in a million years would I have thought that seeing Cecilia again would rattle me so badly. I knew it would hit me hard. The way things had happened, the way I'd loved her and the way the ties between us had been severed meant that it would never be easy to run into her. I hadn't been concerned I'd see her in San Diego because I was barely ever there, but I'd braced for it every time I was in Oregon. I thought that I'd be able to handle it.

Maybe it was the situation we were in that was making things so difficult. The fear I'd felt. The fact that she was standing in the middle of my fucking kitchen holding a goddamn baby.

"That would work," she said cautiously. "Is that okay with you?"

I turned to face her. Fuck, she looked tired. Tired and scared and sad, though I doubted any of the others noticed it. Cecilia had inherited most of her looks from her mother, but the calm, detached expression she wore was pure Casper.

"Yeah," I said with a nod. "Go grab what you need and we'll head out."

After she left the room, Ephraim started chuckling and soon, everyone else was quietly laughing with him.

"Shut up," I said with a sigh, leaning back against the counter.

"Who would've guessed that all we needed to rattle you was a little blonde woman holding a baby?" Lu asked.

"Not just any blonde woman," Siah said.

"*Cecilia*," he and Ephraim sang.

"It's been a long fuckin' night," I replied.

"Gonna be even longer with a baby in the house," Forrest said with a smile. "You see her? Cute little thing."

"How could you tell?" Wilson asked. "She was holding that child so close I couldn't even tell if it had all the requisite extremities."

"It's hers, I assume?" Eli asked me.

"Better be," Josiah said. "Or it puts that nursing Madonna vision we found in the closet into a whole new freaky perspective."

Eli grinned.

"Yeah, she's hers," I replied.

"What's her name?" Lu asked Cecilia as she came back into the room.

"Oh." She looked down at the baby. "She doesn't have one yet."

"You haven't named your kid?" Ephraim said in surprise.

"I'm waiting to see what fits her personality," she replied, the words sounding almost like a question.

"Good luck with that," Eli said uncertainly.

"I think you should name her Cecilia," Lu said, hopping onto the counter next to Wilson.

"So they'll have the same name?" Josiah shot back.

"Men do it all the time," Lu replied with a shrug. I could tell by her tone and the set of her shoulders that she was just winding up, and I didn't want to be there for the eventual debate.

"You ready?" I asked Cecilia.

"Yep. Hopefully, we don't get pulled over," she said as she strode toward me. "I left her car seat behind tonight."

"Shoulda thought to grab it," I replied, opening the door and letting her go ahead of me.

"We'll lock up when we leave," Ephraim called.

"Sounds good," I muttered. I wasn't even sure if he heard me over the sound of Lu defending the merits of Cecilia naming her baby after herself.

"Good thing I have a back seat," I told Cecilia as I led her to my truck. "Probably safer for you two to ride back there."

"Good call," she said. "Thanks for taking me to the store."

"No worries."

I opened the door and spotted her as she climbed in one-handed. I was trying not to stare at her ass, but it was impossible not to notice the shape of her. She didn't look like she'd just had a baby. Sure, she was a little curvier than she'd been when we were kids, but that was normal. No one stayed the same size as they were at eighteen. If anything, Cecilia looked even better now that she had a little extra meat on her bones. She's always been beautiful, but she'd matured into something even better.

I let out a slow breath as I closed the door behind her, determined to stop thinking about the damn shape of her body. It didn't matter what Cecilia looked like. She'd be gone as soon as her parents came to get her and then she'd be out of my life again, and things could go back to the way they'd been before her pop called me.

"You know, I'm not really sure what I'm supposed to get at the store, either," she confessed after we were on the road. "I mean, hypothetically, I know what she needs to survive. Diapers, clothes and food. But what kind? And how many?"

"You'll figure it out," I replied, glancing at her in the mirror. "You just need enough to last until tomorrow, right? Once your parents pick you up, you guys can go back to your place and grab the rest of her stuff." Shit, I was an idiot. "Or we can go over right now, if you want. I should've asked if you wanted me to take you home. I guess I'm so used to imagining you in Oregon, I didn't even think about the fact that you have a place down here."

"That's okay," she said, looking out the window. "I don't really have anything for her at home." She huffed. "I'm woefully unprepared."

"We can go to the store first," I offered. "Get you set up before I take you home."

She was quiet for a while.

"I'd rather stay at your place, if that's okay," she finally said, her voice low. I knew the effort it took to ignore her pride and utter those words. "Just for tonight."

"No worries," I replied, relief hitting me harder than I wanted to admit. "I already made the bed. Someone might as well sleep in it."

We were quiet for the rest of the ride and I tried not to think about the fact that Cecilia Butler, my Cecilia, was sitting two feet from me, and I was backsliding into shit that I thought I'd put behind me years ago. It had taken me a long ass time to get past the fact that she was no longer in my life. Looking back, I'd always assumed that I'd taken it so hard because we'd been so young when it all went down, but now I wasn't so sure. Puppy love doesn't make a man lose focus during a job that he'd done for years.

"So, you guys are mercenaries?" Cecilia asked as we walked into the brightly lit store a few minutes later.

"Something like that."

"Something like that, or exactly that?" she asked as I grabbed a cart.

"We work for a government contractor that primarily does jobs overseas," I clarified.

"And you're the boss, right?"

"No," I replied. "We're a team."

"But you're the leader."

"Not really."

"They call you Chief," she pressed.

"Just a nickname."

"But it seemed like Forrest was in charge tonight," she mused as we headed toward the back of the store. "He was in charge tonight, but they still deferred to you most of the time."

"No one is in charge," I said, leaning my elbows on the handle of the cart. "We're not on a job. When we're on a job, yeah, I usually take the lead."

"Mmhmm," she hummed.

"Does it matter?" I asked.

"Not really," she shrugged. "Come on, baby stuff is this way."

I followed her as she navigated the store and purposefully didn't let my gaze drop below the middle of her shoulder blades.

"Bingo," she announced when we hit the diaper aisle. "Okay, newborn size…shit. There's like forty different brands here."

"Doubt it matters," I replied.

"How would you know?" She sounded slightly panicked.

I stared at her. "They catch shit, Cecilia," I said slowly. "They're all gonna end up in the trash anyway. Any of them should work."

"Good point," she muttered. Dropping her purse into the cart, she turned to me. "Hold her for a second?"

Wait a fucking minute.

"Please," she said. "It'll be way easier if I have two hands."

Without waiting for me to respond, the tiny person was pressed against my chest, and I had no choice but to hold on to her.

"Support her head. I'm going to look at the labels first," Cecilia said as she turned away, completely ignoring the fact that the earth had just tilted on its axis, and I was standing there with what amounted to a seven pound bomb in my hands.

The baby jerked, and I fumbled to catch her little bobble head before it rolled right off the back of her neck. Jesus, she was so small. Her bald head was kind of cone shaped still, and I wondered how long it would be before it rounded out a bit. She didn't look like Cecilia, but I couldn't imagine she looked like anyone. Her features were so tiny, and the only distinguishable feature she had were a pair of pouty lips that I assumed must have come from her dad. She curved back against me and I could feel every vertebrate down her spine beneath the thin blanket and nightgown she had on. She smelled like Cecilia.

"I'm just going to get these ones," CeeCee said, lifting a box of diapers from the shelf. "They're the ones the hospital uses, so they should be a safe bet."

I followed Cecilia around the baby department while she grabbed supplies, growing more and more confused as she filled the cart. When she'd said that she wasn't prepared for the baby, I'd assumed she'd meant that she had some holes in her supplies. From what I was seeing, though, Cecilia must not have had a single thing. Why the hell wouldn't she have been at least a little prepared? Didn't women have baby showers and shit? She'd had nine months to prepare.

"Shit," she said, coming to a stop. She glanced at full the cart. "We should've grabbed the car seat first."

"Pick which one you want," I replied, handing the baby back to her. "I'll carry it."

She walked down the line of strollers and car seats, stopping at each one so she could read the tags. Then she pulled out her phone and started reading something there. Finally, she pointed to the one she wanted.

"That one has the best reviews," she said, her fingers pressed to her lower lip.

The gesture made everything inside me pause. I wasn't even sure if I was breathing as memories flooded back. She'd always done that lip thing, for as long as I'd known her. It was a nervous habit that I wasn't even sure she was aware of. Her Grandma Rose had done the same thing. When they were stressed or worried or thinking about something, they pulled at their lower lip.

"This one?" I asked, the words coming out gravelly.

"Yep." She took a step back so I could grab the box. "It isn't the fanciest one here, but it has the best ratings."

"That's usually a good thing," I assured her, lifting the box. "Middle of the road is usually a safe bet. Just 'cause something's flashy doesn't mean it's the best."

"True," she murmured as the baby started to fuss. "We better hurry. She's getting hungry and we're about five minutes from complete devastation."

Balancing the car seat box in the seat of the cart, I followed her to the front of the store and unloaded the supplies while she grabbed about ten reusable bags from the end of the aisle. Blankets, towels, wash cloths, tiny baby clothes, diapers, bottles, pacifiers, some sort of baby carrier that looked like it would take an hour to put on, nursing pads, the list went on and on. She helped me unload as the baby began to really fuss, and then her eyes widened.

"Shit," she said, bouncing up and down. "I completely forgot—I'll be right back."

She took off without another word.

"New babies are hard," the checker said sympathetically. "Especially ones as fresh as yours."

I nodded.

"She can take her time," the woman continued with a smile as I lifted the car seat so she could scan it. "There's no line and I've got nowhere to be."

"Thanks," I said, glancing back toward the rest of the store. I wasn't sure if I should follow Cecilia or wait while she got whatever she'd forgotten. Deciding to wait, since I wasn't even sure where she'd gone, I shot an uncomfortable smile at the checker.

"First baby?" she asked knowingly.

"Uh, yeah."

"Don't worry, it doesn't get easier," she said, laughing. She leaned against her station. "Just kidding. I mean, it really doesn't get easier, but it changes. Right now, it's all about the lack of sleep and making sure they eat and poop enough. That goes away and you'll wish they weren't pooping so much!" She laughed again. "But eventually, you'll only be worrying whether they're safe and happy."

"Your kids grown now?" I asked.

"Picked up on that, did you?" she said with a wistful smile. "It's cliché and hard to understand when you're in the thick of it, but trust me on this—soak up every second of this stage because before you know it, that baby will be a toddler and then heading off to school and then graduating, and it'll feel like you blinked and missed it."

"I'll do my best," I replied, uncomfortable with the entire conversation. I wasn't about to correct her and embarrass her for assuming, but it also felt really fucking weird acting like I was any part of the baby's life. She was going to be gone the next day and I really *was* going to miss it all.

Just as I finally decided that I was going to find Cecilia and was pulling my wallet out of my back pocket to pay, the sound of the baby girl's cries became audible and they came around the corner.

"Sorry," Cecilia apologized, out of breath. "I forgot to get a few things."

She threw a package of underwear, a bra, a pair of sweats and matching sweatshirt, and a big package of pads on the conveyor belt. My lips twitched.

"Postpartum bleeding is no joke," she huffed, her cheeks a little pink.

"You could've just used the diapers," I joked. "They look about the same size."

Cecilia scoffed, but she was trying not to smile.

"You push something the size of her out the end of your penis and then you can give me shit about the size of my pads, alright?" she said, grabbing her wallet out of the cart.

My hand instinctively went to my junk and she grinned.

"I was telling your man that babies grow so fast that if he blinks, he'll miss it," the checker told Cecilia while she paid.

"That's what my mom always said," Cecilia murmured, shooting her a smile.

"Sometimes, truth is universal," the checker said knowingly. "Have a good night."

"You, too."

As we walked toward the front door, Cecilia pulled a baby blanket out of the cart and ripped off the tags so she could wrap the baby in it.

"I forgot a toothbrush," she said just as we reached the truck. She glanced behind us. "I could run back in—"

"I've got an extra at the house you can use," I said, setting the car seat box on the ground and using my pocket knife to open it. "She's going to burst the blood vessels in her face if you don't feed her soon."

"Good point," she said, doing the bouncing side step thing again.

"Climb in the front," I said, opening the door for her. "Feed her while I get this shit inside and get her seat set up."

"Are you sure?"

"Or we can both stand out here while she screams and then listen to her the entire way back to the house," I said over the baby's cries.

"Right."

The sound of the baby's cries were muted through the window of the truck and it didn't take long before they stopped altogether. As I pulled out the plastic and foam surrounding the car seat, I wondered how the hell Cecilia had gotten herself mixed up in a home invasion and homicide. None of it made sense. She didn't live in the mansion we'd found her in, but she'd been hiding in the nursery. From what I understood, and I assumed Cecilia would have mentioned it, we hadn't left a child behind. Had she been staying there? That didn't really make sense, either—people didn't fully furnish a nursery for their friend's kid. And who the hell were those people, anyway? Friends, maybe, but not the type I would have pictured Cecilia hanging out with. They were fancy wine and dinner parties, and unless things had changed a hell of a lot, Cecilia was more of a good beer and bonfires type.

I jerked my head up as she opened the door again and turned to sit sideways, her feet braced on the edge of the floorboard.

"Thank you," she said. "Again. I swear, by the end of this, I'll owe you so much that I'll never be able to repay you."

"You don't owe me shit," I countered as I worked on the seat. I grimaced as thoughts of just *how* she could repay me flashed in my mind. Jesus, I was an asshole.

"I don't know what I would've done if you guys hadn't shown up," she said quietly.

"He was leavin' when we got there," I reminded her. "You would've been okay."

"Maybe." She was silent for a while. "I probably would've been trapped in that closet until my parents got there tomorrow. I wouldn't have taken the chance to get out."

"Yeah, you would've."

"No," she said, letting out a humorless laugh. "I wouldn't have. I would have stayed in there like a scared little frozen rabbit, too afraid to move."

The words were familiar, but it took me a minute to place where I'd heard them before. When I remembered, it felt like I'd been punched in the gut.

"Cec," I said, straightening up to look at her.

"You know it's true," she said with a shrug.

"It wasn't true then, and it isn't true now," I replied firmly. How many times had we had this conversation? A hundred? A thousand? How many times had I argued that she wasn't a fucking coward for taking cover when she was being shot at? That she'd done exactly the right thing?

"Thank you," she said again.

"Stop fuckin' thankin' me," I snapped, the words sounding different after I knew where her head was at.

"None of this feels real," she said after a moment. "I know at some point it's going to hit me, but I don't think it has yet."

"That's normal," I replied, opening the back door so I could install the seat. "Shock's a funny thing."

"You think I'm in shock?" she asked.

"You've been through a lot tonight," I said. Why the hell did they make these things so hard to fucking install? "Hopefully, that shit *won't* sink in until you've got your people around you to carry some of the weight."

"I haven't seen them in a year, you know," she said. "It never feels that long until I start counting the months. We talk about them visiting me here or me going up there, but then plans fall through and we put it off."

"Bet Farrah isn't happy about that."

"No," she replied. "My mom hates it. I think she was glad at first when I moved so far away, but she wants me home now."

"Didn't your dad get in a pretty bad car accident a while back?"

"Yeah," she said, nodding. "That scared the shit out of me. I swear, I didn't breathe until I saw him with my own eyes."

"Makes sense they'd want you home. You got the distance you needed, but maybe it's time for you to head back."

"You know how it was for me up there," she said softly. "I have no interest in going back to that."

"Maybe it'd be different," I replied as I yanked the seat from side to side. It barely budged an inch. Good.

"I'm different," she said as she pulled the baby up to her shoulder and started patting her back. It sounded like she was thumping her pretty hard and I winced.

"You sure that's how you're supposed to do it?" I asked, shutting the back door.

"It's how the nurses showed me," she said with a huff. "It sounds bad, right? Like a drum."

"Uh, yeah."

"I'm different," she repeated, pulling the conversation back around as she met my eyes. "But I might not be different up there."

"You think you act like someone else down here?" I asked curiously.

"I know I do."

"Huh." I turned away and stuffed all the plastic back into the box and closed it before tossing it in the back of my truck.

"Huh, what?" Cecilia asked as she climbed out of her seat.

"You seem the same to me," I said seriously.

"Gee, thanks," she muttered.

I wasn't sure how to explain that I hadn't meant it as an insult.

★ ★ ★

LATER, AFTER WE'D figured out how to buckle the baby into her seat, drove home while she cried because she didn't want to be in it, dragged all of Cecilia's supplies in the quiet house, and settled in for the night, I laid in bed wondering how in the fuck I was going to sleep.

My bedroom door was open in case Cecilia needed something, but there was no noise coming from the guestroom. She must've gotten the baby to sleep. I hoped that Cecilia was sleeping, too. She looked worn the fuck out by the time we got all of her stuff unpacked from the truck.

Without conscious thought, my mind drifted to the usual memories that helped calm my mind enough to sleep.

Groaning, I reached up and fisted my hand in the pale blonde hair at the base of her neck, pulling her mouth down to mine. Her hips rolled as her mouth opened for my tongue. God, she was incredible. She hadn't been my first, far from it, but she was by far the best. There was something about the way she smelled, the feel of her skin under my fingertips, the way she moved, that outpaced every other partner by a mile. Or maybe, it was because I loved her—the knowledge of that making my skin prickle. Yeah, I loved her, I was more certain of that than I was of anything else in my life. I hadn't imagined love would feel like that, a mixture of possession and protectiveness and tenderness all wrapped up into this weird package that made my tongue too big for my mouth and my chest feel like it was caving in. If I could've stopped it, I would've. I would've never fallen in love with anyone if I'd had the choice. I couldn't help it, though, not with her. She was a force that hit with the strength of a freight train, but instead of running into me, it was like she flowed through me, the particles that made her mixing with the particles that made me. Inevitable. Necessary.

Her nails bit into the skin of my chest as she moaned against my mouth and I hissed, rolling sideways until she was under me.

"Like that?" I whispered into her ear as she gasped. "You want my cock?"

She answered me with a whimper. I hadn't expected anything else. She rarely said anything when we fucked, just random murmurs of my name and the whispered conviction that I was hers. But, while I normally chose my words carefully before I spoke, whenever we were like this, naked and fitted together like puzzle pieces, I couldn't stop the words from flowing out of my mouth. Filthy words that made her tremble and arch.

"Mine," I said into her ear, jerking my hips forward. Blindly, I reached for her legs, pulling them up around my back. "All mine."

She nodded, her breath catching. Within seconds, her hand had found the side of my face, cupping my cheek, and I leaned up slightly, knowing what the gesture meant. Shuddering, her body strung tight as a wire, she came in pulses around me.

I refused to follow behind her as she relaxed beneath me. Instead, as her eyes found mine, I grinned. "Again," I ordered, rolling my hips forward.

A quiet sound came from down the hall and my ears reddened in shame, but it wasn't enough for me to stop the memory flowing through my mind. Eventually, I must have crashed because I found myself in a familiar dream, one I hadn't had for years. I was on my back, staring through tree branches at a powder blue sky dotted with clouds. I knew that I needed to get up, but I couldn't. It was like I was encased in cement and the only part of my body that I had any control over was my eyes. I moaned as the sounds of chatter and laughter were drowned out by the sound of gunfire. I needed to get up. I had to help them. I jerked as the sky went blurry with tears. The sound of a baby crying made me panic and I tried to roll over onto my stomach, but none of my limbs would move. There wasn't supposed to be a baby there.

I woke up in a cold sweat, my heart thumping so hard that I could feel it in my ears.

"I'm sorry," Cecilia said from the doorway of my room. "I thought she might settle down if I walked around with her, but I didn't realize your door was open."

"What's wrong with her?" I asked blearily, leaning up on my elbow.

"Nothing that I can tell," she said. She sounded close to tears herself. "She's just pissed. Every time I sit down, she starts back up again." She was swaying from side to side and the baby's cries turned to whimpers as she spoke.

"Why don't I take her for a little bit?" I said. I wasn't going back to sleep anyway. "You can get some rest."

"No, that's okay," she said as I sat up and threw the bedding back. Her words trailed off and her eyes widened.

I realized way too late that I was sitting there in nothing but a pair of boxer briefs. Thank Christ, my dream had completely obliterated any erection I'd had from my preferred method of falling asleep.

"I'll grab some pants," I mumbled, pushing up from the bed.

"Don't cover up on my account," Cecilia said jokingly, though she sounded exhausted. "Jesus, I didn't even know you were capable of that."

"Of what?" I asked, glancing down to double-check that I wasn't sporting wood as I pulled a pair of sweats out of my dresser.

"That." She waved her hand at me, her eyes focused on the tattoo of her name on my chest before she looked away. "I didn't even know your body could make that much muscle."

I laughed. "It couldn't when I was nineteen."

"Steroids?" she asked in mock understanding. "How're your balls?"

"I don't do steroids and my balls are fine," I shot back, striding toward her. "Boob job?" I asked as I took the baby from her arms.

She gasped and her jaw dropped.

"Actually," she replied, crossing her arms over her chest, "breast-feeding."

I just nodded as I settled the baby against me, gently rubbing her back.

"I can't believe you said that," she said, shaking her head.

"Hey," I murmured. "You opened that particular door asking about my balls."

"I was joking!"

"So was I."

Cecilia stared at me for a moment and then snorted. "Jesus," she said with a sigh, her voice wobbling. Using both hands to comb her hair back from her face, she tilted her head toward the ceiling. "I'm so fucking tired."

I didn't know if it was the memory I'd stupidly conjured up or the fact that she seemed so vulnerable that made me do it, but I reached for her, wrapping my hand around the back of her neck to pull her in, tucking her against my chest next to the baby. I refused to think about all the shit between us, the history, or the fact that she'd be gone the next day.

CHAPTER 5
CECILIA

TREMBLING, I PRESSED my forehead against Mark's chest. Somehow, without even knowing myself, he'd known exactly what I needed.

I was independent to a fault. I never asked for help if I didn't have to, and I handled anything that came my way. But I'd never appreciated a hug more than I did at that moment.

We stood there holding each other for a long time. Mark's hand didn't stray from my neck, and I didn't move my hands from where I'd placed them on his back. He rocked us slowly from side to side, his lips pressed to the top of my head, and eventually, I felt myself start to relax into him more and more.

"Come on," he said eventually, his voice gravelly. "You need some sleep."

I was groggy when he pulled away and it took me a second to get my bearings, but he hadn't gone far. Standing at the side of the bed, his eyes met mine as he lifted the blankets in invitation. It was a bad idea and we both knew it, but I just didn't have it in me to do anything but close the distance between us and crawl into the king size bed.

The sheets smelled like him. Whatever he wore—it was probably just body wash and deodorant—was different than I remembered, but his smell, the scent that was specifically him, hadn't changed. Curling onto my side in the center of the bed, I let out a long breath.

"She's sleeping now," Mark said as he rounded the bed. He laid the baby down next to me so gently that I felt tears sting the back of my nose.

As he walked away, I rested my hand against her chest, comforted by the rise and fall. I was so caught up in watching her, my eyes barely open as the tension finally seeped from my body, that I didn't realize he'd gone to the opposite side of the bed until he was sliding in behind me.

We didn't talk about it. He didn't ask if it was okay. I didn't ask him what he was doing. By unspoken agreement, we just let it be, but I was hyperaware of every move he made. I was conscious of every inch between us. The tension I'd finally released was back, but it was fraught with more emotions than I knew how to name.

I curled my arm up under the pillow so my head rested in the crook of my elbow. He rolled to his side. I pulled my hand from the baby girl's chest and tucked it beneath my chin. He fidgeted with the blankets.

Finally, he pressed forward, his body aligning with mine from knees to shoulders. I let out the breath I hadn't realized I'd been holding.

I rolled slightly forward, straightening my bottom leg while the top stayed bent. Like a key fitted into a lock, his top leg slid over mine, and his weight pressed against my back. I closed my eyes as his hand skimmed my waist and slid beneath my shirt to rest against my ribs.

It wasn't sexual, not in the way it would've been with anyone else. It was comfort. I couldn't remember the number of times we'd slept that way, his body wrapped around mine. Still, I couldn't stop the slight arch of my back and tilt of my hips that lined us up perfectly. His groan was nearly inaudible.

Then, miraculously, we slept.

I woke up later to the baby squirming next to me. She hadn't started crying yet, but by the expression on her face, Armageddon was imminent.

"Where you going?" Mark murmured, his arm around me tightening as I started to slide away.

"Baby's up," I replied. He moved his arm and I crawled gingerly around the baby and off the side of the bed. When I stood, I cringed. Glancing between the baby and Mark, I considered my options. I really needed to get to the bathroom before I had a serious mess on my hands, but I couldn't exactly take her in with me unless I wanted to lay her on the floor. Mark's bathroom was clean, but he was a dude, and I highly doubted it was *that* clean. I could lay her on the guest room bed—

"What's wrong?" Mark asked.

"I need to go to the bathroom."

"So, go."

"Can she stay here with you?"

He stared at me, his expression confused. "Of course."

"Thank you," I said as I hurried around the bed.

"Stop fuckin' thankin' me," he said tiredly, reaching up to scratch at his beard.

After I grabbed my supplies and cleaned up in the bathroom, I rifled through the bags we'd brought back from the store the night before. I'd gone a little crazy there, and I wasn't ashamed to admit it. Okay, maybe I was a little ashamed. When we'd gotten to the baby department, I'd gone a little manic when I'd realized how much shit she was going to need. I'd thrown things in the cart that I knew she probably wouldn't use for a while, but some compulsion to have everything she could possibly need was overwhelming. Maybe it was the *nesting* that everyone had talked about and I'd never felt.

Grabbing a little footie pajama with a matching hat, a diaper, and wipes, I held them to my chest and picked my phone up from the nightstand. My mom had texted me while we slept and thankfully, they were only a few hours away.

After sending a reply, I walked slowly back toward Mark's room.

Now that I was fully awake, I was far more hesitant to just go traipsing around in his space. I didn't belong in there. I didn't even belong in that house.

As much as I'd appreciated the familiar warmth and strength of his body, it hadn't made me any more comfortable in his presence. Actually, it was the opposite. I felt more on edge now than I'd been before.

"You're pretty," Mark said as I stopped in the doorway. He was leaning up on his elbow with his back to me, and his head was tilted down looking at the baby. "Just like your mama. And you're bossy like her, too," he said as she squawked. "I know, I know. You're not bossy, you just know what you want."

I leaned against the doorjamb, unable to move forward as my heart pounded. Jesus, the sight of him leaned over her like that brought back dreams I'd long forgotten—and grief that I'd refused to acknowledge for the last decade.

"She'll be back in just a minute with the goods," Mark said with a soft chuckle. "No need to get all wound up. There you go, princess. Feels good to have a little freedom, huh?" Just as he finished speaking, she let out a wail that could probably be heard from across the street. "Shit," he yelped.

"What happened?" I barked, hurrying around the bed.

"I just unwrapped her," he replied defensively, using one hand to ineffectually try to wrap her back up.

"She's probably just cold," I reassured him, letting out a relieved breath as I lifted her from the bed. As soon as she was pressed against me, her mouth started rooting around at my neck. "Babies like being wrapped up tight because it makes them feel secure. It reminds them of being on the inside."

"Ah, like a halfway house for newborns," he said, leaning back on the pillows to watch me.

"I've never heard it put that way," I replied. "But yeah, I guess."

"You should probably figure out what you're going to call her," Mark said as I laid the baby back down and went to work changing her diaper and clothes. "She needs a name."

"I'll name her when I'm ready."

"Better decide soon or I'm going to start calling her Cecilia," he said, his lips twitching.

"Your friends are a trip," I replied. Every time I tried to thread one of her legs into the little pants portion of the outfit she bent the other one back up against her belly and I had to start the process all over again. I was regretting not just buying her more nightgowns. Her cries turned into wails.

"Cec," Mark said as I grew more and more flustered. He reached over and slid his hands under the baby, lifting her to rest with her butt on his chest. "Just feed her and then you can get her dressed."

He patted the bed beside him and against my better judgment, but following my gut instinct absolutely, I crawled back onto the bed. He handed her over and after a couple attempts to get her all lined up, the room grew silent as she latched on.

"You're a good mom," Mark said, watching me.

"I don't know about that," I huffed. I'd been a mother for less than twelve hours. I had plenty of time to fuck it up royally.

"You're a natural," he murmured.

"No one is a natural," I countered, running my hand over her mostly bald scalp. "It's like all of a sudden this new person is just *there*, and you have to remember all this shit—how to be careful of their umbilical cord, and how to change a diaper, and support their head and don't even get me started on the whole nursing bullshit." I looked at him. "Breast may be best, but it's a fucking nightmare at first."

"Yeah?" He actually seemed interested, so I kept going.

"Oh, yeah." I nodded. "I was only planning on the first couple of days—get her started on the good stuff, you know? But Jesus. She wouldn't latch on correctly and my nipples hurt like a motherfucker for the first two days. Seriously. Agony. And I had all these lactation nurses coming in and out, feeling me up and talking in these super soothing, annoying as fuck tones when I really just needed them to give it to me straight. They finally set us up with these little plastic contraptions that went over my nipples, but then I lost them somewhere and we had to figure out how to do it old school anyway." I shook my head. "Plus, I'm always thirsty. I have to drink a shit ton of water and I hate water." I sighed. "We figured it all out eventually, though." I rubbed at a spot on the side of my breast that ached like someone was pinching me really hard. The first week of baby girl's life had been a whirlwind of nursing and pumping so Liv could give her bottles when I wasn't there.

"Feelin' you up, huh?" he said, lifting his arms up to cross them behind his head.

"Of course that was the part you latched onto."

"Nice pun."

"I thought so," I said, grinning a little.

"Well, she seems to have the hang of it now," he said with a sigh.

"Yeah. It helps that my milk came in, so she's got immediate satisfaction."

"I have no idea what that means, but I'll take your word for it."

We were quiet for a few minutes and I took the time to actually look around his room. Just like in the guest room, the furniture in his bedroom was no joke. It looked heavy and solid and expensive, and I wondered if he'd picked it out himself. There was a chair in the corner that had a pile of folded towels on it and a jacket tossed over the back. The dresser was clean and mostly bare beyond a photo I recognized of him and his mother when he was little. I quickly looked away from it.

"I don't spend a lot of time in here," he said, dragging my attention back to the bed. "We're not home very often."

"Do you like your job?" I asked curiously. When we were young, he hadn't spoken much about what he'd wanted to be when he grew up. He'd always been good with building and fixing anything mechanical, and I guess I'd assumed that he'd work in the club's garage and take his place in the hierarchy. His life now was so far removed from what I'd envisioned for him—for us.

"Yeah, I do," he said, shifting a little on the bed. "It's satisfying and I like never seeing the same thing twice. Shit is always shifting and changing. Keeps me on my toes."

"Is it dangerous?" I asked quietly.

"Life is dangerous," he replied seriously. "No matter what you're doin' with it."

"Fair point."

"I'm good at what I do," he continued. "And my team is the best I've ever worked with."

"They're an odd mix," I replied.

"Probably why they work so well together," he said. "Everyone brings their own shit—faults and assets—to the table."

"Are Josiah and Ephraim brothers?" I asked. "Because they almost seem like they could be twins."

"Cousins, actually," he said in surprise. "Most people don't catch that."

"It's in their mannerisms," I explained. "The way they move, the way they smile, even their voices are similar."

"Get the two of them together and fuck," he said, drawing the word out with a small chuckle. "They could convince the Pope that Jesus was a figment of his imagination."

"Persuasive, huh?" I asked as I brought the baby to my shoulder to burp her.

"Charming is the word you're looking for," he said ruefully. "Snake oil salesmen, the both of them."

"Does that come in handy?"

"More times than you would think."

After the loudest burp I'd ever heard coming from someone so small, I laid her on the bed between my knees, quickly finished dressing her, and wrapped her snugly again. "This is another thing that I had no fucking clue how to do before she came."

"Sure you did," he said, leaning over to look at her. "You've made a burrito before."

I raised my eyebrows in realization. "Well, fuck."

Mark laughed. "Lay back down," he said, his face going soft in a way that was both familiar and brand new. "Maybe she'll sleep for a while."

"The sun's up," I argued, glancing at his windows.

"You got somewhere to be?"

I looked back at him and dropped all protest when his eyes met mine. The pull was as strong as it had ever been, and I was too worn out to fight it. Not now. Not yet.

This time, when I settled the baby on the open space between me and the edge of the bed and laid down on my side, Mark didn't hesitate to curve his body into mine. He reached beyond me and set his hand on the tightly wrapped bundle for a moment before his arm came back around my waist and slid up my shirt.

I didn't bother hiding the arch of my back or the tilt of my hips and he didn't try to muffle his groan. His lips pressed against the back of my neck just before his body relaxed. It didn't take him long to fall back asleep, but I laid there for a while, listening to his breathing.

If someone would have told me a week before that I'd end up in Mark Eastwood's bed again, I would have laughed in their face. I still remembered the devastation he'd wrought, the days I hadn't been able to crawl out of bed and when I finally had, the absolute confusion I'd felt about what I was supposed to do with myself. My world had started and ended with him, and then suddenly, he'd been gone and I'd been completely rudderless. It had taken me a long time to dig myself out of the hole he'd left me in.

Counting on him again was probably a mistake. I knew that. But, as I lay there next to him, I reminded myself that this was temporary. He was an old friend who had come through for me in a big way, but that was all this was. Maybe if I kept repeating that, I'd be able to keep my feelings in check.

I must have fallen back asleep because we woke up later to the sound of my phone ringing on the nightstand.

"Hello?" I answered groggily.

"We're outside," my mom said. "At least I hope this is his house. We've been knocking for five minutes."

"Shit," I sputtered, sitting up. "I'll be right there."

"They're here?" Mark asked, throwing back the bedding.

"Yeah. God, what time is it?" I checked my phone. "Shit, it's almost one."

"They made good time," he said as he got out of bed.

"Oh, my God," I said, realizing that we'd been asleep for over three hours. She never slept that long. Snatching the baby up off the bed, I shuddered. As soon as I had her against me and could feel her breathing, I let out a watery sigh of relief. She was okay.

"What?" Mark said, staring at me.

"She slept for so long."

"That's a problem?"

I didn't answer because suddenly we could hear someone pounding on the front door.

"I have a feeling my dad is done being polite," I said in amusement as I swung my legs off the bed.

"Let's get this over with," Mark said as he led me out of the bedroom.

"Not looking forward to the reunion?" I asked dryly.

"I'm not your pop's favorite person," he muttered. When we reached the entryway, he paused, opening the drawer of a small table behind the couch. My eyes widened as he pulled out a pistol. "Just a precaution," he said easily.

"Uh, you might not want to be holding that when you open the door," I cautioned.

"You might be right," he mused with a chuckle, setting it on top of the table within arms reach.

He unbolted the lock and swung the door open, and there, looking tired and worried, were my parents and brother Cam.

"I swear to God, CeeCee," my mom griped as they came into the house. "You've given me more gray hair than your brother and sisters combined."

She came straight for me, and as soon as she'd reached me, her arms were wrapped tightly around me and the baby. "That was the longest trip ever," she said softly, kissing the side of my head. She leaned back to meet my eyes. "You're okay?"

"I'm okay," I replied.

"I've had the stress shits the entire way," Cam complained as he came up beside us. "Hug me quick so I can find a bathroom."

"Do *not* blow up Woody's bathroom," I warned as he pulled me against his chest.

"Well, I'm not shittin' in the yard," he replied. Wrapping his hands around my skull, he tipped my head back to look at him. "All good?"

"Not even close," I whispered back.

"We'll get ya there," he said, kissing my forehead. "But first, bathroom."

"Down the hall on your left," Mark directed him.

"Hey, Bumblebee," my dad greeted, still standing just inside the door. He was watching me closely, his jaw clenched and his eyes soft.

"Hey, Dad." I tried to smile, but my eyes watered. God, these fucking hormones were the worst.

"C'mere," he ordered, opening his arms.

There was something about the feeling of my dad holding me close that made everything seem safe. The scent of leather and his deodorant, the way he notched his chin above my head and smoothed the back of my hair with his palm, it was one of the most comforting things I'd ever encountered.

"We're here now," he said with a sigh.

"You made good time," Mark said from somewhere behind me.

"We were motivated," my dad replied as he let me go, leaving one arm wrapped around my shoulders. "Fill us in?"

"While I make breakfast," Mark said, jerking his head toward the kitchen. "You guys hungry?"

"Starving," my mom replied.

We followed Mark into the kitchen and my mom started laughing. "Well, this looks familiar," she said, staring at the table covered in car parts.

"Bullshit," my dad argued, leading me to a chair. As soon as I'd sat down, he ran his hand over my hair again before stepping away. "Woman, you have never let me leave any of my shit in the kitchen."

"You have to train them," my mom told me teasingly. "But they eventually learn."

My dad scoffed and turned toward Mark. "You got any coffee?"

I sat back and let their conversation flow around me. For the first time in almost twenty-four hours, I felt like everything might be okay. Not that I'd make it okay, or I'd figure it out, but that it actually was going to *be* okay.

"I'm chafing like you would not believe," Cam said as he came into the room.

"Keep your swamp ass away from me," I replied, trying to dodge his hand as he reached for me. "You better have washed your hands!"

"Of course I did," he said, flicking water in my face.

"Ew," I groaned. "Why didn't you use a towel?"

"I heard something about breakfast and I was in a hurry," he replied, chuckling.

"Help me clear the table," my mom ordered Cam. "We can set this stuff on the counter."

"I can grab that," Mark said apologetically.

"No biggie." My mom waved him off.

I watched as she and Cam cleared the table while Mark grabbed supplies out of the fridge and spoke quietly to my dad. Shit just kept getting weirder and weirder.

"You haven't had any water since you got here," Mark said as he set a glass of ice water down in front of me. "Didn't you say you were supposed to be drinking a lot of it?"

"I've been a little preoccupied," I replied. I tilted my head back to meet his eyes. "Thank you."

"Why are you supposed to be drinking water?" my mom asked, watching us in confusion.

When I didn't answer right away, Mark did it for me.

"Because of the breastfeeding."

"The breastfeeding?" my mom replied. Her eyes shot to the baby.

"It's not what you're thinking—" I said, shaking my head.

"You told us that you had your *friend's* baby with you," my dad said, his voice low and angry.

"Yeah, about that," Mark waded in, pointing at my dad. "You could have filled me in."

"She *is* my friend's baby," I said at the same time. God, this wasn't how I wanted to tell them. My parents were staring at me like they wanted to throttle me, and I couldn't really blame them. I hadn't given them the full story when I'd called them, and now they were having this huge bomb dropped in their lap with no warning.

I looked at Mark, whose face had lost all expression while he waited for me to explain what the hell was happening. I hadn't exactly been straight with him, either.

I looked down at the baby's sleeping face and took a deep breath before lifting my head again.

"I was a surrogate."

Chapter 6

MARK

"YOU WERE A surrogate," Cecilia's mom Farrah said, dropping into a chair at the table.

"Yes," Cecilia confirmed. "I carried her, but she was never supposed to be mine."

"The fuck?" Cam muttered.

"She's not genetically linked to me," Cecilia said, her voice strained. "I was just the gestational carrier. I just, you know, *grew* her because Liv couldn't."

"And Liv's the friend who was gunned down at her house last night?" her dad asked. Casper looked like he was ready to hit something, but he also oddly looked like he wanted to hug his daughter.

"Yeah," Cecilia said. Her fingers started pulling at her bottom lip.

"So—" Farrah started to speak, then seemed to lose her train of thought. She shook her head and ran a hand down her face. "So, she belongs to your friends. Do they have any family? Where is she gonna go?"

If I hadn't known Cecilia so well once upon a time, and maybe if I hadn't been watching her so closely, I wouldn't have seen the way her arms tightened around the baby. She lifted her chin.

"She stays with me," Cecilia announced.

"Don't think it works that way," Cam said, disbelief threading his words. "You can't just take her if she's got family."

"The only family she has is gone," Cecilia shot back. "Cane has a grown son, but Liv was afraid of him. She's not going to him."

"Wait, how old was your friend's husband?" Cam asked.

"You don't get in the middle of family shit, Cecilia," Casper said at the same time.

"Jesus," Farrah muttered.

"Stop," Cecilia snapped, smacking her hand on the table. "None of you have any say in this."

"The hell we don't," Casper replied darkly.

Cecilia rose from the table. "If you wanna go rounds with me," she said softly, staring unflinchingly into her dad's angry eyes, "I'm all for it. But you don't make my decisions for me, and you haven't in a long ass time."

"What you're doin' is wrong," Casper replied slowly.

"That's a little like the pot calling out the kettle, isn't it?" she shot back. Then she turned and left the room.

We all stood silently, digesting everything we'd heard. I didn't know what to fucking think. She'd carried the baby and I knew she loved her, but if baby girl belonged to someone else, it wasn't any kind of right for her to keep her.

"What a godawful mess," Farrah said, running her fingers through her hair the exact same way Cecilia had done the night before. "She can't be serious about keeping that baby."

"I feel for her," Cam said, leaning back in his chair. "She was havin' that baby for a couple that's dead now. She wasn't growin' her for some relative to raise."

"You and Trix had a surrogate and somethin' happened, that woman would sure as fuck not be keepin' my grandkid," Casper said through his teeth.

"I've got no skin in the game," I waded in cautiously. "But I'd give her a minute. Cecilia isn't stupid. She always has a reason for the things she does."

"She's not stupid, but she's selfish as fuck," Cam muttered.

I waited a second for her parents to tell him to watch his mouth and my stomach soured when they didn't.

"Keep your bullshit opinions to yourself," I said, filling in the silence. "You say another word about your sister and you can get the fuck out of my house."

"You fuckin' kiddin' me?" Cam asked, straightening.

"Enough," Casper snapped, pointing at his son.

"I'm gonna check on her," I announced. "Coffee's about done. Mugs are in the cabinet to the left of the sink."

I walked away before I said what I wanted to. Fucking Cameron. Their whole fucking family. I wanted to shake them. It was the same old shit that Cecilia had dealt with when we were young. It was like they thought she was inherently bad or something, like she was just selfish and mean and they just had to deal with it. Never, not once, had they tried to get to the root of the shit she said and did.

Cecilia could be a bitch. Hell, she could be the biggest bitch you'd ever meet—but there was always a reason, even if it didn't make sense to anyone but her. She had never gone around trying to piss people off.

What was that saying? Hurt people hurt people.

And I'd never met someone who hurt as bad as Cecilia and managed to hide it so well.

She hadn't gone into the guestroom. Instead, she was sitting in the center of my bed.

"You here to give me shit?" she asked, looking up from where she'd set the baby between her knees.

"You're in my room," I pointed out, closing the door behind me. "And I figured I'd put a shirt on before I started frying bacon."

Cecilia sighed. "I'm sorry," she said, watching me cross the room. "I swear to God, they turn me into someone even *I* can't stand."

"You let them get to you," I said, pulling on a t-shirt. "And I've never understood why, because in the end, you do whatever the fuck you want anyway."

"Because they're my parents," she said, staring at the baby. "And I still want their approval."

"Not sure you're gonna get it this time."

"When have I ever?" she said, chuckling humorlessly. "Same shit, different day."

"Cec." I sat on the edge of the bed. "She's not yours."

"You know," she snapped, looking up to meet my eyes, "I'm so fucking tired of everyone always assuming that I'm doing the wrong thing."

"This seems pretty cut and dry to me."

"Well, you have no fucking clue," she said. "None."

"Then why don't you tell me?" I said softly.

"It won't even matter."

"Try me."

"When I say Liv was scared of Cane's son, I mean *scared*," she said after a long pause. "She called me to pick her up once from their house. It was before they were married. When I got there, she was shaking. Cane had left for some work thing and his son had shown up. He told her that she'd never marry his dad. That he'd gut her first."

"Jesus Christ," I muttered.

"Yeah. And that wasn't the only time. The guy's a fucking nut job. It got to the point that he wasn't allowed at the house."

When someone knocked on the door, her mouth snapped shut.

"Come on in," I called.

"Hiding out in here isn't going to solve anything," Farrah said tiredly as she swung open the door.

Cecilia stayed stubbornly silent.

"You can't just keep a baby that isn't yours."

"Sit down," I replied, pointing to the open space next to Cecilia.

"I'm guessin' you'll want to hear this."

"Mark," Cecilia said in warning.

I glanced at her and then back at Farrah. "Let her talk."

Farrah nodded and strode into the room. She sat down next to Cecilia and waited.

"After Cane found out that his son, Drake, had been threatening Liv, Cane banned him from the house. He wasn't even allowed on the property. They maintained a relationship as far as I know, but Cane kept things separate. Liv was fucking terrified. She was always on guard. Eventually, after they were married, things settled down and she seemed like she wasn't as worried anymore." I frowned. "If she was, she didn't say anything to me about it."

"He kept seein' his son?" I asked in disbelief.

Cecilia shrugged. "It was his kid."

"Doesn't matter," Casper said from the doorway. "Any man that threatened your mother would answer to me."

Cecilia nodded once at her dad. "When they asked me to be a surrogate, they were concerned. Liv wanted a baby more than anything, but they didn't want Drake to find out and cause problems."

"Fuck," Casper spat.

"So we didn't go through an agency," Cecilia said. "Cane had the money and the connections to do it privately." She met her dad's eyes. "It was all legal and aboveboard. They just didn't want to advertise it."

"They threw you in a lion's den and crossed their fingers that he wouldn't fuckin' notice you," I said, anger burning in my chest. "Jesus Christ, Cecilia."

"She was my best friend," Cecilia replied, crossing her arms over her chest. "And I was in a position to help."

I wanted to believe that was her reasoning, that she'd gone into the thing because of love for her friend and nothing else, but I couldn't shake the feeling that her motivation wasn't quite so clear cut. I searched her eyes for clues and she looked away.

"It all went fine," she said, shrugging her shoulders. "My pregnancy went off without a hitch."

"Yeah, until you had the baby and your friends were shot dead in their house," her dad said, smacking his hand against the doorjamb.

"He couldn't have known," Cecilia said, her eyes widening as she shook her head in denial. "They were waiting to tell anyone. They didn't even come see me at the hospital."

"Timing's a little too coincidental," I told her softly, reaching out to put my hand on her thigh.

"There's no fuckin' thing as coincidence," Casper said. "That shit doesn't exist."

"They had the baby's room all set up," I reminded Cecilia, my gut twisting as she closed her eyes in sad realization. "What's this guy look like?"

I had a pretty good feeling that I could describe him to her, but I waited to say anything until I was sure.

"Dark hair and eyes," she said, her hand lifting to her lips before she deliberately dropped it again. "Mid-twenties. Less than six feet tall, but not super short. He wears his hair brushed back from his face like some old-time gangster and he looks like an idiot. Walks around like he owns the world. *Saunters.*" She scoffed.

"Baby," I said, my tone telling her everything she didn't want to hear. I'd seen that man. He was the douchebag we'd watched leave her friend's house with a box full of shit. No wonder he hadn't robbed the place. As soon as someone found the bodies, it would all go to him anyway.

"Fuck," she whispered, her eyes filling with tears. "Goddamn it."

Farrah reached out to rub her back. "We have to assume he knows about the baby," she murmured.

"But he has no proof," Cecilia countered, sniffling. "She's still legally mine, and I don't think he even knows my name."

"What do you mean?" Casper asked.

"I gave birth to her, so she was legally considered mine. Her birth certificate has my name on it." Cecilia reached out to smooth her hand over the sleeping baby's head. "They could've done a thing called a pre-birth parentage order, but they decided not to. Liv and Cane were going to legally adopt her, instead. I guess they just really didn't want anyone to know until they actually had the baby."

"They never filed any paperwork?" Farrah asked dubiously.

"No," Cecilia replied. "I haven't even sent in the birth certificate yet. Liv hadn't decided on a name, and I didn't want it to be something different than what she chose. We were supposed to sign everything this morning. Cane's attorney was going to come to the house—that's why I was staying the night there."

"So the bodies have most likely been found by now," Casper said quietly. "Anyone else know about all this?"

"No," Cecilia said, shaking her head. "Only the attorney."

"We got company," Cam said from the hallway, his voice low. "Guy's checkin' out the front of the house."

When the doorbell rang a few seconds later, I knew it wasn't one of my team outside. They might hang back for a minute when they noticed the bikes parked out front, but they sure as hell wouldn't have rang the doorbell.

"I'll handle it," I said. I strode to the front of the house with Casper at my back.

"Don't like this," he said quietly.

"Yeah, me, either." Grabbing the pistol off the table near the door, I double-checked that the safety was on and stuffed it in the back of my sweatpants. As soon as Casper was out of sight, I swung open the door.

"Can I help you?" I asked, keeping my expression neutral as I stared at the motherfucker I'd seen the night before.

"Hey," he said, smiling. "Sorry to bother you, but I was thinking about buying that place for sale down the street, and I was wondering how you liked the neighborhood."

"It's good," I replied, hiding the fact that I wanted to grab him up by his scrawny neck and choke the life out of him. "Pretty quiet. No complaints."

"Good, good," he said, still smiling. "Good place for a family, then?"

"Don't have a family," I replied. "So, I couldn't tell you." I looked beyond him, wondering if he'd brought any muscle or if he was arrogant enough to come alone. Unfortunately, I couldn't tell. I wasn't about to put Cecilia and the baby in danger by starting shit when I didn't know who else was watching the house.

"Alright," he chuckled. He stared at me for a moment. "Well, thanks for your time."

"No problem." I shut the door in his face and shoved the deadbolt home.

"Motherfucker had balls, showing up here," I told Casper as he stepped into view.

"How the fuck would he know she's here?" Casper asked.

"No idea, but he sure as hell does," I muttered, looking out the gap in the curtains. He got right back in his car and drove away, not even bothering to continue the buying-a-house-down-the-street cover.

"He got to the attorney," Casper said.

"Sure as shit," I replied. "But how the fuck would he link me to Cec?"

My mind clicked through all the puzzle pieces, trying to find how they fit. Even though he clearly knew who Cecilia was, we hadn't seen each other in over a decade. It would take serious digging and *time* to find any link between us. There was also no way that he could've known that I was one of the team who'd taken her from the house.

Beyond the fact that we'd worn goddamn masks, Wilson had also copied and then wiped the security cameras far enough back that Cecilia couldn't be connected to the crime scene. So, that left what? What did the guy know and how was he getting the information?

"We need to leave," I told Casper as I strode back down the hallway. When I got to my room, Cecilia was pacing, the baby in her arms. She looked up at me when I entered.

"Who was it?" she asked worriedly.

"We gotta go, baby," I told her softly.

"He found us? How?" she asked as I reached her. I pulled her into my arms, the baby tucked between us.

"Don't know yet," I said. "But I'll find out."

"Is he still out there?" she asked, turning her head toward the window.

"Nope, he's gone." I let her go and smoothed my thumb over her cheek. "He'll be back. We're leavin' as soon as we can get packed up."

"Do you have a bag?" Farrah asked Cecilia.

My lips twitched even as I started switching gears. I needed to call my team and we needed to find a place to go. "She's got about ten," I told Farrah. "Your daughter did a little shopping last night."

"Thatta girl," Farrah said, wrapping her arm around Cecilia's waist so she could lead her away. "Where'd you stash them?"

"Somethin' isn't right," Cam said as soon as the women left the room. "We're missin' somethin'."

"Obviously," I muttered, grabbing my go bag out of the closet. I always cleaned everything and stashed it when we got back into town so it was ready and I didn't have to think about it when it was time to leave again, but this time, I was going to need a different supply list.

Kneeling by my dresser, I swung open the door that looked like the rest of the drawers and opened my safe.

"I'm gonna keep an eye on things outside," Cam announced as he left.

Casper watched me from across the room. "Couldn't they just take the whole dresser?"

"Safe's bolted to the load bearing beams," I said distractedly as I pulled out my passport, bank paperwork and a couple stacks of cash. "It's built into the wall and I built the dresser around it."

"Nice work," he mused.

"Gonna call my team," I said as I zipped my bag and got to my feet. "I wanna be out of here in five minutes."

"We're set," he replied. "I'll go help Farrah get CeeCee ready."

"No one goes outside until we're ready to go," I ordered, pulling my phone out. "No reason to let them know we're goin' before we do."

"This ain't my first party," Casper said in amusement as he walked away.

Crazy bastard. I swear, the more hectic things got, the easier going he seemed. For as long as I could remember, he'd been that way. We'd be holed up at the club because they were dealing with some heavy bullshit, and Casper would be strolling around the room like he didn't have a care in the world, pinching his wife's ass and laughing with the boys. It was a show he put on, and I knew it, but it was still hard to see any cracks in the façade.

"We've got trouble," I told Forrest when he answered.

"Hell, boy," he said with a sigh. "I knew this was comin'."

"The fucker we saw at the house last night just showed up at my door."

"No shit?"

"No shit," I confirmed. "I've got no clue how he found Cecilia, but he did."

"You know who he is?" he asked in surprise.

"Son of the dead man," I replied grimly.

"Ain't that some shit," he muttered. "What do you need?"

"I'll spread the word," I told him as I grabbed clothes out of my dresser. "Siah and Eph, here. They can wait it out and see who comes to play. You, Eli, and Lu, meet up with us. Until we know what we're dealin' with, probably best if we all lay low."

"You think they got a look at us?"

"No clue," I replied, pulling my jeans on. "Wilson took care of the cameras, but there's a chance. Very few ways he could've linked me to Cecilia, and that's one of them."

"Gotcha."

"Meet you in the desert," I said, referring to one of the safe houses we'd bought as a group. There were four, spread out as randomly as possible.

"Roger that."

As I got dressed, I called the rest of the team and let them know what was happening and where they needed to be. Thankfully, none of them said a word of complaint. We all knew at some point we'd be caught up in some shit. We'd just never realized that it wouldn't be connected to one of our jobs.

"All set?" I asked, meeting everyone in the kitchen.

"She's going to be hungry soon," Cecilia said as she fussed with the baby's blanket inside her car seat.

"You can feed her on the road," I replied. I picked up a few of the bags that were waiting on the kitchen table.

"Farrah's riding with you," Casper announced as he lifted the baby's car seat. "Me and Cam will follow."

With a nod, I led the group out of the house.

"How you doin'?" I asked as I helped Cecilia into the back seat of the truck. She had just enough room to slide her feet in. An uncharacteristic rain shower meant I couldn't put her stuff in the bed of the truck and the floorboard was covered with bags full of baby supplies.

"I'm scared," she said, her hands clenched into fists. "Pissed. And I feel like shit for dragging everyone into this."

"Don't," I replied, brushing her hair away from her face. I left my hand there for longer than necessary, because her skin felt hot.

"Let's move," Casper called as Farrah hopped into the front seat of the truck.

"It's gonna be fine," I told Cecilia.

I slammed her door and climbed in the driver's seat, the back of my neck tingling. Someone had their eyes on us. As I pulled out of the drive and headed toward the freeway, I kept a look out for anything out of the ordinary and didn't find a damn thing. Whoever was helping the motherfucker was damn good at their job.

I was going to have to be better.

Chapter 7

CECILIA

We drove for a long time. Mark took residential streets, backtracking and going in big circles before hopping on the freeway headed west. As time passed, I got more and more antsy. Sure, I'd grown up in an environment where bad shit happened and my family was constantly watching their backs, but I'd lived a relatively normal life since I moved away. I never could have imagined that becoming a surrogate for my best friend would somehow morph into running from a fucking madman.

Drake was creepy as hell, no doubt about it. He was just one of those guys that constantly gave off a bad vibe—well-dressed and seemingly normal, but you'd still cross the street in broad daylight so you didn't have to pass by him. Still, I would've never guessed that he had it in him to kill Cane and Liv.

"How you doing?" my mom asked, turning in her seat to look at me. "Alright?"

"I'm fine," I lied, forcing a smile.

"Bullshit," she scoffed. She wrapped her arms around the back of the seat and got comfortable. "Did you know that my boyfriend before your dad was shot right in front of my apartment building?"

"What?" I asked, my jaw dropping. I'd never even heard a whisper of that story.

"Yeah," she said with a sigh. "A drive-by. It was—" she paused and shook her head. "It was different than what happened when you were a teenager. We lost family then, but it was almost like the grieving was postponed because we had so many living family members that we had to worry about. When Echo died, it was the opposite. Overwhelming. Immediate. Me, your dad, and your Aunt Callie were all there. She practically tackled me to keep me from going to him before it was over."

"Holy shit," I replied. "Why didn't you ever tell me this before?"

Mom shrugged. "It wasn't relevant. Ancient history."

"Still," I said.

"And your dad never liked him," she said with a crooked smile. "Thought he was too old for me—which he was—and thought he didn't treat me the way he should've—which he hadn't."

"That's crazy, Mom," I replied. "I'm sorry."

"Feels like a different lifetime, now," she said with a sigh. "I just wanted you to know that I've been in that place—losing someone important and being helpless to stop it. It's one thing when you're literally diving for cover, it's something different when you're watching a bad thing happen from the sidelines and there's nothing you can do about it."

"Maybe I could've," I murmured.

"Nope," she said simply. "You took care of their child instead, and coming from a mother—the best one you'll ever meet, thank you very much—if I had a choice between someone coming to help me or someone saving one of you kids? Please. All day, every day, no question, keeping you safe is what I'd choose."

"So humble," Mark said, his eyes crinkled in amusement as they met mine in the rearview mirror. My mom huffed and swatted his shoulder as she spun to face forward again.

"How much longer?" I asked him. Baby girl had slept the entire time we were in the car, but I had a feeling she'd be awake soon.

"Still gonna be a while," he said apologetically. "An hour and a half, maybe?"

"Where are we going?" I asked tiredly.

"Arizona," he replied. "Not too far over the border."

"Why the hell are we going to Arizona?"

"The team's got a house there. It's not in any of our names, no ties to us at all. Hopefully, we can stop there for a minute and figure out what the fuck is going on."

"Your team is meeting us there?" I asked.

"Most of them. Eph and Siah stayed behind to keep an eye on my place."

"Do you think he'll go back there?"

"Absolutely," Mark replied. "Probably tonight when he thinks we're sleepin' and he'll have the upper hand."

"I don't want anyone getting hurt because of me," I said worriedly.

Mark chuckled. "They'll be fine," he assured me. "Alone, either of them could handle that fuckwad without breaking a sweat. Together? If someone shows up, they'll have him and whoever he brings with him crying for their mamas."

I didn't bother replying. It wouldn't have made a difference anyway. They were going to do things the way they thought was best, and because I didn't have any experience, my opinion wasn't going to amount to much. It didn't matter that we'd all seen men I thought were invincible taken down by asshole twenty-somethings, or that sometimes, no matter how much experience you had, shit just happened.

I turned and looked out the back window. My dad and Cam were riding side by side, bandanas covering their faces and no sign of their colors—the beat-up leather vests that marked them as part of the Aces and Eights Motorcycle Club. It was weird seeing them on their bikes without them, but it made sense. I didn't know who ran that part of California, but I did know that the Aces didn't have control of anything south of the Sacramento area. My dad nodded at me and raised a hand to where his mouth was hidden behind the black fabric. He pressed it to his mouth and then flipped his hand outward. Smiling as my eyes filled with tears, I blew a kiss back to him before turning back around.

At some point, with my body aching and my head throbbing, I fell asleep.

★ ★ ★

"We're here, Cec," Mark said, waking me up as he unbuckled my seatbelt. "Baby made it the whole way here without a peep."

"Is she okay?" I asked, startled. I looked toward her seat, but it was no longer in the truck.

"She's fine," he replied. "Your dad carried her inside. Come on."

He helped me out of the truck and led me toward a two-story house. It wasn't massive, but it was definitely big enough for the group of us to stay comfortably. The landscaping left a lot to be desired and the sidewalk out front was cracked all to hell, but as we walked in the front door, I realized that there was a reason it looked a little worn down on the outside. No one driving past would guess that the place was fully furnished and sported some serious tech inside.

"Welcome," Wilson called out, crossing through the entryway with a computer monitor in his arms. "Eli is playing chef if you're hungry."

"Thanks," Mark replied. "Any problems?"

"It was a quiet and delightful drive," Wilson said as he disappeared down the hallway.

"Bet your parents are in the kitchen," Mark said, grabbing my hand. "Let's grab something to eat."

He pulled me past the main room of the house and rounded a corner into an enormous kitchen. The previous owners must have really cared about where they'd be cooking, because the space was gorgeous, and the appliances probably cost more than my car.

Damn, I missed my car. I missed all of my stuff.

"Eli made Pad Thai," Lu called out from her seat at the island.

"Grabbed some groceries when I knew we were headed here," Eli said as we made our way toward him. "I fuckin' love this kitchen."

"CeeCee," my mom interrupted from the kitchen table, where she was pulling the baby out of her car seat. "She's soaked and going to be pissed in about three seconds."

"I'll grab some food while you get her," Mark told me, squeezing my hand before letting it go. "Gimme two seconds and I'll take you up to a room so you can get her changed and shit."

A wail split the air and I hurried across the room.

"Hey," I cooed, taking the baby from my mom. "Are you wet?" I grimaced as I realized that she'd wet through her diaper and it was seeping from her clothes to mine.

"Here," my mom said as she moved things from one bag to another. "I grabbed some diapers and wipes and some clothes for her."

"I'll take it," Mark said, grabbing the bag from her while he held a plate of noodles in the opposite hand. "Come on, baby."

He walked away and my mom elbowed me. "*Baby*, huh?"

"Shut it," I hissed.

"Didn't know you were *baby* again."

"Seriously, Mom," I snapped. I wasn't even sure how I felt about the endearment.

She snickered as I followed Mark out of the room and up the stairs.

"This place was a foreclosure," he explained. "And thankfully, the previous owners weren't assholes and didn't trash the place before they left." He opened a door, and strode inside. "They even left behind some furniture."

"Is that a fucking canopy bed?" I asked in disbelief.

"Without the canopy," he confirmed.

The entire room was pink, and the light fixture was an actual chandelier.

"Well," I said, looking around. "I feel like a princess."

Baby girl screamed while I changed her, no surprise there, but as soon as she started nursing, the room was quiet again. The bed dipped a little as Mark sat down facing me.

"Have a bite," he said, offering up a forkful of noodles.

"You don't have to feed me—" My last word was cut off as he pushed the fork so close to my face that I had no option but to take a bite.

"I know," he said while I chewed. "But you must be fucking starving."

"Actually," I said while he took a bite, "I'm more tired than anything. I feel like I'm getting a cold or something."

"Yeah." He fed me another bite. "You felt warm earlier. Maybe you're coming down with something."

"I hope not," I muttered around my food. "That's the last thing I need."

The baby took that moment to stretch out her legs, and the moment one made contact with the breast she wasn't nursing on, I yelped.

"Shit," I barked, blocking her foot.

"What's wrong?" Mark asked, setting the plate on the bed.

"This boob hurts like hell." I reached up and pressed on it. "It aches really bad, especially on the side."

"Is that normal?"

"How the hell should I know?" I replied. I pressed it again, harder, and groaned. It reminded me of a toothache—it hurt to touch it, but the pressure also felt almost good.

"Hopefully, it stops," he said, offering another bite. "I don't like you hurting."

He kept feeding me bites, one for him and one for me, back and forth until the food was gone. By that time, baby girl was finished nursing and snuggled up against my chest, wide awake.

"Want a tour of the house?" Mark asked, getting to his feet.

"Sure." I followed him out of the room and listened while he told me about buying the house for a song and how they hadn't had to do much to it because it was half furnished when they got it. He pointed to the rooms everyone was staying in, but didn't open any doors if they were closed.

"Not much privacy with everyone livin' on top of each other," he explained. "Closin' the doors gives everyone their own bit of space."

I followed him downstairs and through the short hallway Wilson had disappeared into when we'd arrived.

"Hey," Mark greeted as he strode into a huge room.

"I'm busy," Wilson replied, his fingers flying over the keyboard in front of him.

"Whoa," I breathed, looking around the room. "This is insane."

"This is the only house we have with this much hardware," Mark said, looking up at the wall of screens. Two of them were playing different news broadcasts, muted, with the captioning on. Another four had stuff that I couldn't make any sense of. The last one showed what Wilson was working on because I could see the letters and numbers appearing on the screen, but I couldn't make any sense of it, either. It looked like some kind of code.

"The news reported Cane Warren and his wife Lavinia were found deceased in their home this morning," Wilson said, not looking up from his keyboard.

"They mention anything else?" Mark asked.

"Authorities believe that it was a home invasion, possibly a burglary gone wrong." Wilson's inflections were slightly off, and I realized after a moment that he was mimicking the newscaster exactly. He'd memorized what they'd said.

"Alright. Meet us in the kitchen in five," Mark ordered.

"If I'm finished," Wilson replied.

I followed Mark out of the room, my feet practically dragging. I was so fucking worn out. I wasn't sure if it was because I'd just had a baby or everything else that had happened, but I seriously just wanted to go back to the bedroom and lay down. The baby tilted her head back, completely awkward and uncoordinated, and I swallowed hard as I kissed her forehead.

I was doing a pretty fantastic job not thinking of anything beyond keeping her safe, but eventually, I knew that I was going to have to deal with the fact that her mother was dead. My best friend, who'd wanted her so badly, would never get to watch her grow up. She'd never get to dress her in all the frilly outfits she'd bought, or go for mother-daughter pedicures, or help her pick out her outfit for the first day of school, or all the other things Liv had told me she was excited for.

"Did you eat?" my mom asked as we walked into the kitchen.

"Yeah." I let her pull the baby out of my arms.

I hoped that at some point I'd take to motherhood as well as my mom had. I don't know if it had been the fact that she'd helped out with my cousin Will before any of us kids were born, or if she was just a natural, but she'd always seemed at ease with us. Like she knew exactly what to do, no matter the situation we found ourselves in.

"Round table," Mark announced to the room. "We've got shit to go over. Where's Cam?"

"He went outside to call Trix," my mom replied, her cheek resting on the top of the baby's head while she swayed from side to side. "He'll be back in a minute."

"You name that baby yet?" Eli asked as he sat down at the kitchen table.

"I still say you name her Cecilia," Lu said as she hopped up on the island.

"Ooh, after you," my mom pointed out, raising her eyebrows.

"That's the idea," I replied, my mouth twitching. "I'm not naming her that."

"Why?" she said. "It's a beautiful name. You can carry on the tradition."

"Tradition?" Lu asked.

"Cecilia was named after me," my mom said proudly.

"Not exactly," I argued.

"I thought your name was Farrah?" Eli asked. "Shit, have I been callin' you the wrong name?"

My dad chuckled.

"No, Farrah is my name," my mom clarified. "But my dad and step-mom actually named me Cecilia. I was raised by my mom, and she named me Farrah." She shrugged.

"See?" Lu said just as Cam came through the door.

"Everything all right?" my dad asked.

"Yep," Cam replied. He made his way over and slung an arm over my shoulder.

"Wilson," Mark called over his shoulder. "Get your ass in here."

We waited.

"You know he ain't comin' in here until he's damn well ready," Forrest said with a grin, leaning his chair back on two legs. "You wanna get started, I'll fill him in later."

"He's a serious pain in the ass," Mark muttered.

"But he gets the job done," Forrest replied.

"We need to lay out everythin' we know and everythin' we don't know," Mark said. He looked at me and paused. "You need to sit down before you fall down."

"What?" I looked at him in confusion.

"You okay?" my mom asked. "He's right. You look like you're going to tip over."

"I'm fine," I replied.

Mark didn't continue speaking, he just stood there staring patiently at me.

With a huff, I pulled away from my brother and sat down in one of the kitchen chairs.

"So," Mark continued, "we know that the couple in the house were named Cane and Lavinia Warren—"

"Hold up," my dad said, raising his hand in a stop signal. "*Cane Warren?*"

"That name mean somethin' to you?" Mark asked.

My dad met my brother's eyes across the room and my stomach sank.

"You could say that," Dad said, leaning forward to rest his elbows on the table. "He's the head of the Free America Militia. Shit, I'd forgotten those fuckers even existed." I recognized the look in his eyes. Something was clicking into place, like he'd just put the final piece in a puzzle.

"You gonna fill the rest of the class in?" Mark asked.

My dad didn't answer.

"Right," Mark spat, clearly frustrated. "Okay, is there anything else you can tell me?"

"They're a bunch of skinhead white supremacists," my dad replied darkly. He looked at me. "I'm guessin' he had no idea that you were part Mexican."

"It never came up," I said softly, the realization making my stomach churn.

What the fuck? *What. The. Fuck?* Cane was a white supremacist? I'd willingly eaten at his table and hung out with him and *carried his baby.* My mouth started to water as bile burned the back of my throat. Had Liv known? Had she married the guy knowing that he believed in some master race bullshit? The world spun.

"She's going down," Lu barked.

Within seconds, someone pressed my head between my knees, the hand on the back of my neck cool and comforting.

"Shit," my brother said from somewhere above me. "She's definitely got a fever." Ah, it was Cam's hand on my neck.

"A fever?" my mom asked. "What? She's sick?"

"Come here, baby," Mark said into my ear as he lifted me into his arms. "Why don't you lay down for a while?"

"We're having a meeting," I argued weakly. If I was being honest, I didn't give a shit about the meeting. I *did* just want to lay down for a little while.

"Wilson didn't show up, either," Mark said as he carried me up the stairs. "We'll brief you both later."

"I'm sorry," I sighed as he laid me on the bed. "I feel like shit."

"Don't worry about it," he replied. He strode over to the closet and pulled out a pillow wrapped in plastic and a blanket. "Just get some rest."

As he unwrapped the pillow and put it under my head, I groaned. It felt like it had been days since I'd gotten any rest instead of just hours. After covering me with the blanket, he left the room, leaving the door cracked open.

I stared at it for a long time, my mind racing, and when I finally closed my eyes, all I could see was Cane, laughing at something I'd said.

He hadn't looked like a monster.

Chapter 8

MARK

"IS SHE OKAY?" Farrah asked as soon as I got back to the kitchen.

"Yeah," I replied, scratching at the whiskers on my cheek. "She's laying down."

"Well, let's get this over with so I can go up there," she ordered.

"Okay, so Cane's the head of the… what?"

"Free America Militia," Casper supplied.

"Alright. We know anything about them?"

"Not much," he grumbled.

"I'll get Wilson on that, pronto," Forrest chimed it.

"Right. So, we can probably assume that his kid is a member, too."

"Fair to assume his kid is *leadin'* it now," Casper corrected. "I'm bettin' it's run like a monarchy."

"Put's a different spin on things," I mumbled.

"Spin on what?" Lu asked.

"Cecilia was a surrogate—"

"Oh, shit," Lu mumbled, her eyes widening.

"What?" Eli asked, looking between us.

"She carried the baby, but it's not hers," Lu said to Eli. "Safe bet it was the Warrens'."

"Yep," Cam said, shaking his head. "Fuckin' Cecilia."

"You know what, man—" I growled. I was stressed, tired, and overwhelmed, I sure as hell wasn't in the mood to listen to Cam listing all of Cecilia's faults again.

"Enough of that shit," Casper snapped at Cam. "You don't got somethin' helpful to add, keep your goddamn mouth shut."

"Cody," Farrah said softly.

"No," he replied. "I'm done with that shit."

Jesus Christ. Finally, when Cecilia wasn't even around to hear it, the man spoke up. I scrubbed my hands over my face.

Forrest waded into the awkward as fuck silence. "So, the kid's after the baby, then."

"Yeah." I grabbed a kitchen chair and spun it around so I could sit down. "Legally, the baby is still Cecilia's. The way it works is the parents were supposed to legally adopt her after she was born."

We went over everything, turning and twisting it so we could try to see it from all angles. After almost an hour of talking it out, we still hadn't figured out much beyond probable motive. We had no clue how the son had found Cecilia at my house so soon.

"I'm going to go check on her," Farrah finally said. "Who wants the baby?"

"I'll take her," I replied, lifting my arms. As soon as Farrah had handed her over, I felt a weird sense of relief. Discussing her fucked up family had made me antsy as fuck, and the warm weight of her calmed me.

And wasn't that some shit?

"We need to get her back up to Oregon," Casper said after Farrah had gone. "We've got the resources up there to keep them safe."

"We've got resources down here," I argued.

"Man," he replied, shaking his head, "you're all in a motherfuckin' safe house because you don't know how they found you."

"Wilson's workin' on that," Forrest pointed out.

"You'll be doin' the same damn thing," I said to Casper at the same time. "You'll lock them behind the clubhouse gates until you end this shit."

"At least she'll be at home."

"That hasn't been home to her in over ten fuckin' years," I shot back.

"And whose fault is that?" he asked quietly.

"Don't put that shit on me," I replied, my voice just as low. "She was tryin' to escape that place long before anything happened with us."

Casper opened his mouth to speak, but didn't say anything as Farrah came back in the room.

"She's got a nasty fever," Farrah announced. "Does anyone have something she can take to bring it down?"

"Fever?" Forrest asked.

"I'll get something out of the med pack," Eli said.

"It must be at least one-oh-one," Farrah told Forrest. "She's warm."

Forrest looked at me.

"Go check her," I ordered.

"Why you sendin' him?" Cam asked.

"Because he's a doctor—was a doctor."

"No shit?"

"And why isn't he one anymore?" Casper asked.

"Because in his last year of residency, he tore his meniscus," I replied, holding his stare. "And got a taste for narcotics."

"Clean now?" Casper asked.

"As a whistle."

"Got a soft spot for disgraced doctors, do ya?" he said, fighting a grin.

I stood without replying and headed upstairs. I wasn't going down that road with him. My father didn't have any bearing on why Forrest was a part of the team. It hadn't even been my decision when we'd been placed together the first time. The fact that both Forrest and my father had gone all the way through medical school and ended up with no letters after their names was the only similarity between the two.

"You have any other symptoms?" Forrest was asking Cec as I stepped into the bedroom.

"No, I just feel like shit," she replied, shifting a little, like she couldn't get comfortable.

"What about your tit?" I asked, making everyone look in my direction. "Didn't you say it was hurting?"

"Yeah," Cecilia said. "It's just sore."

"Is it hot to the touch?" Farrah asked. "Do you think you have a clog?"

"A what?" Cecilia asked in confusion.

"A clogged milk duct."

They went back and forth discussing Cecilia's breasts until Forrest interrupted.

"If you've got a fever and you feel like shit, it's probably more than a clogged duct," he said. "Sounds like mastitis."

"Shit," Farrah muttered.

"What?" Cecilia looked between them. "What's that?"

"It's an infection. You'll need antibiotics," Forrest replied.

"We need to call your—" Farrah stopped mid-sentence. "We call your doctor, there's a damn record."

"I can get 'em," Forrest said.

"I'm not taking some random pill that you pull out of your pocket," Cecilia argued. "I'm not an idiot and I'm nursing."

"He knows what he's doing, Cec," I said. I looked at Forrest. "Do your thing, man."

He nodded at me before leaving the room.

"He's a doctor," I told Cecilia and Farrah.

"I thought he worked with you," Cecilia said.

"He does. Long story."

She didn't reply, just reached out her arm and beckoned for me to give her the baby.

"You need to try and nurse her on the side that's hurting," Farrah advised. "And Jesus, you need to name that child already. I'm sick of calling her *the baby* and *her*. So, what's it gonna be?"

"I was thinking Olive, after Liv. I mean, her name was Lavinia, but she never liked that name. She always went by Liv," Cecilia said, looking down at the baby. She looked back at her mom. "Even if her parents were complete assholes," she cleared her throat and swallowed hard. "Even if Liv wasn't who I thought she was—she still loved their baby more than anything and she was so excited to meet her."

"I think Olive is the perfect name," Farrah said calmly. "Olive Cecilia has a nice ring to it."

"You don't give up, do you?" Cecilia said with a watery chuckle.

"Never," Farrah whispered, leaning down to kiss the side of Cecilia's head.

"Olive," I said, trying the name out. "I dig it."

"Oh, well, if *you* like it," Farrah mocked jokingly.

"Hey, now," I replied. "Me and Olive are best friends."

"Well, your best friend needs to eat and it's going to be a complete shit show in here while Cecilia tries to take care of this clogged duct, so out you go."

She ushered me out of the room and shut the door in my face.

★ ★ ★

HOURS LATER, CECILIA wasn't feeling much better, but she came down to have dinner with the rest of us. We'd spent all day researching the Free America Militia, and I had to admit, it was nice to sit around the table and *not* talk about the shit we'd found.

It turned out that FAM had people all over California, but their main compound was just south of the Oregon border. And compound was the correct word for it. According to the land sale records, they owned a little less than a hundred acres in the middle of nowhere where entire families just seemed to disappear. Literally. The men popped up eventually in the form of traffic tickets and gun sales, but the women and kids were never heard from again.

From what we could uncover, once they moved onto the compound, they never left again. It made my skin crawl.

"You have any luck with those antibiotics?" Farrah asked Forrest as we dished up the spaghetti Eli'd made.

"Meetin' up with my supplier tonight," Forrest replied.

"Good friend to have," Casper said.

"Know him from way back," Forrest said with a nod. "Good people."

"Have you heard anything from the guys at your house?" Cecilia asked as I sat down beside her at the table.

"They haven't seen anything," I replied, putting one of my pieces of garlic bread on her plate. "Eat."

"I have my own food."

"You barely got anything," I argued. "You need the fuel. Eat."

"I don't remember you being this bossy before," she said.

The words dropped like a cannon ball between us. From the minute I'd seen her again, we'd carefully and deliberately skirted around what we'd been before. Beyond her teasing me about my muscles, which had been light, we hadn't gone there. Honestly, I'd wondered how long we could maintain it. There was just too much shit between us to ignore, too much history, too many hurts.

"I've always been bossy," I said, moving my attention back to my own plate. "Part of my charm."

"Charm?" Lu asked, sitting down across from us. "You've never been charming. Intelligent, yes. Handsome, yes. Hell on wheels with a rifle in your hand, definitely. But charming? Nope."

"I'm not even sure if that was an insult or a compliment," I replied honestly.

"Just take it as one," Eli said as he dropped down in the chair beside her. "That's what I always do."

"And how's that working out for you?" Lu asked.

"Pretty well, actually," he replied, stuffing an entire piece of garlic bread in his mouth.

"You're a Neanderthal," Wilson said as he sat down with us. "At least chew before you attempt to swallow that."

"This table is great," Farrah said as she sat down on the opposite side of Cec. "We need one of these at our house. It fits everyone!"

"We don't have room for a table the size of a yacht, Ladybug," Casper told her as he took the seat next to her.

"Well, we should make the space."

"All our kids are outta the house but one," he said easily. "I'm sure as shit not addin' onto the place."

"We'll see," Farrah mused.

"You get pregnant and I'm movin' out," he muttered, making Farrah laugh.

"If I get pregnant at my age, we're calling the news because it's a goddamn miracle," Farrah cackled. "And we're naming the baby Jesus."

"I like you," Lu said, pointing at Farrah across the table.

"Back atcha, honey," Farrah said easily. "And I'd love to get my hands in your hair."

"Say what?" Lu asked as Cecilia started to giggle beside me.

"It's gorgeous, but you're doing yourself no favors by pulling it back so tight," Farrah said. "By the size of your bun, I bet it's super long. Am I right?"

"Jesus," Cecilia whispered in embarrassment.

"Wait," Eli said, laughing. "Is she talking about your hair or your ass? I have noticed your buns are—"

"Finish that sentence and die, dipshit," Lu replied, pointing her fork at Eli. She looked back at Farrah. "It's down to my waist."

"Oh, nice," Farrah said.

"I've just gotten used to keeping it back for work. Can't do my job if my hair's flying everywhere."

"You'll have to show it to me after dinner," Farrah said loftily. "And if nothing else, let me give you a trim. It really is gorgeous."

"Thanks," Lu said happily.

"You'd never know that my mother used to be the asshole in the Callie-and-Farrah duo," Cecilia said to me out of the side of her mouth. "I wonder if it's old age?"

"I heard that," Farrah said.

I laughed.

The situation we were in sucked. I'd finally got a handle on shit, and I felt like I was making decisions and thinking things over with a clear head now, but it didn't really make things any easier. I was still in close proximity to Cecilia. Still dealing with the mess she'd gotten herself into. Still spinning my wheels trying to figure out how to fix it. On top of all that, she was still so fucking beautiful it hurt to look at her and I was seeing her tits on an almost hourly basis when she fed Olive.

But even with all that, it felt kinda good to sit around the table with people from my past and friends from the present. Weird, yeah, but good. For years after I'd left Oregon, I'd missed the sounds and the feel of the big gatherings they'd have at the clubhouse. Even when there wasn't an event, I could've shown up at any time and had a group of people to hang with. It was impossible to replicate, but I'd found something close with my team. Dinner that night was like the best of both worlds, even if there was a shitstorm gathering outside.

"God," Cecilia said as conversation at the table flowed around us. "This is the worst possible time to feel like crap."

"Did you get the uh, clog taken care of?"

"Nope," she said, leaning back in her chair. She raised a hand to the baby she'd somehow strapped to herself with the carrier. "I had to nurse her on my hands and knees, with my boobs just dangling there."

"Now, that I'd like to see," I said with a chuckle.

"Oh, I bet." She rolled her eyes.

Suddenly, I was transported to the past, Cecilia staring up at me.

"I seriously love that bikini," I said, *looking down between us at the triangles just barely covering her tits.*

"This is the last time I'm wearing it," she huffed, *pulling at the strap.* *"I let them convince me to jump off the rope swing one last time before I left, and the entire thing came undone when I hit the water."*

"Now, that I'd like to see."

"Oh, I bet." *She rolled her eyes as I leaned down to kiss her.*

★ ★ ★

LATE THAT NIGHT, I sat in the communications room with the team. Ephraim and Josiah had called in to touch base, but they hadn't had anything to report. Everything was quiet back in San Diego, which made the hair on the back of my neck prickle.

"I've spent hours searching through public records," Wilson said, tilting back and forth in his computer chair, making it squeak. "Free America Militia doesn't own a damn thing."

"Great," Eli muttered.

"*However*," Wilson said smugly, "I did uncover some properties that were owned by Mr. Cane Warren, one of which is a large tract of land near the Oregon border."

"We knew that," Eli said.

"Furthermore," Wilson said with forced patience, "I cross referenced that with the owners of land that abut Mr. Warren's property. That's where things became slightly more interesting."

"Good call," Lu said.

"As always, your praise is effusive and heart warming," Wilson told her. "I realized that Warren's property wasn't nearly as large as we'd anticipated, which got me wondering who owned the property surrounding it. Friends, meet Richard Campbell, Cody Howser, and Benjamin Morris."

He clicked a key on his computer and three mug shots popped up larger than life on the screens. "Richard, here, was arrested for domestic violence, but lucky for *Dick*, the charges didn't stick. Probably because less than a month later, he and his wife and children dropped off the face of the earth. Wonder where they went?" he asked sarcastically. "Cody Howser, arrested for assault in a bar fight, did two years in the pen, and somehow had the funds to buy the property within a year of his release. Interesting, no? Last, but not least, we have Benjamin Morris. Benny, here, is a real peach. He found Jesus while doing six years in federal prison for robbing a bank. His rap sheet is quite the novel. Robbery, assault, attempted murder, drunk driving, intent to distribute—meth, I believe—and various other misdemeanors. He also fell into some cash and was able to buy a large tract of land bordering Warren's property."

"Well, aren't they the picture of Aryan health," Lu grumbled, staring at the photos. Each man was pale, blue eyed, and handsome. Each had absolutely nothing behind their eyes.

"Warren and his wife obviously never met Cecilia's parents," Forrest said, glancing at me. "Hard to miss that her daddy ain't white."

"You see her face when she found out Warren was a card carrying racist asshole?" Eli asked. "Shit. I've never seen someone's face pale that quickly."

"It's fucked up," I said with a sigh. "She had no fuckin' clue—but I'm not surprised. Livin' and workin' in southern California, doubt Cane advertised his shitty world view."

"So what are we lookin' at here?" I asked Wilson. "What kind of resources do they have?"

"A lot of them," Wilson said simply. He spun back toward his computer and started typing. "I looked into the son, and he's a real fuck—a rich one. He got kicked out of so many schools, his father must have paid a fortune to get him to graduation. His accounts are mostly overseas, and they're hefty and diversified."

"Shit."

"And they're nothing compared to Cane Warren's," Wilson said darkly. "He's set to inherit millions."

"Which he's not going to split with a baby," Lu said.

"I've been looking at missing persons databases, narrowing it down to only Caucasian families, then cross checking those with fathers who'd been in the California prison system in the past fifteen years. There's… a lot."

"How many?" I asked.

"Hundreds," Wilson replied. "So, I cross checked it again with those who would've been inside with our terrible trio up there." He jerked his chin at the screens. "Narrowed it down to less than a hundred."

"That's good," Forrest said.

"Not good enough," Wilson countered. "It's going to take time for me to filter through all of these."

"So, we know who some of the main players are, and we know there's a shit ton of money at stake. Do we have any idea if they've got connections anywhere?"

"I am a miracle worker," Wilson said. "Not a superhero. This type of investigating takes time. It doesn't help that Casper—that surely isn't his real name—isn't telling us what he knows."

"Bottom line," Forrest said, "Warren's son has the money and loyal manpower to keep searching for Cecilia and the baby. He's not going to stop, not with that kind of money on the line."

We were all quiet.

"Then it looks like we're going hunting," Eli said quietly.

"You don't have to—"

"Shut it, Chief," Lu interrupted. "Even if you weren't making googly eyes at the woman, none of us would leave her to the wolves."

"Especially not to these particular racist wolves," Wilson added.

"I'll call HQ and put us on leave," Forrest said. "We've all got time coming anyway."

"Thank you," I said, leaning back in my chair. "Shit."

"We'll end this," Lu said, patting me on the shoulder awkwardly.

"Heads up," Forrest said, lifting his phone into the air. "It's Siah."

"Nothing's happening here," Josiah said as soon as Forrest put him on speaker phone. "And when I say nothing, I mean *nothing*. Somethin' ain't right. It's too fuckin' quiet. No one's comin'."

"Wait it out," Eli replied.

"Of course," Siah said. "We aren't goin' anywhere. But, I'm tellin' you, man, no one's even watchin' the house."

"You sure?" I asked.

"Positive. I can feel a sniper's stare from five hundred yards away. There's no one here."

"Fuck," Lu breathed.

"Stay until mornin' and then head our way," Forrest ordered. "Make sure no one's followin'."

"Will do," Siah muttered before hanging up.

"Was anyone followed?" Wilson asked, looking around the group.

"Of course not," Eli replied.

"No," Forrest said.

"I rode the bike," Lu said. "Unless they were riding, too, no way could anyone have followed me through traffic. I practically had wings."

"I didn't see anything," I added. "And I had Casper and Cam watching my back."

"They must've seen you leavin' the house," Forrest said. "Know you're not there. Doesn't mean they know where you are now."

I nodded. It was past midnight and I was dragging ass. Part of me wanted to stay in that room and go over everything that Wilson had uncovered with my own eyes, but the rest of me just wanted to lay down for a bit. After years of working with the man, I knew I wouldn't see anything that he hadn't. The guy had a photographic memory and the ability to make connections like no one I'd ever seen. Okay, that wasn't true. I'd seen Casper do the same thing. It was fucking weird.

"I'm going to stay at it," Wilson said as we all began to move around. "See what else I can uncover tonight."

"I'll stay up with you," Eli replied. "Got some television to catch up on."

"I'll assume you want to use one of my screens," Wilson grumbled. "Fine. Take the one on the far right. It's the least accessible when I'm at my keyboard."

"You mean you have to turn your head to see it?" Eli asked, deadpan.

"Yes," Wilson hissed. "Now stop talking so I can work."

As Lu, Forrest, and I filed out of the room, we met Casper and Farrah in the hallway.

"Hey," Casper said. "Was just comin' to find you. Any news?"

I filled him in as we strode back toward the massive kitchen.

"So you've got the names of his highest in command," Casper said when I'd finished. "That's good."

"Any information is good," I replied. "But this shit will get us nowhere. Just because we know who they are doesn't mean I know where they are or what they're doin.'"

"Chances are, those men were loyal to the father, not the son," Casper said, rubbing his chin. "Wouldn't be pleased with that particular patricide."

"Assuming they know," Forrest replied. "Which they probably

don't."

"So, maybe we need to make sure they do," Casper said.

"Again," Lu said tiredly, "if we knew where they were, that would be a possibility. Maybe. But we don't. Those men have pretty much disappeared."

"On the compound?" Casper asked.

"Probably," I replied.

"They stole one of our trucks," Casper told me, his tone grim. "Didn't sell the contents."

"That's fuckin' fantastic," I replied sarcastically.

"Only one," Casper said, like that made it any better. I knew exactly what the Aces bought and sold, and that kind of firepower in the hands of an adversary was not a good thing.

"We're not going to figure out anything more tonight," Lu said, stretching her arms above her head. "Let Wilson do his thing and we can meet up again in the morning."

"Works for me," Forrest said. He looked at me. "I'm gonna head out for a bit—get Cecilia those antibiotics."

"Thanks." I turned to Casper. "Fill Cam in?"

"I'll do it in the morning," Casper replied. "He already crashed for the night."

"I swear," Farrah said, wrapping an arm around her husband's waist. "We raised a bunch of weaklings. Who goes to sleep before midnight?"

We went our separate ways and I grabbed a bottle of water for Cecilia before going upstairs. She'd been in bed for hours already, but I knew she'd be up with the baby throughout the night. When I opened the door to her room, she was already awake.

"Hey," she said softly. "How'd your meeting go?"

"It went," I said, closing the door behind me. "Wilson's digging deep, but finding anything out takes time."

Cecilia shook her head. "I still can't believe this. No good deed goes unpunished, right?"

"We'll get it figured out," I assured her, setting the water bottle on the nightstand. "How're you feeling?"

"Like I got run over by a truck," she said with a little groan. "But my mom found some bedding, so at least I've got that going for me."

"I see that," I replied. The bed had been made up with sheets and a comforter, and she was tucked inside, lounged back on a couple of pillows with Olive asleep against her chest.

"All this stuff was brand new," she said, patting the bedding on her lap.

"Lu must've bought it," I said as I kicked off my boots. "The rest of us would've been happy with sleeping bags."

"Oh, whatever," she joked as I sat down beside her. "I've seen your house. You like expensive shit."

I let out a startled laugh. "What?"

"You've got expensive furniture," she pointed out. "And your bedding is soft as a baby's ass."

"I made the furniture," I said, leaning against the headboard with a sigh. "And bought the only bedding I could find that didn't have flowers or cartoon characters on it."

"You made it?" she asked in surprise. "Really?"

"I like working with my hands," I replied, flexing my fingers. I lifted them up a little from my lap and showed her the tiny scars from all the times I'd nicked and sliced them up working on various projects. "It relaxes me."

"I get that," she said. "I like to quilt while I'm binge watching TV."

"Quilt? Seriously?" I could not imagine the wild girl I'd chased all over Eugene quilting.

"My gram and great aunt taught me," she said with a shrug. "I have a hard time sitting still. If I'm not doing something while I watch TV, I fall asleep or get bored."

"Now, that I can believe," I replied.

"I'm not great at it," she said, leaning her head back tiredly. "But they're functional when I'm done."

"That's pretty cool. Do you make designs and shit?" The conversation was surface, a throwaway exchange of words, but Jesus, I wanted to know everything about her. The thought made my stomach twist with excitement and sink at the same time.

"Yeah," she said. "Nothing fancy, though. You should see some of the handmade quilts my gram's mom and sisters used to make. They're incredible. My mom gave Cam one when he was a kid, and I think she and my Aunt Callie inherited some more when my gram died."

At the reference to her gram's death, we both went quiet. Neither of us would forget that day. We were never the same afterward. Both of us had our own demons to work through, but that hadn't stopped us from clinging to each other like lifelines. It had made for a messy as fuck relationship, but a solid one, all the same.

"I liked your gram," I said finally, breaching the silence.

"Everyone liked my gram," she said with a quiet chuckle. "She was a goddamn saint."

"Fair point," I said in concession. "She used to make the best cucumber salad." I groaned. "To this day, it's still my favorite food."

"Cucumber salad? Really?" Cecilia smiled. "That's so simple to make."

"You know how to make it?" I asked, my mouth watering.

"It's not hard," she replied. "It's just cucumbers, red onion, vinegar and dill."

"Maybe it was the ratio," I said defensively. "Because I've had it since, and no one makes it as good as your gram did."

"It was all that love she put in it," she joked.

"Hmm," I squinted my eyes. "That's what love tastes like?"

"Depends on who you ask," she replied dryly.

She laughed when I raised my eyebrows.

"Get your mind out of the gutter," she admonished. "I meant that cucumber salad isn't everyone's favorite food."

"Uh huh, sure." I climbed off the bed and walked to the end of the room to where I'd stored my bag.

"What are you doing?" Cecilia asked, sitting up.

"What does it look like I'm doing?" I asked as I tugged off my t-shirt.

"It looks like you're stripping." She paused. "If this is a show, at least do a little dance."

I huffed in amusement as I pulled off my jeans, *not* doing a little dance.

"I'm not sleepin' in my clothes," I said as I strode back toward the bed.

"You're sleeping in here?" she asked as I slid into the bedding beside her. "My parents are here."

I couldn't help the loud bark of laughter that left my mouth. She'd sounded so scandalized and worried, so not like the Cecilia I'd known. Hell, we'd once had sex against the outside wall of the clubhouse while everyone—including her boyfriend at the time—partied inside.

"Shut up," she grumbled. "It's just that my mom is already saying shit."

"Like what?" I asked curiously.

"Nothing," she replied. "Just little comments."

"Cec," I said patiently, trying not to laugh, "I didn't give a shit what your parents thought when we were kids, and I give less of a fuck now."

"Well, I give more fucks," she said quietly.

I thought it over for a moment. "Here's the thing," I said, leaning up on my elbow. "If somethin' happens, someone needs to be in here with you. If you'd rather share a room with your parents, you can do that. Or Lu—she probably wouldn't mind."

"No, it's fine," she said. "Do you think something will happen?"

"Nope," I lied. "It's just a precaution."

I couldn't know if they'd find us, not without knowing how they'd found Cecilia in the first place. The house was secure, with silent alarms and—if I knew Wilson—booby traps, but that didn't mean that they wouldn't show up. It just meant we'd have a little warning before they got in.

As Cecilia got herself and the baby settled, I turned off the bedside lamp, leaving the room aglow from a light in the closet. I knew better than to pitch the room into darkness. Neither of us had ever discussed it, I hadn't wanted to broach it, and she'd never offered the information, but I'd always known that Cecilia was afraid of the dark.

It was just one more thing that she hid from everyone and hadn't been able to hide from me.

"My parents are going to want to take us home soon," Cecilia said after I'd curled into her, the curve of her ass cradling my dick and her legs tangled with mine. "Do you think he'll search for us in Oregon?"

I couldn't lie that time. "He'll search until he finds you," I said carefully. "No matter where you go."

Cecilia sniffled. "She doesn't even have any legal tie to Cane's money," she said in frustration. "And we don't fucking want it."

"It's a lot of money."

"I have money," she said. "More than we need."

"You cut a lot of hair?" I asked.

"I'm damn good at it," she replied, elbowing me in the gut. "But Cane and Liv also paid me for being a surrogate."

My head jerked in surprise. "They were buying Olive from you?"

"No," she said with a huff. "It was payment for a service, in this case, growing their child. It's completely normal and not at all shady or weird."

"Sounds weird."

"Well, it wasn't," she said. "Surrogates get paid for their time and energy and trauma to their bodies, and emotional upheaval of having a child for someone."

"Okay," I replied. "I get it."

"Though, I doubt most get paid as much as I was," she mumbled.

By the time I grew the balls to ask just how much she'd gotten paid for having Olive, she was already asleep. I laid there for a long time, listening to her breathe. The situation she was in was so extreme that we seemed to have fallen back into something that we'd lost years before. It was an easy camaraderie, but I knew it wouldn't last. At some point, things were going to calm down and we were going to have to face the things we were choosing to ignore.

I tightened my arm around her. Eventually, she was going to come to her senses and not let me anywhere near her. I could feel it coming like an axe being swung at my neck. Because, even though she trusted me to keep her safe—Cecilia was never going to forgive me for what I'd done.

★ ★ ★

THE NEXT FEW days passed pretty slow. Cecilia spent most of her time in bed with the baby, which, along with the antibiotics Forrest had picked up, was exactly what she'd needed. Wilson had even set her up with a laptop—warning her not to check any social media or search anything to do with the Warrens or herself—so she could stream movies. And she'd been telling the truth about falling asleep, whenever I checked on her, she'd passed out with Olive, whatever show she'd been watching still playing. The only time she was able to stay awake was when she was taking care of the baby.

Wilson was making progress on the FAM, but it was slow going. Every thread he pulled connected to five others that he'd have to follow.

Most of them were dead ends, but we'd found a few land mines. One of Richard Campbell's daughters had shown up at a police station the year before, reporting that she and her mother and younger siblings had been held hostage on her father's property for years. Unfortunately, when the police had gone to follow up on her claims, all they'd found was a saccharinely happy family with stories about how unstable the oldest daughter was. Even if she hadn't gotten the outcome she'd hoped for, the daughter, Kaley, had at least put herself on the state's radar, which meant that she'd been able to escape the FAM's hold with little repercussions, and was now living somewhere in Eastern Oregon.

Because she had insider knowledge of the workings inside the FAM, Wilson had started immediately trying to contact her, but hadn't had any success so far.

Things were pretty quiet for the most part, with everyone researching and calling contacts for information—but we hadn't found much. Warren's group was surprisingly quiet for a bunch of white supremacists, which I was pretty sure worried all of us.

We were sitting around the kitchen table Monday afternoon, eating some sort of chicken bake Eli had concocted, when Forrest's chair dropped down onto all four legs. The noise got my notice, and when my head snapped up, I realized why he'd come to attention.

Casper had stepped just inside the back door with his phone clenched in his fist, tension radiating from him in waves. "Cam, Farrah," he called. "Need a word."

They were up and out of their seats immediately, and even though he hadn't asked us, Cecilia and I followed.

"Rose and Mack are missing," he said without preamble once I'd closed the door behind us.

"What?" Farrah replied, gaping. "Together?"

"That's what it looks like," Casper responded. "Went outside during one of Rose's breaks at the bar and never came back in."

"Jesus Christ," Cam snapped.

"What do they know?" I asked.

"Nothin,'" Casper growled. "Haven't heard a fuckin' whisper."

"We need to get home," Farrah said, looking from her man to Cecilia. "Are you ready to make the drive?"

"As long as I'm not the one driving," Cecilia replied. "I can sleep most of the way."

"We can follow you up," I said, my stomach twisting. "More eyes and ears, just to be safe."

"Appreciate that," Casper replied. "We'll leave in the morning."

"We're waiting?" Cam asked, surprise and frustration making the question sound more like a pissed off statement.

"Your sister is sick as fuck and she's got a newborn," Casper told him. "And we're gonna have to stop a fuckin' million times on the way up. I'm gettin' some sleep before we head out."

Casper and Farrah walked back into the house and Cecilia turned to Cam, who had walked to the end of the patio and was staring out at the sandy yard.

"I'm sorry," she said with a sigh. "I know you'd rather be up there helping."

I bristled as Cam turned, his scowl so nasty I was surprised when Cecilia held her ground. Before I could say anything, his face softened.

"I'm right where I'm supposed to be, little sister," he said quietly. "Takin' care of you. We'll all head up tomorrow, yeah?"

"Yeah," Cecilia replied.

Cam threw his arm over her shoulder and led her into the house.

Jesus, sometimes I was glad to be an only child. By the way Cam bitched about Cecilia, it was easy to assume he couldn't stand her—but I guess the truth was never that simple. The bond they had, even when they didn't get along, was still solid. He'd known just what to say to her.

It made me wonder why for so many years, he'd never realized that there was something wrong.

"All good?" Lu asked as I came back into the kitchen.

"Change of plans," I said, sitting back down. Casper, Farrah, Cam and Cecilia must have gone upstairs. None of them had even bothered to clear their plates. "We leave for Oregon in the morning."

"Somethin' happen?" Forrest asked.

"Cecilia's cousin went missing," I replied.

"Shit," Eli said, drawing out the word. "That family has a lot of drama."

"They're part of an outlaw motorcycle club," Wilson said, striding into the room. "It's not a lifestyle that promotes stability."

"He's not wrong," I mumbled into my food.

"I will not be traveling to Oregon in the morning," Wilson said as he grabbed a plate of food. "I assume you all can make it without me."

"What's up?" Forrest asked him.

"I believe that I've found Richard Campbell's daughter, Kaley," Wilson replied. "I'll continue trying to make contact and follow up on leads from here."

"Sounds good," Eli said.

"So glad you approve," Wilson replied emotionlessly.

I wolfed down the rest of my food and went searching for Cecilia. When I found her, she was sitting on the edge of the bed, her phone in her hand.

"Whatcha doin'?" I asked, closing the door behind me.

"I was trying to work up the courage to call Lily," she said with a self-conscious huff. She flicked at the charger connecting the phone to the wall. "My phone was dead, so I plugged it in, but then I chickened out."

"I bet she'd be glad to hear from you," I said, sitting next to her.

"No, she wouldn't," she said simply. "Did you know she's with Leo now?"

"No shit?" Cecilia and Leo had been a thing when we were kids.

He'd been the one to look the other way while Cecilia ran around with me.

"No shit," she confirmed. "I always kind of saw it coming."

"Really?" Lily was around five years younger than us, and had been just a kid when I'd left.

"Not when she was little. Gross." She wrinkled her nose at me. "But later, yeah. They just always had a connection."

"Huh," I said, trying to wrap my head around it. "Still, you're her sister. She'd want to know you're thinking about her."

"She was always closer with Rose," Cecilia argued with no heat. She set the phone on the bedside table. "She's probably really freaked out. I'm not going to bother her."

She twisted on the bed and laid down with her back to me, pulling the covers up to her shoulder.

"You want me to take Olive so you can get some rest?" I asked, glancing at the squirming baby. Olive was busy kicking her legs and waving her arms in front of her face.

"If you don't mind, yeah," Cecilia said from beneath the covers.

I stared at Cecilia's back for a while, wondering if I should crawl in behind her. Cecilia and Lily's relationship was complicated, and I knew that was mostly because of the woman curled into a ball in front of me—but I also knew that she didn't want it to be that way. Sometimes, people just fell into patterns that were nearly impossible to get out of. I hated that she didn't even feel welcome to call Lily when her family was going through something so terrifying.

Olive started to fuss and when Cecilia didn't even reach for her, I made my decision. I picked up the baby and left the room, closing the door behind me so her mother could rest.

"You want a tour?" I asked Olive quietly as I strode toward the stairs. Her little body felt good against my chest, and for the first time in a couple days, it felt like I could exhale.

Later, I'd be grateful for that little piece of calm before the storm.

Chapter 9

CECILIA

I STARED AT a small drip of paint on the windowsill, millimeters away from where it met the wall. It was almost perfectly formed, like it had been caught mid-roll and was now stuck in that same position forever, marring the nearly pristine paintwork. A mistake that was now permanently part of the room.

How fitting.

It had always been amazing to me how a word of praise can be forgotten in an instant, but a harsh word is remembered forever. I'm not sure if it's a defense mechanism protecting someone from being hurt again, or if we as humans just choose to remember the shitty parts of someone rather than the good ones. Whatever the reason, I felt like I'd been dealing with it my entire life.

I was the family fuck up. Mean. Wild. Selfish. Liar.

For a long time, I'd owned it. I'd played into the role that I'd been cast because honestly, there hadn't been a different role to play. My older brother Cam was the child my parents had chosen. They'd adopted him after his entire first family had died, and he'd been fully formed when they added him to our family, his personality already set. He was a leader. Before he became my brother, he'd already been the oldest child, the oldest sibling. He was patient and helpful and he adored my mom, which meant he always went out of his way to make her happy.

My little sister Lily was different. Where Cam was a natural born leader, Lily was a follower. She was easy, because she was so damn sweet. From the minute she was born, it was like our world revolved around her. And I understood it, I really did. She was brilliant, really and truly brilliant, like my dad. Her intelligence was intimidating, but she never held it over anyone. It was like she didn't even realize how much smarter she was than nearly everyone around her. She was just sweet, in a way that wasn't grating or annoying. So when she lost her sight at eleven years old? It rocked our family to the very foundation and what little attention hadn't been focused on her before, became hyper-focused on her afterward.

I also had another little sister, Charlie, who came after Lily became blind.

Rubbing my fingers over my lips, I fought against the urge to cry.

I didn't know Charlie very well. She was born when I was nearly out of the house, and most of my memories with her were when she was still called swimming, *fimming*, because she couldn't make the *s* sound. She was a really cool kid, I knew that much, but we hadn't spent much time together since I'd moved away. It was my fault. I hadn't made an effort.

I'd escaped Oregon because I'd been the fuck up. Because I had put so much importance on getting my parents' attention—on getting *anyone's* attention—that it was suffocating me.

I was the middle child and because of that, I'd naturally found myself doing anything and everything to get my parents' attention and affection. Hell, even their anger had been better than feeling ignored. And when I was young, it hadn't been terrible. I'd been bratty, sure. But it wasn't until the early summer day when our family had been attacked, and I'd found myself stumbling through the carnage, that things had changed.

No one came to me. No one asked if I was okay. No one held me.

Because I wasn't bleeding, they'd just assumed that they didn't need to console me. Not then, and not afterward, when everything had settled back into a new normal. I'd been overlooked, again, but it was so much worse that time because I'd needed them so badly.

Mark, who'd been in the hospital for weeks with gunshot and knife wounds, had been the only one who'd asked if I was okay. He'd been the only one who'd held me as I cried. The only person I'd confided in about those moments when I'd thought I was going to die.

Everyone around me had assumed I was jealous. I'd heard the things they said—that I was a self-centered brat, that I didn't care about anyone but myself, that I couldn't stand the fact that Lily got all of my parents' attention. And I'd fed into the bullshit for a long time, believing all of it, because it was easier than facing the truth.

It had actually been the opposite.

I'd been terrified for my little sister. I'd adored her. But I'd also been doing anything I could to get my parents to look at me and see that I was drowning.

"Hey," Mark called, startling me as he put a hand on my hip. "I've got a hungry baby here."

Internally shrugging off the memories, I turned to him.

"Thanks for taking her for a while," I said, lifting my arms for Olive. "Is she getting cranky?"

"Cranky, no," he said with a weird look on his face. "But she started trying to suck on my neck."

I huffed out a surprised laugh.

"I might have a hickey," he said, leaning his head to the side to show me.

"You don't have a hickey," I replied, pushing myself up.

"Thank God." He sat down on the edge of the bed. "I usually make them buy me dinner first."

I was surprised at the small twinge of jealousy that flared in my belly. I didn't want to think of Mark with anyone else, even if he was joking.

"So," he said uncomfortably, "your parents are pretty much set to leave, but we need to pack up your stuff tonight so we can hit the road early."

"We?" I asked as Olive started to nurse. "You're coming with us?"

"We're all going," Mark said. He laid down on his side and propped up his head with his hand. "Just because there's shit happening in Eugene doesn't mean that fuckwad is going to stop messin' with you. If you guys need to head north, we're headed north."

"You don't have to do that," I said quietly. "Once we're there, you know I'll be safe."

"Can't take the chance," he said, his expression grim. "Not willing to."

As I stared at him, I remembered all the different ways he'd made me feel safe when we were young. The way he'd always been so attuned to me that he would notice when I was upset from across a crowded room. How intently he used to watch me when I talked, like nothing was more important than what I had to say. And then, like a blow to the windpipe, I remembered when he'd torn that all away.

"Cec?" He must have seen something in my expression, because he sounded both worried and guarded.

"I can't believe Rose is missing," I said, bringing the conversation around to what was really important. "Have they heard anything else?"

"No," Mark said with a sigh. "They don't know shit. Literally nothing except that she disappeared from work and she was with Mack."

"I thought they'd broken up," I mused.

"Guess not," Mark said with a shrug. "That shit's never black and white."

"Sometimes it is," I murmured, not meeting his eyes.

He sighed and sat up. "Yeah, sometimes it is. You want me to send your mom in to help you pack up?"

I looked over to the bags neatly lined up against the wall. We hadn't unpacked anything, I'd just been grabbing supplies as I needed them. Surprise, surprise, I hadn't touched half of the crap I'd bought during my manic spending spree.

"Sure," I said as he reached the door. He didn't even turn to acknowledge my answer.

"Maybe I shouldn't have said that," I whispered to Olive, running my fingertips over her scalp. "But sometimes you have to face reality, you know? He's handsome and he smells good, but don't get used to him, okay? He won't be around much longer." I ran my finger over the tiny whorl of her ear. "He's not for us."

Hours later, after my mom had carried all but one bag down to Mark's truck, we'd eaten dinner, and I'd nursed Olive to sleep—I ignored the warning I'd given the baby as Mark slid into bed behind me and wrapped his arm around my waist.

He may not be for us, but I couldn't find the willpower to keep my distance until he disappeared from our lives.

"How you feelin'?" he asked, his breath tickling the back of my neck. "Any better?"

"A little," I replied in a whisper. "I think that medicine your friend got is working."

"You say that like you're surprised," he said with a small chuckle. "It's antibiotics, Cec, just like you'd get from your doctor."

"Bought in some back alley," I muttered.

"Since when are you too snobby for illegal meds?" he asked, a smile in his voice. "Pretty sure my pop supplied you with quite a few of them when we were kids."

"That was different," I argued. "Number one, I knew Doc. Number two, I was a kid and didn't know any better. Number three, I pay through the nose for insurance so I don't have to buy black market antibiotics."

"Well, we just saved you a co-pay and the cost of prescription meds."

I didn't reply, because he kind of had a point. Instead, I finally said out loud what had been playing on a loop in my head for hours.

"I'm scared for Rose," I confessed, closing my eyes. "I know they're doing everything they can to find her, and I'm sure she's fine, but I'm terrified."

"I know you are," he replied, kissing my head.

"She doesn't even like me," I said quietly enough that I could pretend he might not hear me. "She wouldn't give me a second thought if the roles were reversed."

"You don't know that," he argued.

"Yeah, I do."

Mark was quiet for a while as he let that sink in.

"Does she not remember what you did for her?" he finally asked, his entire body throbbing with tension.

"I'm sure she does," I replied.

"Then what the fuck?" He scoffed. "Jesus, if it wasn't for you, she'd be dead."

"Don't say that," I said quickly. "Don't."

"You know it's true."

"I don't want to talk about it."

"Well, maybe you should," he said angrily. "Because I'm tired of this shit."

"It doesn't have anything to do with you," I argued.

"Jesus Christ, Cecilia," he said with a long sigh. "Why the fuck don't you stand up for yourself?"

"Because it doesn't matter," I replied. "They're always going to think whatever they want about me. It hasn't changed in fifteen years, and it's not going to change now."

He growled against my neck, but thankfully let it go. I didn't want to talk about the way my family viewed me. I'd done that before, told him all of my secrets, all of my hurts, every bad thing they'd said when they thought I couldn't hear them. He didn't get that from me anymore.

As I slowly drifted off into a fretful sleep, I relaxed into his body. This was the only thing he got from me—the comfort of my body against his while we slept. We both knew he didn't even deserve that much.

★ ★ ★

I HAD NO idea if it was hours or just minutes later when I woke up to Mark's hand over my mouth and his lips at my ear.

"They're here," he said softly. "Grab Olive and get up."

I nodded, and as soon as he let me go, I was climbing off the bed with Olive in my arms. The bedroom door was still shut, and the only light illuminating the room came from inside the closet.

"How do you—"

"Silent alarm," he said, cutting me off as he ushered me toward the closet. "See it in the corner?"

Up near the ceiling was a small, blinking white light. If I hadn't known it was there, I would've never noticed it.

"White means they haven't made it into the house yet," he said, grabbing my bag off the floor. "We have time."

"What are you doing?" I asked as he knelt inside the closet.

"Another reason we got this place," he said as he ran his fingers along the carpet. After a few seconds, he found what he was looking for and pulled, opening a trap door in the floor.

"In," he ordered.

I looked around the bare closet. "No," I spat. "I'm not hiding in a fucking closet again."

"Get in, Cecilia."

"No, I—"

Mark looked beyond me and cursed. Following his gaze, I watched as the light that had been white only seconds before blinked red.

"Get the fuck in," he ordered again. "Or I swear to God, I'll knock your ass out and put you in."

"What does red mean?" I asked as I stepped toward the opening.

"Get in."

I scrambled to the opening and sat down, my feet hanging over the ledge. The floor beneath me was close, and I slid down until I was standing, half in and half out of the small space.

"What does red mean?" I asked again, my heart pounding.

"There's a reason we put you in this room," he said quickly, dropping my bag in the hole. "Sit down."

I crouched down and curled my legs until I was seated, staring at his face.

"What does red mean?"

"Stay in here until I come for you," he ordered. "Don't fuckin' move."

"What does red mean?"

His eyes met mine. "They're in the house."

Then he swung the door closed and the darkness surrounding me was absolute.

Slowly, I inhaled through my nose, ignoring the way my skin crawled. It was just darkness, the absence of light. I'd been in the dark before. It wasn't anything that I couldn't handle.

They were in the house. They were *in* the house. *They were in the house.*

The words played over and over in my head as Olive stirred and I began to rock back and forth.

It was happening again. I was hiding again. Just like the first time. Just like the last time.

I flinched as a loud thump came from somewhere in the house.

It was happening again.

I began to hum as more thumping and thudding and crashing reached my ears.

It was happening again.

Something slammed downstairs, shaking the floor I was sitting on.

It was happening again.

Memories I'd tried to bury flashed through my mind. Rose's wide eyes as she stood frozen. The weight of her as I dragged her away. The feeling of bullets hitting the tree against my back. The feel of her fingernails digging into my arms. The burn of a bullet passing so close to my shoulder that it cut a hole in my t-shirt and left a welt on my skin.

Gunshots.

I couldn't figure out if they'd been part of my memory, or if I'd actually heard them.

It was happening again.

I rocked faster. Hummed louder. Olive began to squirm against my hold on her.

Footsteps overhead.

Then, like someone flipped a switch, there was nothing.

No fear, no memories, no fight.

Blissful, *nothing*.

Chapter 10

MARK

I MEMORIZED HER face, the fear in her eyes and the tension in her jaw and the way her lips had flattened into a thin line as she braced herself. Then, I closed the trap door between us and took a few precious seconds to make sure that the seam in the carpet was invisible. After I knew she wouldn't be found if the worst happened, I was on the move.

I didn't have time to get dressed, but I threw on a black hoodie over my bare chest, hoping for at least a little concealment considering the way my pasty-as-fuck skin practically glowed in the dark. The light in the closet went out and I let out a breath, knowing that Wilson had cut the power. I hadn't heard anyone else moving around, which I expected, and I had to assume that everyone knew what was happening.

I didn't need sight to grab a pistol from my bag and quickly add a suppressor. There was no need to scare Cecilia even more with sounds of gunfire. Then, just in case, I pocketed my switchblade. I'd had the thing since I was a kid, and while it wasn't something I'd had to use often, it worked in a pinch.

I quietly made my way to the door and opened it wide, immediately seeing a shadow in the darkness.

"Woody," Casper breathed.

"All set?" I asked. His shadow nodded.

"Cam's stayin' up here in case one of 'em gets past us."

"Won't happen," I murmured. Then I shut my mouth and led him to the top of the stairs.

If I knew my team, they were already positioned around the first floor, and I listened for any whisper of noise that would tell me where the intruder had entered the house. For Cecilia's sake, I hoped that we could end this shit quickly and quietly.

As we reached the bottom of the stairs, a lanky shadow emerged on our left and I lifted my hand to keep Casper from hitting him.

"Rock and roll," Wilson breathed, his shadow becoming clearer as he stepped closer. Then he started singing, the sound barely audible.

Ignoring him, I took the lead as we made our way toward the entryway. The front door was slightly cracked, and I let out a slow breath as I moved in that direction. The living room was the only place between me and the door, and I really fucking hoped that the motherfucker was in there. If he wasn't, that meant he was somewhere behind us.

Wilson went low and I went high as we cleared the room.

"Shit," Casper said under his breath.

We spun back toward the front door and I silently closed it and slid the deadbolt home. Leaving it open had either been sloppy or easy access for whoever he'd left outside, and I sure as fuck wasn't going to make it easy for them to send in reinforcements.

Just as we'd rounded the corner and hit the dining room, a flash of light came from my right and I swore as the bullet hit my shoulder and knocked me back a step.

"Mine," Casper said, returning fire. The thud of the body hitting the floor sounded at nearly the same time as his gunshot.

"Kitchen," Wilson said, taking the lead. We followed him, and found Lu on the floor and Forrest slicing the throat of another man.

"There's two?" Wilson asked as Forrest dropped the body.

"Four," Forrest replied.

"Fuck," I whispered, dropping to a knee to check Lu's pulse. It was strong and I couldn't see any blood, but she was completely out.

"I got her," Forrest said as I stood. "Go."

The only thing I had ever hated about the house was the sheer number of rooms it had. While it was good for holding larger groups of people, it was also a logistical nightmare. As we cleared room by room, I grew more and more anxious.

They couldn't have made it past us and up the stairs, but I fucking hated the fact that it was taking so long to find the motherfuckers.

"—*in the name of love*," Wilson whisper-sung as we moved. "*Pour some sugar*—gotcha." In less than a second, he was reaching into the darkness, moving so fast that I didn't even have a chance to respond. The third man was a little harder to take down, and as Wilson fought him, still singing, I cleared the rest of the room. Unfortunately, he was the only one in there.

"Double back," Casper said, tapping me on the shoulder.

I nodded as we moved back toward the front of the house.

The hallway leading to the command room was empty, and I knew without checking that the room itself was empty. Wilson had installed fingerprint locks that were only used in case of a breach, and he would've activated them before he left his lair.

How the fuck we'd missed the last man as we'd searched the house was beyond me, but he hadn't been in the living room when we'd been in there before. As we rounded the couch, we found him lying flat on his back, partially hidden in the shadows. I would've liked to question him, but when I saw his pistol pointed in our direction I didn't hesitate. The first shot hit exactly where I'd aimed. I probably didn't need to shoot him the second time. I did anyway.

"All clear," Eli said, strolling into the room.

"Where the fuck have you been?" I asked, letting Casper take the pistol from my hand so I could put pressure on my shoulder.

"Takin' care of business outside," Eli replied calmly. "They won't be reporting back, but I have a feeling they'll be missed sooner rather than later."

"We gotta go," I said, hurrying toward the stairs.

"Need to get a look at that shoulder," Forrest said as he led Lu out of the kitchen.

"Alright?" I asked her.

"Just pissed," she replied in disgust. "Must have been in the bathroom when the silent alarm tripped. Asshole knocked me out when I went to get a glass of water."

"I do not appreciate visitors showing up unannounced," Wilson said as he joined us. "It's just poor manners."

I ignored him as I took the stairs two at a time, Casper on my heels.

"That kid is fuckin' weird," he said. "Was he singin'—"

"Def Leppard," I replied. "Yep."

We parted ways as we reached our rooms and the lights came back on just as I reached the closet. Kneeling down, I winced as I reached for the carpet with both hands, sliding my fingers across it until I found the seam. I could feel the blood dripping down my arm inside the sweatshirt, but I ignored it and the burn of my shoulder as I found the seam and dragged my finger under it until I found the latch.

I swung open the door and the relief at finding Cecilia and Olive safe warred with the dread that hit me as she tilted her head up at the light.

Her face was completely emotionless. Blank.

"Come here, baby," I said softly, reaching for her.

Her hand met mine instantly and she let me pull her to her feet.

"It was dark in there," she said distractedly, laying Olive on the floor so she could crawl out of the hole.

"I'm sorry," I said, watching her closely as she picked Olive back up.

Cecilia didn't respond. She just stood there, rocking slightly.

"Jesus," Farrah said as she came into the room behind me. "I'm getting too old for this shit. Are you okay?"

"She's fine," I responded when Cecilia didn't. Reaching into the space, I grabbed her bag, gritting my teeth as my shoulder protested the movement. "We're leavin' now."

"Cody told me," Farrah replied with a nod. She looked back and forth between me and Cecilia, her brow furrowed. "CeeCee?"

"Yeah?" Cecilia asked easily, looking over at her mom.

"You okay, sweetheart?"

"Yeah," Cecilia replied as I gently walked her out of the closet.

"Chief," Forrest interrupted, barging into the room. "I need to take a look at that shoulder. Sit." He pointed to the bed.

"It's fine," I argued, urging Cecilia forward with my hand at the small of her back. "You can look at it later."

"Boy," he said, half amused and half pissed. "Sit your ass down."

"Take her out of here?" I said quietly to Farrah.

"Sure thing." She grabbed the bag from my hand and wrapped her arm around Cecilia's shoulders. "Come on, let's find your dad."

"Mark?" Cecilia asked, looking over her shoulder at me, her face still void of any emotion whatsoever.

"I'll be right out, Cec," I replied, jerking my chin toward the door. "Go with your mom."

"She's in shock," Forrest said after Farrah walked Cecilia out of the room. "There a reason you didn't want her in here for this?"

"She's seen enough gunshot wounds," I said, unzipping my hoodie.

"Damn," he said, nodding his head to the matching scars on each shoulder, one of them just inches from the new wound. "Yours?"

"Mine," I confirmed, trying and failing to block the memories of that day. "And others. Too many."

"Well, this'll be a nice scar to add to your collection," Forrest said in disgust as he pulled out a roll of bandages and an assortment of other supplies. "At least it's a through-and-through. Barely missed your clavicle. Couple inches to the left and we wouldn't be havin' this conversation."

"Can you stitch it?"

"Not in the next ten minutes," he replied. "But a bandage should hold it until I've got some time to work."

"That's fine," I said, staring at the open doorway.

I'd expected Cecilia to be freaked the fuck out. I'd even expected her to be pissed. But I hadn't prepared for her to be unfazed. No, not unfazed, it was like she was completely unaware of everything that had happened.

"You know, if you didn't have so much muscle, the bullet would've missed you," Forrest mused. "Lucky shot."

"Doesn't feel lucky," I said as he pressed a bandage to each side of my shoulder.

"They never do," he replied dryly.

As soon as I was wrapped like a mummy and taken whatever pills Forrest had dropped into my palm, we grabbed our things and left the room, not bothering to clean up the mess Forrest had made as he took care of my shoulder. A cleaning crew would come in later, people we trusted, to take care of the blood and bodies. Wilson had probably already called them—he was usually Johnny-on-the-spot with that shit.

Everyone was clustered in the garage when we got downstairs, probably because most of the rooms had dead men in them. Cam eyeballed me as I strode toward them and gave me a short nod.

"Siah and Eph will meet us up north," Eli informed me. "They'll check on your place again before they go."

"Have them grab a truck," I said, watching as Casper rubbed Cecilia's back. She still wasn't really responding to anything around her. "Tell them to head to Cecilia's place and pack it up."

"You sure about that?" Cam asked.

"She's not gonna be back for a while," I replied. I turned back to Eli. "Don't bother with the furniture, but everything else goes, including her car."

"Oh, they're gonna love that," Eli said with a chuckle.

"They can suck it the fuck up," Forrest said, his eyes on Cecilia. "She's gonna need her things when she lands."

"Due to the hostile working conditions of this property, I'm going to relocate back to San Diego," Wilson said, crossing his arms over his chest. "I can get more accomplished there anyway."

"Keep trying to reach Richard Campbell's daughter," I ordered.

"Her name is Kaley," Wilson replied.

"Don't care. Find her. Make contact. We need to cut the head of this fucking snake."

"I'll fingerprint the visitors before I go," Wilson replied. "See if we can get any new information from them."

"You're gonna fingerprint dead men?" Casper asked blandly.

"Yes," Wilson replied.

"We need to move," Lu chimed in. Her face was drawn and her jaw was tight as she leaned against the wall.

"You're ridin' with me," Eli informed her.

"My bike's here," she argued without any heat.

"And it's gonna stay that way. We'll store it in here," Eli said firmly, shouldering his bag. "No way you're ridin' like that. Come on."

We filed out of the garage, leaving Wilson inside to finish up, and as soon as Casper handed Cecilia off to Farrah, he met me at the hood of my truck.

"Our best bet would be to make it to Sacramento in one shot. As soon as we meet up with the chapter up there, we're golden," he said, handing me Olive's car seat. The baby was completely passed out, a little pink hat covering her head and a small yellow blanket tucked around her. "The boys know we're on our way."

"Good," I said. "I'm not sure how often we'll have to stop. I'll tell Cec to feed and change Olive on the fly so we're not stopping for long periods."

"That's what I'd do," Casper said. "Jesus, how the fuck is he tracking her down?"

"I've got no clue, but the man must be connected in a big way."

"No shit," Casper muttered. "Can't tell you how much I fuckin' hate feelin' like we're runnin.' I've never run from a fight in my entire goddamn life."

"You've got shit happening back home," I replied. "Can't be two places at once."

"Problem is, we're just bringin' the problems down here and addin' them to the ones we've got up there."

"You hear anything?"

"Not a goddamn thing," he spat. "People don't just fuckin' disappear. I have no idea what the hell is goin' on up there."

"Two days, and you'll be there to sort it."

"I fuckin' hope so," Casper said. "Keep your eyes sharp. I'll catch you on the other side."

He went around the truck to kiss Farrah goodbye and I strode to Cecilia's door. She was sitting sideways in the seat, waiting for Olive. As soon as I got close, she hopped down so I could put the baby's car seat inside.

"You got everything?" I asked her, reaching up to push her tangled hair out of her face.

"Yeah, we were already packed," she replied. "I had Lu grab me a blanket so I could sleep."

"Good idea." I stared at the dark shadows beneath her eyes and the sharp ridge of her cheekbones. "You need the rest."

"We're headed north?" she asked.

"Yep. Oregon or bust," I joked.

"Okay." She gave me a wan smile and turned away, climbing gingerly into the truck. When she sat down, she winced.

"You alright?"

She nodded as she buckled her seat belt. "Just sore."

I closed the door as she pulled the throw blanket up around her shoulders. Yeah, I bet she was sore. I couldn't imagine that any of the activities over the past week had been easy on her healing body. On top of everything else, I hated the fact that she didn't even have time to recover from giving birth.

She was riding the razor's edge, and everyone could see it. She'd held up, no one could argue that—keeping a cool head, doing whatever was asked of her, and never complaining or breaking down. It was coming, though.

Some point soon, she was going to lose it, and I was super fucking concerned that none of us were going to know how to help her when she did. Crying, screaming, throwing shit—I could calm that down. But the brittle way she was moving? The blank stares? The calm, almost robotic responses? They scared the hell out of me.

We didn't bother going in circles or trying to lose any potential tails—it was too late for that—instead, I drove straight to the freeway and hauled ass west. Cecilia and Olive slept until we'd hit California and were headed north.

"There's nowhere to change her back here," Cecilia complained, rifling through a bag to find supplies.

"Just lay her on your knees," Farrah replied, turning in her seat so she could watch. "Make it work."

"I don't want to make it work," Cecilia mumbled tiredly. "I want to be sitting on a couch somewhere, with space to spread out."

"You'll get there," I reassured her, glancing in the rear view mirror. "Just a couple more days."

I kept my eyes on the road as Cecilia pulled Olive out of her seat and got her changed. Our plan to keep going while she took care of the baby had seemed like a good one at the time, but I had to admit that in practice, it was more nerve-wracking than I'd thought it would be. Freeway drivers were assholes, and I was constantly cursing under my breath as they did stupid shit—cutting each other off and generally driving like idiots at eighty miles an hour. On top of that, Olive seriously didn't like being changed, and the cab was filled with screaming so loud that it made my ears ring. I'd never been so glad that my truck was considerably bigger than most of the cars surrounding us.

"Finally," Farrah said with a laugh when Olive stopped wailing.

"It's hard to maneuver back here," Cecilia replied. "She doesn't like being undressed."

"You were completely the opposite," Farrah mused. She propped her chin on the seat back. "Probably because your skin was so sensitive. We even had to use cloth diapers because anything else gave you a rash."

"I didn't know that," Cecilia said. "Was it a total pain in the ass?"

"Yeah, at first," Farrah said with a nod. "But once we had it figured out, it was no big deal." Farrah chuckled. "I was glad we didn't need to use cloth with Lily, though. By that time, I was up to my ears in laundry already."

"These diapers don't seem to bother Olive," Cecilia said with a sigh.

"You're doing a good job, you know," Farrah said quietly. "Especially for someone that had no idea they were going to be a mother."

"All I have to do is feed her and change her," Cecilia replied. "It's not exactly rocket science. I have plenty of time to screw shit up."

"True," Farrah said. "But that doesn't mean you will."

"Come on," Cecilia said with a scoff. I looked at her in the mirror. "You know it's only a matter of time before I do." She looked dully out the window.

"I *don't* know that," Farrah argued, her voice still soft. "You've never given yourself enough credit."

When Cecilia didn't respond, Farrah turned forward and settled back in her seat. The cab was quiet beyond the sound of the freeway as Cecilia finished feeding Olive and buckled her back into her seat. Not long after, the sound of Cec's quiet snores drifted to the front seat.

"You ever think that maybe she's never given herself enough credit because none of you have, either?" I said finally, the quiet words falling like a bomb between us.

"You got something you want to say?" Farrah asked, her voice both amused and hard at the same time. I was walking into a minefield that I had no business being in, but Christ, I was too fucking old to ignore the bullshit anymore.

I chose my words carefully.

"She's not the same person she was when we were twenty years old," I said, switching lanes to pass a car that wasn't keeping up with the flow of traffic. "And even if she was, all of you acting like she's some selfish brat is getting real fuckin' old."

"You might want to stop there," Farrah replied flatly.

"Why?" I said with a grunt. "I've already started, might as well lay it all out."

"Oh, please, tell me how *I've* done Cecilia wrong," Farrah snapped. "I'd love to hear it."

"I know you love her," I said, making Farrah laugh derisively. "But Jesus, I've never met a group of people so willing to believe the worst about a person."

"I don't believe the worst of Cecilia."

"Don't you?" I asked, glancing at her. "If Cecilia was saying something shitty, she was the asshole—it didn't matter who she was speaking to, or what they'd said about her. If she was teasing Lily, she was a bully. If she was making nasty comments, even just to defend herself, she was mean. From what I saw, you gave up on her instead of figuring out why she was doing the shit she was doing."

"You have no clue what you're talking about," Farrah replied.

"Don't I?" I shook my head. "Who do you think she was talking to back then? It wasn't you. It wasn't Casper. It sure as fuck wasn't Leo."

I jerked as a hand settled on my shoulder. "Enough, Mark," Cecilia warned sleepily. "That's enough."

I opened my mouth to argue and then snapped it shut. She was right. It wasn't my place to educate Farrah on all the ways she'd fucked up back then. I knew she'd done her best, slogging through the devastation after the shooting in her back yard and trying to take care of everyone at the same time. Cecilia had told me things in confidence, and even if the promises I'd made were half a lifetime ago, I still needed to keep them to myself.

I reached forward and turned on the radio, gesturing for Farrah to pick a station. Thankfully, the olive branch worked, and she leaned forward to fiddle with the dials. I had a feeling that we weren't done with our conversation, but at least for a while, we were calling a truce. Once we were out of the truck and Cecilia was out of earshot, I was pretty sure Farrah was going to tear me a new one.

Conversation was spotty for the next couple of hours. Cecilia drifted in and out of sleep, Farrah did word search and crossword puzzles that she'd pulled out of her purse, and I kept my eyes on the road, both ahead and behind us. Cam and Casper switched between leading the way and following behind the truck. Eli's car and Forrest's SUV stayed visible, but I didn't notice any other cars that seemed out of place. Beyond the fact that we were trying to reach Sacramento as soon as possible, it was a pretty uneventful and boring drive.

Just outside Bakersfield, we finally stopped for fuel and so everyone could stretch their legs. As I climbed out of the truck, I kept my head on a swivel. The gas station we'd pulled into was busy, but thankfully, I didn't see anyone that seemed out of place or seemed to be watching us.

"Wilson's been tryin' to reach you," Forrest said, his mouth set in a grim line as he strode toward me. "Call him."

Chapter 11
CECILIA

"I NEED TO go to the bathroom," I told my mom as I handed Olive to her. "Pronto."

"Alright," she replied. As I turned to get my supplies out of the truck, she called for my dad. "Cody, we need an escort to the ladies room."

"Announce it to the world," I mumbled.

"I knew Casper wasn't his real name," Eli said as he walked toward us.

"She's the only one who calls him Cody," I replied as I slung my purse over my shoulder. "I wouldn't try it."

"Of course not," Eli said with a shit-eating grin, raising his hands in surrender.

"You're pretty," my mom said in amusement, looking him up and down. "Too bad me and my girls already found our other halves."

"Um, excuse me?" I asked, raising my eyebrows.

"Oh, please," Mom said with a scoff. "The only people who haven't figured it out is you two dumbasses."

Eli laughed and I glared at him. "She's right," he said sympathetically, raising one eyebrow as he rubbed his chest in the exact spot my name was permanently etched on Mark's chest.

"Bathroom," I reminded my mother, choosing to ignore the entire conversation.

"I'll walk you," Eli offered.

"Cody," my mom called again. When my dad didn't turn to look at her, she rolled her eyes. "Just go with the pretty one," she told me. "Your father is clearly preoccupied."

"Fine."

Mom looked at Eli, all joking gone from her expression. "If something happens to her, you'll be the first to die."

"Whoa," Eli muttered, his head jerking back in surprise.

"Ignore her," I told him as I started toward the building.

"I think my balls just shriveled up into my stomach," he said as he caught up with me. "Seriously." He reached down to the zipper of his pants. "They're gone."

"Just walk me to the bathroom," I replied. "You can search for your balls while I'm in there."

"You realize that if there's more than one stall, I have to follow you in, right?"

"You realize if you follow me in, my mom isn't the one you'll have to worry about, right?"

"Point taken," he mumbled, opening the glass door to the mini-mart. "I'll just check it out and then stand outside."

"Good idea."

I got the key from the guy at the cash register and did my business quickly, anxious to get back on the road. God, I hated this. I felt like shit, my vagina throbbed constantly, and I just wanted somewhere to lay down and rest for at least a week. My mind wandered to Liv while I washed my hands, and I ruthlessly jerked it back to the present. The only thing I would focus on was getting us to Sacramento. There was nothing I could do to change the past, or to make us any safer, or to somehow untangle the mess my life had become. I refused to even think about it. I'd deal with it all later. Much later. Maybe never.

"All set?" Eli asked as I came out of the restroom.

"All set." I followed him back out to the vehicles, and my stomach tightened as I got a look at Mark's expression.

"Where's your phone?" he asked, his hand out palm up. "In your purse?"

"Yeah." I glanced at the other people in the group, all of them wearing the same grim expression. Reaching into my purse, I blindly searched for my phone and pulled it out.

"Give it here," Mark snapped. As soon as I'd handed it over, he was completely dismantling it.

"What are you doing?" I blurted, reaching for it.

"It's how they've been tracking us," Mark replied flatly, handing back the phone without a battery. "You know Warren had a big stake in the telecom industry?"

"I had no idea where he got his money," I replied honestly.

"Well, he did. So does the son. We figure that's the only way he was able to track your phone so fast. When you own the business, it's easy to throw your weight around."

"With that much cake, we should have realized it sooner," my brother spat.

"Money makes the world go 'round," Lu grumbled.

"But we were at the house for days—" I snapped my mouth shut when I realized that my phone had been dead until I plugged it in to call Lily.

"Let's get back on the road," my dad ordered. "We're wasting time."

It didn't take long before we were loaded back up and headed north again. I closed my eyes and leaned my head against the window, letting the cool glass soothe the headache that was forming at my temples. I just wanted it all to be over. I wanted to get settled somewhere in a little house where we could rest and I could relax, even for a few minutes.

The rest of the drive seemed to take forever, and I spent the last hour trying to keep Olive calm in her car seat, but eventually, we pulled up outside a garage on the outskirts of Sacramento. As a large gate with barbed wire across the top rolled open, I sat up straight in my seat.

I hadn't been to the Sacramento clubhouse since I was a kid. Back in the day, my parents had brought us with them when they'd come down to visit, but as we'd gotten older, they'd started leaving us behind with various friends and family, usually my Gram.

"I swear, this place never changes," my mom said as we rolled into a parking spot out back. "It's like walking into a time warp, every time."

"You're from down here, aren't you?" Mark asked as he shut off the truck.

"Yeah." Mom sighed and sent him a tired smile. "Eugene is better."

"Of course it is." He chuckled, then met my eyes in the mirror. "You all set?"

"I just want out of this truck," I said, stretching my arms over my head.

As soon as we'd climbed out, we were surrounded by people that I barely remembered. Old men with long beards passed my mom around, giving her hugs and kissing the top of her head, like she was a long lost sister. Cam had disappeared into the crowd, probably to call Trix, and my dad was shaking hands and giving back-slapping hugs of his own. As I stood there holding Olive, I realized that, while I felt completely out of place, my family knew these people and felt comfortable in their company.

Mark's arm slid around my shoulders until his forearm rested against my upper chest, and his solid form pressed against my back. If we'd been anywhere else, I would've laughed at the blatant show of possession, but standing in that courtyard, I was thankful for the solidarity.

"Well, I'll be damned," an old timer said, grinning as he looked at the two of us. "You have to be Doc's kid." He laughed, reaching out to shake Mark's hand. "I'd recognize that face anywhere."

"Yup, that's Woody," my dad said, a small smile tugging at his lips.

"Your old man was a good'un," the old guy said. Then his eyes came to me. "And you have to be CeeCee. You look just like your mother did, way back when."

"Lucky girl," my mom sang, making everyone laugh. "What? You know it's true."

"Hey," I said, smiling at him.

"Who's the little one?" He shifted his head to the side, trying to see around Olive's blanket.

"This is Olive," I said, pulling the blanket down to show her face.

"Well, hello, Olive," he whispered. "I'm Chunky." He leaned back and whistled. "Hell, girl, that's a fresh one. Shouldn't you be in bed?"

"Well, now that you mention it," I joked.

"Well, come on inside," he said to the group. "We'll get you settled and make introductions then."

"His name is Chunky?" Eli asked in amusement as we followed the group. "Do you think at some point he actually was?"

"He was bigger when we were young," Mark replied. "Think he had a bout with cancer a few years back."

"How do you even know that?" I asked in surprise, looking up at his face.

"Poet likes to talk," Mark said, his lips twitching. "I barely get a word in when I call to catch up."

"I miss him," I said with a sigh. I had to admit, that was one thing I was looking forward to when we got to Eugene. Poet and Amy. They were old as dirt and a couple of the kindest people I'd ever met. They'd seen everything and nothing I'd ever done had surprised them or made them look at me differently.

"He misses you, too," Mark murmured, kissing the side of my head.

The inside of the clubhouse was both familiar and completely alien. I had flashes of memory, running around the pool tables and hiding from Cam underneath the bar, but the strongest sense of recognition came from the smell. Hardwood and beer and leather and grease with just a hint of sweat. Just like the clubhouse in Eugene. Jesus, it was like coming home.

"Hey, mama," a rounded woman with short, salt-and-pepper hair said as she reached us, giving my mom a sweet smile. "You're a sight for sore eyes."

"You cut that glorious hair," my mom replied, smiling huge. "And it looks goddamn fantastic. I hate you."

The woman laughed as my mom hugged her, and something in me settled as they held the hug longer than necessary, whispering into each others' ears as they rocked side to side. When they finally pulled apart, they both turned to look at me.

"CeeCee, this is Eileen. You probably don't remember her, but when you were little, she used to carry you around all damn day." Mom chuckled. "At one point, she strapped you to her back just so she could get things done."

"You must be exhausted," Eileen said. "Poor thing. Come on, I'll get you settled in a room."

Mark's arm tightened and Eileen's mouth twitched. "We're not goin' far," she told him. "But she's dead on her feet."

"I'll be in soon," Mark murmured into my ear. "I need to have Forrest check on my shoulder." I nodded. Part of me wanted to giggle at the fact that he thought I needed some sort of protection. I was as safe as I'd ever been in my entire life, surrounded by these people. It didn't matter how far I'd run or how long I'd been gone, we both knew these were my people. My tribe. But the other part of me was comforted to know that he wasn't just going to disappear now that I was safe. I didn't let myself dwell on that realization.

"I can show you a room, too," Eileen said to Lu, reaching out to shake her hand. "I'm Eileen."

"I'll stay out here," Lu said politely. "But thank you."

"She's one of the boys, Ei," my mom said with a smile at Lu.

"Right on," Eileen said, nodding. "Well, if you need anything, you let me know."

"I'll do that," Lu replied.

"Hey, what about if I need anything?" Eli asked, grinning.

"You come to me, pretty boy," a large man replied, making Eileen laugh as she looked over her shoulder at him.

"Oh, honey, I couldn't even keep up with this one," she told the man, pointing her thumb at Eli.

The man chuckled. "Baby, you know that ain't true," he shot back.

Mark leaned down to my ear. "Home sweet home," he said in amusement, giving me a little tap on my ass to get me moving. "I'll find you in a bit."

I followed my mom and Eileen through the room, and as we got to the hallway where the bedrooms were located, I felt my entire body grow heavy. I guess knowing that I was so close to somewhere I could rest had somehow triggered a physical response.

"Now, don't you go tellin' anyone, but I got a bathtub in our room and I keep it sparklin' clean. You feel like a soak, you just let me know," Eileen said. "I'd imagine that would feel real nice right about now."

"Jesus," I mumbled. "Are you an angel?"

Eileen laughed and looked at my mom. "She's yours, alright."

"I think she's a clone," my mom said proudly. "Didn't even need Cody for this one."

They both chuckled.

"You're stayin' in here," Eileen said as she opened a door. "When your pop called, we got to work. All the boys with homes in town gave up their rooms and we got 'em cleaned and ready for visitors."

"You mean they're not staying here?" my mom asked, a thread of steel in her voice.

"Oh, they're stayin' here," Eileen said with a smirk. "But they've got bedrolls they know how to use. The boys who're here full-time have too much shit in their rooms, so we didn't bother tryin' to move 'em."

"Ah." Mom nodded.

"And some of the boys headed north to help with the search," Eileen said quietly. "But we've got plenty left down here."

"Thank you," my mom said with a sigh. "When it rains, it fucking pours."

"It's what family's for, mama," Eileen replied, reaching out to give my mom's arm a squeeze. She turned to me. "This one's a queen, so you and your man should fit. Might be snug though."

"Oh, he's not—"

"He probably won't be sleeping much," my mom said, cutting me off. "I have a feeling they'll be up most of the night trying to figure shit out."

"You're probably right," Eileen replied ruefully. "I brought in a portable crib—" She pointed to it in the corner. "Wasn't sure if you'd use it or not, but just in case. And we've got plenty of babies around here if you find you're needin' somethin' else you hadn't thought of."

"Thank you," I told her, growing more and more comfortable with each word. *This*, this was what everyone else felt when they went home. This sense of belonging and safety and camaraderie. It had been longer than I could remember since I'd felt it, and I found myself swallowing against a lump in my throat.

"Here, sweetheart," my mom said, setting the diaper bag on the bed. I hadn't even realized that she'd been carrying it the whole time. "You two get comfortable while Ei shows me where your dad and I are staying. I'll be back in a few minutes."

"Thank you, again," I told Eileen as they moved to the door.

"It's good to see you again, lovey," she replied warmly.

As soon as the door was shut and I was alone in the room, I let out a sigh that felt like it came from the deepest parts of my chest. Finally, I could breathe again.

"I know it's been a long day," I said to Olive as I laid her down on the bed. "But at least tonight, we have some space to spread out and get some rest. First, though, I need to find a bathroom."

She definitely wasn't going anywhere, but I still put pillows on each side of her before grabbing my supplies and heading back into the hallway. The clubhouse was shaped differently than the one back home, but the logistics of the building were basically the same, and it was easy to find a bathroom. I smiled as I closed myself inside and inhaled the scent of cleaner. Eileen hadn't been joking when she'd said they prepared for our visit. The bathroom looked like it hadn't even been used since they'd cleaned it from top to bottom. I hurried through the motions and looked longingly at the shower before heading back to our room. The thought of a long shower where I could shave my legs and let the hot water soothe my muscles sounded like heaven.

"Hey," Mark said, startling me as I entered the room. He was sitting at the foot of the bed, his feet on the ground and his shoulders drooping. "How you doin'?"

"Tired," I replied honestly. "A little relieved. How's your shoulder?"

"Fine," he replied, brushing off the question. "A couple stitches. Hurts like a bitch, but I heal quick." He was quiet for a minute. "It's amazing, huh?" he mused, leaning forward on one elbow, the other resting on his thigh. "Doesn't matter how long you're gone, moment you step foot back on Aces' ground, it's like you never left."

"You noticed it, too?" I asked as I put down my purse.

"Hard to miss. Gotta say, I never really thought I looked like my pop, but apparently, I do."

"Really?" I asked in surprise. "You definitely look like him. It's the mouth."

"This damn mouth," he grumbled, making me laugh.

"Hey," I said, pushing his shoulder. "I like your mouth."

"You do, huh?"

I rolled my eyes. "Stop fishing."

"You're more relaxed here," he said quietly, reaching out to grab my hips. "I can see the difference already."

"I'm—" I paused to try and find the words. "I'm relieved. We made it. And inside these walls, it feels like we're safe."

"You are safe."

"For now, yeah. For tonight. After that—" I shrugged. "It'll all still be there in the morning, like a tidal wave waiting to drown us."

"Nobody's drownin'."

"Not yet."

"Not at all."

"You can't know that."

"I'm not gonna let anything happen to you."

"Until you bail again," I replied, the words out of my mouth before I could stop them. Both of us froze.

"Deserved that," he said, his voice low as he dropped his hands from my hips.

"I still shouldn't have said it," I backpedalled. Jesus, he'd gone all commando and saved me and I was bringing up ancient history. "You've gone beyond what anyone would expect from—"

"Don't start that shit," he cut me off, rising to his feet.

"Don't start what?"

"Don't make this some altruistic—"

"Well, your vocabulary has definitely improved—"

"Goddamn it, Cecilia," he snarled. "Jesus Christ. I've been in love with you since we were kids. You know, you *know* I would've come for you no matter what, no matter where, no matter the circumstances."

"Let's not pretend that has *ever* been the case," I shot back.

"I was twenty fucking years old!"

"So was I!" I yelled, my hands clenched into fists.

"You want to get into this now?" he asked, his voice scarily quiet. "We both knew it was coming, so let's get it over with."

"There is no *getting it over with*," I hissed. "It won't ever be over."

"Well, you sure as fuck got that part right," he muttered.

His hands came up to cup my head, and before I could push him away or say anything else, his lips were on mine.

CHAPTER 12

MARK

IT WAS A spectacularly bad idea to kiss Cecilia, but goddamn did she taste good. I wasn't sure how she managed it, the rest of her was a mess, but her mouth tasted clean with a hint of chocolate from the candy she'd had while we were driving. It was incredible, and she'd been right about the drowning—I sure as hell felt like I was drowning then.

Her hands came up to grip my forearms, the nails pressing into my skin, and I shuddered. It had been so fucking long since anything had affected me that much. Hell, I'd had sex that hadn't rocked my world the way one taste of Cecilia's mouth did. Tilting my head, I pressed deeper into her mouth, the memory of how that used to make her groan swirling in my head—

"Am I interruptin'?" Forrest drawled from the open doorway, making Cecilia tear her mouth away.

I was going to kill him.

"What?" I snapped, not bothering to raise my head. I was too busy staring at Cecilia, who looked like she couldn't decide whether to bolt or hit me.

"Just lettin' you know they brought in some pizzas. Time to eat," Forrest replied, his voice laced with amusement.

"Got it."

He didn't leave.

"Is there a reason you're still standing there?" I asked through gritted teeth.

"Nope," he answered, coughing to hide a chuckle as he walked away.

I sighed as Cecilia stepped away from me, avoiding eye contact as she reached for the diaper bag.

"We'll finish this later," I told her as she carefully unwrapped the baby to change her diaper.

"There's nothing to finish," she replied. "In a few days, you'll be back in California, and I'll be back in hell. Just drop it."

"You know that's not going to happen."

"I'm going to get some pizza," she mumbled, giving me a wide berth as she headed for the doorway, Olive snug in her arms.

I followed her out to the common area and watched as she was swallowed up by the crowd. No matter what she thought about the club or her place in it—the woman belonged with these people. Most of them hadn't even seen her since she was a toddler, and they still treated her like a long lost daughter.

"This place is a trip," Lu said around a bite of pizza as she walked up beside me. "The men look at me like they can't figure me out, and the women don't bat an eyelash."

"That's because most of these guys don't have any clue how much the women pitch in," I replied quietly. "These women have been kicking ass and taking names for years, they just do it from behind the scenes."

"Yeah, that's the vibe I've been getting."

"When I was a kid, the men in the club paid an interest—especially after my pop died—in teaching me how to work on engines and fire a weapon. Hell, one of the boys taught me how to drive. But it was the women who pulled me into the fold—made sure I had clean shit to wear, kept me fed, made sure I was doing alright."

"Men did the surface shit, women did the real heavy lifting," Lu said with a hum.

I chuckled. "Pretty much, yeah."

"But you lived with your mom, right?" she asked.

Cecilia was handing the baby off to someone and I paused until I realized it was Eileen. "Yeah," I told Lu distractedly. "But she worked two jobs, so I went to my pop's a lot, and later, to different club members' houses. I spent most summers there."

"Like a big, extended family," Lu mused.

"Pretty much."

"Must be nice. It was always just me, my brother and my mom. Now it's just me."

"It's not just you," I argued, throwing my arm over her shoulder. "You've got your niece up north, and the team, too."

"True—if her mother would answer my calls. Do I have to claim Siah, though? I'd rather not."

"If I had to pick and choose, I'd leave out Wilson," I joked.

"Nah, Wilson may be a pain in the ass, but he doesn't go out of his way to irritate me."

"Fair point."

"We've got an audience," Lu said under her breath. "Better keep your hands to yourself."

I scoffed, but dropped my arm. I'd felt the stares, too, I just hadn't paid them any mind. The club was like a big family, and because of that, everyone talked about everyone else. It was par for the course.

"In order to keep things simple, Casper told the boys I was Cecilia's man. I'm always welcome, but I don't know these guys like I know the ones in Eugene, so they would've been leery to let the team camp out here."

"Politics," Lu said, nodding her head.

"Something like that."

"I'm telling you, don't even make eye contact with any of the women," Eli told Forrest as they strode toward us. "I thought that monster with the pot belly was going to gut me."

"They don't give a shit about me," Forrest said, irritated. "It's your pretty face that's makin' 'em jumpy."

"And the way you check out every female you meet," Lu added as they reached us.

"I can't help it," Eli complained, shrugging. "I love women, and every single one of them has at least one attractive attribute. Farrah, for instance—"

"I'll stop you there," I said, crossing my arms over my chest. "Casper really would gut you—and no one would ever know because your body would never be found."

Lu laughed, but Eli turned a little green.

"Casper likes me," he argued.

"He don't like anyone that much," Forrest said with a chuckle. He turned to me. "We still leavin' bright and early?"

"That's the plan. Why?"

He jerked his head toward Cecilia. "Just thinkin' that a little more time to rest and feel comfortable would be good for her. She can make another day trip, but by the time we get to Oregon, she's gonna be worn the fuck out. Those antibiotics are only gonna do so much—she needs to rest."

"Thought she'd be feeling better by now," I replied. Cecilia was picking at her food, shoulders slumped and eyes tired, even though she was smiling at the people talking to her.

"A couple'a days here isn't gonna hurt," Forrest said. "Just a thought. Give us some time to hear from Wilson, too."

"You're forgetting that they've got an emergency up in Oregon," I replied. "Cecilia's cousin is still missing."

"Right," he muttered. "But she ain't our mission. Your girl is."

I nodded and slapped him on the back as I moved toward the group gathered around the massive pile of pizza boxes.

"You guys all know Doc's son, Woody, right?" Farrah asked, smiling up at me from her seat next to Cecilia.

"Don't think we've ever met," an older guy said, reaching out to shake my hand. "I'm Throttle."

"I didn't spend much time down here," I replied, as I shook his hand.

"Lost your old man pretty young," he said in understanding. "Tough."

"It happens when your old man was old as shit before you were born," I replied, making him laugh a little.

"You got a point there," he said, nodding in agreement. "Never figured out how the man did it—and I understand it even less now. Randy old bastard."

A few others introduced themselves and I went through the motions, but my attention stayed focused on Cecilia. She was practically falling asleep in her chair.

The second time her eyes closed for a few seconds before she jerked them open again, I'd had enough. Rounding the table, I didn't bother arguing with her, I just grabbed her hand and tugged her up beside me.

"What are you doing?" she asked with a yelp.

"Takin' her to bed," I told Farrah, ignoring Cecilia. "Can you bring Olive in?"

"Yep," Farrah said with a nod. "As soon as she starts fussing. Give you guys a little time first."

"Perfect."

Cecilia was silent as I towed her through the clubhouse. I wasn't sure if it was because she didn't want everyone hearing our argument, or if she was just so wiped out that she was relieved I'd made the decision for her. Probably the former. She used to hate when her parents would get into loud arguments in front of everyone—it embarrassed the shit out of her—which was actually pretty funny since nothing else seemed to phase her.

"You need sleep," I told her as we had some privacy.

"I need a shower first," she said with a sigh. "I'm not climbing into bed like this."

I thought about it for a moment, wondering just how far she was willing to argue. By the mutinous set of her mouth, pretty far.

"Alright, what do you need from the truck?"

"I can go," she said, reaching up to rub at her eyes. "I need a bunch of crap and it's all in different bags."

"What do you need?"

"I can—" Her eyes met mine and her mouth snapped shut. She sighed. "I need a new pair of underwear, another sports bra, shirt, pants, and socks."

"You need that baby soap we got at the store?"

"No." She sat carefully on the bed. "My toiletries are in the diaper bag."

"Alright."

"You don't have to wait on me," she said softly.

"I don't mind goin' to get your stuff," I said, reaching out to run my hand over her hair. God, she looked so worn down. I'd never seen her look so drained. "I'll be right back."

It took me longer than I wanted to find everything she'd asked for because my shoulder was throbbing like a bitch and I had to baby it—but eventually, I'd packed her an overnight bag and headed back toward the building. I didn't notice Casper standing outside until he called my name.

"What's up?" I asked, stopping a few feet away.

"Can't thank you enough for all you've done," he said, his words coming out with a billow of smoke. I glanced down at the joint in his hand and he raised it in invitation.

"I'm good," I said with a shake of my head.

"Helps me sleep," he said, leaning back against the brick wall. "Took sleepin' pills for a bit, but they made me groggy as fuck. Plus, I'm not a fan of big pharma tryin' to shove pills down my throat when this works better."

I just nodded. I wasn't sure where the conversation was going.

"You came through in a big way," he said, nodding. "And I gotta ask, man, what now?"

"What do you mean?"

Casper grunted. "I mean, we get to Eugene and then what? You leavin'?"

I didn't respond.

"If the past is any indication, you're gonna take off and I'm gonna have a daughter in my house that's inconsolable, angry at the world, and never leaves her room." He took a hit off his joint, paused and then let it drift out his nose and mouth. "But from what I'm seein' now, that might not be the case. Just tryin' to get the lay of the land."

"I don't know," I replied honestly. "There's a lot of history there."

"You're tellin' me," he chuckled humorlessly. "But fuck, man. That shit never comes easy. It just don't. Doesn't matter what kind of history you got."

"I think ours is probably worst than most."

"Yeah," he said. "You'd think that. But I know a few couples that had it worse, and they're still fallin' asleep together every night."

I just stood there. I had no idea what the fuck I was going to do. Part of me wanted to put a fucking brand on Cecilia's forehead so everyone knew she was mine. The other part wanted to get her where she needed to be and then go back to my boring, drama-free life.

Shit.

"Yeah, I see the wheels turnin'," he said. "Think on it."

He strode away into the darkness and I turned toward the door. I guess I was lucky that he hadn't punched me while he had the chance. I'd always kind of been waiting for the payback, the retribution for completely fucking up his daughter's life—but it never came. He'd always been civil, even when I'd come back to visit the year after it all went down.

Without conscious thought, my first instinct when I stepped into the common area was to find Olive. Farrah was holding her, swaying side to side, and I let out a breath. I knew she was fine, she was as safe as she could be in the middle of the clubhouse, but there was this weird, constant niggle in the back of my mind to know where she was at all times. It was like needing to know where my wallet was, but a fuck of a lot stronger.

"CeeCee sleeping?" Farrah called out as I made my way through the room.

"She wants a shower first," I replied, gesturing to the bag in my hand.

"Okay, when she's done, this sweet thing's getting hungry."

"Alright. I'll come get her as soon as Cec is finished," I said.

"He's a cutie," I heard Eileen say as I left the room. My lips twitched. I didn't know if I'd ever been called a *cutie* in my life. I'd been an awkward kid and then a pretty solidly built man. Cute was for round cheeks and charm, neither of which I'd ever had.

"Hey, baby," I said opening the door to our room. "You ready?"

Cecilia's eyes popped open as she sat up. "Yeah, all set."

She followed me groggily to the bathroom, clutching her toiletry bag against her stomach, then stood there awkwardly as I turned the shower on for her.

"You can just put the clothes on the toilet," she murmured finally. "I got it from here."

I laughed. "No way am I leaving you in here to pass out alone in the shower."

"You're not staying."

"I am," I said flatly, sitting down on the closed toilet lid.

"I can shower by myself."

"Not happening."

She stood there staring at me like the force of her gaze could get me to change my mind. I wasn't sure why, since it had never worked in the almost twenty years we'd known each other.

"You want me to go get your mom instead?" I asked.

She grimaced. "No."

"Then you've got me."

Cecilia let out a loud sigh and I felt my lips twitching as I tried not to smile.

"At least give me five minutes alone to go to the bathroom," she said mutinously.

"Fine." I got to my feet and set her clothes on the counter. "But if you lock that door, I'll break it down."

"You're an asshole," she muttered in exasperation, clearly frustrated that I'd known what she was up to.

"Been called worse," I said as I slid around her to the door. "Keep this unlocked."

By the time I opened the door again and stepped inside, she was already in the shower. I was both relieved and a little disappointed, but the frosted shower door didn't hide much. I tried to give her some privacy, averting my eyes as I leaned against the counter, but I couldn't seem to stop my gaze from darting back to her silhouette over and over again. Hell, I *was* an asshole. But Jesus, it had been nearly a decade since I'd seen her naked, and I was jonesing big time for another look.

When the shower finally shut off, I grabbed a towel from the shelf above the toilet and handed it over the door.

"Thanks," she called wearily. "Did you bring my bag in with you?"

"Yeah, I got it," I said to the wall, my back to her.

She was silent for a few moments. "Okay, can you hand me the underwear and bra?"

"You're gonna get dressed in the shower?" I asked doubtfully.

"I'm all dried off," she replied. "You can just toss them over the door."

I laughed as I grabbed her underwear from the bag. No way was I tossing them to her. She'd never been able to catch anything, her hand-eye coordination was the equivalent of a four-year-old. "Here," I said, keeping my eyes on the wall as I handed them over.

A few curses from the shower later, I was sidestepping to get out of her way as she swung the door open.

"Damn, it's cold," she complained, shivering as she bent down to the bag on the floor. She swayed a little. "Can you give me a minute to get dressed?"

"You're standin' in front of me in your underwear," I replied, trying to ignore the changes I could see, the ones I wanted to map with my hands. "Why do you need a minute to get dressed? What's left to hide?"

I knew I should probably give her some privacy, but the way she was swaying worried me. I wasn't about to leave her alone and have her go down when I couldn't catch her. In all honesty, I also wasn't sure that I could drag myself away at that point.

"You know what?" she snapped. "Nothing at all."

Then, without any kind of hesitation, she reached into her toiletry bag.

When we were young, we'd been adventurous, to put it lightly. I'd seen Cecilia naked in every position known to man, and probably a few that we'd invented ourselves. But it was almost an out of body experience as I watched her pull her underwear down around her thighs and place a pad in the crotch, situating it just so. It was more personal, more intimate, than anything I'd ever experienced. I felt it like a blow to the solar plexus, that small peek into something so private. Swallowing hard, I watched as she pulled the underwear back up around her hips.

She stood up defiantly, her arms dangling at her sides, and I was toast.

"You're the most beautiful woman I've ever seen," I blurted, staring at her as I tried to figure out what the fuck I was feeling. She was Cecilia. I knew I loved her. I'd always known I loved her. So why the fuck did I feel like my chest was about to cave in? Why the hell was it so hard to breathe? It was like an earthquake was rumbling beneath us and I was struggling to plant my feet.

"You must not get out much," she replied, crouching down to rifle through the bag I'd brought. She barely had any room to move because I seemed to be incapable of giving her space, but she got dressed quickly anyway. "Come on," she said, running her fingers through her hair. "We can't stay in here all night."

I nodded dumbly and led her out of the bathroom.

Farrah was waiting in the hallway. "Sorry," she said, bouncing on the balls of her feet. "She's about fed up with me, she needs Mama."

Cecilia froze for just a second before moving toward her mom. "That's okay, I'm all done anyway."

"Did you get a good shower?" Farrah asked, her eyes meeting mine as she handed the baby over.

I felt the back of my neck and my ears heat in embarrassment, something that hadn't happened since I was a teenager.

"I feel so much better," Cecilia replied, missing the exchange. "Now I just need to get her changed and fed, and I can crash."

"We're just two rooms down," Farrah said, reaching out to cradle CeeCee's head in her palm as she kissed the opposite side. "We'll probably be up visiting for a while, but let us know if you need anything."

"I will."

Farrah looked at me. "You in for the night, too?"

"Nah," I shook my head, still a little dazed. "I'll be out in a while."

I followed Cecilia into our room and sat on the edge of the bed while she got Olive ready for bed. The baby was seriously pissed, and the second Cecilia put her down she let loose with an ear-piercing wail.

"I'm hurrying," Cecilia called as she pulled supplies out of the diaper bag. "Just give me one second."

"I don't think she cares that you're hurrying," I joked over the noise. I was so fucking raw, I wasn't sure what to say or how to say it.

"I think she's tired of my shit," Cecilia said with a humorless chuckle. "But I'm all she's got."

I watched her change the baby and wrap her back up, her movements gentle and confident. By the time Cecilia got situated and Olive was nursing quietly, I finally opened my mouth again.

"Why do you say stuff like that?" I asked, leaning forward to rest my elbows on my knees. I was starting to feel as tired as Cecilia looked.

"Like what?" she replied in confusion.

"Why do you put yourself down? She's lucky to have you."

"Lucky would've been Liv," Cecilia said flatly. "Lucky would've been sleeping in that nursery that her mom spent months working on, and getting on some kind of schedule, and being rocked to sleep in a rocking chair. Lucky would've been two parents that loved her and wanted her so much that they went to pretty great lengths to get her. She's not lucky."

"I think you're forgetting something."

"Oh, yeah?" Cecilia said, dryly. "What's that?"

"That her parents were white supremacists and her dad was the head of an organization that pretty much disappears entire families when they try to escape their fucked up lives," I said, not bothering to pull any punches. "That her older brother is a fucking murderer that killed her parents and would've killed her. She's goddamn lucky that you're the one who saved her, that she has all these people—good people—

that will have her back. What kind of life would she have had if the Warrens had lived?"

"I wasn't planning on being a parent," Cecilia murmured. "This was never in the cards."

"That would've been a fucking shame," I said baldly.

"I wasn't cut out for this."

"Bullshit," I practically spit. "If ever there was a woman who should be a mother, it's you."

"How do you figure?"

"Cecilia, you are one of the most loyal and protective people I've ever known."

She laughed. "Yeah, right."

"Don't pull that shit with me," I said, sitting up straight. "Don't forget who you're talking to right now."

"How could I?" she mumbled. "You're literally the only person on the planet who would ever say that."

"That's because I know you better than anyone else on the planet does."

"You hadn't even seen me in years."

"People don't change that much," I said with a sigh. I should've added stubborn to her list of traits. "Who they are, the root of them, doesn't change. You haven't changed."

"Yes, I have," she said, staring into my eyes.

"I see you," I replied, holding her stare. "I've always seen you. I'm not someone you can hide from."

"Then you should see that—"

"Cec," I said quietly, not letting her finish whatever bullshit she was about to say. "I see the girl who ran into danger to save her cousin and protected that cousin with her own body."

"It was only a couple steps," she whispered.

"And I see the girl who didn't bother to tell anyone about the gunshot she got in the process—"

"It was only a graze. It was nothing."

"And I see the girl that has lived her entire life feeling guilty for shit that was completely outside her control."

"I don't want to talk about it."

"I see the girl who's entire family was in crisis and she still went and sat by some kid's bedside so he wouldn't be alone."

"Shut up."

"A girl who put up with every dirty look and every stare because she refused to leave that kid behind, even though her people wanted her with someone else."

"I'm serious, Mark. Be quiet."

"I see the girl that didn't tell anyone how bad she was hurting because she didn't want to burden them. Who shut everyone out, every single person, except me."

"Don't make me into some saint," she spat, lifting the baby to her shoulder to burp her. "You know the shit I pulled."

"Of course you're not a saint," I scoffed. "No one is. You're mouthy and rude as fuck, and you say shit before you think about the destruction it would cause when we both know if you'd just take two seconds to think it through, you wouldn't say it. You're stubborn and independent to a fault, which is irritating as fuck."

Cecilia nodded, like I was finally reading her right.

"When you feel cornered, you lash out. You hate confrontation, and if someone forces it, you say the absolute worst thing you can—not to hurt them, but to get them to back off," I continued. "You don't want people to see that you're kind because then they'd expect more from you. They'd expect you to talk and work shit out, and you refuse to let anyone in that far."

"You don't know what you're talking about," she muttered, wrapping Olive back up in her blanket.

"I know I've never loved another person as much as I love you," I confessed so quietly I wasn't even sure she'd heard me. "And I don't think I ever will."

Chapter 13

CECILIA

I STARED AT Mark, completely at a loss. What the hell did he think he was doing?

"I'm not sure what I'm supposed to say to that," I said finally.

I wanted to rage. I wanted to hit him. I wanted to pull him under the covers with me and let him whisper all of those things to me while I raked my nails down his back and bit him for it.

"You don't have to say anything," he replied with a sigh.

My rage built.

"How dare you," I whispered, my voice cracking. "How dare you say that to me now."

"Cec—"

"No, now you get to listen," I ordered, raising my hand in a *stop* motion. "I cannot take one more thing. Do you get that? I cannot handle one more single thing. *I am at my limit.* This is it. Okay?"

"I don't expect you to handle anything," he shot back.

"You just drop that bomb on my lap, and what? I'm supposed to ignore it?"

"I didn't drop a bomb, and it wasn't the first time I've told you I loved you."

"This, whatever this was, it was different and you *know* it."

He reached for my face and I jerked my head back. No. He didn't get to do this now. He didn't get to make this about him. Not again.

"I'm not sure what you expected," I said, my voice hard. "That I'd confess my undying love and we'd ride off into the sunset? That somehow, now that you'd told me you *loved* me, that we could just start back where we were before?"

"No, I didn't think that."

"You left me pregnant and alone," I said, my voice vibrating with the anger and resentment I was trying so hard to control. "Because *you* weren't ready. Because *you* wanted to get out of Eugene. Because *you* wanted to play soldier. You. You. You. Would you like to know what I see when I look at you? Because *I see you*, too. I see a person that goes out of his way to help others because he wants other people to think well of him, but deep down inside of him is pure self-centered selfishness. Someone who has no idea what it means to stick it out long-term. Who didn't even go home to take care of his sick mother until it was time to put her in the ground. That's what I see when I look at you."

Mark's face paled and lost all expression. Without a word, he got to his feet and left the room.

And I sat there, breathing like I'd run a marathon, my ears ringing and my heart pounding.

Fuck him and his declarations of love. They were years too late. Couldn't he see that I couldn't take anymore? I was so close to my breaking point, I was half tempted to walk outside the gates and yell for Drake to come and get me just so we could finish the cat-and-mouse bullshit. I just wanted it to be over. I didn't want to be scared anymore, and it felt like I was scared of everything.

After the shooting, I'd been terrified. Every noise, every sharp movement, going to school, driving in the car, even the dark had made me want to crawl out of my own skin. It had taken years for me to get past it, years before I'd even been able to sleep with a nightlight instead of a lamp. I'd deliberately put myself into dangerous situations until I'd become numb to self-preservation. I would've rather died than go back to how I'd felt back then.

But I hadn't died and I was right back where I'd started anyway, and it was a thousand times worse now. I looked down at Olive.

Somehow, in the span of a little less than two weeks, my priorities had completely changed. It wasn't about me anymore. It was her. Only her. I'd kill for her. Die for her. Sacrifice anyone else for her. The terror that gripped me when I imagined Drake getting ahold of her was debilitating. I found myself counting the steps to the doorway, cataloging all the exits, paying attention to the places we could hide and filing them away, just in case. I would do anything, literally anything, to keep her safe.

Protecting Olive held all of my focus. I'd always be thankful to Mark and his team for coming to get us and protecting us when there was no one else. That was a debt I'd never be able to repay. But that didn't mean that I forgave him for abandoning me all those years ago. Frankly, I didn't know when I'd have the emotional space to even contemplate it.

I looked up as someone opened the bedroom door. "What happened?" my mom asked quietly, coming into the room. "Mark just borrowed a bike and took off."

"Nothing," I said, rolling my eyes at the drama of it all. "I just laid out some difficult truths."

"Difficult truths or typical Cecilia-style-annihilation?" my mom asked, sitting down on the bed.

"If you can't take it, don't dish it," I replied stonily.

Mom inhaled slowly and let out a long breath. "We haven't really talked about it—"

"I feel like this is kind of obvious, but now is not the time," I replied before she could finish her sentence.

"Maybe now is the perfect time."

"It isn't."

"Really?" she said curiously. "Because he's *here* now. The man you never got over."

"I'm over him."

"If you are, then why have you never had another serious relationship?" she asked pointedly. "Don't try to pretend that you're immune. We can all see that you aren't."

"Maybe not," I conceded. "But I can't handle anything else right now."

"Baby," she said gently. "You let him in, and half that shit is lifted off your shoulders. Trust me on this."

"If I let him in," I countered, "it's going to be a million times harder when he bails again when I need him."

"I don't see him going anywhere," she replied.

"Give it time."

"I swear to God, you have both your father's stubbornness and mine, combined."

"You saw the aftermath last time, why are you even bringing this up?"

"Because I *did* see the aftermath," she said, shaking her head. "I saw the way it wrecked you. I also saw him come back, heart in his hands, and you wrecked him right back."

"He left me," I said, my voice rising in disbelief. "And then he came back afterward like he could just fix everything."

"Life isn't black and white, CeeCee," she said. "Everyone screws up."

"It wasn't a screw up," I said flatly. "He left, and I was so terrified and helpless and without options that I had an abortion. There's no coming back from that."

"You had options," my mom pointed out. "You were never alone."

I leaned forward and squeezed her hand. "I know I wasn't. But we also both know that neither of us believed that I was ready to raise a child on my own."

"Your father and I would have."

"I know. I knew it then and I know it now. But I was an adult, and I had to make that decision. It wasn't your responsibility to carry."

Mom nodded and swallowed hard, her eyes growing glassy. "I always wished that I could've done more. Done something."

"You did exactly what you needed to," I argued. "You held my hand and you supported me, even if you didn't agree. That's all I needed."

"I was terrified that you'd regret it," she said, her voice almost a whisper, "and that it would make you spiral even worse than you already were."

"I don't think anything would've made me worse," I replied. "God, I was snorting so much coke." I shook my head. "That was part of the reason I made the decision to go through with it. Who knows how much damage I'd done by that point?"

"I didn't know that."

"Oh, yeah," I said with a huff. "I was doing anything and everything. I wanted to tear down the world, but I was content with self-destruction."

"Jesus."

"I'm past it," I reminded her. "I've been past it for a long ass time."

"You're so much like me, you know?" She smiled sadly. "I wish that we could pass down all of our wisdom to our kids in a way that they'd actually pay attention. I never wanted you to go through the shit I went through."

"We all have to figure things out ourselves," I replied. "Thankfully, most of us do—eventually."

"Ladybug," my dad called, poking his head in the door. "I thought you might be in here. Everything alright?"

"It's fine," I replied as he came inside the room. "Just visiting."

"What'd you do to Woody?" dad asked, stretching out on the bed with us, his back against the wall and legs crossed at the ankles. "He tore out of her like his ass was on fire."

"You two are a bunch of Nosy Nancys," I complained without heat.

"We're your parents, we have the right."

"The right to ask? Sure," I joked. "The right to an answer?" I tilted my head from side to side like I wasn't sure, snickering when he let out an annoyed huff.

"Plan tomorrow is to get to Eugene as fast as we can," he said, changing the subject. "It's gonna be another shitty drive, but nothin' for it. Once we're back home, we'll take care of this shit for good."

"I don't know how you'll do that," I said quietly.

"You let your pop worry about that," he replied. "You just keep your head down until we get you two safe."

"I can't believe they were tracking my phone," I said, cringing. "I'm so sorry about that."

"Forget it," Dad replied with a wave of his hand. "None of us knew it. That shit is usually the way cops track people—not normal, run-of-the-mill fuckwads. Pure chance that they had clout at your cellphone company."

"I guess I should've used throw-aways like you told me to."

Dad laughed. "Are you tellin' me I was right about somethin'? Ladybug, write this shit down, I wanna remember it."

"Shut up," I joked, nudging his leg with my foot.

"It's gonna be okay, CeeCee," he said, grabbing my foot and giving it a squeeze. "You're with us now and everything's gonna be fine."

"I know," I said, only partially lying. I didn't know how he was ever going to make things okay again. It didn't seem possible. But I did know that I felt safer now, especially in the clubhouse, than I had since it all began. There was a security that came with being surrounded by my people.

"We better let you get some rest," my mom said, getting to her feet. "Ollie's going to be hungry again before you know it."

"Ollie?" I said in amusement.

"Olive is an old lady name," she replied, lifting her hand to stop me as I started to argue. "Not that there's anything wrong with old lady names. But she's the size of a sack of flour—she needs a kid name."

"Ollie's a boy's name," my dad said, groaning as he got to his feet.

"Who says? I like Ollie."

"Can we just call her Olive?" I asked as my dad slapped my mom on the ass.

"*You* can," mom replied. She leaned down to kiss my forehead. "I'll see you in the morning."

"Love you, princess," my dad said as he kissed the top of my head. "Get some rest."

"Love you, too. I will."

I nodded when my dad put his hand on the light switch and looked over his shoulder at me. Then let out a long breath as the room was plunged into darkness, the only light coming from the moon shining in the window. Carefully, I slid down in bed, laying Olive between me and the wall.

"We're almost home, kid," I whispered, fixing the fold on her little hat. "then we'll figure out what we're going to do."

Once I'd scooted away from her and got comfortable, I laid there thinking about what our life was going to look like once all of this was behind us, and how Mark would fit into that, if he fit in at all. I imagined the way my reappearance would piss people off back home, the shit I'd have to deal with and what I was willing to take before I pushed back. I wondered how I would fit back into our family. Eventually, though, I couldn't keep my eyes open any longer, and I passed out.

★ ★ ★

IT WASN'T THE cool air, or the lack of sounds, or the presence of someone else in the room with me that woke me up. It was the absence of light coming in from the window. Something was blocking it. Less than a second later, I felt a fist in my hair.

"Get up and keep your mouth shut," a voice whispered into my ear, as he dragged me from the bed.

As I arched, trying to relieve the pressure on my scalp, I pulled the blankets up over my pillow.

"Fuckin' bitch," he hissed as he pulled me painfully to my feet. "You think you're safe here? You ain't safe anywhere."

His breath was hot and wet and as I turned my face, trying to get away from it, I caught a glimpse of a knife in his right hand.

"Baby ain't in the crib. Where's the baby?" he asked, the point of the knife poking through the clothing at my ribs. "Huh? Which room?"

Somehow, he hadn't seen her. Deliberately keeping my eyes forward, I clenched my teeth and firmed my lips. The knife pressed closer and, magically, it strengthened me.

"I'm not playin' around with you. Where's the fuckin' kid?"

Everything I'd done to that point, every mistake I'd made, every scrape I'd escaped from, every bridge I'd burned, every relationship I'd ruined and mended, every decision I'd ever made, coalesced into that single moment. He could do anything to me. I wasn't going to say a single goddamn word. Not one.

Any parent would tell you that they'd die for their child. I was one of the few who would ever put that into action. And honestly, I was ready.

He was being quiet so he wouldn't be caught. I would be silent for a very different reason. I couldn't scream, not without alerting him to where Olive was. I couldn't fight him for the same reason. Any noise could wake her up. The only weapon I had was my silence.

"Bitch, he wants you alive," he said, sliding the knife along my ribs. My heart thundered in my ears as I felt the sting and then the wetness.

"But he said to get that kid by any means necessary."

Silence.

His hand went to his waist, and before I could brace myself, he swung me wide and the impact of his fist against my cheekbone was almost as startling as it was excruciating. The only sound in the room was a dull thud. I didn't even whimper.

He paused. Then, another hit. Another pause. Another hit, this one to my stomach.

I wheezed as I instinctively curled forward and was pulled straight by the hand in my hair.

"You think you'll win this?" he asked, yanking me forward until our faces were just inches apart. I memorized his face. "Tell me where the kid is."

I gasped and relaxed as much as I could, letting out a long slow breath. Then I spit in his face.

I'm not sure how long it went on. At some point, I lost track of everything except the overwhelming need to stay silent, to stay on my feet, to stay away from the bed. I focused on each point of pain as he paused, his words holding no meaning before the blows began again.

Then, like the sun coming out from behind the clouds, the door to the bedroom swung open and light from the hallway shined inside.

The loud report of a gunshot made my ears ring, and I dropped to my knees as the man in front of me went down, his hand still around my throat.

Olive's high-pitched wails filled the room.

I'd done it. She was safe.

Chapter 14

MARK

"How the fuck did they get inside?" Casper bellowed as the sound of footsteps filled the hallway. I ignored the noise around me as I focused on Cecilia, waiting for her to say something. Anything.

I'd known something was up when I'd pulled in the front gate. Something was off. The back of my neck had started tingling and my gut had twisted, both signs that I'd learned to pay attention to, but I couldn't see anything out of place. Boys were still manning the gate, a few old timers were sitting out front in lawn chairs passing around a joint, the main space of the clubhouse was empty, but still held the feeling of being occupied.

Not knowing what else to look for, but still feeling uneasy, I'd headed straight to our room. Just to check. Just to make sure.

My hand was on the doorknob before I'd heard the sounds. Thumping, but not with any sort of rhythm. I'd paused, trying to figure out what the noise was. I'd always hate myself for that pause.

Then I'd reached into my holster as I opened the door. And thank fuck, I had.

It had taken me less than a second to process what was happening, and in that small snapshot of time, I'd pulled my weapon from the holster, my body knowing what to do before my mind could even catch up. I hadn't worried that I'd miss him, not at that distance. I'd fired without hesitation.

"Cec?" I'd called as they both dropped. I knew I hadn't hit her, but she didn't respond.

That's when all hell had broken loose and men began pouring out of the bedrooms, most of them naked and armed to the teeth. The sound of gunshots inside the compound wasn't unheard of, but inside the clubhouse? That was something else entirely.

Cecilia hadn't answered me when I lifted her into my arms and sat down on the bed so I could pull the blankets off of Olive. She'd just reached for the baby, pulling Olive against her chest in relief.

It had been an hour since I'd found her, and she still hadn't said a word—not while Forrest looked her over, not while her mom paced back and forth trying to settle Olive down, not even when her dad came and knelt in front of her, asking if she was okay.

She was with it. Her eyes were clear, even if her face was badly bruised, and she hadn't lost consciousness at any point, but she wasn't speaking. She wasn't making a single sound, even though I knew it must've hurt like a motherfucker for Forrest to stitch up her side.

Wiping a hand over my forehead, I grimaced. I'd broken out in a cold sweat the minute I'd seen Cecilia being attacked, and while I was no longer cold, I was still sweating like I'd just finished working out. It was fucking disgusting.

"Can I talk to you for a sec?" Eli murmured, setting his hand on my shoulder.

I nodded. "I'm gonna go have a chat with Eli, baby," I told Cecilia, brushing her hair back from her face. "I'll be back in a minute."

I paused, waiting for a response that didn't come before getting to my feet. We'd been in Casper and Farrah's room while everyone searched the grounds, and I was happy to take a step away for a few minutes. The air in there was thick with worry and fear and helplessness. My job had been to guard Cecilia and make sure she was alright, and I wouldn't have wanted to be anywhere else, but it was still hard as fuck not to be one of the ones searching.

"Yo, we're not finding anything," Eli said quietly. "Not a single fucking thing. Nothing on the security videos, no holes cut in the fence, not a single member that remembers seeing anything out of the ordinary."

"How is that possible?" I muttered.

"You know how it's possible," Eli said apologetically. "They've got someone here."

"Nope." I shook my head.

"Look, man, I know you got history with this place," Eli replied. "And I'm sure most of these men have your back, and by extension, ours. But the least complicated explanation is usually the right one, and you know it. Someone let that fucker onto the property."

"Fuck," I breathed, looking over his shoulder at the men who were still roaming around, looking for any type of clue or threat.

"They might not see it, or just don't want to admit it," Eli said. "But we've got a problem. We can't stay here."

"We weren't planning on staying," I pointed out.

"Yeah, I know," he agreed. "But we were planning on having bikers escort us to Eugene."

"And if we tell them we don't need them, they'll know something's up," I said. "Goddamn it."

"Pretty much."

I wasn't sure what the right call was. On one hand, I felt a loyalty to the club that had been ingrained in me since birth, but on the other hand, I couldn't ignore what was looking me in the face. We had a mole, and worse than that, we had someone willing to risk getting caught in order to bring the enemy inside the gates.

"We need to talk to Casper," Eli said. "Now."

I nodded. "Grab Cam, too."

"Will do. I'll round everyone up."

"Make sure you do it quietly," I said as he turned away. "No need to make people nervous."

"I've got it handled," he replied dryly.

I wiped at my face again as I strode back toward Casper's room. Jesus, how much pull did this Drake guy have, and how the fuck had he gotten to one of the members so quickly? Was there some kind of connection that predated this shit with Olive? And how the fuck were we supposed to find that connection?

Farrah's hand was on the pistol in her lap when I re-entered the room.

"How's it going?" I asked, leaning down to kiss Cecilia's bent head. Olive was nursing sleepily, and I breathed a sigh of relief that at least that was going okay.

"She's still quiet," Farrah said cautiously, her worried eyes meeting mine. "But we've got the baby settled now, so that's good, all things considered."

"That is good," I said, sitting down carefully next to CeeCee.

The slice along her ribs was superficial, thank Christ, but I couldn't imagine how badly it had hurt. The thought of how scared she must have been made my skin crawl, and watching her stoically let Forrest stitch it had been one of the worst moments of my life.

"How you doing?" I asked, wrapping my arm around her back. I let out a breath as she silently leaned against me for support, her head resting on my shoulder.

The door opened, and Farrah's head jerked up, her hand back on the pistol.

"Just me, Ma," Cam said, coming into the room. "You can put that thing away."

"I think I'll keep it where it is," Farrah retorted.

"You're surrounded by armed men."

"So was Cecilia," Farrah reminded her son darkly.

A few minutes later, Casper came in, Eli behind him.

"I left Forrest and Lu out with the others," Eli told me, leaning against the closed door. "I can fill them in."

"What's going on?" Farrah asked, looking from one person to another.

"You know what's goin' on," Casper said with a frustrated grunt. "Can't stay here."

"We aren't," Farrah replied. "We're leaving in a couple hours."

"And takin' half the club with us?" Casper said. "Possibly the man that let that motherfucker in to terrorize my daughter?"

"*Our* daughter," Farrah muttered.

"We need to find out who the fuck it was before we leave," Cam said, crossing his arms over his chest.

"No," I said firmly. "Not with your sister and the baby here. Not with your mom here. We don't have the time and we don't have the fucking resources."

"So what's your big plan?" Cam shot back.

I kept my mouth shut. I didn't have a goddamn plan.

"Well," Eli drawled from the door, "I have an idea."

Casper looked at him in surprise, like he'd forgotten Eli was there.

"We've got three rigs," Eli said quietly as he stepped further into the room. "You two stay on your bikes. Me and Lu take mine. Forrest takes his. Farrah rides with Cecilia and Chief."

"And how does Lu switching rigs change a goddamn thing, exactly?" Cam asked.

"You didn't let me finish," Eli said with a short bark of laughter.

★ ★ ★

Two hours later, we were loaded up and almost ready to head out.

"You sure, man?" Chunky asked Casper as they stood next to the long row of motorcycles. "Seems like a bad fuckin' idea to leave with no backup."

"I'm sure," Casper said, reaching out to shake the man's hand. "Best bet is to keep shit as quiet as possible. Drawing attention to us with a big convoy of bikes is just gonna put a bullseye on our backs."

Chunky nodded slowly. "I'll take care of shit here," he said quietly, as if Casper's decision was finally coming into focus. "I'll keep you updated. You let me know if there's anything I can do to help."

"Absolutely," Casper said. He moved toward where I'd been eavesdropping and slapped my shoulder as he passed me.

"You ready?" I asked as I turned to follow him to the trucks.

"Don't like it," he muttered. "But I don't see a better way."

"On that, we agree," I said.

I climbed into the truck and checked on Cecilia. She was crammed into the back seat again, surrounded by the car seat and baby supplies, but she didn't seem bothered by any of it. All of her attention was focused outside the window.

We were quiet as we pulled out of the front gate.

"This better work," Farrah said, her shoulders stiff as she stared out the windshield.

"It will."

Fifteen minutes later, Eli and Lu pulled away from the caravan with Cam following behind them. Five minutes after that, Forrest did the same. Then it was just us, Casper following behind as we headed north.

"Take care of my granddaughter," Farrah whispered, leaning her head back against the headrest.

When I looked back at Cecilia, her hand was resting inside the empty car seat and tears were rolling down her cheeks.

★ ★ ★

FOUR HOURS LATER, we stopped for gas. Farrah and Cecilia stayed inside the truck as planned, and I hurried through the motions so we could get back on the road. Inside the cab was eerily silent, and as I waited for the tank to fill, I pressed my hand to Cecilia's window. When she looked over, I pressed my lips against it in a kiss. Her lips curved up slightly as she rolled her eyes. I considered that a win.

I jerked in surprise as Casper came jogging around the pump.

"What's up?" I asked, my head snapping up to scan the surrounding area.

"Found 'em," Casper said, out of breath. "Rose came tearin' through the gate not twenty minutes ago."

"No shit?"

"No shit," Casper replied, nodding. "On their way to get Mack now."

"That's good news," I said with a grin. "They're okay?"

"Far as I know," he said, slapping me on the shoulder. "I'm gonna let Farrah know."

He rounded the truck and I looked over to meet Cecilia's eyes. She smiled with her mouth, but the rest of her face and body practically radiated a mixture of fear and helplessness. I had a feeling that any relief about finding Rose was being completely overshadowed by the fact that Olive was probably a hundred miles from us by now.

We'd agreed to go radio silent until we met up that night, and I knew it was absolute torture for Cec. I had to admit, it wasn't real fun for me, either. Not knowing where Olive was, how she was doing, or if the plan would work was really wearing on me. It also didn't help that our truck was technically the bait truck. Anyone who didn't know what we'd done would assume both Cecilia and Olive were with me, driving north to the clubhouse in Eugene.

Only our small group knew she was in a box on the passenger seat of Forrest's SUV. Not the safest way to travel, but we were pretty much beyond that worry.

"Let's head out," Casper said, meeting me back at the pump. "Got a lot of road to cover before we get there tonight."

"You think this'll work?"

"Pretty damn sure," Casper replied. "Long as they don't try to ambush us on the road. Only a few people know about Poet's place on the coast and the security is prime. Even has safe room."

"Haven't felt like I'm being watched since we left the clubhouse," I said quietly. "It can't be that easy."

"It might be," he said with a shrug. "They think we're headed to Eugene—and a straight shot up I-5 means we'd have to drive right through the territory they're controlling. No need to follow if they know we're headed right for 'em."

"Let's hope you're right."

We were on the road again pretty quick after that, and I let myself relax just slightly into my seat. If we could all just get to the house on the coast, we could figure out what to do next.

"What's wrong?" Farrah asked, turning in her seat to look at Cecilia. "You okay?"

I looked in the mirror to find CeeCee crying silently, shaking her head in dismissal. She'd been in tears most of the drive, but something about those tears were different.

"You need to pump?" Farrah asked, rummaging through the bag at her feet. "I washed everything after you used it this morning, so it's ready to go."

Cecilia waved the contraption away.

"Cec," I said, getting her attention. "Forrest said you need to pump while you guys are apart unless you want to get another clog."

"Yeah, or have your supply tank," Farrah said, pushing the hand-pump at Cecilia.

She just stared out the window.

"Should I pull over?" I asked Farrah. It wasn't a good idea—actually it was a terrible one—but if Cecilia needed to stop, I'd stop.

Silently, CeeCee yanked the pump out of her mom's hands.

"Threatening to pull the car over never stopped you from being a punk when you were a kid," Farrah said, still twisted in her seat. "Glad to know it does now."

Half an hour later, a little bottle of milk was passed to the front of the cab and Farrah stashed it in a cooler at her feet. When I glanced back at Cecilia, her head was resting against the window, her eyes closed.

"Only an hour left before we get to the house," I said quietly to Farrah in case Cecilia was able to get some rest.

"Yeah, then we'll have somewhere to pace until everyone else shows up," she said in frustration, running her hands through her hair. "But at least we know that Rose and Mack are safe back home. Might help my ulcer, some."

"Can't imagine how hard it's been for you and Casper," I replied.

"Hard's an understatement," she said quietly. "Rose is like one of our kids. And we know that she had the whole club up there searching, but it's been pretty much an impossible situation not knowing whether or not to haul ass north or play it safe."

"Being pulled in two different directions," I muttered.

"Yep. This shit is far from over, but it's a bit of a relief to have one fucked situation to deal with at a time."

"I bet."

We were quiet for a few minutes.

"I was sorry to hear about your mom," Farrah said out of the blue. "Don't think I ever told you that."

"You don't have to say that," I replied, glancing at her. "I know you weren't her biggest fan."

Farrah huffed out a laugh. "Bit of an understatement," she said ruefully. "But I *am* sorry you lost her. Losing a parent sucks, doesn't matter if they were a good one or not—and from what I understand, she did her best with you."

"She did," I replied.

"People react differently to shit," Farrah murmured. "Cam and Trix were different, but I can't imagine telling him to bail when he told us Trix was pregnant."

"That's not exactly how it went down."

"Close enough," Farrah said, shooting me a look. "But she'd had a different experience with the club. Couldn't have been happy that you knocked up some club brat."

"I think she regretted it later," I said quietly. "Once she saw how bad it fucked me up."

"Water under the bridge now," Farrah said with a sigh. "I never understood why she hated everyone so much, but still sent you to us all the damn time."

"I have no idea," I said, shaking my head. "I think she was just desperate for help."

"The boys probably didn't give her much of a choice, either," Farrah replied ruefully. "They weren't about to let you fall through the cracks."

"My dad seemed to attract that kind of loyalty," I agreed.

"Not just your dad, kid." She slapped me lightly on the arm with the back of her hand. "Seems to me you've got that same pull."

I shrugged.

Time seemed to speed up as we got off the highway, following Casper as he led us down back roads, circling and backtracking through small towns along the coast. When we finally turned onto a long, gravel driveway, I sat up straight and stretched my arms over my head.

The house was small and covered in wooden shingles, and it looked ready to fall over, which made the high tech alarm system seem seriously out of place.

"Only you would remember the code to this place," Farrah called to Casper as we climbed out of the truck.

"You complainin'?" he called back, opening the front door.

I grasped Cecilia's hand as we walked up the steps to the porch and was kind of surprised that she didn't pull away. Shit had been happening at lightening speed, but I was still highly aware of the fight we'd had. Did I really think that she believed all the garbage she'd spewed at me? Partially. But I didn't think she would've ever said it if I hadn't been pushing. It didn't let her off the hook—she didn't just get to say whatever hurtful crap popped into her head without consequences, but the conversation could wait.

Flat out—I loved her, even the shitty parts of her, and we had more important things to deal with at the moment.

"I'm gonna find a burner and call the club," Casper said. "Open a couple windows we can keep an eye on—air the place out."

The house was as small as it looked on the outside, but it was cozy. A small bedroom off to the left side had a queen-sized bed covered in a drop cloth and a small closet without any doors. The living room furniture was also covered in drop cloths, and as Farrah took care of the bedroom, me and Cecilia uncovered the couch and a recliner.

"No TV," I said, looking around the room.

"I doubt they're watching TV down here," Farrah said. "Here, I'll stash those canvases in the closet with the other one." She pulled the rolled up fabric from my hands. "See if there's anything in the kitchen—I'm starving."

I followed Cecilia into the postage stamp sized kitchen, wrapping my arm around her waist as she stopped to look out the window. The house was small, but the real estate must have been worth a fortune because the back deck butted right up to the beach.

"Maybe we can take a few minutes once Olive gets here," I said, resting my chin on the top of CeeCee's head. "Bring her down to the water."

Cecilia didn't reply.

"Why aren't you talking?" I asked, not expecting an answer. "I need to hear your voice, baby."

She still didn't reply, but her hands came to the arm around her waist and squeezed before lightly rubbing back and forth.

"I'm sorry I wasn't there," I said into her hair. "I shouldn't have assumed you'd be safe. I fucked up."

Her hands squeezed again.

"All of this is going to be over soon," I promised. "And then we can find a little house for you and Olive. Someplace close to your parents, but not close enough that your mom stops by every single day." Her body shook with a half-hearted chuckle. "And we'll make sure you have a yard so you can lay out and get a tan while Olive plays in one of those little plastic pools."

Cecilia tilted her head back to look at me, her eyes full of emotion.

"They'll be here soon," I said, reaching up to run my thumb over her cheek. "I trust Forrest more than any other person on the planet. I wouldn't have sent Olive with anyone but him."

"Toss me your keys," Casper said, coming up behind me. "I'll store your truck in the garage."

I threw the keys to him and he left the room, but the moment between me and Cecilia was over. Not even a second later, Farrah came bustling in.

"Did you find anything to eat?"

"We didn't check," I replied. She huffed.

"There's gotta be something." She started opening cupboards. "Eureka!"

"What'd you find?" I asked as she started pulling cans out of the cupboard.

"Chili and chicken noodle soup. Good enough for the people we know!" she joked.

"You better check the dates on those," I warned.

She paused, looking at the cans. "Yep. All good until next year."

"I let the boys know we're here," Casper said, coming back into the kitchen. The space was getting really crowded with all four of us in there. "They found Mack, and said he's in pretty rough shape, but the doctors are working on him. Rose is physically okay, but takin' all of it hard."

"Uh, yeah," Farrah said. "She was fucking kidnapped."

"It sounds like she held her own," Casper said with a small sigh. "Now they're just waitin' on news from the doctors."

"You told them not to mention where we are?" I said, hating that I had to. We knew there was a mole in the Sacramento chapter, and we couldn't just assume that's where it ended.

"I did," Casper replied. He looked at Cecilia. "The boys know what's happenin' down here, but they're keepin' it to themselves. Once we're home, we can decide who needs to know what."

Cecilia nodded.

"Can't keep this level of shit to ourselves," Casper continued. "Even though you asked me to."

Cecilia nodded again before pulling out of my arms. Crossing her arms over her chest, she left the room, closing herself into the tiny bathroom.

"Keeping this to ourselves seems counterproductive at this point," Farrah said, leaning back against the counter. "We've got other kids back home wondering what the hell is going on. Charlie we can keep in the dark—but Lily's not going to be put off much longer."

"Now that things are calming down a little back home, I think Lil's gonna have her hands full with Rose. We got time," Casper replied.

"I just wish she didn't feel so determined to keep everything a secret," Farrah said, looking at the bathroom door. "It's not like she'll be able to keep things to herself once we get back."

"She knows," I said quietly. "She's struggling with that, too."

"We love her. Her aunts and uncles and cousins love her. Her sisters and brother and nephews love her. It's like she's forgotten that."

"There's a lot of hurt feelings on both sides, I think," I said quietly as Cec came out of the bathroom.

"We're going to have to figure out the food situation," Farrah said without missing a beat. "We've got some canned stuff, but not enough to feed all of us."

"I can send Lu later," I replied. As soon as the words were out of my mouth, we heard the sound of a car out front. I barely got an arm wrapped around Cecilia's waist as she bolted for the door.

"Let your dad get it," I said as she tried to pull away. "Give him just a second."

Casper looked out the window, then unlocked the front door and swung it wide.

"How was the drive?" he called out as we all moved toward the front of the house.

Cecilia slumped back against me as she realized it was Eli and Lu walking up the steps, not Forrest.

"All good," Eli said. "Your boy's right behind us—I think he was making an extra loop."

Casper nodded as the sound of Cam's bike came from the end of the driveway.

"Forrest get here yet?" Lu asked as she came inside.

"Not yet," I replied.

Cecilia dropped onto the recliner, covering her face with her hands.

"She needs a break," Lu said quietly to me. "I can't imagine how she's still upright."

"No idea," I replied. "I just keep thinking if we can get her home, she can rest. But I don't know. There's a lot of history up there, so she'll be safe, but—"

"Emotionally, it's a minefield," Lu said in understanding. "Well, we'll deal with that when it comes."

My phone rang in my pocket and for a second, I froze.

"Answer it, dumbass," Lu said, shoving me lightly.

Pulling the phone out of my pocket, I checked the caller ID.

"How's it going?" I asked Josiah as I walked out to stand on the back deck.

"We're on the road," he replied.

"He even bought me road snacks!" Eph sang happily.

"Oh, great," I muttered. "I'm on speakerphone."

Josiah laughed. "We got her stuff packed up," he said. "Did you know she keeps a bug-out bag? No shit. Found it in her closet. Spare change of clothes, extra magazines for a .37, shotgun and a box of shells, couple of burner phones, the works."

"I'm guessing that was a gift from her dad."

"Father of the Year," Josiah said approvingly.

"No doubt," Eph agreed.

"You're headed north?" I asked.

"Yeah, man. We'll be in Eugene tomorrow. What do you want us to do when we get there?"

"Get a cheap room and wait," I said. "Not sure when we'll be there, but we'll get there eventually."

"You know, rainy ass Oregon is not where I'd choose to go on a winter vacation," Eph said conversationally. "I like the sun."

"Yeah, man, I get it," I said with a sigh.

"Just fuckin' with you," Eph said with a laugh. "I'll be a happy man if I can find a place with a hot tub and room service."

"I thought I said *cheap*?"

"Got bedbugs from a cheap room in Abilene one time," Josiah said.

"Never again," he and Ephraim vowed at the same time.

"Whatever. Just find a place to hole up and wait for us."

"Will do," Josiah said. "Uh, hey Chief?"

I stiffened at his tone. "What?"

"Didn't seem worth gettin' everyone worried, but thought you should know that her place had been tossed."

"Say what?"

"They didn't break anything, but they weren't careful, either."

"Not knowing what was there before made it impossible to tell if they'd taken anything," Ephraim added. "But we found a small safe tucked up into the box spring under her bed that they must have missed. Hopefully, that's where she keeps anything important."

"Shit," I said, turning to look into the kitchen window.

"She didn't have a ton of sentimental stuff, but we made sure to wrap anything that could get ruined in transit," Eph said.

"There's a reason I hire moving companies when I change domiciles," Josiah said primly. "Packing sucks."

"I owe you guys."

"Nah, she didn't have much," Josiah replied. "And since we didn't move any furniture except the quilting frame, it went pretty fast."

"The quilting frame was super light, anyway. Didn't really count as furniture," Eph pointed out.

"She has a quilting frame?" The idea of my wild Cecilia that could never sit still and was always looking for the next big thing, sitting down in front of a damn quilting frame, made me want to howl with laughter.

"Yeah," Josiah said, sounding impressed. "It's actually a pretty decent design, too."

"Our gran had a wood frame that had been passed down a couple generations—" Eph said.

"But it wasn't nearly as multi-functional as this one," Josiah cut in. "Your girl made hers out of PVC pipe, and—"

"Yeah, I bet it's awesome," I replied. "We've got shit going on here. All good on your end?"

"Roger that. Yep, we're solid. I'll let you know if that changes," Josiah said, once again all business. "I'm not anticipating any problems."

"Alright. Let one of us know when you get there and where you're staying."

"Will do."

Ephraim's voice poured into the phone singing *On the Road Again*, with an exaggerated southern drawl before the sound cut off.

Since I was already outside, I rounded the house and went inside the garage to grab a couple of Cecilia's bags. I needed a minute of quiet to think. At some point, I was going to need to tell Cec that her shit had been ransacked, but now definitely wasn't the time. Eventually, though, we'd have to figure out if anything was missing, and she was the only one who could tell us that.

When I got back inside, Cecilia was still sitting, still as a statue in the recliner.

"Hey," I said, crouching down in front of her. "Why don't we check out that cut and see if we need to change your bandage?"

She looked over my shoulder at the front door.

"Better to get it done now before she gets here," I said, pulling her to her feet. "That way you don't have to put her down later."

I led her into the bedroom and closed the door behind us.

"It probably doesn't need checking yet," I said as I set the bags on the bed and sat down next to them. "But I'm always extra careful. The guys give me shit for it." I copied Eli's inflections. *"Hey, Chief, better make sure that doesn't scar your pretty skin."*

Cecilia shot me a brief smile as I pulled her to stand between my knees.

"They're good guys," I said as she lifted her shirt, holding it high so I could check out Forrest's handiwork. "When I got out of the military, I was pretty aimless. Wasn't sure what I was going to do, you know?

Going from the club to the Marines meant I always had my group, always had built-in brothers." I carefully pulled the tape away from her skin, working my way around the edges of the bandages. "So when the company I'm working for now started headhunting me, offering the same environment but considerably more money, I was pretty stoked about it."

The cut looked a little angry and red, but nothing I thought we should worry about. I let out a quiet breath of relief. Knife wounds could be gnarly, especially if the knife wasn't clean. Grabbing a tube of ointment from the bag, I used a piece of gauze to smear it along the wound.

"My first team was alright. Not great, not what I'd been hoping for, but okay. They just didn't mesh well, too many cooks in the kitchen, if you know what I mean. Forrest was with me on that team, and Eph and Siah for a while. But then a few years back, some shit got switched up and we ended up with a new group—the one we have now."

Cecilia wasn't responding, but one of her hands had come to slide gently through my hair.

"There were some growing pains at first," I said as I pulled more gauze and tape out of the bag. "I didn't like Eli, and Lu and Josiah butt heads about anything and everything, down to what we eat for dinner. But eventually, things settled into a groove. We got to know each others' strengths and weaknesses. Shit that bothered us in the beginning started to matter less as we got to know one another. Eventually, our team turned into one of the best—not only because we're all good at what we do and trust each other, but because we know each other, good and bad, and we naturally pick up the slack if someone's lacking—if that makes sense."

She winced as I taped the bandage back on, but didn't shy away.

"I shouldn't have trusted anyone outside our circle. It was stupid. But between my team and your family, we have this handled," I said, looking up into her face as she let her shirt drop back down to her waist. "I promise I won't let anything else happen to you."

Her hand came down to cup my cheek, and I sat still as her thumb slid over my cheek and down over the beard at my jaw.

"Why aren't you talking?" I asked gently. "It's just me and you in here. You can talk to me."

She opened her mouth like she was going to answer me, then shut it again, her jaw flexing with frustration.

"Are you hurt?" I asked in confusion, looking down at her mouth.

Chapter 15

CECILIA

Was I hurt? Yes. My ribs throbbed every time I moved and the cut along my side stung and pulled. My cheek and jaw ached every time I made any expression. My mouth felt like raw hamburger from the inside of my cheeks being forced against my teeth. My stomach still churned from being hit, and even water made me nauseous.

I knew what he was asking, though. Was there a physical reason I wasn't speaking?

No.

I just couldn't make myself do it. I'd open my mouth to say something, to argue or agree, and I couldn't. It was as if when I'd trapped all the sounds inside myself, I'd locked the door and lost the key. They were stuck inside my head and every time I tried to let them out, everything just shut down.

I couldn't fix it no matter how hard I tried. Not even when they'd come up with the plan for Olive to travel separately from me. I hadn't even been able to tell her goodbye, and that killed me.

"It'll come back to ya," Mark said, his hands smoothing over my hips. "Just give it a little time."

I hoped he was right.

"Sounds like another car is pulling up," he said. I was swinging open the bedroom door and flying through it before he'd even risen from the bed.

The front door was already open and my dad was standing in it. Beyond him, Forrest was climbing out of his SUV.

"All good?" my dad called, stepping out onto the porch.

"Yep," Forrest called back.

I slid past my dad and hurried down the steps as Forrest lifted Olive from the box on the passenger seat.

"Here you go, mama," he said, handing her to me. "I fed her that milk you pumped this morning, but it's been a couple hours and she's about ready again, I think. She's a good road trip partner, slept most of the time and didn't bitch once about my music."

I barely heard him as I lifted Olive close to my face, running my cheek along hers. The weight and feel and smell of her comforted me in a way I couldn't explain. Relief hit me so hard I found myself swallowing back a sob.

"Your music sucks, Forrest," Lu said, coming up behind me. "Come on, hun. You guys better come back inside."

I nodded and let her lead me back to the house.

"How's she doing?" my mom asked as I sat down in the recliner. "She doesn't look any worse for wear."

Setting the baby down with her tush against my belly and her head near my knees, I unwrapped her. Forrest was a doctor, or at least had the training, and he knew how to take care of a newborn, but I still had an almost overwhelming urge to make sure everything was as it should be. I needed to be one hundred percent sure.

"All limbs, present and accounted for," my mom joked. She squeezed my shoulder. "I know today was hard, sweetheart, but you did good."

I nodded, still focused on Olive. Her little legs were bent at the knee against her belly and her ankles were crossed, and I didn't know if I'd ever seen anything that was more wholesome or cute or made me feel more protective. God, she was so small, and she had no idea what was happening around her. Had she missed me while she was with Forrest? Had she panicked when she realized I wasn't right there next to her? The thought of that made my chest hurt.

Diapers and wipes were set down on the arm of the chair and I looked up in surprise.

"Forrest said she probably needs a change," Mark said. He dropped down on his haunches and laid his hand gently on her chest. "I didn't like having her away from us today," he confessed. "Can't imagine how it was for you."

I couldn't have even begun to explain how excruciating it had been for me. The irony was that when she was born, I'd been fully ready and willing to give her up. That had been the plan all along, and while the thought of it had hurt—it hadn't felt overwhelming. She hadn't been mine. But somewhere between her birth and sitting in that beach house in Northern California, things had completely shifted. I couldn't imagine my world without her, I didn't want to.

I changed her diaper and wrapped her back up, resting her against my chest as I leaned back in the chair. Finally, I could breathe again.

"We need to figure out something to eat," my mom said as people trickled into the room, leaning against walls and sitting on every available surface. "And how we're going to get home."

"We will," my dad replied.

"If I could make a suggestion?" Forrest drawled from his place on the couch.

"What's up?" Mark asked.

"She needs to rest," he replied, pointing at me. "I've been sayin' it for days, and no one seems to be hearin' me. Look at her. How much weight you think she's dropped since we found her in that house?"

I frowned at him. It couldn't be that much, all my clothes still fit the same. Besides, I'd just had a baby, of course I was going to start losing weight.

"A couple pounds a day," Lu said quietly, looking at me. "At least."

"Her appetite is gone, she's barely sleepin', we're draggin' her all over hell and back, and on top of that, she's nursin'," Forrest said. "It sounds like shit ain't gonna slow down much once you're home, either."

"What are you suggesting?" my dad asked, his face expressionless. Oh, no. I knew that tone. It usually sent me and my siblings backpedalling before we ran for cover.

"I'm suggestin' that we stay here for a bit. Let her rest, take a walk on the beach, bond with the baby, finish those fuckin' antibiotics I brought her. We need to figure out our next steps, anyhow, and this place is as good as any. No one knows we're here," Forrest replied, obviously unfamiliar with The Tone.

"Problem," Eli said, dryly. "Where are we supposed to sleep?"

Lu laughed. "Man, I've seen you sleep in a damn culvert," she said jokingly. "I'm sure you can figure it out."

"Couple of sleepin' bags, and we're fine," Forrest said, shooting Eli a look.

"Well, I've got a bad back," my brother said with a sigh, his eyes dancing.

"Boy, you think you're takin' the couch or the bed, you've lost your damn mind," my dad said, raising his eyebrows as he gave my brother a good-natured shove.

Forrest dug his hand down in the couch cushions. "Good news," he said, grinning. "It's a pull-out."

"Dibs," my mom said quickly.

"Probably a good idea," my dad said, meeting my mom's eyes. "Give the family some time to get past the shit they're dealin' with before we bring more to their doorstep."

"Sounds good, baby," she said softly.

I leaned my head down so I could rest my cheek against Olive's head, my lips tipping up in the corners. I didn't know what it was about old Poet's beach house, but it was like all of us were breathing a sigh of relief. I'd felt safe in the Sacramento clubhouse. Surrounded by people who were willing and able to put themselves between me and danger had been so comforting… until it wasn't. But when we were there, we'd all been anxious to get moving, to get north and find Rose. Now that she was safe and we were getting good news from my uncle and aunt, that pressure was gone.

Here, it was like we were hidden at the end of the world where no one could find us.

Olive began to fuss so I carried her into the bedroom and sat down on the bed to nurse her. At some point, I knew I'd be able to nurse her in company without a second thought, but it still felt like we were figuring it all out, and I didn't really feel like flashing my dad for a solid five minutes while she tried to navigate my nipple and determine exactly what she was supposed to do with it.

When she was finally latched on, I leaned back against the headboard and sighed, listening to everyone discuss logistics in the living room. I probably should have been out there and part of the conversation, but honestly? I could barely even follow it. I was so worn out, any attempt to help would probably be useless.

"I'll go," Lu said. "If I curl my hair and put on some make-up, I doubt anyone would even recognize me if they saw me."

"That's flat out untrue," Forrest argued.

"That's a good idea," my mom said at the same time. She laughed. "You men have no idea how much of a difference a little cosmetics can make."

"I'll go with you," Cam said. "We can drive pretty boy's car."

"Hey, now," Eli complained. "That's going a little too far."

"No, that's a good idea," Mark said. "Then if anyone's asking about your rig and their descriptions, they won't put it together."

"I would," my dad pointed out.

"But you're not the average bear, Cody," my mom said. I couldn't see them, but I imagined she was patting his chest proudly.

"I'm gonna need a list," Lu said. "We need sleeping bags."

"New burner phones," Cam added.

"Groceries," my mom and Eli said at the same time.

"Toilet paper," Forrest drawled. "There's a lot of people here."

My dad chuckled. "You all figure it out. I'm gonna make some calls, let the boys know we're stayin' here for a bit."

"That a good idea?" Forrest asked cautiously.

I could only imagine the look on my dad's face.

"We're not spreadin' it around," he said finally. "Only a few of us know what's happenin', and for now, we're keepin' it that way."

The room grew quiet.

"Forrest has brass ones," I finally heard Eli mutter. "Seriously. Can I see them?" I heard a thump and then Eli complaining and laughing at the same time. "Ow! You know you were all thinking it."

My eyes grew heavy as I pulled Olive up to my shoulder to burp her. A few minutes later, just as I'd put her on the bed next to me and laid down, Mark came into the room.

"You want me to take her?" he asked quietly, resting his hand on my hip as he leaned over to look at Olive.

I shook my head. I wasn't ready for her to be out of my reach yet. I wasn't sure if I'd ever be.

"Alright," he said. He rounded the bed and gently climbed in behind her. "Go to sleep," he whispered. "I'm just going to lay with you guys for a while."

Within minutes, I was out.

★ ★ ★

"WHAT DID WILSON say?" Lu asked as my mom passed out plates of pigs in a blanket and macaroni and cheese.

The sun was setting and the darkness was making me a little jumpy, but I was doing my best to hide it. The sun went down. It happened every day without fail. I needed to get a handle on my nerves.

"He's been talking with Kaley Campbell for a couple of days. He said that at first she thought it was some sort of trap, but it sounds like she's cooperative now," Forrest replied, setting his plate on his knees. "She's full of information. Turns out, if the rest of the militia knew it was Drake that took out his pop, the man wouldn't have long to live."

"The problem with that is they're not gonna believe a word we say," Cam said. He looked up as my mom handed him a plate. "Thanks, Ma. This looks great."

I rolled my eyes. He was such a kiss-ass.

"And who knows how they'd feel about Olive," Mark said. "Could want nothin' to do with her, could see her as the princess and want her with them."

"Is there any way we could get word to them and somehow leave Olive out of the equation?" Lu asked.

"Could be," my dad said. "But makes it less believable since Olive's birth was the kid's motivation for offin' his pop."

"Even if we get this shit sorted and the Warren kid's no longer a problem," Eli said quietly, "the more we find out about these people, the less inclined I am to do nothing."

"How do you mean?" my mom asked, sitting down between my dad's feet, her back against the bottom of the couch.

"There's whole families in there," Eli said, looking down at his plate. "Women and children with no way out."

"You're talkin' about war," my dad replied flatly.

"Yes," Eli said simply, lifting his head to meet my dad's gaze.

"First, we make sure Cec and Olive are safe," Mark said firmly. "That's the mission."

"Fuck—" Eli began to argue.

"I'm not sayin' never," Mark cut in. "I'm just sayin' not yet. Our priority is Cecilia and the baby."

"Patience," Forrest said quietly, reaching out to thump Eli on the back.

"That's not one of my strengths," Eli mumbled.

"Yeah," Lu said dryly. "We know."

They continued throwing around ideas about how we could tell the Free America Militia that the prince had killed the king, but no one knew a fail proof way to do it. Even reaching out to them put me and Olive in danger, because as far as we knew, the group had no idea we existed. It was decided that Drake must have hired the men who were helping him. According to Wilson, the dead men he'd fingerprinted—ew—had no ties to FAM that he could find, and the woman he'd been talking to hadn't recognized any of their photos. Apparently that was a good thing, because men who worked for money were far less likely to stick around when shit went south than men who felt loyalty to their leader.

I figured it didn't really matter either way. Things hadn't gone south for them. We were still being hunted.

I picked at my food, wondering how long we'd be able to stay at Poet's little house. While it was a relief to be there, it was temporary. Soon, we'd be on the move again, racing toward Eugene and a whole group of people who would both fight to the death for me and didn't want anything to do with me. I was anxious to be there, safe behind the walls of the clubhouse, but I also dreaded it.

I could only choke down a few bites of my food before I couldn't make myself eat any more. Folding my plate in half to hide the leftovers, I got to my feet and carried it into the kitchen garbage.

"You have to eat more than that," Mark said softly, his hands wrapping around my waist from behind. He was always gentle and avoided my stitches, but I still cringed until I realized that he hadn't hurt me.

I nodded and sighed, gingerly leaning back against him. I was so angry with him, but I was so glad for his presence. Our conversation back in Sacramento had opened wounds that I'd thought were healed. It had been years since I'd let myself think about the way he'd left me, about the helpless rage and panic I'd felt, about the decisions that had come afterward.

I was also so grateful he was with me that I could've fallen to my knees and wept. He made me feel safe. Having my brother and dad around comforted me, too, but it was a different kind of safety with Mark. He knew me in a way they didn't, even after all those years apart.

"I think we're going to try to make contact," Mark said, leaning forward a little so his cheek was against my temple. "Anonymously reach out to the highest men in the organization with what we know."

I fought the tensing of my muscles as he spoke.

"If they aren't receptive, we'll do it another way," he said, his thumb gently smoothing back and forth over my ribs. "But, best case scenario, they take care of it in-house and we don't have to deal with any of it."

I wanted to argue, to tell him that I'd never be safe that way. That even if Drake was dead, we didn't know whether or not the militia would come after me and Olive anyway. If Drake was dead, all of the Warren money would be legally Olive's, and while I never planned on going through the channels to get it, the fact that she was out there with that kind of power may be reason enough for the militia to hunt us down. I wanted to point out that telling them about Drake might not have the effect they were hoping for because Cane was financing them. If Drake was dead, that money flow would dry up instantly. It would be infinitely better for them to keep Drake alive.

I opened my mouth and nothing came out. Not a single noise. My hands fisted at my sides. I needed to *speak*. I reached out and smacked the countertop hard, the sound reverberating through the small house.

Unfortunately, it didn't relieve the frustration I was feeling. Instead, the noise scared the shit out of me and I froze, my heart racing as I fell into a full-blown panic attack.

I shouldn't have done it. I shouldn't have made that sound. My eyes went to the darkness outside the window. There were no curtains, and the feeling of being watched became so strong that I jerked out of Mark's arms and dropped to the floor so I couldn't be seen.

"Cecilia? What the fuck?"

"What happened?" my brother asked from somewhere above me.

"I have no idea," Mark replied. He reached for me as I curled myself into a ball against the cupboards. "She smacked the counter and then dropped."

"Is she okay?"

"She did it on purpose," Mark said in confusion.

I watched as my brother's eyebrows furrowed and he strode toward the back door. "She see something out there?"

"I was lookin', too," Mark said in frustration as I slapped his hand away from my arm. "I didn't see shit."

"I'll check, anyway," Cam said, stomping outside.

"CeeCee?" my mom asked. "What's going on, honey?"

I looked past her. Olive was asleep on the bed all the way across the house. She was all alone in there.

Still conscious of the watchers outside the window, I started crawling toward the bedroom.

"The fuck are you doin'?" my dad asked, getting up from his seat.

I ignored him, jerking away from Mark as he tried again to lift me to my feet. My focus was absolute, even as I felt the stitches pulling against my movements and my head throbbed. I just had to make it to the bedroom without anyone outside seeing me. If they saw me, they'd know where she was.

"She's trying to get to Olive," Lu said hoarsely, her tone one I hadn't heard before. "Mark, stop. Just let her get to the baby."

By the time I reached the bed, my knees felt bruised and my hands were red and dirty, but I didn't even notice as I pulled Olive gently onto the floor with me. Scooting on my ass, I pressed us into the corner between the bed and the wall and let out a long breath of relief.

"Don't," my mom said to someone in the living room. She'd placed herself in the doorway, keeping everyone out. "I've seen this before." Her voice broke. "If one of you steps inside that room, you won't be coming out on your own two feet."

"Ladybug?" my dad said in confusion.

"Callie almost shot Grease when he tried to get to her," my mom said, her voice low. "You have no idea what a wounded animal will do when it's cornered. Give her a minute to breathe."

I lifted my head to look across the bed. My pistol was in my purse on the opposite side of the room. I calculated how long it would take me to get there and back while holding Olive and decided it was too risky. As long as we were quiet, we were safe in the corner. The minute we moved, we'd be in danger again.

Chapter 16

MARK

I STARED AT Farrah guarding the bedroom door. I could make it past her—I was fast and she wasn't expecting it—but the minute I got inside, I knew Casper would be dragging me back out. He wouldn't be pleased that I'd manhandled his wife or ignored her orders. I silently debated back and forth whether or not the drama would be worth it, and eventually came to the conclusion that it would make an already fucked up situation a hundred times worse.

I couldn't believe the way Cecilia had snapped. One second, she was standing in my arms listening to me talk, and the next she'd been on the floor like she was dodging bullets. I'd never seen anything like it.

We'd done rescues before where the people were seriously fucked up. Tortured, brainwashed, the whole nine yards—but I'd never seen anyone snap the way Cecilia just had. I'd known it was coming, that eventually she'd hit her breaking point, but I still hadn't been prepared for it.

"How long am I supposed to wait?" I asked Farrah flatly, watching Cecilia over her shoulder.

"Give her a minute," she said stubbornly.

"Five," I replied. "Five minutes, and then I'm going in there."

Casper huffed.

"I'll go through both of you if I have to," I told him quietly. I respected the man, and I liked him, but there wasn't a single person on the earth that would keep me away from Cecilia. Not even her parents.

"Didn't see a thing," Cam said as he came back in the house. "It's quiet out there."

"Don't think she was respondin' to a threat," Casper said wearily. "Least not one anyone else can see."

"I'm gonna need to check those stitches," Forrest said apologetically. "She might have ripped a couple open."

"I'll check," I told him, still watching CeeCee. My skin felt tight as I crossed my arms over my chest. It had to have been the longest five minutes of my life. "No one goes in there but me."

"Wait a second," Cam started to argue.

"Leave it," Casper ordered. "If that was Trix in there, you'd be sayin' the same damn thing."

"Not the same, and you know it," Cam shot back. "I didn't leave Trix and completely fuck up her life."

"You did plenty," Casper replied calmly. "And if I remember right, you weren't real pleased when Dragon put himself in the middle of that mess."

"Dragon?" Eli whispered in disbelief. "*I need a fucking nickname.*"

"None of this is helping," Farrah said in exasperation. She stepped to the side. "Go ahead," she told me.

She'd barely gotten the words out before I was striding past her into the room. I slowed as I got closer to Cecilia, watching carefully as I crouched down in front of her.

"Hey," I said softly. I wanted to pull her into my arms, but I had no idea how she'd react. "Cam checked outside. There's no one there."

Her eyes met mine and I jerked back like I'd been sucker punched. Fuck. The fear in her eyes was so overwhelming, it made me sick to my stomach. Dropping to my ass, I carefully scooted forward until my knees bracketed hers.

"You're safe," I said, cautiously smoothing her hair away from her face. "I'm right here, Cec. You and Olive are safe."

There was no indication that she'd even heard me.

"You know, there's a safe room behind the closet," I said, sliding my hand to her shoulder. I rubbed her neck soothingly with the side of my thumb. It took everything inside me not to pull her toward me. "We can put you in there if you'd feel safer. If I know Poet, it's probably got at least a chair in there for you to sit on."

"I don't know what the hell to do," Farrah hissed from the doorway, clearly replying to a comment I hadn't heard. "Wait?"

"You're scaring everyone," I told Cecilia. "We need to know you're okay, baby."

My stomach twisted as her eyes shot to the doorway and then back to me.

"You want me to shut the door?" I asked. I waited for any indication that was what she'd been trying to tell me, but she didn't move. "Okay, I'll shut the door."

I got to my feet and, ignoring Farrah's look of astonishment, closed the door in her face. When I turned back around, Cec and Olive were still in the exact same position.

She could stay there as long as she wanted. If she needed me to sit with her, I would—all night if that's what it took. But, I needed to check those stitches on her side, and I hated to acknowledge it, but at some point, Olive was going to start fussing to be fed and changed, and I had no idea how Cecilia would react.

"Baby," I said, crouching down in front of her again. "You need to get out of this corner."

She just stared at me.

"Cecilia," I said, more firmly. "Come on."

I reached for her arm, and was surprised as hell when she didn't pull away, letting me tug her to her feet. Her gaze darted around the room, but she allowed me to help her onto the bed. A little progress, at least. She was no longer curled up in the corner.

Sitting down beside her, I rubbed my hands over my face. I suddenly felt weary all the way to my bones. I had no fucking clue how to help her. No idea if I should be pushing or leaving her alone. No idea what to say to snap her out of whatever had happened in the kitchen. I was at a complete loss, and I felt my throat grow tight as I dug my fingertips into my eyelids.

"You know," I said, after the quiet became so absolute that you could hear a pin drop, "I knew it was a mistake the moment I left you. No, that's not right. It took about an hour. I was stepping onto the plane when I realized how badly I'd fucked up."

I glanced at her, but couldn't meet her eyes when I realized she was watching me.

"But by then," I continued, "my course was set. I didn't have any choice. I'd signed a contract to go." I huffed out a breath. "I told myself that I'd make it up to you. That as soon as I could, I'd go back home and get you. It was only three months. I convinced myself that three months was nothing if we had our whole lives together."

When I looked at her again, her eyes seemed clearer. She was staring at me, and while the fear wasn't gone, it was now mixed with sadness.

"I didn't let myself think about the fact that you were pregnant," I confessed, forcing the words out. "It didn't feel real. So, instead, I thought about things going back to exactly how they'd been before. I was so sure you'd forgive me. I was so sure that I could fix it. The few times I did go down that road, trying to imagine what a baby would mean for us, I'd picture you meeting me at the airport, your belly sticking out and a big smile on your face."

I laughed derisively. "It was three months," I ground out. "It was only three goddamn months."

I cleared my throat and fought against the urge to hit something. This was why I refused to let myself think about the past—because the guilt was impossible to live with. I froze when Cecilia's head met my shoulder, her body leaning into mine.

"If I could relive it, I would," I told her, kissing the top of her head. "If I could go back and change it, I would. I know I was the reason that shit went south, but fuck." I took a deep breath. "I've never regretted anything the way I regret that."

Cecilia turned and kissed my shoulder before raising her gaze to mine.

She was with me, one hundred percent, and I let out a small breath of relief. Who would've guessed that ripping my guts out and handing them to her would be what pulled her out of the fog she'd been in? Afraid of letting her fall back into that hole, I kept going.

"I wrote you," I said as she pushed herself backward until she sat cross-legged in the middle of the bed. "Every day. I told you about everything that was happening, all the shit I had to deal with, the plans I'd made about how I was going to come get you and leave Eugene. About how we'd get married so you could live in San Diego with me. That you could get a job down there, or go back to school—whatever you wanted, we'd figure it out. God, I fuckin' missed you. It was like a physical ache." I shook my head at the memory. "But I didn't have your address. I didn't have anywhere to send the letters. I kept them, you know?" I met her eyes. "I held on to them, planned on giving them to you when I got back to Oregon."

Uncomfortable with the memory, I scratched at the back of my neck and stared at the floor. "We both know how that played out. Jesus, I'm lucky I didn't kill Leo that day. I could've. With my bare hands. But it was you that stopped me. The look on your face. Fuck, you *hated* me. The whole time I was planning on how I'd make it up to you, you were figuring out how to live without me."

"I had to," she whispered, making my head jerk up in surprise.

"What?" I croaked.

"I had to figure out how to live without you," she said, her voice almost soundless. "The other choice wasn't an option."

"I thought you'd wait."

"If you'd have given any indication that I should," she said gently, "I would've."

"Fuck," I whispered. *"Fuck."*

"I was never with Leo," Cecilia said, her voice still low. "Not after you. He was just a good friend that knew seeing you was going to hurt me. He made it easier the only way he knew how."

"By acting like the two of you were together?" I asked in disbelief.

"By making sure that you wouldn't come back," she clarified.

"He did that," I confirmed. After I'd left the club that day, I'd avoided going back for almost two years. I couldn't stand the thought of Cecilia and Leo together. Imagining it *still* made my guts twist.

"You broke me," she said simply, "and I needed the space to piece myself back together again."

"That was never my intention," I replied. I didn't know how to explain that I'd been immature and stupid, that I'd convinced myself everything would be okay, that somehow, I'd deluded myself into thinking that she'd still be there when I got my shit together. I honestly hadn't even realized back then that I'd had the power to break her.

"Intention matters less than people think," she said quietly. "I *needed* you."

"I know."

"Do you know what it was like?" she asked, her voice still quiet. "Calling your mom's looking for you, only to find out that you'd left? You didn't even tell me."

"I was afraid you'd talk me out of it, and I knew it was the right thing to do," I said hoarsely.

"No," she hissed with a jerk of her head, the Cecilia I knew finally shining through. "The right thing would've been to tell me that you were leaving, but that you'd be back. The right thing would've been to say that we were in it together, even though you had to leave for boot camp or whatever the hell it was called. The right thing would've been to grow a pair and tell me to my face that you'd made a decision that was going to completely change our lives, and let me decide what I wanted to do about it."

"I know that now."

"I would have followed you to the fucking moon," she said, her voice almost pleading. "And you left me without a word."

I could feel my pulse pounding in my head as her words sunk in deep. I'd known it all along. I'd known it, because if I hadn't, I wouldn't have assumed that she'd be waiting on me with open arms. I'd taken advantage of that fact, deciding to ask for forgiveness instead of permission, because I'd been so fucking weak and unsure of myself that I'd been afraid that her disappointment would make me change my course. I'd known, and that's why I'd been so blindsided when I'd come back and she'd wanted nothing to do with me.

I'd known my entire adult life that I'd screwed Cecilia over and I had no one to blame but myself for our relationship imploding, but it wasn't until that moment that I realized just how deeply I'd betrayed her. My breath sawed in and out as I tried to drag enough air into my lungs.

"Looking back," she said, her voice steady, "we weren't ready for a baby, not even if you'd stayed."

I swallowed hard against the bile rising in my throat.

"Please don't feel guilty about that," she said softly, looking down at Olive. "It wasn't meant to be."

"For fuck's sake," I whispered, gripping my hair in my fists. "Stop, Cecilia."

We sat there in silence as I tried to get myself under control. I'd deliberately pushed those memories to the past for so long, convincing myself that, sure, I'd fucked up—but it just hadn't worked out, that the realizations hitting me made it feel like it had happened yesterday. The shame of what I'd done was suffocating.

"How can you even be in the same room with me?" I asked in confusion.

"Because I love you," she said with a small huff. "And you came through when I needed you."

"Don't fucking say that," I replied.

"What? That I love you?" she asked, tilting her head to the side. "So you can say it, but I can't?"

"I don't have anything to be angry about," I said. I remembered the day I'd come back for her, how pissed I'd been that she would barely look at me. How much I'd hated her in that moment, believing that she'd moved on, not having any idea that it was self-preservation. That hate had been the only thing that had kept me going in the following months, the only way I'd justified what I'd done. At some point, that feeling had faded completely. I hadn't owned up to what I'd done, but I hadn't been able to blame Cecilia. Not for any of it.

"I don't know that I'll ever forgive you," she said. "But that doesn't mean that I stopped loving you. Loving you just *is*, it always has been."

I let her words sink in. Our relationship may have imploded years before, our lives going in completely different directions, but in this one way, we were still the same. Loving Cecilia wasn't a choice for me either, it just *was*.

Finally, I nodded. "You know, you scared me there for a minute."

"I scared myself," she replied, her eyes haunted. "When that guy came into the room, he was looking for Olive."

My body tensed until even my toes pressed hard against the floor.

"He kept asking where she was," she said, her arms tightening around the baby. "I guess he hadn't seen her on the bed because of the blankets."

"That was smart," I said, my voice gravelly. I cleared my throat. "I saw the way you'd put the blankets over her."

"I knew if I yelled for help, I'd wake her up," she said softly. "So, I didn't." Her eyes met mine. "I didn't make a sound."

I closed my eyes in understanding and disgust, imagining the beating she'd taken before I'd gotten to her. It had to have been nearly impossible to stay silent. I wasn't sure I'd be able to do the same thing.

"When it was over—" She shook her head. "It was like I couldn't force myself to speak. The words were there, but—"

"Understandable," I said roughly. "If I'd known all it took to get you talking was needing to set the record straight about our past—I would've brought it up in the car, even with your mom there."

Her lips tipped up at the corners at my joke. "I think it was the lost puppy expression on your face that did it."

"Liar," I teased. "You just couldn't resist the urge to argue with my version of the story."

She shot me a tired smile. "It still feels like they're everywhere," she confessed, looking at the window. "Like Drake's just waiting for the right moment."

"No one knows we're here," I replied. "We've been super fucking careful, okay? I swear to God, Cec, we'll end this. You and Olive are safe."

"I don't think anyone is ever safe," she mused with a sigh. "Look at me—I moved a thousand miles away from the chaos, and still ended up right in the middle of it again. I'm so fucking tired, Woody."

The nickname hit me with the force of a sledgehammer.

"Then rest, baby," I said gently, reaching out to run my thumb over the soft skin of her cheek. "I'll be right here, keeping the monsters away."

Chapter 17

CECILIA

EVEN THOUGH I believed that no one knew where we were, my paranoia that we were being watched never faded. It didn't matter whether I was inside the crowded house or sitting on the deserted beach, that feeling never left. I had trouble sleeping at night, and usually had to rest during the day in order to function. I lost more weight, even though I tried to make a conscious effort to eat. Basically, I was a mess, which only added to the guilt I felt every day we were at the beach house.

I knew everyone wanted action. They wanted to end the threat to me and Olive so they could get on with their lives. Instead, we holed up in the beach house for almost two weeks in an attempt to give me some time to recuperate and get my footing again. It didn't seem to be working, though. I was still as exhausted, anxious, and depressed as I'd been when we arrived, the only difference is I'd found my voice again.

"Family meeting," Eli called cheerfully from the back door, interrupting my hour of staring at nothing. "We've got news."

"I'll be right in." I brushed the sand off my legs and heaved myself to my feet. Even while the rest of my body seemed to be consistently weary, thankfully, I was healing from Olive's birth. My clogged duct had cleared out and my vagina no longer felt like a war zone, which, I had to be honest, was a huge relief. You always imagine that things are going to be wonky for a while after pushing a human out of there, but until you're in the midst of it, you don't realize just how tore up you'll be. I liked that part of my anatomy, and at some point, I was going to want to use it again.

"What's the big news?" I asked as I stepped inside the house. Everyone was gathered around the kitchen area, leaving barely any room to stand.

"Olive smiled," Mark said, grinning at me. "Heard my voice and smiled."

"It was probably gas," my mom said.

"It wasn't gas," Mark argued.

"That's the news?" I asked. The look on his face was adorable, but I'd been hoping for something bigger. I didn't have the heart to tell him that she'd been smiling at random for the past few days.

"No, that's not the only news," Forrest drawled. He looked like he was about to either start laughing or roll his eyes. "Wilson and that woman from the FAM have been doin' their thing—"

"Turns out *Kaley* is a hacker," Lu said, grinning. "Between her and Wilson, they've been all up in FAM's shit. Bank records, Web history, you name it, they've seen it."

"And?" I asked.

"Looks like Warren kid is off on his own," my dad said. "While the group is trying to find out what happened, he's been puttin' 'em off, wheelin' and dealin', and generally makin' himself look real guilty."

"That's good news," Eli said when my expression didn't change. "Means there's an opening for a few words from a concerned party."

"You're going to make contact?" I asked, my stomach twisting with anxiety.

"Wilson is," Mark said, his eyes meeting mine. "On your go-ahead."

"Why mine?" I blurted.

"Because it's your ass in a sling," Forrest said. "We think this is the way to go, but if you're not comfortable with it, we'll find another way."

"Is there another way?"

"I can find him and take care of it," my dad said flatly. "Give me about a week, and this is over."

"And then you've got a target on your back for every racist white kid on the west coast," Cam retorted.

"No one would see me," my dad said, brushing him off.

I looked at Mark again. "What do you think?" I asked quietly.

"I think we make contact," he said firmly. "We'll go from there."

"Okay," I said with a nod.

Forrest immediately pulled out his phone, and the rest of us spread out around the house and outside. The place was way too small for eight people and a baby, but somehow, we were making it work. Thankfully, we'd had some breaks in the nearly constant rain, so we could at least hang outside occasionally.

"How you feeling?" Mark asked, dropping down next to me on the couch. Olive was curled up against his chest sleeping, and I couldn't help but lean down to look at her face. She was such a calm baby, it was amazing to me that she didn't seem to realize that she was surrounded by turmoil.

"I'm okay," I answered as I leaned back up. "I hope Wilson contacting the militia doesn't backfire."

"Either way, Drake Warren's a dead man," Mark said with a sigh, leaning back against the couch. "Only thing up in the air is who's gonna do it."

"Maybe I should have let my dad—" I stopped mid-sentence and shook my head. "I'm not putting that on his conscience."

"Not sure it would even be a blip on his radar," Mark mumbled dryly. "You just worry about you, yeah? We'll do what we have to."

"We don't even know where he is," I pointed out. "I don't know how any of you are going to find him."

"That was the other part of Wilson's news," Mark replied.

"What?"

"The Campbell girl." He smiled, and a hundred memories raced through my mind of when he'd given me that exact same look, right before he'd gotten away with something he shouldn't have. "She's a serious hacker. She got into Warren's cell phone."

"No fucking way," I breathed.

"Yep. They're keeping an eye on it, and they know exactly where he is."

"Where?" I asked instantly.

"Central California, last time I talked to Wilson."

I let out a long breath. He was hours away.

"Those burner phones my dad always gives me suddenly don't seem so crazy," I murmured.

Mark laughed. "What?"

I shook my head, relief and something like hope making me feel almost dizzy. "Every time I see him, he gives me a burner phone and tells me to stop using a plan," I replied, rolling my eyes. "He even sent me one in the mail a few times."

He laughed again.

"I just gave them away," I said with a shrug. "Why the hell would I need a burner? No one is looking for me, or hacking into my shit." I widened my eyes and lifted my eyebrows.

"Jokes on you," he said teasingly.

"I still don't understand how all of this happened," I said, shaking my head.

"You've got a big heart," Mark replied. "And you always see the good in people."

I scoffed.

"Don't make that noise at me," he said, reaching over to give my knee a squeeze. "You might be a porcupine, but you've got a soft underbelly."

"Bite your tongue," I joked.

"If you didn't," he pointed out, a small smile playing on his lips, "you wouldn't forgive people so easily."

"I don't," I replied stubbornly. "I hold grudges forever."

"Bullshit," he said with a laugh. "How many times did you make nice after hearing someone say shit about you at the club? A hundred? A million?"

"Making nice isn't the same as forgiving."

"Fine," he said raising a hand in surrender. "You're a monster and I don't even want to sit by you."

He stared at me expectantly.

"You can get up, then," I said, pulling my feet up so I could curl my legs under me. "I'm comfortable here."

He grinned wide. "You're a pain in the ass."

"You dig it," I replied drolly.

"Jesus," he said, shaking his head. "I do. What the fuck is wrong with me?"

"You two done flirting?" my mom asked, strolling into the room. "Because that recliner is calling my name."

"Is it?" I asked, watching her fall dramatically into the chair.

"Yes," she replied, kicking her feet up. "Farrah," she called breathily. "Farrah, come sit on me."

"Is it just me, or does that sound faintly pornographic?" I asked Mark.

"I was trying to ignore it," he whispered back.

"Whispers don't make friends, Woody," my mom called, her eyes closed. "Share with the class."

"I need to piss," he said, handing Olive to me.

"Coward," I called after him as he practically ran out the front door.

"Why is it that men cannot pee inside?" my mom asked, her eyes still closed. "Are they like dogs, always needing to mark their territory?"

"Actually," Eli said from the kitchen, "someone blew up the bathroom. I wouldn't advise going in there."

"New question," my mom said with a sigh. "Why are men so disgusting?"

"Well—" Eli drew the word out.

"Shut it, Eli," me and Mom both called at the same time.

She opened her eyes and grinned at me. "Mini-me."

I snorted.

"I think this is going to work, you know," my mom said, her voice growing serious. "But even if it doesn't, that man will never get anywhere near you and Olive again."

"You can't be sure of that," I replied.

"If I have to, I'll kill that motherfucker myself," she said with quiet intensity.

The chair protested with a loud screech as she abruptly sat forward, kicking the leg rest back into place.

"Dad would never let you anywhere near him," I said, giving her a crooked smile. "But thank you."

"I'll always protect you with everything I have," she said, holding my gaze. "And if ever there's a time when one of us isn't there to help you—you know what to do. Don't hesitate, Cecilia. Not for a second."

I swallowed hard. When I was a baby, Cam's biological dad had kidnapped us and drove us into the mountains with some batshit crazy idea of making us his family. There was a whole lot of other things happening behind the scenes, but bottom line, he'd lost his mind. The pistol my mom kept in my diaper bag was the only thing that had saved us. Well, that and my big brother, who'd been the one to use it. My mom had grabbed Cam, picked me up, and walked miles back down the mountain until the police found us. From then on, Cam was a part of our family. Legend was that she'd thrown herself in front of my big brother when the cops had drawn their weapons, literally shielding him with her body while threatening the men with complete annihilation. I didn't know if it had happened exactly like that, though. In deference to Cam and the impossible decision he'd had to make—my parents rarely spoke about it.

Afterward, my mom had never again went anywhere without a handgun in her purse, not even the grocery store—and she'd passed on that habit to me.

"Did you know that someday, I'd need to know how to shoot?" I asked curiously as Olive began to fuss.

"I prayed you wouldn't," my mom said. "What's that saying? Hope for the best, prepare for the worst."

"I hate that saying."

"Everyone hates that saying," she said, kicking back in the chair again. "No one wants to prepare for something bad to happen." She closed her eyes and made a shooing motion with her hand. "Go feed your child, she's starving."

"You're not starving," I mumbled to Olive as I carried her into the bedroom.

The next few hours passed so slow that it felt like days. On top of worrying that Drake Warren would find us, I now had the added worry that his group of skinhead pals were going to be searching for us, too. While we waited for news from Wilson, I watched everyone act like they weren't trying to find things to pass the time. The almost two weeks we'd been in the house, my group of protectors had been vigilant, but I'd also noticed that they'd used the time to unwind a bit from their hectic lives. Lu did yoga every morning. Forrest read through Poet's fully stocked bookshelf. Eli hung a portable hammock from the deck railings and laid in there for hours. My brother tinkered with his bike. My mom and dad went for walks along the beach—holding hands. And Mark kicked back in the recliner and held Olive, sometimes for hours.

Now, though, everyone was antsy. They paced around the house and checked their phones. No one stayed still for long, including me. The nervous energy was catching, and I was far from immune.

Finally, Forrest raised his hand for quiet, even though none of us were really talking, and answered his phone.

"You're on speaker," he said.

"Lovely," Wilson said flatly. "I've spoken with someone who refused to give me his name, though I was unflaggingly polite. While he didn't seem to be very receptive to the news that perhaps the assassination—his word, not mine—of their leader was an inside job, I do believe that I planted a seed of doubt in his very small brain."

"What does that mean?" I asked Mark. He shook his head.

"He has agreed to take the news to the rest of his terrorist group," Wilson continued. "Though, I don't know if that will help the situation."

"So, we're exactly where we started," I said bluntly, looking around the room. "Great."

"Not quite," Wilson replied. "Hello, Cecilia. I hope you're feeling better."

"I'm fine."

"Good. We're not exactly where we started. Dialogue is important in negotiations."

"We don't negotiate with terrorists," Cam spat.

"Correct," Wilson replied. "However, they *do* believe they're negotiating with us, which works in our favor."

"Did you set up another time to make contact?" Mark asked.

"Tomorrow," Wilson replied. "They prefer to call me."

"They probably shit their pants when he called," Eli said to Lu. "Bet he did that thing where he tells them all about something he shouldn't know about, but somehow does."

"And now they're wondering how he found out," Lu replied.

"And checking their security and locking their doors," Eli said.

"I get results," Wilson said, clearly annoyed.

"Keep doin' what you're doin'," Forrest told Wilson.

"If I could make a suggestion?" Wilson said, the sentence posed as a question, but definitely not one. "Leave for Oregon. If I'm right, and I usually am, the Free America Militia will be calling Mr. Warren in for a meeting that he cannot refuse, in which case, he'll be headed north in a matter of hours. Dependent upon what they decide once they've spoken to him, you could have a bigger problem on your hands than the son and his goon squad."

"Will do," Mark said, glancing at me. "We'll keep you posted."

"Do that," Wilson replied before hanging up.

My heart started to thump and my skin felt hot. The time I'd had to get my shit together was over.

"Cecilia," my dad called, looking at me from across the room. "Got no choice. I'm callin' in the boys, just in case."

"Have them meet us," Forrest said as he got to his feet. "By the time they get here, we'll be long gone."

Dad ignored him, still looking at me.

"Okay," I said softly. "Call the boys."

Mark wrapped an arm around my shoulder and gave me a squeeze.

★ ★ ★

DURING THE FINAL leg of our trip to Eugene, we didn't bother with stealth and subterfuge. Our main goal was speed. It barely took any time to pack up our things, and in less than an hour, we were headed north. Olive and I rode with Mark, but my mom insisted on riding with Eli. In her words, if we ran into trouble, he'd need someone riding shotgun. My dad hadn't appreciated that comment at all.

"You ready to be home?" Mark asked.

I didn't answer him right away because I was leaning over the seat to check on Olive in the back. It felt weird not riding beside her.

"Home is San Diego," I said as I dropped back into my seat. "And no, I'm not ready."

"It's gonna be fine."

"I'll survive," I said with a humorless laugh. "I mean, hopefully."

"Not funny."

"I'm always funny."

Mark shot me a frustrated look.

"Fine," I said with a sigh. "No, I'm not ready. I don't want to go there. I don't want to see anyone. I don't want the whole club in my business and discussing how I've brought hell and damnation home with me, or debating my motivation for literally every move I make. But I'll handle it."

"You've been gone a long time," he replied. "I think you might be surprised by how this all plays out."

"I was just home after my dad's car accident," I reminded him. "And not much had changed. I was still the – God, what do you call a person when everyone else are black sheep?"

"The white sheep?" he said with a chuckle.

"Definitely not that," I said with a huff. "The llama."

"Huh?"

"They're the black sheep, and I'm the llama. I don't fit…and I spit at people."

"This metaphor has gone in a really weird direction," he mused.

"You know what I mean. When I was there, Lily wanted nothing to do with me—even though I made a serious effort to make things right between us. Everyone stared, waiting for me to cause a scene or something. It was complete bullshit. I was there for my *dad*. What did they think I was going to do, start a brawl with my baby sister over a guy that I hadn't wanted when I was 16, and still don't want now? So ridiculous."

"Just take it one day at a time," he said, setting his hand on my thigh, his thumb rubbing back and forth over the seam of my sweats. "It'll be fine."

"At least I've got you with me," I said, holding back a smile. "They'll be so busy wondering if me and you are together that they won't be taking bets on when me and Lily will get into a fistfight."

"Puhlease," he said, making me laugh. He paused. "Like Lily would ever get into a fistfight."

"Hey!" I said, swatting at him.

"What? Have you ever met a sweeter person? She's the least confrontational person I know."

"To you, maybe," I muttered. Though, I knew he wasn't wrong. The idea of getting into a physical fight with my sister seemed as likely as being abducted by aliens. "Still, they'll be waiting for some sort of drama that they can blame me for... beyond the drama I'm bringing with me, I mean."

"I think they might surprise you," he mused. "They're dysfunctional as fuck, but when someone's in trouble, they circle the fuckin' wagons."

I sighed. "I know. I just never wanted them to do that for me."

"They already have," he pointed out, glancing at me. "They didn't cut me out back when I bailed on you, but not one person set me straight on you and Leo. They let me believe it."

"I think they believed it," I confessed, watching him drive. "At least for a while. They just assumed, and we didn't correct them. Plus—" I swallowed hard. "I used it—you know? During arguments and shit. I used Leo as a shield to keep people from fucking with me."

Sometimes I forgot how much I owed Leo. He'd come through for me in a way that defied comprehension. There was nothing in it for him at that point. I'd already completely screwed him over. He should have hated me. A familiar memory hit me, and my lips twitched as I tried to hold back a laugh.

"You're being surprisingly cool about this," I said, failing to keep the surprise out of my voice.

"I look like the jealous type?" Leo asked. If I was being honest, yeah. Yeah, he did. When the right woman came along, I had a feeling that Leo would be jealous and possessive as hell. He just wasn't that way with me.

Leo hadn't held a grudge when I'd started screwing around with Mark and inevitably left him behind, and I'd never really understood it until years later, when I'd seen him with my little sister. Me and Leo just hadn't fit, and we'd both known it. Ironically, he'd fit with my baby sister—who was my complete opposite.

I started to stretch to look over the back of the seat again, but Mark held me still with the hand on my leg.

"Stay put, yeah?" he said, glancing in his rearview mirror.

Alarm thrummed through me.

"Why?" I looked in my own rearview mirror, but couldn't see anything.

"Just noticed a pickup that's been with us for a while," he said, giving my leg a squeeze. "Could be nothin,' but no reason to highlight exactly where Olive is, yeah?"

"Fuck," I breathed, clenching my fists on my lap.

"Should be meeting up with the boys in the next hour," he said, switching lanes. He gave a chin lift to Forrest as we passed his SUV. "They're probably freezing their asses off in this weather."

"I know. Just another reason for everyone to be pissed at me," I said dryly. "Hooray."

"Nah," he said, smiling. "They're probably happy to ride, even in the shit."

"Until one of them goes down because it's fucking snowing."

He leaned forward to look at the sky above us. "I think we'll make it through before it gets bad," he argued. "Rain's nothing. They're used to it."

"I'm going to miss the sun," I said wistfully. "But it'll be nice to have actual seasons again if we stay that long."

"Yeah," he agreed. "That's one of the things I missed most. The fall when it starts getting cooler and everything smells like wet leaves. You never really get that in San Diego."

"And Christmas trees," I said, looking in the rearview mirror again. Mark seemed calm, but I was still on high alert. "They're so expensive in San Diego."

"I know, right?" he replied. "Nothing like paying twenty bucks to some roadside stand for a seven-foot tree."

"In San Diego, I always paid at least a hundred for a small one for my condo," I confessed. "The fake ones just don't do it for me."

"They don't smell," we both said at the same time. Mark laughed.

"What's the point of a Christmas tree if it doesn't make the house smell like Christmas?"

"Agreed," he replied.

We lapsed into an easy silence, and long before I was ready, we took an exit that led to a rest stop right off the freeway. Sitting up straight, I stared through the front windshield trying to see something beyond the rain. Suddenly, a whole row of headlights flashed on, and I felt tears clog my throat.

I hadn't wanted them there. I still didn't want them involved. But, Jesus, it felt good to know that they were.

"Say hello to the cavalry," Mark mumbled.

Though he'd never say so, and would probably deny it, I could tell he was bracing himself for whatever came next. He was on good terms with the club, he always had been, but he also wasn't one of them. It had been his decision, but I imagined it still probably stung a little.

"We're not stopping long," he said as I grabbed my purse from the floorboard. "Quick hello and we're back on the road again."

"Got it," I said, throwing open my door. "But I'm not going anywhere without a weapon."

Mark grinned. "Smart girl."

"Woman," I corrected.

"*My* girl," he argued. He turned and hopped out of his side of the truck, leaving me there with my face slack and a warm feeling burning up my chest. Dammit. I threw the hood of my sweatshirt up and stepped out into the rain.

"These are Woody's people," my dad was saying as I rounded the hood of the pickup.

"Hell," my Uncle Grease said, reaching out to shake Mark's hand and slap him hard on the shoulder. "I thought we were your people."

"Always," Mark replied with a smile. "This is my team—Forrest, Eli and Lu. The others will meet up with us in Eugene."

"There she is," my cousin Tommy said happily, throwing his arm around my shoulder. "Long time, no see, cousin."

"Jesus, Tommy," I complained. "You're soaked."

"Is that a problem?" he asked as he held me tighter, wrapping his other arm around me. "I'm not getting you wet, am I?"

I could feel the water soaking through my sweatshirt, and I squirmed to get free.

"She's been sick," Mark said, his tone far from amused. "Not a good idea."

"How's it goin', Mouth?" Tommy asked. I pinched him hard in the side. He *knew* Mark had never liked that nickname. He was being an ass on purpose, but he let me go, anyway.

I looked around the group. My Uncle Grease, cousins Will and Tommy, the Aces' president Dragon and his son, my ex, Leo, had all ridden down to meet us. I was surprised that they hadn't brought more men until my dad spoke.

"Kept this quiet?" he asked Dragon.

"Just like you asked," Dragon confirmed. "Any problems?"

"Fuck," my dad muttered, shaking his head as he drug the word out.

"Like that, is it?" Dragon replied, glancing at me. I stiffened.

"I'll fill you in when we're not getting' pissed on," my dad said, gesturing to the rain.

"Sounds good," Dragon said. He nodded at me and Mark and headed for his bike.

"That went well," I mumbled under my breath.

"Good to see you, sweetheart," my uncle said, coming forward to give me a hug. "Missed you."

"Missed you, too. How's Rose?" I asked, breathing in the scent of leather and tobacco smoke.

"She's doin' good," he said with a squeeze. "Thankfully. We'll catch up more when we get home, yeah?"

"Okay," I said with a smile as he pulled away.

As the little crowd dispersed, my cousin Will reached out and shoved me gently, his big paw still making me side-step a little. "Everything's gonna be good," he said. "Don't worry."

"Sure," I replied, taking a step backward toward the truck.

I looked over at the bikes, where Leo and Dragon were already waiting. To be honest, I'd never expected a warm reception from anyone in the club and it was always a surprise when I got one, but the fact that neither of them had said a word to me stung.

"Forget it," Mark said as we climbed into the truck.

"What?" I asked blankly, peeling off my soaking wet sweatshirt.

He started the truck and reached forward to crank the heat. "Forget it," he repeated. "That wasn't about you."

"What wasn't about me?" I asked, checking on Olive. She was still completely passed out.

"That Leo bullshit," he said. His hand was so tight on the steering wheel that his knuckles were white. "That was about me, not you."

"Why would it be about you?" I asked, dropping into my seat.

"No love lost, you know?" he said, running his hand through his hair. "He's always had a problem with me."

"That's stupid," I huffed.

"No," he said quietly, glancing at me. "That's loyalty, baby."

"To who?"

"To you."

"Bullshit," I said with a laugh.

"It's not bullshit."

"Uh, yeah," I argued. "It is. If my family has no issue with you, then why would he?"

"Don't know," Mark said with a shrug. "Just is."

As landmarks grew more and more familiar, I sat trying to figure out why Leo would have any loyalty for me. We hadn't spoken much since I left for California. Like I'd told Mark, even my family had let the stuff from the past stay in the past—from what I could see, they weren't holding any grudges. So why the hell would Leo? It didn't make any sense.

Whatever Leo's issue was, I hoped that he'd keep it to himself when we got to Eugene. I was going to have a hard enough time making nice with Lily without her boyfriend causing a bunch of bullshit. My stomach knotted in a mixture of anxiety and excitement. I'd always want to see my siblings, no matter how fucked up our relationship was, but I also dreaded it.

It was impossible to explain the feeling of being an outcast in your own family to people that hadn't experienced it. Knowing that they loved you, but didn't necessarily want you around was… heartbreaking. It made you unsure of yourself in a way that you hadn't been before. It made you question your worth.

"First hurdle is over," Mark said, reaching out to cover my hand with his. "Painless, right?"

I didn't have the heart to burst his bubble. I hadn't been worried about the men. It was the women who'd make snide remarks and talk shit about me behind my back. Before I could say anything, Olive's wail filled the cab of the truck.

"Just climb back," Mark said, glancing in the mirror. "We're not stoppin' until we're behind the gates."

"Never in a million years," I grumbled as I climbed over the seat, "did I ever think I'd be nursing a baby in a moving vehicle like it was 1972."

"Cost-benefit analysis," Mark said, leaning out of my way. "Better to keep moving."

"I know," I replied. I shushed the baby as I unbuckled her seatbelt and pulled her into my arms. "I promise it won't always be like this," I crooned. "Some day, I'm going to nurse you in a rocking chair, with sun shining through the window and the Beatles playing."

"The Beatles, huh?" Mark said.

"What can I say," I said with a shrug. "I'm a fan."

"No lullabies?"

"I doubt I even know any," I replied as I quickly and awkwardly changed Olive's diaper. "Farrah wasn't really a lullaby type of parent, but I can probably sing every Beatles song from start to finish."

"My mom was more of an Alabama fan," Mark said.

I didn't respond. I wasn't really sure what to say, because anything even remotely nice would've sounded insincere. At some point, maybe I'd be able to say something kind about Mark's mother, but not yet. Not when I could still remember the satisfaction in her voice when she'd told me he'd left me.

"Dad was more of a Zeppelin guy," he said, clearing his throat. "The Who. Pink Floyd. Bob Dylan. Creedence."

"Really? I would've thought The Monkees," I replied sarcastically.

Mark barked out a laugh. "Oh, they were top ten, for sure."

We discussed different bands we liked, both old ones and new, while I fed the baby. By the time I'd buckled her back in and was climbing into the front, we'd moved onto movies.

"*Back to the Future* was ahead of its time," he said, pointing at me.

"Was that an intentional pun?" I asked with a laugh. "Plus, there's no comparison. How you could think that B*ack to the Future* is even close to being as good as *Dirty Dancing* is beyond me."

Mark scoffed.

"*That* was a movie that dealt with social issues—"

"And was sexy as fuck," Mark cut in.

"Well, yeah," I drawled. "Patrick Swayze was fucking delicious."

"Jennifer Grey," Mark said, smacking his lips. "When she's in those shorts, dancing down that little bridge thing? Damn."

"That does it for you, huh?" I asked with a laugh. "Cut-offs and a pair of white sneakers?"

"If you hadn't noticed," he said, turning his head to give me a look. "I had a type."

"What?" I practically screeched. "I don't look anything like Jennifer Grey—before the nose job or after."

He laughed. "I didn't mean your face." He shrugged.

I snickered as I realized he was right. In my late teens and early twenties, I *had* been shaped like Baby in *Dirty Dancing*.

"Well," I said with a shrug, "too bad I couldn't fit in those cut-offs now if someone paid me."

"Fuck," he spat with a huff. "Kill me if you're ever shaped like that again."

"Hey," I said, a little confused and offended.

"Cecilia," he said, his voice deepening, "you're ten times sexier now than you were then. Jesus, I want to bite your ass every time you turn your back to me."

I choked a little on the spit in my mouth.

"Too much truth?" he asked in amusement.

"No," I wheezed.

"Good." His hand came across the seat and gripped my thigh, and I was acutely aware of how close his pinky was to the seam of my pants. "Just so you know, I've never wanted anyone the way I want you—not even when you're putting on a pad the size of a diaper just to prove a point."

My cheeks burned with embarrassment, but I shrugged.

"I want to see a red mark the shape of my hand on your ass," he said, his eyes on the road. "I want to put hickeys on the insides of your thighs. I want to feel your tits against my face as I'm fucking you. God, I want to fuck you so bad, my teeth ache."

Chapter 18

MARK

I SNAPPED MY mouth shut and waited for Cecilia to put me in my place. We may have cleared the air back at the beach house, but we were far from a place where I could tell her I wanted to leave hickeys on her goddamn thighs. The back of my neck grew warm with a mixture of arousal and embarrassment, but I refused to back-pedal. Not when I could see Leo's bike a few car lengths ahead of us.

Fuck, I hated that guy. I'd be lying if I said that spelling out exactly what I wanted had nothing to do with the douchebag. His presence reminded me of every insecurity and fear I'd had as a kid. He'd been the chosen one. The one who'd always fit in. A natural born leader. A complete fuck. And, he'd had Cecilia, at least before she'd realized that I'd fucking worshiped her.

Knowing that they hadn't gotten back together after I'd left didn't lessen my hatred. If anything, it made it worse. I hadn't tried again because I'd thought she moved on. I hadn't gone back on my hands and knees and begged for her forgiveness because I was angry.

Cecilia still wasn't saying anything and I risked a glance at her.

"Are you marking your territory?" she asked, fighting a smile as she tilted her head to the side.

God, it was fucking annoying that she could still read me like a book.

"No," I lied.

"Good, because you know he's with Lily," she chuckled a little.

"You know, my *sister*. And if that wasn't enough, I didn't want him when he was single."

"I can't want you because you're *you*?" I dodged. "Why's it gotta be that I have some ulterior motive?"

"I didn't say that."

"That's what it sounds like."

"Oh," she sang, throwing her hands up in the air. "Put me on the defensive. Good move!" She dropped her hands. "It's not going to work, though. We saw Leo and you're suddenly all fired up to—to fuck me."

"Been a while, sweetheart?" I teased. "Can't even say the words?"

"None of your beeswax," she shot back, making me laugh. "I can say the words. You want to put hickeys on my thighs," she said, jokingly drawing out the words. "You want to spank me."

She was joking, teasing me, and I still couldn't help but get hard at the words coming out of her mouth.

"You want these big, new breasts in your face while you're fucking me," she said, leaning back against the seat. "Which is odd, because if I remember correctly, it was all about the doggie-style with you when we were teenagers."

I huffed out a surprised laugh and looked at her. "It was any way I could get you when we were teenagers. Usually, that meant we were outside, and I didn't want you to have to lay on the ground, so missionary wasn't my go-to."

"Oh," she said, crossing her arms over her *big, new breasts*. "Well, that's actually kind of sweet."

"Mmhmm," I hummed.

"We've gotten off track," she said. "Why now?"

I tried to think of a way to change the subject, but by the stubborn set of her chin, I knew she wasn't about to let it go. Instead, I went with honesty. "We're almost to Eugene," I said, keeping my eyes on the road. "And you're gonna be surrounded by family and the club, and I know you." Her hand covered mine on her thigh, and she slid her fingers between mine. "You're gonna start talking about how I don't need to be there. That you're safe. That I should get back to my life."

"You know it's true," she replied quietly.

"I don't know it's true," I said, tightening my fingers around hers. "I don't know what the fuck is true right now. All I know is that they'd have to drag my ass away from you at this point, and I wouldn't make it easy for them."

Cecilia didn't say anything, so I left it at that. I considered telling her that I didn't just want sex from her, but I dismissed it. She already knew that. It had never been just sex with us, not even when we were two horny nineteen-year-olds with a lot of time on our hands. At the risk of sounding like a complete fucking sap, our connection was about more than that. We'd understood each other in a way that other people didn't—the every-other-weekend kid that never felt like he belonged anywhere, and the misunderstood brat that acted out because she felt like no one saw her.

"I wonder where they're going to have us stay," she said after a while. "It's not like I can stay in the clubhouse long-term."

"Probably at your parents' place," I replied, instinctively cringing at the thought.

"God, I hope not. That place has had enough chaos. I can't believe they never moved."

"Me, either."

"After the shooting, my dad said that some pencil-neck fuckers weren't going to scare his family from their home," Cecilia said dryly. "It was his big stand. But all the kids are gone now, you know? Only Charlie's still at home, and she wasn't even alive then. What does he have to prove at this point?"

"Maybe they just love the place," I replied.

"Well, I don't. I don't give a shit if they redid the backyard. It's still the place where our lives fucking exploded."

As we got closer to Eugene, Cecilia's hand went to her mouth, her fingers pulling at her bottom lip over and over. By the time we took our exit, her knee was bouncing with anxiety and her hand was holding mine so tightly that my fingers had begun to ache. There wasn't anything I could say that would calm her down, and I wondered how in the world she'd forced herself to visit in the past if it made her that nervous.

When we pulled through the gate of the Aces' compound, it was like a switch flipped. Cecilia's hand slid away from mine as she sat up straight and ran her fingers through her hair. She quickly pulled her sweatshirt back on and found a tube of lipstick in her purse, smearing it on without bothering with a mirror. By the time she'd settled back into her seat like she was out for a Sunday drive, it was like I was looking at a completely different person than I'd spent the last few anxiety-filled hours with.

As we pulled to a stop in the forecourt and I put the truck in park, Cecilia looked at me.

"Showtime," she said quietly. Then, without waiting for me, she hopped out of the truck and immediately opened the back door for Olive.

"You want me to grab her seat?" I asked as she climbed inside.

"No, I'll just grab her without it," she said as she unbuckled the baby. "But can you grab the diaper bag? She needs a diaper change."

"No problem."

After I'd grabbed the bag from the backseat, I met Cecilia at the hood of the truck. It was so late that I swore I could see the sky growing light, but by the number of people streaming out of the clubhouse, everyone had waited up for the convoy to get back.

"Give me my grandbaby," Farrah ordered as we made our way toward the front door. "I wanna show her off."

"Later, Mom," Cecilia said with a shake of her head. If you looked closely, you could see the tension in her shoulders and in the movement of her body.

Unsurprisingly, no one noticed but me.

"Such a party pooper," Farrah said lightly, bumping Cecilia with her hip. The tension that Farrah had been carrying seemed to have melted away now that we were behind the safety of the Aces' gates.

"It's not a party," Cecilia ground out. The tension in her had magnified.

We were swallowed up as the groups mingled, and not for the first time, I noticed the way Cecilia stood apart. Not geographically, we were right in the middle of it all, but emotionally.

"You're a sight for sore eyes," Poet said as he stepped in front of us. "Look at the three of you."

"Good to see you, old man," I said, grinning as he slapped me on the shoulder.

"You need to call me more often," Poet replied. He pointed at Cecilia. "This one never calls."

"I didn't know I was supposed to," Cecilia said in amusement.

Poet harrumphed. "Like you've ever done what you were supposed to anyhow," he said, reaching out to cup her cheek. "Beautiful, as always. You call me anytime you want to hear an old man blather."

"Make sure you've got the time," Amy said, coming up behind her husband. "He'll keep you on the phone for hours."

"Hey, Amy," I said as she smiled at me.

"Hey, yourself." She shook her head. "Should've guessed when you were eating us out of house and home that you'd grow into such a giant. Every time you come home, I'm surprised again at how damn tall you are."

She turned to Cecilia. "Hi, sweetheart," she said, her voice gentle.

"Good to have you home."

"It's good to see you," Cecilia replied. She didn't say it was good to be home.

"You sure know how to make an entrance," Amy said, grinning. "Let's get you inside out of the weather so you can show me that baby of yours."

"Cecilia!" a voice called over the crowd. I looked up from Amy to find Cecilia's aunt Callie hurrying toward us. Within seconds, she'd wrapped Cecilia in a hug with Olive pressed between them.

"Goddamn it," she said, her voice muffled by Cecilia's head. "I can only take one of the kids getting into trouble at a time." She leaned back to look at Cecilia's face. "You okay, baby?"

"I'm okay," Cecilia replied hoarsely.

"Thank God. Come on, let's move this party inside."

I fell into step behind the row of women, Amy on one side of Cecilia and Callie on the other. The sight was enough to make it appear like Cecilia had just been welcomed wholeheartedly back into the fold—but I knew better. These older women, who'd been through hell and lived to talk about it—didn't have the time or the inclination for petty bullshit. Cecilia hadn't been worried about her reception with them.

"You did good," Poet said, striding along beside me. I slowed my gait so he could keep up. While I'd never say it, the old man wasn't moving like he used to.

"What?" I asked, watching Cecilia move further away.

"Goin' to get her," he said jerking his head toward the women. "Bad deal. Glad you were there."

"Me, too," I replied.

"I bet," he said with a sly grin.

I shook my head.

"You've got a prime opportunity to make things right," he said seriously. "Don't fuck it up, boyo."

"You just gonna leave us standing outside?" Eli asked, jogging up to us. "I see how it is."

"Shit," I muttered. I'd totally forgotten that my team was even there, I was so caught up in seeing the old crew and watching out for Cecilia. "Poet, this is Eli." I looked up to see Forrest and Lu walking up behind him and introduced them, too.

"Welcome," Poet said, shaking everyone's hands. "Real grateful you took care of our girl."

"Glad we were in the right place at the right time," Forrest replied.

I spent the next twenty minutes saying hello to people I'd known forever, but hadn't seen in years. It was wild to be in the same place with so many of the kids I'd grown up with and their partners. Hell, even Tommy had settled down, which I'd assumed would never happen. Okay, *settled down* wasn't the correct term, I thought as I watched him pretend like he was humping his wife, complete with dramatic ass-slapping as she bent over to pick something up. When his wife realized what he was doing, she shot up straight, and from what I could see from across the room, it looked like she gave him a titty-twister in retaliation.

My gaze automatically strayed to Cecilia. She was still standing with her aunt Callie and Amy, but her mom had joined the group. They were cooing over Olive like they'd never seen a baby before, and the proud look on Cecilia's face made me smile.

"Know that look," Grease said as he came up next to me at the bar. "Think I've worn it myself once—or four times."

"What look is that?" I asked, dropping onto a bar stool.

"The *Proud Papa* look," he said dryly. He lifted his hand to stop me from replying. "Yeah, yeah, I know she's not yours, and you and Cecilia haven't gotten your heads out of your asses yet."

"Jesus Christ," I swore. "Does everyone have an opinion on this?"

"Nah," Grease answered with a laugh. "My daughters-in-law don't even know you."

"From what I remember, none of you wanted us together in the first place," I shot back.

"Shit," he drawled, shaking his head. "It wasn't that we didn't want you two together, dipshit. We could all see Cecilia racin' toward the edge of a cliff, and her obsession with you was bound to end badly. I always thought you two'd end up together eventually, but that girl needed to get her shit straight first."

"Maybe if you'd done something to help her," I ground out, anger boiling in my belly, "she wouldn't have been racing toward the edge of anything."

Grease shot me a look. "Before or after I got done buryin' my youngest son and takin' care of my wife's gunshot wound?" he asked. "I get where you're comin' from, man, I do, but you're barkin' up the wrong tree with that shit. I loved Cecilia and supported her the best I was able at the time."

"Shit," I replied, reaching up to press my fingers into my tired eyes. "I apologize."

"Nothin' to apologize for," he said, taking a sip of his coffee. "I'da felt the same way if it was Callie. Just be mindful of who you go mowin' down with righteous anger, yeah? We were all doin' the best we could back then."

As he walked away, I turned back to watching Cecilia.

"Got you some coffee," Lu said, handing me a cup as she sat down beside me. "That old guy Poet is a hoot. He introduced me to literally everyone in the building. Hard to believe he used to be the VP around here."

"Don't be fooled," I murmured. "He's no angel."

"Now that's a life story I'd like to hear," she mused.

"Don't ask him," I warned her. "Where'd the boys go?"

"Bathroom," she said, rolling her eyes. "Apparently, they needed to go together."

"Trust most of these men with my life," I said seriously. "But it goes without saying to watch your six while you're here. Probably not a bad idea to stick together."

"Seriously?"

"Do I think you're gonna be attacked by a member?" I replied. "Doubt it. But I also thought that Cecilia was safe at the club in Sacramento, and look how that turned out. I know the old timers here, but I don't know the new ones. We gotta work on the assumption that there's a mole, even if there isn't."

"You know I can take care of myself," she said, stopping when she saw the look on my face. "Yeah, okay, I hear you. I'll keep my eyes open."

"Good."

I sighed as I took a sip of my coffee. Damn, I was tired. We'd driven through the night, and now that the sun was beginning to rise, exhaustion was riding me hard. I could go days with no sleep, and I'd had to do that sometimes in the past—my line of work meant you slept when you could, not when you wanted—but being home, in the safety of the clubhouse, was like a warm blanket on a cold day. Instant drowsiness.

"Hey, stranger," Brenna said as she strode toward us. "Nice of you to stop in and say hi."

"Hey Brenna," I said, accepting the hug she offered. The smell of her took me back to being 12 and riding in the car with her to the mall because she'd noticed that my toes were wearing holes in the ends of my shoes. I still remembered every piece of clothing she'd bought me. New sneakers and a pair of flip-flops. One pair of jeans and three pairs of shorts. One hoodie, three t-shirts and two tank tops. All name brands. All things my mother would have never been able to afford.

She must still wear the same perfume.

"You guys must be beat," she said, reaching out to squeeze my arm. "Why don't we get you settled in some rooms? We've got some open ones."

"Sounds good," I said as I stood. I finished off my coffee in three gulps, grimacing as it burned all the way down.

"You could've brought it with you," Brenna said with a laugh.

"It's habit," Lu said with a smile. "Finish it up while you can—don't know when you'll have another opportunity."

"I have a feeling you have tons of stories about this one," Brenna said, pointing at me. "I'll have to pick your brain later."

"Hey," I complained.

"I've got some doozies," Lu agreed.

"Well, if you'd visit more than once a year," Brenna said as she led us to the hallway, "I wouldn't have to ask your friends about your life."

I glanced across the room, checking on Cecilia one more time. She'd handed Olive to her aunt and was standing with her arms crossed over her chest. There was nothing about her posture that indicated how uncomfortable she was, but I could just tell. Something about her stance made me want to pick her up and drag her out of there.

Lu elbowed me in the side.

"I'm right here," I said to Brenna, paying attention to the conversation again. "Ask anything you want."

"I'll hold you to that," she replied. "So, me and the girls got this bright idea to start remodeling some of the rooms. Just new paint and carpet—no big thing—but it's taking a lot longer than we expected with everything that's been happening. That's why we've got a couple empty rooms. I hope you don't mind the smell of fresh paint?"

"As long as it's not still wet," I said as she opened a door.

"Nope. And the smell really isn't bad—it's been a few days."

"It smells like a new apartment," Lu said with a smile. "Not bad at all."

"Good," Brenna replied. "We have three rooms, so however you want to divvy them up is fine."

"Forrest and Eli can share," Lu said instantly. "That way me and Chief have our own."

"Chief?" Brenna asked, raising an eyebrow.

"Just a nickname," I said, shaking my head.

"That should work," Brenna said, getting back to the conversation. "I'm sure CeeCee can stay in her pop's room—"

"She stays with me," I said, cutting her off.

Brenna laughed. "Now why did I know you were going to say that?"

Lu snickered.

"I'll let you two have this room since it's the biggest—barely," Brenna told me, smiling. "Come on, Lu, I'll let you pick between the other two."

"Your dad wasn't lying, you really *are* the best," Lu said, following her out of the room.

I needed to get back out to the main room to keep my finger on the pulse of what was happening, but I couldn't resist the lure of the freshly made bed. Brenna had been downplaying the remodel she was trying to achieve in the rooms—I'd definitely never seen a club room with a headboard and a comforter before.

Dropping my ass to the bed with a sigh, I ran my hands through my hair and scrubbed them over my beard. It was so weird being back and knowing that I'd be staying at the club, even for a little while. Anytime I'd visited in the past, I'd spent a few hours saying hi and visiting on the compound, and then almost always had dinner with Poet and Amy before heading to a hotel. It was nice to catch up, but I was usually ready to go back to my life after an afternoon being surrounded by the old crew.

Something was different this time. It didn't feel like I was back to see some old friends. It felt like I was *home* for the first time in a long time. It felt natural and comfortable, and beyond the fact that we had some seriously big shit that needed to be dealt with—almost relaxing.

As I stood up from the bed and pulled my hoodie off, I tried to figure out why this trip to Eugene was so different. It wasn't necessarily because of the circumstances or the fact that I knew I'd be staying a while. Any other time, I still would've been itching to leave even if I knew I had to stay.

Then, as Brenna walked by the doorway and gave a little wave, I realized what the difference was.

Cecilia.

It wasn't because she was in trouble, it was because she was *there*. Eugene hadn't felt like home in years because Cecilia hadn't lived there for years. This was the first time we were both at the club at the same time. God, I was an idiot. *Cecilia* felt like home, especially in the middle of our family and friends, in the place where we'd fallen in love.

I hurried back to the main room.

CHAPTER 19

CECILIA

I SHOULD'VE PUT on more makeup. Out of all the things I'd learned from my mother, one of the lessons had always stuck with me – *never go to war without your war paint*. I'd taken the time to swipe on some lipstick as we'd pulled up the gravel driveway, but as I stepped inside the clubhouse doors, I realized it hadn't been enough. I felt exposed. Naked.

I recognized the old, artificial holly garland draped across the bar and the biker Santa perched on top of the sound system, but the familiar Christmas decorations that I'd loved as a kid did nothing to calm my nerves. If anything, their worn condition highlighted how long I'd been gone. I couldn't even enjoy the way the strings of colored lights made the room seem like it was glowing as my gaze scanned the room.

"I'm so glad you're home," Aunt Callie said, ushering me into the room. "The men will get everything figured out."

I smiled, but didn't reply. I wasn't sure how they were going to figure anything out, and honestly, I was more concerned at the moment with the sweat that was making my t-shirt stick to my skin. It wasn't even very warm in the clubhouse. They kept it cool because the temperature always rose a lot when you got a big crowd of people inside one room.

"I know you're probably overwhelmed," Amy said to my quietly, as Aunt Callie turned to yell at Will across the room. "But it's going to be okay, honey. You're home now, for what that's worth, and at least you'll have some time to rest."

"Thank you for letting us use the beach house," I replied, tucking Olive closer to my chest. "It was such a relief to have a little time off the grid."

"Absolutely," Amy said. "We don't use it much in the winter anyway." She waved her hand in dismissal. "My car doesn't do well in the snow, so we stick close to home."

"You need to get something with all-wheel drive," I said as my aunt turned to me, wiggling her fingers in a give me gesture. I handed Olive over, and without the weight of her in my arms, I felt even more uncomfortable. It was pretty pathetic that I was using a baby as my shield, but beggars can't be choosers, right?

"Honey, I'm old as dirt," Amy said with a laugh. "I'm not buying a new car when I won't even have time to enjoy it."

"Don't say that," I yelped. "Ugh. Don't even think it."

"We all die, CeeCee," she replied, patting my arm. "I've had a good run."

"Jesus, I thought you were trying to make me feel better! What the hell?"

"Well, some things never change," my mom said, choosing that moment to join our conversation.

"She's talking about dying," I replied defensively.

"You're going to live forever and that's final," Mom said to Amy, poking her in the chest. She turned to Aunt Callie and started cooing at Olive.

"She is the sweetest baby," my mom said with a happy sigh. "Seriously. If I'd had one like her, we wouldn't have stopped at four."

"Hell," Amy said. "I was happy with the one. He still keeps me on my toes."

"Nix is fantastic and you know it," Aunt Callie argued. "I can't imagine he ever gave you any problems."

Amy laughed.

"Oddly enough, Tommy was my easiest baby," Aunt Callie said as my cousin Tommy shouted something filthy across the room. "And look how that turned out." She met my eyes, grinning. "Good luck."

"Oh God," I mumbled, making all of them laugh.

"Don't worry," Amy said, reaching out to rub Olive's back. "This one's too sweet to ever shout obscenities across a crowded room."

"I wouldn't count on that," my mom said with a laugh. "In this family, you haven't reached adulthood unless you've swore like a trucker at someone across a crowded room."

I grimaced. She wasn't wrong. My parents hadn't ever told us that swearing was bad, they'd just taught us to know our audience. We'd known to only curse at each other until we were old enough that it wasn't seen as disrespectful to other adults. I was pretty sure I wasn't going to be quite as progressive with Olive. There was something inherently gross about hearing a four-year-old dropping f-bombs, even if it was funny.

"Hey, I almost forgot—Cam said to tell you he'll see you in the morning. He went home to see Trix and the boys," my mom said.

"He couldn't say goodbye?" I asked, glancing over my shoulder to see if I could catch him.

"He's been gone for over two weeks," my mom answered unsympathetically. "He wanted to see his woman and his kids."

I swallowed back the urge to snap at her as guilt made my stomach churn. I understood, so clearly, what she was insinuating. *I* was the reason he hadn't seen Trix or the boys in two weeks. I had no right to get bent out of shape because my brother had left without saying goodbye. I had no right to make any demands at all—not when all of these people would be rearranging their lives to help me.

"I was surprised I didn't see her here," Aunt Callie said.

"After all of the stuff with Rose," my mom replied with a grimace, "she didn't want to freak the boys out by dragging them to the club in the middle of the night."

"Where is Rose?" I asked. I'd noticed that she still hadn't appeared. I'd also noticed that Leo had vanished the moment we got to the clubhouse, and I hadn't seen Lily. I didn't ask about her, though. Beyond the fact that my pride wouldn't allow me to ask, hearing that my sister didn't care enough to be there when I got home was something I wasn't up to dealing with at the moment.

"Rose's home with Mack and Kara," Aunt Callie replied. "Rebel and Charlie were spending the night, too, so they said they'd see everyone tomorrow."

"I hope Molly doesn't drink tonight," my mom said. "I'm going to need her help on breakfast."

"Everyone's coming for breakfast?" I asked, my stomach knotting. I was having a hard time dealing with the partial crowd that was surrounding us.

It felt like too much information, too many moving parts. After being away for so long, the sheer number of people to keep track of was overwhelming. I knew, of course, who belonged to who, and I could list off every single person in our extended Aces family—but actually being in the center of it was completely different.

"Yep," my mom replied. "Brunch, really. I'm not waking up before noon."

"She says that like it's surprising," Aunt Callie said to Amy.

"I always get up before noon," my mom argued.

"Always?" Aunt Callie countered. "That's a bit of a stretch."

"Nine times out of ten," my mom said.

"Two times out of ten," Aunt Callie said with a laugh.

My mom looked at me. "Hello, a little loyalty here?"

"I haven't lived here in almost a decade," I replied with a shrug. "I have no idea when you wake up."

"How are you my daughter?" my mom asked, looking at the ceiling. "How did I raise such a Benedict Arnold?"

"You need sleep," Aunt Callie said with a laugh. "You're getting loopy."

"That's fair," my mom grumbled. She reached over and pulled me into a tight hug, kissing my temple. "Brenna got you set up?"

"Not yet," I said, scanning the room over her shoulder. I couldn't see Brenna, but I was sure she'd find me eventually.

"She's got some rooms ready," my mom said as she let go. "Sleep good, sweetheart. I'll see you in the morning."

"Afternoon," Aunt Callie joked out of the side of her mouth.

"Get some rest," my mom said, ignoring Aunt Callie. "You're home safe now."

After quick hugs with Aunt Callie and Amy, the former including a pinch on the ass that made Aunt Callie yelp, my mom sauntered away. I loved that she always seemed like she fit right in no matter where she was. She was comfortable in her skin like no one else I'd ever met, but I also envied her confidence. Of course, she *would* feel comfortable in the Aces clubhouse—my grandpa had been the president before he was killed—but her ability to stride into a room and make it her bitch didn't end at the gates.

Brenna strode up as Aunt Callie gave Amy a turn holding Olive.

"Hey, doll," she said, pulling me into a hug. "It's good to see you."

"Even if I bring doom and destruction with me?" I asked dryly. I couldn't help myself. Brenna had always been kind to me, but I sometimes wondered if it was all a show to keep the peace. She had to get along with my mom and aunt, not only because their men worked so closely together, but also, she was my brother's mother-in-law. But she was also Leo's mom—and I wasn't exactly kind to him when we were kids, especially after the shooting.

Brenna let out a little noise of surprise and leaned back, keeping her hands on my shoulders. "Hell, honey," she said with a little chuckle. "Everyone else has done it at one point or another, myself included—I'd say you're due."

I couldn't help the startled laugh that fell out of my mouth.

"I know you're always nervous when you come back here," she said quietly. "But don't be. You belong here as much as anyone else, okay? You keep your chin up and don't take any shit."

"Okay," I whispered, so quiet I wasn't sure if she'd heard me until she winked and nodded in approval.

"Introduce me to your daughter," she said, letting go of me as she turned toward Amy.

"This is Olive," I said, unable to keep the pride out of my voice.

"Oh, she's beautiful," Brenna said, leaning down to run a fingertip along the top of Olive's hand. "What a sweetheart. How's she sleeping?"

Aunt Callie laughed. "We always ask that," she said, shaking her head. "Like it matters."

Brenna chuckled and glanced at me. "That's true," she said, grinning. "It doesn't matter if she's sleeping a ton or keeping you up at all hours. She's still a good baby, either way, and I promise it doesn't last forever."

"I think it's just a roundabout way to ask the mama if she's gettin' enough rest," Amy said, swaying from side to side. "Don't be afraid to ask for help, if you aren't," she said to me. "There's plenty around here that'll hold her for a while if you need a nap."

"Shit's been so crazy," Mark said from behind me as he slid an arm around my waist. "Don't know if this one's rested since she gave birth."

"Well, that'll change now," Aunt Callie said. "I can't imagine not having a home base while the kids were newborns. It's good you're home."

The conversation continued and I was thankful for Mark's arm around me as my mind wandered. Aunt Callie was wrong—I still didn't have a home base. I didn't have a home. The clubhouse wasn't somewhere I could stay indefinitely, and I knew without a doubt that I couldn't stay with my parents, either. They would let me—no doubt about that—but I refused to move back into that house. The thought of sleeping with the scene of the shooting right outside my window made me want to barf.

"You ready for bed?" Mark said quietly into my ear.

I nodded. "Hey, Brenna, where should me and Olive sleep?"

Brenna looked from me to Mark, then rolled her lips in to keep from smiling.

"She already set us up in a room," Mark said. "I'll show you which one."

"Oh, we're sharing, are we?" I asked, more to tease him than because I cared. I was actually thankful that he'd be close.

"That's right," Amy said proudly. "Make him work for it."

"You should be on my side," Mark replied, acting thoroughly betrayed.

"Girl power," Amy replied simply.

I laughed as Amy handed Olive back to me.

"I'll see you guys in the morning," I told the women. "Well, *later* in the morning."

"Sounds good," Aunt Callie said with a smile.

Mark threw his arm over my shoulder as he led me across the room toward the archway that led to the back hallway. As we passed the table where Will was sitting with Molly in his lap, talking to Tommy and Heather, I waved but didn't make eye contact—I was too worn out to actually engage in conversation with anyone else.

"Was it as bad as you thought it'd be?" Mark asked as he led me into the room we were staying in.

"No," I said with a sigh, laying Olive on the bed. I stretched my arms above my head—my shoulders were sore from being tensed up for the past two weeks. "But Rose and Lily aren't even here, neither is Trix, and I didn't talk to either of my cousins' wives."

"You think that would've mattered?" he asked curiously, sitting down gingerly on the edge of the bed.

"Probably," I replied. "It would've been nice to get it all over with at once. Now I have to do it all again in the morning."

"I think you'll be pleasantly surprised," Mark said.

"What gives you that impression?" I snapped, frustrated with his optimism. "Was it the fact that my brother left without saying goodbye? Or that my cousins' wives didn't come over to say hello? Maybe it was the fact that the club had to ride down to meet us, but my sister didn't even bother to show up to, you know, say hello or *make sure I was okay?*"

"Cam didn't say goodbye?" Mark asked. "That's kind of shitty."

"He doesn't owe me anything," I said, shaking my head. "My mom made sure that I remembered that."

"What do you mean?" Mark asked, frowning. "What did she say?"

"It doesn't matter."

"Maybe Lily had good reason for not showing up," Mark said reasonably. "Maybe she wanted to be here."

"Just stop," I said, my voice almost pleading as any frustration I'd felt was replaced with weariness. "She didn't come to see me because I was an asshole, okay? Before I left, I was an asshole. Not once—*all the time*. I was unhappy and I made everyone around me as unhappy as I was. She didn't want anything to do with me the last time I was home, and she doesn't want anything to do with me now."

"That was years ago," he said softly, getting to his feet. "How long do you think you need to be punished for that?"

"I left," I replied, taking a step back as he reached for me. "I wasn't ever punished for it. I left and I never had to atone for any of it."

"You don't think banishment was atonement?" he asked softly.

"Banishment?" I scoffed.

"Yeah." His eyes were kind as he stood there, letting me have my space. "There's a reason why it was a punishment used by different cultures around the world. Separating a person from their family and everything they've ever known is one of the most painful punishments there is."

"I was the one who left," I reminded him around the lump in my throat.

"Which is even worse," he said gently. "Because you did it to yourself."

I dropped my face into my hands as his words sunk in. The first sob was a hiccup, but as he wrapped his arms around me, I lost it.

He was right.

I had been punishing myself. I'd been keeping myself away because I'd known how awful I'd been, and I couldn't stand to take my family down the dark hole with me. I felt like I'd deserved to be alone. That I'd deserved to be separate from my family and the people who loved me, but had no idea what to do with me. Hell, I still felt that way. They didn't deserve to deal with the mess I was in. It was *my* mess.

God, it hurt that Lily hadn't come to see me. I couldn't imagine not being the first one out of the clubhouse doors the minute she arrived if the roles were reversed. Even the thought of something bad happening to her made me panicky. In the early days in San Diego, I'd let the anxiety of not being there if she needed me swirl around in my brain until it was nearly debilitating, and I'd had to find out ways to cope so that my thoughts wouldn't even go there. I'd gotten the fear under control until the last time I was home, when she'd been caught in a house fire. I'd been one of the first people at the hospital then, so frantic to make sure she was okay that I'd parked behind the ambulance and they'd towed my rental car. The never-ending fear cycle had started up all over again when I'd gone back to California. It was a nightmare.

So, the fact that she'd refused to even pretend to care whether or not I was home safe made nausea burn in my stomach. Did she really still hate me that much? Even after I'd apologized and tried to make things right? I'd barely spoken to her outside the holidays when my parents passed the phone around when I called, but I thought we'd figured things out the last time I'd seen her.

"Shh," Mark said, his hand running soothingly over the back of my head. "It's okay, baby. Shh. You're gonna make yourself sick."

He shushed me over and over again, but he never let go or stopped running his hand over my hair until I'd cried myself out.

"I'm done," I finally rasped out just as Olive began to stir. I wiped at my face as I pulled out of his arms.

"Hey," he said, catching me before I could turn away. His hand cupped my cheek as our eyes met. "Everyone's done shit they're not proud of, Cec. Give yourself some grace, yeah?"

"I'll try," I replied.

He huffed. "Good enough." Leaning down, he pressed his lips softly against mine. "I'm gonna go get our stuff out of the truck. You need anything while I'm out there?"

"Could you grab me some water?" I asked.

"Of course. Be right back." After stealing another kiss, he left the room.

Turning to Olive, I sighed. I hated that everything about her first month of life was being overshadowed by the monster stalking us. Even introducing her to my family felt strange. I wasn't ready to show her off, comfortable in our surroundings and sure of our welcome. Even with the older crowd welcoming me back warmly, I still felt like an interloper.

I also wondered if she'd feel like she was cursed when she was finally old enough to learn about this time in her life—the same way I'd felt cursed when I'd learned about being kidnapped as a baby. I hoped not.

It took having Olive to realize that what had happened to me, Cam, and my mom as a kid just sucked. There was no rhyme or reason for it—just a douchebag with a grudge. Somehow, I'd have to make that clear to Olive, too.

"How you doing, sweet thing?" I cooed, leaning over the bed to stare into her slate gray eyes. "Are you getting hungry?"

She answered me with flailing fists, and I couldn't help but grin. Even with everything happening around us, she was like sunlight chasing away the clouds. It was a miracle that I'd grown something so perfect. I couldn't even keep plants alive, and yet here she was, strong and healthy and getting bigger every day. Even if I got nothing else right for the rest of my life, I was suddenly certain that this was one arena in which I would excel. I wouldn't allow myself to fail.

"Jesus," Mark mumbled as he came in the room a few minutes later. "Seeing you with her is like a punch to the chest."

"I'm not even sure how to respond to that," I replied, taking the diaper bag out of his hand.

"You don't need to respond," he said, rubbing his sternum. "I'll just have to get used to it."

"You're a big softy," I said quietly, turning back to the baby.

"Only when it comes to you," he said, stepping in behind me so he could kiss the back of my neck.

"You know I can't have sex, right?" I blurted, refusing to look at him as I changed Olive's diaper. "Not for another month—at least."

Mark's hand tightened on my hip before letting go.

"Where'd that come from?" he asked, moving across the room to drop the rest of the bags on the floor.

"You're being sweet," I replied. I lifted Olive into my arms and turned. "And you were saying all of that stuff in the truck."

Mark scoffed. "Cecilia, even if you were all healed up and wet as a rainstorm, I wouldn't fuck you tonight."

I jerked in surprise.

"You're dealin' with a lot of shit right now. It's not the time to start any of that."

"Then why are we sharing a room?" I asked, both relieved and slightly humiliated. A part of me understood what he was saying, but my pride wanted to tell him that I wouldn't have sex with him *ever*.

He looked at me like I was stupid. "I'm not sleepin' without you," he said simply.

"That makes absolutely no sense," I argued as Olive began to fuss.

"You want me out?"

"I never said that," I replied mutinously. Olive started to cry in earnest, her mouth gaping like a little fish.

"What is your problem?" he snapped.

"*What's your problem?*" I snapped back.

"Jesus Christ," he said over the noise. "Fuckin' feed her already."

"Don't tell me what to do," I spat, even as I sat down on the bed and lifted my shirt.

"I forgot about this," he said, shaking his head. "The bullshit fights that never ended because they were *bullshit*."

"You know where the door is," I said flatly as Olive began to nurse and the room got quiet.

"Yeah, I've already been through that door," he said, staring at me with his arms crossed over his chest. "Even with the bullshit, it's better in here."

His reply completely took the wind out of my sails. Well, shit.

"You wanna argue with me, fine," he said quietly. "You wanna take your shit out on me because your family is bein' assholes—do it. Nothin' I haven't dealt with before. But don't tell me to leave, Cec. You've only told me that once before, and I listened to you. That's not happening again."

"Fine," I muttered, even though my stomach gave a little flutter.

He sat down on the bed next to me and let out a long breath. "I want to lock us in here and fuck you for a week straight," he said evenly, though one glance at his hands tightened into fists indicated he wasn't as calm as he seemed. "But this was a big night for you. Shit, it's been a massive few weeks. We both know that the minute we fall into bed again, everything's gonna be so heightened and fucking intense that everything else will fade."

"Sounds nice," I replied, making him chuckle.

"Yeah, it does." He leaned over and kissed the side of my neck. "But you need to figure this shit out with your family, and I've still gotta make sure you and Ollie are safe."

"Do you think she'll ever be safe?" I asked, cupping her head in my hand. It was so small and fragile that I could see her pulse thrumming in her soft spot.

"Yeah, baby, I do. I'll make sure."

We sat quietly while Olive nursed, both of us watching her. It seemed inconceivable that anyone would want to hurt someone so innocent and new.

My eyes were drooping, and I was leaning heavily against Mark by the time Olive was finished. Honestly, even the thought of having to stand up to pull back the blankets so I could crawl in bed seemed like too much work. Mark laughed at me as I groaned.

"Come on," he said, helping me to my feet. He pulled the blankets down and helped me sit again before kneeling at my feet.

"What are you doing?" I asked tiredly.

"Takin' off your shoes," he replied, nodding at my feet.

Tears made my nose sting as I stared at him. It was such a simple gesture because he knew how tired I was, but it felt big. Really big. Down on one knee, big. Because if a guy that's been up just as long as you have, and is just as tired as you are, still takes the time to kneel down to remove the shoes that you could easily toe-off yourself—you've hit the jackpot.

"I still have to run to the bathroom," I cried, unable to stop my voice from wobbling.

"Aw, sweetheart," he said reaching up to wipe my tears away as he fought a smile.

"It's not because I have to go to the bathroom," I tried to explain through my blubbering as he got me back on my feet. "*You tried to take my shoes off.*"

"I know," he said, though he clearly had no idea what I was rambling on about.

After grabbing the diaper bag, I clenched my teeth and stiffened my spine while he escorted me to a bathroom I'd been in a million times before. If we ran into anyone, I wasn't going to let them see me losing my shit. I reminded myself of that as he gently took Olive from my arms and gave me a pat on the butt to get me moving. When I got out of the bathroom, he was holding a lamp in his free hand.

I looked at him curiously, but didn't say anything as we went back to the room. Then I almost lost it again when he laid Olive on the bed and plugged in the lamp, throwing a t-shirt over the shade to dim it, before turning off the bright overhead light.

Within minutes, I was back in bed, with Olive on one side of me—closest to the wall, and Mark on the other side, his body lined up perfectly with mine. For the first time in hours, I found myself relaxing.

"Mornin' is gonna come early," he murmured into my hair. "Turn that brain off and sleep."

"I'm trying," I replied in a whisper. "You got me a nightlight."

"You don't like the dark," he replied easily. Within seconds, his breathing had evened out and his arm around my waist relaxed as he fell asleep.

I knew that the next day was going to be pretty horrible, even if it went better than I was expecting. Seeing everyone and being surrounded by the people I'd left behind was going to be hard, no matter how it played out. It always was. Even knowing that, it wasn't long before I passed out, too, but before I did, I laced my fingers through his. Just to make sure that he'd be in the same position when I woke up.

Chapter 20

MARK

"WHY CAN'T WE be in there?" Eli asked, jerking his head toward the room behind the bar.

"Nobody goes in there," I muttered back tiredly.

"*They're* in there," he pointed out around the toothpick in his mouth.

Swear to God, he was needling me just because he could see how very uninterested I was in dealing with his shit. We were sitting in the empty main room of the clubhouse, waiting for Dragon and the boys to come back out and give us a rundown. I wasn't sure what exactly they had to discuss beforehand, but honestly, I didn't really give a shit unless it directly involved Cecilia. Olive had been up repeatedly throughout the morning, and me and Cec hadn't gotten much sleep. It hadn't helped that we'd gone to bed as the sun was coming up.

Forrest checked his watch. "They better get a move on, this place is gonna start fillin' up with women and kids at noon."

"I'm starving," Lu said, knocking her knuckles on the table. "I hate waiting on other people to get shit done."

"The wait'll be worth it," I told her with a sigh. "They go all out when everyone's here for a meal."

"This place is different from the club down in Sacramento," she replied. "More family oriented or something."

"You can thank Brenna for that," I said. "Callie and Farrah, too. They made it a family meeting place."

"Brotherhood's the same, though," Forrest said.

I nodded.

"I really wanna see inside that room," Eli said as the door behind the bar opened and the men filed out.

"Don't even think about it," I warned, shooting him a look. "At best, you'd have broken bones if you tried it."

"At worst?" he asked, grinning.

"You been waitin' long?" Dragon asked as he pulled up a chair at our table.

"Not long," I replied, hoping Eli would keep his mouth shut for once. I didn't worry about Lu and Forrest—they were like chameleons, they could read a room and blend in anywhere.

"First off, I wanna thank you for everything you've done," Dragon said seriously as the rest of the men found seats. I braced. If the next words that came out of his mouth were anything close to telling us to leave and let them handle the Free America Militia, we were going to have problems.

"Of course," I said, realizing that he was waiting for a reply.

"We don't usually bring outsiders in on shit that's happenin' with the club," Grease chimed in.

"I'm well aware," I replied flatly. Seriously, if they thought they were going to cut us out, shit was going to get nasty.

Grease's mouth curled up in amusement.

"With that said," Dragon murmured, "we realize that this is a different situation—not only because you came through in a big way for Casper. Hell, boy, we raised your ass. You can't trust your children, you ain't any kind of parent."

"Boys have been fillin' me in on what I missed while we were down south," Casper said. "I'm thinkin' that, while we were dealin' with the head of the snake down in California, they were dealin' with the rest of it up here."

I sat up straight as the implications of that sunk in.

"Mack and Rose were kidnapped by a couple of skinheads," Grease said darkly.

"Excuse the interruption," Forrest drawled, "but skinheads are a dime a dozen. What makes you think it's the same group, and not a couple'a good old boys with a flare for dramatics?"

"Two things," Casper said. "One, that Copper, a former brother and Rose's ex, is the one who hired them, and two, that FAM had some information on a shipment that they couldn't have gotten anywhere except from inside the club. The Free America Militia had an inside man up here, an inside man in Sacramento, and a random pair of skinheads kidnapped my niece and her man? No such thing as coincidence."

"Copper was your inside man up here?"

"Yes," Dragon said.

"How can you be sure?" Lu asked, staring at Dragon.

"We're sure," Grease replied firmly.

I shot Lu a look before she could say anything else. By Grease's tone and body language, Copper must've given them plenty of information—and it didn't matter how many times Lu asked, there wasn't a man in that room who would tell her how that had come about. There also wasn't any way that our team could interrogate him. The man was definitely already dead.

"From what Copper said, those boys he hired were low-level shitheads and the only people he was in contact with," Dragon continued.

"Do you know who the leak in Sacramento is?" I asked.

"Got some ideas," he replied enigmatically. "Nothin' concrete."

"Yet," Casper added.

"From what Casper said, you were thinkin' of goin' around the big man and usin' his group to take him down," Grease said. "Smart move."

"But that ain't gonna work for us," Dragon said. "Might make Cecilia safe, might not, but either way, it's not a long-term solution. Creatin' a power vacuum in a white supremacist group is askin' for more trouble."

"What do you propose?" I asked cautiously.

I knew in that moment that whatever they decided, I was in. As far as I was concerned, the less power the FAM had, the safer Cecilia and Olive would be. However, I didn't know that my team would be behind me. I couldn't blame them. We were venturing into dangerous territory with an outlaw motorcycle club, and while we'd all skirted the law for a greater good in the past, this was different. There was a level of immunity that working for a government contractor gave us, and we'd be completely without that cushion if something happened.

"We go to them," Cam said, speaking for the first time since they'd come into the room. "No more waiting for them to strike."

"Because they will," Grease said. "Sure as I'm sittin' here, once they realize we know that it's all connected—Cecilia, Rose and Mack, and Copper—they'll be on their way."

"How the fuck is it all connected?" Eli said, his face screwed up in confusion. He lifted his hand when Casper started to explain it again. "No, I get it. I see the connections. What I mean is, how the fuck did Cecilia somehow get caught up with this shit at the same time that you're dealing with those asshats up here? No coincidences, my ass. This is the weirdest shit I've ever heard, and I have a grandpa that's also my uncle."

Every man sitting at the table stared at him.

"His mother's mother married his father's brother," Lu said nonchalantly. "They're from a small town. It's not as incestuous as it sounds."

"And I thought we had a tangled family tree," Tommy said with a laugh.

"They knew where I was from," Cecilia said from the edge of the room, making most people in the group glance at her in surprise. Everyone knew we were in the middle of a sit-down, so they'd steered clear of the room. I wondered how long she'd been eavesdropping. I was actually impressed by her nerve—if Olive would've started fussing, it would've given them away instantly.

"Explain," Dragon said, waving her toward us.

I stood from my seat as she got closer and put out my hand. As soon as she'd laced her fingers through mine, I pulled her close.

"Thought I told you to stay in the bedroom?" I murmured into her ear.

"I thought you knew by now that I don't take orders from you?" she replied easily. She lifted her head and gave me a quick kiss right there in front of everyone before handing Olive to me and sitting down in my chair.

Lu must've noticed the stunned expression on my face, because she leaned over and drug a chair closer so I could sit. "Here, Chief," she said in amusement.

"Thanks." I dropped into it and, holding Olive against my chest with one arm, I laid the other across the back of Cec's seat.

"Cane Warren," Cecilia explained. "The head of the militia? He knew where I was from. Who my family is."

"He knew your pop was in the club?" Grease asked.

"Yeah," Cecilia replied, nodding. "It wasn't a secret. I mean, I didn't talk about it with Cane, but I'm sure I talked to his wife Liv about it. She was my friend for years, so of course it came up."

"What else you tell them?" Dragon asked. I could see that he was trying to keep his voice level, but the tension in the room had grown thick.

"That's it," Cecilia said with a shrug.

"You think it's smart to go around tellin' people that your pop's an

Ace, especially in San Diego?" Leo asked. It was the first thing he'd said to her since she got back, and she stiffened, which made me tense.

Cecilia's hand gripped my thigh before I could say anything.

"I wasn't out at the bar boasting about my daddy being in a motorcycle club," Cecilia said through her teeth. "Liv was one of my best friends, who I'd known for years. Our families came up a few times."

"From what I remember, once you were drunk, you weren't too careful about what you spread around the bar," Leo said, his voice flat.

I was on my feet before he'd finished speaking. The only thing that stopped me from hopping over the table was the baby in my arms.

"You ain't helpin'," Dragon barked at his son. "You got shit to say to Cecilia—you bring it up when we're not discussin' shit more important than your high school drama."

"Sit, baby," Cecilia said to me quietly, tugging on my belt loop.

"And I'd have a word with Lil before you do it," Casper said, staring Leo down. "Think she might have something to say about it."

I slowly lowered myself back down into my seat.

"So, they knew you were Casper's," Grease said.

"I didn't specify who my dad was," Cecilia said with a shrug. "But, I mean, we have the same last name, so it wouldn't be a jump to figure it out."

"'Specially with the last name Butler," Grease murmured, running a hand over his beard. "Been a number of years, but I'm bettin' those stories are still circulatin.'"

"What stories?" Will asked in surprise.

"Our uncles were notorious," Casper said dryly. "And so was your great grandmother."

"Gram?" Cecilia said in disbelief.

"Still waters," Grease said, his lips tipping up in a smile. "Your gram was a badass."

"Well, we knew that," Tommy said.

"I'd like to hear this story," Eli said, nodding his head. "But what does that have to do with what's goin' on now?"

"Could be nothin'," Dragon said. "Just tryin' to get all the information."

"You think Liv hooked up with you because she knew who you were?" Casper asked Cecilia gently.

She jerked back in surprise and paled. She was silent for a long moment, before shaking her head. "No." She shook her head again. "No, we met at work way before she got with Cane. That came later."

"Could he have been usin' her to get to you?"

"They were together for years. He was playing a really long game if that was the case," she replied.

"Did he hit on you?" Lu asked quietly. "Before or after he got with your friend?"

"No way," Cecilia said with a nervous laugh. "Never. It was always Liv. He worshipped her."

"Alright then," Dragon said. "We'll take your word for it."

"Even if he didn't plan it," Casper said, leaning back in his chair, "opportunity dropped in his lap."

"How so?" I asked.

"Well," Casper replied, "he's got his people up here, makin' friends with members and then stealin' from us, and he's got my daughter down there, close as he can get her, carrying his child."

Cecilia's face scrunched up in disgust. "Can we not phrase it that way? It makes it sound like I had sex with Cane." She shuddered.

"Sorry, Bumblebee," Casper said with a bark of laughter. "Still, we retaliated up here and he woulda had the perfect set up to fuck with you, and if you tried to fuck him over down there, he had the means to retaliate up here."

"Smart," Forrest said to himself with a huff.

"So, now what?" I asked. "The man's dead."

"Now we take care of the rest of 'em," Dragon said.

As the group tossed out ideas about how we'd take care of the Free America Militia, Olive woke up and started to squirm.

"I'm going to take her back to the room," Cecilia said as she took the baby from me. "You guys don't need me for this."

"Always need you," I teased quietly.

"Come find me when you're done," she said with a small smile. "I'll hopefully be the one napping."

"Lucky," I said, squeezing her hip as she stood. "You want me to wake you up when the food's ready?"

"Sure."

I watched her walk away until I couldn't see her anymore, and when I turned back to the table, I met Leo's eye. He wasn't glaring, but his expression wasn't exactly welcoming, either. Yeah, we were going to go rounds if he didn't get his shit straight. Out of respect for his dad and the grounds we were on, I'd never put a hand on him in the past—but I was just about at the end of my patience. If he didn't keep his mouth shut, I'd shut it for him.

"What do you think?" Dragon asked Casper, dragging my attention back into the conversation happening around me.

"If they don't get back to Woody's whiz kid today," Casper said, tilting his head to the side, "then a show of force would be the right way to go about it. Chances are, the son won't be there—but we can make it clear that we're watching them."

"You think it'll matter?" Cam asked.

"I think that they believe they're flyin' under the radar at this point, and it would be in our best interest to let them know they aren't."

"Wouldn't it be better to let them go on believin' it, and let them come to us?" Tommy asked.

"It would," Grease said, "if they lived by the same set of rules that we do—they don't. They've already come after your sister and your cousin. Don't know who they'd fuck with next, and don't wanna find out. I'm ready to put a stop to this bullshit now."

"And let 'em know that if one of our kids falls off their fuckin' bike, their heads will roll for it," Dragon said firmly.

"I bet the militia will send thousands of feet of gymnastics mats if that's the way they word it," Eli whispered to Lu, making her grin.

"You'll let us know when your man calls?" Dragon asked me.

I nodded. "Of course."

"Alright," he said. He glanced up and over my shoulder. "Perfect timing, where are my grandsons?"

I looked behind me at Trix, who was pushing through the doorway with a big platter in her arms.

"They're out front waiting for the girls," she replied, rolling her eyes. "Rose and Mack were right behind me."

"I'm gonna go hide out in my room so I don't get pulled into helping with breakfast," Lu said, elbowing me in the side.

"Coward," I said as I got to my feet.

"I don't do that female bonding shit," she said, standing up. "If they were going to grab a beer, I'd be down. I'm not cooking for a big group of men."

"Is that feminism?" Eli asked, cocking his head to the side. "I can't tell if it's feminism or bitchy-ism."

"It's self-preservation," Lu said, shoving him away from her. "I'm not taking the chance of killing one of these guys with my cooking."

"You're not that bad," Forrest said, fooling none of us.

"Woody," Casper said, rounding the table as the group dispersed. "Keep it locked down until this shit is over, yeah?"

I didn't have to ask what he was talking about. "You realize I'm not the only one you should have to say that to, right? Where the fuck is Cam in all that? Or her cousins? Or you, *her father*? Why am I the only one that wants to knock his teeth down his throat?"

"Think we just hide it better than you do," he replied, his lips twitching.

"Doubt it," I shot back. "Leo better keep his fuckin' distance."

"If Rose is here, then Lily isn't far behind," Casper said with a slap to my shoulder. "She'll keep him in line."

"Right," I said with a scoff.

"Hey, Casper?" Forrest said. "Josiah and Ephraim are in town with Cecilia's stuff, you think we should get a storage unit, or you guys got some place to put it?"

Lu smiled at Forrest, knowing just like I did, that he'd chosen that moment to bring it up because he was trying to smooth shit over, and not because the boys were in any kind of rush to unload the truck.

"Nah," Casper said. "No use wastin' money on a storage unit. I've got room in my garage—we can put it there. Let your boys know we've got food on, and afterward, we can head out to our place."

"Sounds good."

"Why do you look like someone just kicked your puppy?" Eli asked, throwing his arm around my shoulder as Casper was called across the room.

"The fuck are you talkin' about?"

"You don't want to go to Casper's place?" he asked, holding tight to my shoulders as I tried to shrug him off. "I do. I have *got* to see where a man like that lives."

"It's a fuckin' house, Eli," I said, succeeding in getting him to let go of me. "It's white and it's old and it's got a big front porch."

"Oh, yeah? Huh." He looked over at Casper. "Seems alright. Why don't you want to go there?"

"Leave it," Forrest ordered Eli. "Go call the boys, would you? Tell 'em to get over here."

"Fine," Eli said with a sigh. "Though I hope you realize that means less food for us."

"He's in fine form today," Forrest said as we watched Eli leave the room.

"It's 'cause we haven't had shit to do," I replied. "Boredom is kicking in."

"Yup. God, I can't imagine livin' with that guy. You think anyone will ever marry him? How the fuck would she handle the day to day monotony?"

"Earplugs?" I joked.

"I'm gonna go ask if the ladies need any help," Forrest said, scratching at his beard as he smiled ruefully. "And after they kick me out of the kitchen, I'm gonna take a shower."

"I'm gonna lay down with Cecilia," I replied. "Wake us before the food's gone?"

"You got it," he said with a nod. "She's good for you, you know? Puts you off your game a bit—makes you human."

"Yeah, I know," I mumbled as I left him. "See you in a bit."

I waved at Poet as he came in the front door, but I didn't slow down as I made my way back to our room. Suddenly, I couldn't get back there fast enough. I had a feeling that it wouldn't be long before everyone was ready to eat, and I wasn't going to get any sleep, but I craved the feeling of being wrapped up under the covers with Cec. If FAM didn't get back to Wilson by the end of the day, shit was going to get messy tomorrow, and I *needed* the calm before the storm.

"Hey," Cecilia whispered groggily as I entered the room, unbuckling my belt. "Is it already time to eat?"

"No," I whispered back, stripping out of my clothes. "Thought I'd come lay with you for a bit."

"Oh, okay," she said with a sleepy smile over her shoulder. "Hopefully, it takes them a while."

"We have at least half an hour," I replied as I slid in behind her. "Go back to sleep."

She relaxed into me as I wrapped around her waist, but stayed awake. Eventually, she sighed.

"I can't wait for all of this to be over," she breathed, her voice so low I barely heard her.

"I know," I replied kissing the back of her head. "Soon, baby."

"Do you really think Cane was using me to get at the club?" she asked.

I thought about it before I answered. I wasn't going to lie to her, but I also didn't want to make the whole situation even worse than it already was. Cecilia carried more guilt than anyone I'd ever met. Half of the shit she felt guilty about had nothing to do with her—I wasn't going to add to that unnecessarily.

"I think that he saw an opportunity and took it," I said finally. "I don't think he was using you to get to the club. Honestly, from what you've said about him and how he felt about your friend, I'm guessing that he figured the club was insurance to make sure you didn't screw them over."

"I wouldn't have," she said thickly. "I wouldn't have agreed to carry Olive for them if I—" She stopped and swallowed. "I gave up an entire year of my life to help them."

"I know you did," I said, tightening my arm around her waist. "But men like that—especially rich ones—see enemies everywhere, even if they look like friends."

"I wonder if Liv knew."

"I doubt it," I replied. I guess I *was* going to lie. I would've bet my left nut that her friend had known exactly what her husband was up to. She'd just been so desperate for a baby that she'd fed into the illusion that they had to have leverage on Cecilia to keep her honest.

"Talked to your dad," I said, changing the subject. "After breakfast, we're gonna put the stuff from your condo in his garage. Siah and Eph are coming for breakfast, and we'll head over after that."

"You don't have to do that," she said, turning carefully so we were face to face. "Let the rest of the guys do it."

"I don't mind goin' over there," I replied.

"Bullshit," she shot back. "You don't like being there any more than I do."

I huffed as I got comfortable, folding my pillow in half to prop up my head. "It's not my favorite place in the world, but I've been to worse ones," I conceded. "It's not like we'll be there long. Just unloading the truck."

"I'm going with you," she said firmly.

"Stay here and rest," I argued. "Let the ladies watch Olive so you can get some real sleep."

"I don't want real sleep—" Her words cut off as she realized how ridiculous she sounded. "I want to go with you," she said instead. "Plus, I need some of my stuff. Clothes and shoes, at least."

"Fine," I said, brushing her hair back from her face. "But I think Olive should stay here."

"Do you think something's going to happen at my parent's house?" she asked, leaning up a little in alarm.

"No," I replied, running my hand along her back until she settled back in. "But if something did, she'd be safer at the clubhouse."

"Yeah, you're right," she said with a sigh. We lay there quietly for a while, just breathing the same air, and I felt something inside me settle for the first time in years.

"Hey, you have a new scar right here," she said softly, running her finger under my chin. "I didn't notice it before now because your beard covers it."

"Got a lot of new scars," I said with a laugh. "That one's from a fist fight." I closed my eyes as she ran her fingers down the front of my neck. "Fucker wore a ring the size of Texas."

"Ew," she said. "Any man that wears a ring other than his wedding band is afraid that any punch he throws won't be hard enough to do the job."

I laughed and opened my eyes. "Where'd you hear that?"

"My mother," she said with a chuckle. "Probably true, though."

"I've seen the rings your dad wears," I pointed out.

"He didn't wear them for a week after she said it," Cecilia replied, giggling. "Until he realized she was just fucking with him because some woman had hit on him, not noticing his wedding ring."

"He should've known that already," I said dryly.

"You'd think so, wouldn't you?" she said as her laughter faded. "Now that I think about it—he probably did it to needle her back—she loves his rings."

"That sounds familiar," I said. "Remember when you gave me shit for wearing basketball shorts to pick you up after school?"

She wrinkled her nose at the memory. "You looked like a fucking snack that day," she said grumpily. "I didn't like all the other girls looking at you."

"So I stopped wearing them," I said, shrugging.

"Until I asked why you weren't," she said, realization dawning as her eyes widened. "You punk!"

I chuckled as she poked me in the chest.

"Hey," I joked. "Careful, I'm injured."

Cecilia grimaced. "Does it hurt?" she asked, smoothing her hand gently over the bandage at the top of my shoulder.

"Nah, I'm just teasing you," I said, pulling her tighter against me. "It's barely a twinge anymore."

"You've barely even mentioned it," she said softly. "I'm sorry. With everything else, I just—"

"Hey, stop it," I ordered. "It's nothin.' Promise. Forrest has kept an eye on it, it's not a big deal."

"You were shot," she said flatly.

"Wasn't the first time," I replied. "This one's nothin' compared to the others."

I regretted the words immediately when Cecilia flinched.

"Wrong place at the wrong time," I said softly, leaning forward to kiss the tip of her nose.

"You were there because I'd set you up with a tent and food," she said, emotionless. "You wouldn't have been there if I'd told you to go home and deal with your mom."

"You thought you could boss me back then?" I replied in disbelief. "Cec, if you hadn't fed me, I'da just grabbed food somewhere else. Still woulda camped out there."

"Bullshit," she said with little heat. "You were there because of me."

"And you couldn't have convinced me to be anywhere else," I replied firmly. "Jesus Christ, why do you have to take everything on your shoulders? I thought we'd talked this out years ago."

"Just because I stopped arguing didn't mean I agreed with you," she said. "I just didn't want to argue about it anymore."

"None of that shit was your fault," I said, raising my voice slightly. "Not a single goddamn thing."

"Well, I remember it differently," she snapped back.

"Well, your memory is bullshit and you know it. When are you gonna let it all go, baby? Fuck."

"I'm not."

"Cecilia," I said, grabbing her chin as she tried to turn away. "It was *my* decision. Mine. I coulda stayed with Poet and Amy and they woulda smoothed shit over with my mom, and I *knew* that. I chose to camp out on the back of the property because I didn't want my mom to know where I was. I was an asshole kid, and I was trying to punish her."

"I helped you do it."

"Sometimes back then, sweetheart, seeing you was the only thing I had to look forward to," I whispered, pressing my forehead against hers.

"If you woulda taken that away? No. You didn't do anything wrong. Not a single fuckin' thing."

"Maybe we're just toxic together," she said softly, her voice wobbling. "Maybe the universe just keeps telling us to stay away from each other. Look at everything that's happened up to this point."

"No," I argued. "Look at all the shit we've survived to this point."

"I'm terrified," she whispered tearfully.

"Jesus, me, too," I replied honestly. "I don't know what the hell I'd do if somethin' happened to you or Olive. I'm gonna make sure nothin' does."

"I—I know you are" her voice caught, and she stopped to clear it. "Before, I knew that you were out in the world somewhere, even if you weren't with me. I can't imagine a world where you aren't in it… especially if I'm the reason. I don't think I could survive that."

"I'm not goin' anywhere," I replied. "I'm good at what I do, baby. You just gotta trust that."

"I'll try," she replied.

"I hate it when you say that," I said, making her laugh a little. "We're gonna figure this out and then we're gonna figure *us* out, alright? One thing at a time."

"First thing is breakfast," she said with a sigh, as the noise outside our room got louder. "Sounds like everyone is here."

"You ready?" I asked.

"Yeah," she replied. "Just need to do my makeup."

I grinned.

Chapter 21

CECILIA

IGNORING THE WAY Mark watched me from the bed, I carefully ran liquid eyeliner across my lash line. Foundation, powder, blush, highlighter, bronzer, brow powder, eyeshadow and liner, mascara and finally, lipstick. I could've followed the steps in my sleep, but repeating them as I stared into the small compact mirror centered me.

"You don't need all that, you know," he said, reaching out to run his finger down my spine.

"It makes me look like myself," I said simply as I put the eyeliner away.

A knock interrupted him as he opened his mouth to speak. "Yeah?" he called out quietly.

"Food's on," Forrest said as he opened the door. His eyes widened when turned. "Damn, woman," he said, whistling appreciatively.

"Put your tongue back inside your mouth," Mark told him dryly.

Forrest grinned and laughed uncomfortably. "Excuse me, ma'am," he apologized. "You're always beautiful. Just surprised me is all."

"Don't call me ma'am," I said, turning back to my mirror. "And thank you—there's only so much I can do when the only clothes I have are sweats."

"Don't think the clothes much matter," he replied.

"Yeah, we get it," Mark said, chuckling as he sat up in bed.

"Glad I showered," Forrest said. I glanced at him in the mirror as he gestured toward me. "Didn't know we were gussying up for brunch."

Mark lifted his arm and sniffed his pit. "Eh, I'll do."

"That's disgusting," I said, trying to keep a straight face as I applied mascara.

"What?" Mark asked innocently. He sniffed his armpit again. "I smell fine. Here—"

"I'm not going to smell your pits," I replied, scrambling across the floor as he leaned toward me. I laughed as he wiggled his eyebrows up and down.

"There's a lot of people out there," Forrest said, leaning against the doorjamb. "Kids all over the place."

The words should have ramped up my anxiety, but they didn't, and I smiled to myself as I tossed the mascara back in my bag. Mark's little armpit sniff had done its job distracting me. A quick swipe of red lipstick and I was done.

"I'm going to get Olive dressed and then we're ready," I told Forrest.

She was lying quietly on the bed, her eyes unfocused and her binky bouncing a little every time she sucked on it.

"Hey, you," I said softly. Kneeling next to Mark, I pulled her slowly toward me. "You ready to party?"

"She's in a good mood," Mark said.

"Thank God," I said as I started stripping her down. "All I need is a crying baby to top off the coming-home-with-a-killer-chasing-me shit sundae."

Forrest choked out a laugh. "They seem like they're glad you're here," he said, the words coming out questioningly.

"The oldies are," I replied as I worked. "They like all the chicks in the nest, especially if shit's going down. It's not them I'm talking about."

"Family politics?" Forrest asked.

"Something like that."

"Neither of us were crowd favorites when we left," Mark said in amusement.

"Oh, please," I argued as I dressed Olive. "They liked you fine. The only reason they would've been pissed was because you left *me*, and since there's no love lost there—they didn't care."

I paused as Mark's hand wrapped around the bottom of my jaw, turning my head gently toward him.

"You're wrong about that," he said, his thumb smoothing over my skin.

"I guess we'll see," I replied with a shrug.

Lifting Olive, I got to my feet and ran my hand through my hair, tousling it. "I'm ready."

"Seriously, woman," Forrest said, shaking his head. "*Damn.*"

"Seriously, Forrest," Mark said. "Shut the fuck up." He was grinning.

My confidence boosted by Forrest's words and the look in Mark's eyes, I scooted past the man in the doorway and led them toward the main room of the clubhouse.

Makeup had never made me feel pretty—or at least not any prettier than I was without it. It was just window dressing, like wearing a dress instead of sweats. Instead, each step of the makeup process made me feel braver. Strong. Prepared. It was armor, and it was fully intact as I stepped into the room full of people sitting at tables and filling their plates with food from the row of platters on the bar top.

"Steady," Mark murmured in my ear as he threw his arm over my shoulders and kissed the side of my head. "Anybody gives you shit, just remember I'm right behind you… staring at your ass in those pants. Mmm."

I laughed and elbowed him in the side as he led me across the room.

"CeeCee!" a young voice squealed.

Turning toward the sound, I grinned as my baby sister Charlie threaded through the tables toward me.

"Hey," I said as she threw her arms around me, careful of Olive as she laid her head on my shoulder. "I missed you, kid."

"I didn't know you were coming!" she said, leaning back. "You had a *baby*?"

"I did," I said with a chuckle.

"What the fuck?" she asked, her face screwed up in confusion. "Did Mom and Dad know?"

"She's definitely your sister," Mark said, trying to hide his laugh with a cough.

"No, they didn't," I replied to Charlie. "Surprise."

"Oh, man," she said, grimacing. "Is this the dad?"

I rolled my lips inward to keep from giggling. Mark was right, she reminded me a lot of me at her age.

"No, he's not."

"But he's your boyfriend, right?" she asked out of the side of her mouth. "He's got his hands all over you. *He* knows he's not the dad, right?"

"I'm aware," Mark said dryly. "And if I hadn't been, the cat would've been out of the bag now."

Charlie snorted.

"You remember Mark, right?" I said, gesturing to him. "I know he's been back to visit a few times."

"We've probably met," she said with a shrug.

"It's been a few years," Mark said. "Good to see you, Charlie."

"Well, he clearly remembers me," she said, raising an eyebrow.

"Oh, for fuck's sake," Mark mumbled. "You look exactly like your sister, so yeah, I could pick you out of a crowd."

Charlie cocked her head to the side. "Eh, I don't see it."

"Stop bein' a pain in the ass," my dad said, pulling on Charlie's ponytail. "You and Cecilia both look just like your mother, and you know it."

"Hey, Dad," I greeted.

"Hey, sweetheart. You get some sleep?" he asked, putting his hand gently on Olive's back.

"A little."

"Well, bring Olive to me later. She can hang with Papa so you can get a nap."

"Aren't you guys going to the house to unload the truck?" I asked, ignoring the sight of my cousin Rose at the corner of my eye. I couldn't tell if she was looking at me, so I deliberately kept my eyes averted.

"Where we going?" Cam asked as he joined our little huddle.

"CeeCee's stuff is here," my dad answered. "We're gonna put it in the garage at the house."

"Oh, cool. Let me know when you're leavin.'" Cam looked down at Charlie. "You seen the boys?"

"Yeah." She looked at me. "You're staying for a while right?"

"Yep."

"Cool, I'll see you later." She turned to Cam. "They're eating outside with Reb and Kara," Charlie said as they walked away.

"It's pissin' rain," Cam replied.

I didn't hear what Charlie said back, but it made Cam shake with laughter.

"I thought the youngest would be the easiest," my dad said, jerking his head toward my brother and sister. "Apparently, it doesn't work that way."

"You can't improve on perfection," I said with a wide smile and a tiny curtsy.

Dad laughed. "You two go get some food," he said, shaking his head. "We're gonna head out in half an hour."

"Sounds good," Mark replied.

We made our way over to the mostly deserted bar and stood behind my cousin Tommy's wife Heather while she stared at a platter of pancakes.

After waiting for a while, Mark cleared his throat. "Uh, you need some help?"

Heather jumped and turned toward us, her face pale. "No," she said, backing up a step. "No, I'm not hungry." She let out a breath of air like she was blowing out a candle. "Thanks, though. It's good to see you back home," Heather said to me, trying and failing to smile. "It's been a while."

"Yeah, how's your house? Almost finished?" I asked as Mark lifted two plates and started filling them with food.

"Pretty much," Heather said, rolling her eyes. "Just cosmetic stuff left. Tommy insists on doing everything with cash, so we're still missing some trim and shit like that."

"That's awesome. I know you guys have been working on it forever."

"You should come see it while you're here," she said, exhaling through her lips again. "We'll have dinner or something."

"Sounds good—"

"Sorry," she blurted, cutting me off as she strode quickly out of the room.

"Congratulations," I said under my breath as I turned toward Mark.

"Not so bad, right?" he asked, glancing at me. "But she must've had a rough night." He laughed.

I shook my head. "Pregnant," I said quietly.

"Really?" he looked in the direction Heather had gone. "How could you tell?"

"I know the signs," I replied dryly, grabbing us some silverware. "She didn't even mention Olive, and everyone coos at babies unless they're deliberately trying not to. Plus, if it was a hangover, she'd look haggard and be drinking a Bloody Mary. Hair of the dog, and all that."

"I'll take your word for it," he said. "You want fruit?"

"Yes, please," I replied. "I wonder if Tommy knows?"

"If he did, everyone would," Mark said in amusement. "He'd be shouting it from the rooftops."

"Or *he'd* be the one puking," I joked.

"Yeah, I can see that." He grabbed our plates and turned toward the tables. "Where you wanna sit?"

Turning with him, I took a deep breath. My brother and Trix were sitting on a couch in the corner with Will and Molly on the opposite couch and as I watched, Tommy crawled over the back of Will and Molly's couch and planted himself between them. Poet was making the rounds, carrying a cup of coffee. Amy sat at a table with Dragon, Brenna, and my Aunt Callie sitting on my Uncle Grease's lap. My parents were sitting with Lily, Leo, and Leo's son. I swallowed hard as I scanned the rest of the room full of people, jumping over Rose's table without looking too closely.

"Come on," Mark said when I didn't answer.

I followed him to one of the closest tables, sitting down next to Lu.

"You've been hangin' with me for weeks," she said in surprise. "Don't you want to—" she gestured to the rest of the room.

"Not especially," I said under my breath. I looked up as Mark set my plate in front of me. "Thank you," I said, tipping my head back to meet his eyes. He gave the back of my neck a squeeze and rounded the table.

"This is so much better than continental breakfast," Ephraim said, digging into his food. He looked up and grinned. "Good to see you guys in one piece."

"Thanks for driving my stuff up," I replied, looking from him to Josiah.

"No problem," Josiah replied for both of them, big hands wrapped around a cup of coffee. He sniffed it appreciatively. "Worth it for this right here."

"Right?" Forrest said, nodding. "I need to see who made it and what they put in it."

"Cinnamon?" Josiah asked.

"Could be," Forrest replied, lifting his own cup to take a drink.

"Girl," Lu said, dragging the word out as she looked at me. "You brought your A-game today."

"What?" I asked, shaking off the feeling of someone watching me. They probably were. So what?

"Makeup," Lu said. "Looks good."

"Oh, thanks."

"You put on makeup?" Eli asked, tilting his head as he stared at me. "Why?"

"Why'd you put all that product in your hair?" Lu snapped back. "Mind your business."

"I don't have product in my hair," Eli said in confusion as Lu turned back to me.

"The guy could tell you every bra size in this room," she said to me, shaking her head. "But the subtleties of makeup are lost on him." Lu bumped her shoulder against mine. "Families are hard, man," she said. "Especially ones that are this big."

"Not all of them are family," I said as I adjusted the way I was holding Olive so I could eat. "I barely know some of them."

"Like *four* of them aren't family," she joked. "Your family tree's a spiderweb with this club at the center."

"You're not wrong," I replied, as I forced myself to take a bite. I should've spoken to Lily before I sat down to eat, now I wouldn't be able to think of anything else until I did. Ripping off the Band-Aid would be a lot less painful all at once, and I was more aware than anyone how awkward it was that I hadn't said hello to everyone.

After a few minutes of halfheartedly picking at my food, Mark tossed his napkin on his empty plate and stood. "Come on, Cec," he said, putting his hand out to me. "This is getting' painful to watch."

"Thank God," Forrest said, shoveling a huge bite of potatoes into his mouth. "She was givin' *me* a nervous stomach."

I got up without argument and let him lead me through the tables.

"There she is," my mom said, wiggling her hands in a give-me motion. "Have you eaten? I can hold her while you get some food."

"We got some," I said as I handed Olive off. I braced myself as I turned to Lily.

"Hey, little sister," I said softly.

"It took you long enough to come over here," she said, jumping to her feet. "Jesus, it's like I have the plague or something."

I let out the breath I'd been holding as she wrapped her arms around my waist and pulled me into an awkward hug.

"Missed you," I said, leaning my head against hers.

"Missed you, too," she replied, letting me go. "Back to cause trouble, huh?"

The words were offhand. Her tone and body language were easy and friendly. Everyone *knew* it was a joke.

But I still felt my hands curling into fists and my spine stiffening. "No use coming back otherwise," I replied, my tone and manner just as easy as hers.

Except, suddenly, the entire feel of the table changed.

"Let's just *not*," Rose called out from her place at the next table. "I'm too fuckin' tired to deal with it."

"Not sure what you have to deal with besides your boyfriend's wrecked leg," I said back, meeting her eyes.

"Yeah, say thanks to your baby daddy for that," she said drolly, leaning back in her seat.

"Baby," Mark said in warning, his hand fisting in the back of my shirt.

"That's enough, Rose," my mom said.

"You've got to be kidding me," I spat, looking at Rose. "From what I understand, your ex is the reason your boyfriend's walking with a limp. At least your taste has improved, but hey, it couldn't have gotten any worse, right?"

She was on her feet before the words had even left my mouth.

"Sit your ass down," Grease ordered, pointing at his daughter. "Jesus Christ, it's like you're in high school again."

"Maybe you should head back to San Diego and deal with your own shit," Rose said as she dropped back into her seat. "Looks like you've got your old bodyguard back anyway. Hey, Mouth."

I could take the way she was looking at me, the way she felt the need to chime in when I was trying to talk to my sister, even her bullshit about Olive's father—but the way she'd looked at Mark and said the nickname that Leo had used to make fun of him when we were kids—put me right over the edge.

"Jealousy is a stinky cologne, Rose," I said, glancing at Olive. "You should try to cover that up with something."

Her face paled as she stared at me, and even though she didn't say anything back—I didn't feel any satisfaction. I never did after I'd finished verbally sparring with my family. The only thing I felt was relief that it had ended, and guilt about what I'd said.

Rose and Mack had broken up before they were kidnapped because he refused to have any more kids. As far as I knew, that was the only reason they'd been apart—and I'd just used that information that I shouldn't have known in a way that I knew would shut her up.

"CeeCee," Lily said, sitting back down beside Leo, "for fuck's sake."

I was strung so tightly that I couldn't even respond. I hated that I'd lost control of my temper so easily. That I'd let Rose goad me into snapping back at her.

"It never fucking ends, does it?" my mom asked tiredly as she got to her feet and handed me Olive. "Just stay away from her while you're here, alright?"

She walked away from us and I looked to my dad, who got up to follow her. He just raised an eyebrow as he passed me. I ignored the pang of guilt I felt as they walked away. I shouldn't have used information my mom told me in confidence about Rose, especially when everyone knew my mom was the only one who would've told me about it.

"You know," Leo said conversationally, leaning back in his chair. "You'd think you'd be a little nicer when you're asking people for help."

"I didn't ask her for shit," I shot back. "And I didn't ask you, either."

"No, I guess you didn't have to ask," he replied. "You didn't have to, because you know if you call crying to your pop, you've got the whole club behind you no matter what."

"Stop," Lily said, reaching out to grab Leo's thigh.

"Fuck you, Leo," I replied through my teeth.

"Our son is sitting *right* here," Lily shot back. "That's *enough*. I'm glad you're here, but maybe we can catch up later, okay?"

"Come on," Mark said, tugging me away.

"I want to go back to the room," I said quietly as he led me through the tables. I refused to cry in front of everyone and I could feel the tears stinging the back of my nose.

As soon as Mark had closed the bedroom door behind us, I spun to face him. "What the fuck?" I said, my voice shaking. "Seriously. What the fuck? This is why I didn't want to come back here. This is exactly why."

"You held your own," he said crossing his arms over his chest. "Breathe, baby."

"Fucking *Rose*," I gritted out. "I couldn't get one fucking conversation with my sister, not even one, without her snarky ass commentary."

"It's like instinct for her," he said calmly. "You know that. It's always been that way. The minute she thinks Lily's in trouble, she steps in."

"In trouble from me?" I said, pointing at myself. "Me. Her sister."

"Didn't say it was logical," he replied.

"And Leo," I hissed.

"Let's leave that one for now," he said grimly.

"What?" I paused in my ranting to meet his eyes.

"You were holdin' your own," he replied. "So I didn't knock his teeth down his throat—but it was a close thing. So, baby, I'll stand here all day and listen to you get this shit off your chest, but I'd rather leave the Leo conversation for a different time. When he's not within walkin' distance."

My lips twitched. "You wanted to knock his teeth down his throat?" I said, raising my eyebrows.

"The fact that he's breathin' your air makes me want to do that," Mark grumbled. "That shit he was sayin' just intensified the urge."

"I hate it here," I said with a sigh.

"It'll calm down," he reassured me. "Give it some time."

Olive started to fuss, so I dropped onto the bed and pulled my t-shirt up to nurse, glad for the distraction as my heart rate finally started to slow down.

"What was that jealousy shit about?" Mark asked, laying down beside me.

I grimaced. "Rose's boyfriend refused to have kids—which is why they broke up. They must be back together now."

"Cec," he groaned.

"I know, okay?" I said defensively. "She shouldn't have called you Mouth."

"That's why you said it?" he asked, leaning up on his elbow.

"She can fuck with me all she wants, but she's sure as hell not going to fuck with you," I replied flatly.

Mark chuckled. "That name stopped bothering me a long ass time ago," he said, patting my leg. "Right about the time I realized just how much you liked my mouth."

Chapter 22

MARK

Cecilia grinned at me slyly, and just as I rose up to kiss her, my phone rang.

"Fuck," I muttered, pulling it out of my pocket. I glanced at the screen. "I gotta get this."

I stood from the bed and kissed Cec on the top of her head as I answered.

"What's up?" I asked, walking toward the door.

Most of the time, I wouldn't care if Cecilia sat on my lap with her ear pressed to the phone—but the fact that Wilson was calling me so soon after Forrest had heard from him made the hair on the back of my neck stand up.

"Warren's phone was shut off," Wilson replied in frustration. "It was like two hours man—that's it."

"And you didn't say somethin'?" I barked, striding down the hallway.

"It was two fucking hours," he ground out.

"And?"

"He must have a goddamn helicopter," Wilson said grimly. "Because he is currently in Eugene."

I came to a stop with my hand on the door leading to the field behind the clubhouse. "Say again?"

"Drake Warren's cell phone is in Eugene, according to the GPS coordinates I just uploaded."

My mind raced. How close was he? I glanced back at the room where I'd left Cecilia and Olive. "You got anything more precise?"

"With the technology at my disposal, that's not possible," Wilson replied. "Shit, Chief," he said, his words coming out far more informal than usual, making him sound like the kid he was. "I fucked up."

"Call Forrest and fill him in on the particulars," I said, spinning on my heel and striding back toward the center of the club. I didn't have it in me to offer him absolution—not when the devil was knocking on our goddamn door.

I found Casper and Dragon standing at the bar. As soon as I got close, their conversation stopped, and both men looked up in surprise when I joined them.

"Warren's in Eugene," I ground out.

"Course he is," Dragon said, watching me closely. "You surprised by this?"

"Warning would have been nice," I replied.

Casper chuckled. "Yeah, man, it always is." He slapped me on the shoulder. "You've been spoiled with gadgets and backup too long. Welcome back to reality, where fuckers jump outta the shadows."

"We planned for this," Dragon said calmly.

"We plan for everything," Casper added. "But knowing he's here now, we can adapt a bit. Here's what I'm thinking—"

The longer I stood with them, listening to Casper as he laid out the plan for the day, the more my shoulders relaxed. They really did try to plan for all contingencies. All that calm disappeared in an instant when Casper said Cecilia's name.

"You want to what?" I barked.

"She's gotta come with us," Casper said. "Highly visible."

"No," I replied.

"You think I'm happy about this?" he shot back. "You think I'd ever put one'a my kids in danger? This is the only way to draw them away from the club. They don't need to take any of us out—at least not at this point. He's after CeeCee and Olive, and for this to work, he's gotta think that he's got a chance to get one of them."

"We risk the chance of them tryin' to get onto the property," Dragon said. "And we could hold 'em off—but I've got a feelin' that they'd just come back. How long you think we should play that game? Can't keep the women here indefinitely."

"Sure as shit can't keep them inside indefinitely," Casper added. "He's not gonna stop."

"So we take Warren out," I said.

"The militia hasn't gotten back to your friend," Casper said calmly. "And they let Warren leave. They're in this shit. You think takin' one man out will stop this shit?"

"His goon squad isn't part of the militia—"

"They're still gettin' paid," Dragon said reasonably. "Even if Warren's dead. I'd put money on it."

"Militia will take care of that," Casper agreed. "Hamstring us and claim plausible deniability. Exactly how I'd play it."

I ground my teeth together and stared at the rows of booze behind the bar. I knew they were right. We had to draw the fight away from the clubhouse full of women and children, and we had to make it so that they couldn't retreat and regroup. That didn't mean that I could agree to putting Cecilia right in the middle of the fight we were about to invite.

"We'll get her to the house and inside with Cam," Casper said. "She'll be in the open fifteen seconds tops from the truck to the front door."

"Fifteen seconds is a long motherfucking time," I bit out.

"You got a better idea?" Dragon asked. "I'm all ears. You don't? Get your shit straight and back us the fuck up."

"Cecilia know about this?" I asked Casper. If she knew, there was no way I could put a stop to it, short of tying her down.

"Do I know about what?" Cecilia asked, coming up behind me.

"Fuck," I breathed, closing my eyes in frustration.

"Warren's in Eugene," her dad replied, not bothering to sugarcoat it. "We're gonna draw him away from the clubhouse."

"How?" she asked quietly. "What do you need me to do?"

"You've got to be fuckin' kiddin' me," I bit out.

"Olive stays here?" she asked her dad, looking straight into my eyes.

"Of course," her dad replied.

"Then I'll draw that asshole a map straight to me," she said.

I held her gaze, the muscle in my cheek jumping as I forced myself not to shout at her. We could do this without her. I wasn't sure how yet, but I knew there was a way, I just had to find it. Unfortunately, the only idea that kept popping into my head was cutting Farrah's hair short like Cecilia's and taking her instead—which I knew Cec would never allow in a million years. Maybe if I put the idea to Farrah instead. When it came to a showdown between Cec and her mother, I honestly didn't know who would come out on top.

Cecilia turned to her dad and Dragon. "If something happens to me—"

"It won't," her dad said instantly.

"If something does," she continued, ignoring his reassurance, "Olive goes to Mark."

I choked on an inhale, my entire body locking in surprise.

"If something happens to Mark," she said, her voice less steady. She looked between the men and swallowed hard. "She goes to Lily and Leo."

"Not gonna happen," Dragon said quietly. "Nothin's gonna happen to you, CeeCee."

"Baby girl, you think I'd okay this if I thought you'd get hurt?" her dad asked, staring at her in wounded surprise.

"Now nothing will happen to Mark, either," she joked flatly, shrugging her shoulder. "Lily is my first choice if we're dead, but Mark would never let Olive go to Leo."

My stomach churned with nausea as she walked away, her back straight and her chin high.

"She's exactly like her mother," Dragon mused.

"I'm aware," Casper said emotionlessly. He finished his cup of coffee and set it hard on the counter. "I'll round up the boys and let them know what's happenin'."

"You don't lock that down, you're a fuckin' moron," Dragon said to me, gesturing toward Cecilia before turning back to the bar.

I didn't bother answering. I wasn't even sure if I could speak. I hadn't felt this kind of helpless frustration in more years than I could count. I knew, flat out *knew*, that I could stop Cecilia from going, even if I had to kidnap her ass. I also knew with complete certainty that type of interference would sever any chance of a relationship going forward. Could I live with that if it meant Cecilia was safe? I shook my head. She wouldn't be safe, not unless we ended the threat—and if I interfered with what they were planning, I wouldn't be around to protect her anymore. I strode toward the back hallway, my hands fisted at my sides.

★ ★ ★

"Forrest filled us in," Lu said when I found the team in her room. "What's the plan?"

"We're going to use Cecilia as bait," I said, making my decision as I said the words.

Lu nodded as Forrest swore in two languages.

"Don't like that," Eli said, crossing his arms over his chest.

"It's her monster," Lu replied, going to her stack of things in the corner of the room. "She deserves to be a part in taking him down."

"I agree with the sentiment," Forrest said politely as Lu opened a case holding a dismantled sniper rifle. "However, allowin' her to be present durin' a confrontation may not be the best way for her to do that."

"Let her kill him once we have him," Josiah said flatly.

"That's fair," Ephraim added, his voice low.

Forrest looked at me.

"She wants to do it," I said quietly. "I might be able to stop her this time, but I won't be able to next time. She'll make sure I'm nowhere near her the next time."

"Understood," Forrest replied. "Fill us in."

★ ★ ★

AFTER I'D FILLED my team in on strategy and objective, we agreed that they would leave long before me and Cecilia. When it came to a *confrontation*, as Forrest put it, their strongest asset was stealth. While the Aces relied on brute force in most cases, our team was built differently. They'd take care of the players from a distance, toppling them like the pieces on a chessboard.

"See you later, Alligator," Eli said as I opened the bedroom door.

"Catch you on the flip side," I said as I left the room.

"You're supposed to say, *After a while, Crocodile*," he called out behind me.

My lips twitched as I went to find Cecilia. I was strung too tight to laugh, but I was thankful for the familiarity of Eli acting like a dumbass before a mission. He could be staid as a priest when he needed to be, but up until that point, he'd act like a punch-drunk seventeen-year-old boy that had been up all night drinking Mountain Dew and gaming. It had driven me crazy until I'd realized that it was his own way of keeping everyone calm when nerves were a problem. He could pinpoint which person was thrumming with the most tension, and he knew exactly how to get their attention enough to piss them off or make them laugh, easing that tension. It was a skill that came in handy, even if it was irritating as hell.

"Hey," I said in surprise as I saw Farrah in the hallway carrying Olive. "You know where Cec is?"

"I think she just went in to shower," she said, her expression taut with worry. "I can't believe you're allowing this bullshit."

"You think I could stop it?" I asked seriously.

Farrah paused. "No," she griped, shaking her head. "I told Cody it should be me."

"The thought crossed my mind," I said, a little guiltily. If Farrah went in Cecilia's place, she'd be in the exact same danger.

Farrah huffed out a small laugh. "I bet it did," she said knowingly. "But Cody was right. CeeCee would never allow it. We'd have to literally lock her in here."

"Yeah."

Farrah stood there for a moment, her eyes unfocused. "It feels like I just got her back, you know?" she said, shooting me a helpless look. "It took years to get to where we are now. If we forced her to stay here—"

"I get it," I replied. Farrah and Casper were in the same boat I was, and the knowledge of that pissed me off even more. It was like we were walking on eggshells to keep Cecilia happy, and that didn't sit well with me at all.

"It is what it is," she said. "This isn't the first time I've disagreed with a club decision and it won't be the last."

"More than a club decision," I pointed out.

"Haven't you learned yet," she said, no trace of bitterness in her voice, "in our family, everything's a club decision?"

"You're okay with that?" I asked curiously.

"Cecilia was in trouble and she had somewhere to go," Farrah said. "A place where she knew the people would protect her, or die trying. That's worth it, don't you think?"

I didn't reply.

"She's in the bathroom next to your room," Farrah said with a sigh. "You might be able to catch her, if you hurry."

She left me standing in the hallway by myself, turning her words over and over in my head. Logically, I knew that Cecilia could've gone to the police. They would have protected her as much as they could. I also knew, in my gut, that Farrah was right. No one would protect Cecilia more diligently or wholeheartedly than the Aces—not even my own team. She was one of them, for better or worse, and they protected their own.

As I turned on my heel and headed for the bathroom, I thought about the times when I'd gone to the club, knowing that I was welcome, no matter what. The way they'd paid for my medical bills when my mom couldn't—not only after the shooting, but before that, too. Amy and Brenna had taken me to get almost all of my vaccinations growing up. I grimaced, remembering the time I'd ended up in the hospital at fourteen. Cam had driven up to Salem, where I was living with my mom, and beat the shit out of my dealer—ensuring that he'd never sell mushrooms laced with poison again. They'd even taken care of those hospital bills.

"It's me," I said, opening the door to the steam-filled bathroom. I stepped inside and closed it behind me as Cecilia poked her head out from behind the glass shower door.

"Everything okay?" she asked, her eyebrows rising as I stripped off my t-shirt.

"Room in there for two?" I asked. The question was rhetorical, and I didn't wait for an answer as I toed off my boots and stripped off the rest of my clothes.

She was still healing, and I needed to keep my head on straight for the shit we were facing, but there was no way in hell that either of us was leaving that bathroom until I felt her skin against mine. Enjoying

Cecilia naked and wet wasn't an opportunity I was willing to let pass—not anymore.

"Are you bigger?" she asked, pressing her lips together to keep from grinning as she stared at my dick. "Because I don't remember you looking like *that*."

"You know just the words to make a man feel ten feet tall," I replied, climbing into the shower. "Or two inches tall—depending on the situation."

"I've always excelled orally," she replied in mock seriousness.

I couldn't have stopped the laugh that came from deep in my throat. Reaching out, I slid my hands into her hair, gripping her skull in my palms. Jesus, she was so tiny compared to me. Her bruises were gone, and Forrest had removed the stitches across her ribs, but I'd never forget the way she'd looked when I'd found her that night—her face swollen and her shirt covered in blood. I'd mostly been able to put it into the back of my mind, she didn't need me losing my shit every time I looked at her—but *Jesus*. The human body was so fucking fragile. Having her bare in front of me, slender and dainty, reminded me of that in glaring Technicolor.

"We can come up with a different way," I said, running my lips down the bridge of her nose.

"I just want to get it over with," she replied, her hands coming up to rest on my chest. "I can't keep waiting for the next shoe to drop."

"I'll finish it," I promised, pressing my forehead against hers. "You stay here, and I'll take care of it."

"If you thought that would work, you'd already be gone," she said. Sliding her hands up my chest, she softly scratched her nails through my chest hair, up over my shoulders and down my arms, her hands finally coming to a stop wrapped around my forearms. "It's going to be okay."

"I got a bad feeling about it," I replied, breaking my own rule about saying that type of shit right before things got messy. "Don't do it, Cec."

"I have to," she said simply. "I promise, I'll stay out of the way. I'll be fine."

"There's no way to know that," I spat, letting go of her to run my fingers through my hair. "You've seen how fast shit can go bad."

Cecilia's expression darkened. Before she opened her mouth, I knew she'd moved beyond trying to calm me and I braced.

"I do know," she said, raising her chin. "We weren't ready, and we didn't see it coming. I can't live my life waiting for that to happen the next time I let my guard down. I won't."

"I'd never make you," I shot back. "There's other ways to finish this."

"Today?" she asked. "Because if I do this, Olive is safe *today*."

I inhaled sharply, fury making every muscle in my body tense. I breathed in once, then twice, but it didn't calm me enough to stop the urge to slam the side of my fist against the wall of the shower.

"Feel better?" she asked, not even flinching.

"What's she gonna do without you?" I asked. "Somethin' happens to you, and then what? All because you couldn't be patient enough to wait for a few goddamn days so I could plan somethin' different?"

"That's not fair and you know it," she spat back, her voice steadily rising with every word. "And if something happens to me, then you better buy some baby books so you can figure out how to change a fucking diaper."

"I'm supposed to raise her without you?" I yelled back. "Are you out of your fucking mind? What did I tell you? I'm not leaving you again. Where you go, I go, *goddamn it*."

I was still breathing heavily, my hand fisted in her hair when she lunged. I went back a step as her mouth hit mine, but within seconds, I had control of us both, pressing her into the wall of the shower, one hand still in her hair and the other gripping her ass. Her hands were everywhere, scratching down my back and digging into my ass cheeks, gripping my sides and finally rising to my shoulders. I boosted her up easily and groaned into her mouth as her legs wrapped around my waist.

As her hips started to roll, I ripped my mouth away. "We can't do this."

"I know," she gasped, still grinding against me, "but I'm so close."

"Fuck," I breathed, kissing her again.

Shifting slightly, I held my breath as her pussy slid up my cock and back again, over and over. Shit. With every movement of our hips, I was more and more convinced that she wasn't the only one who was going to get off. Pressing my face against her neck, I sucked the skin between my teeth, biting down slightly.

Cecilia hissed in a sharp breath as her hips lost their rhythm and she pressed down hard against me. The change in movement shifted us just enough that I barely slid inside, and I cursed as I jerked my hips back and came against the wall between her legs.

We both froze when it was over, breathing heavily.

"I'm going to be sore as hell," she said finally, laughing a little as she tipped her head back. She sighed. "Worth it."

"Fuck," I muttered, shuffling back so she could drop her feet to the floor.

"We better finish up," she said, giving me a half smile as she stepped backward into the spray. "I was almost done."

I just barely kept my hands to myself as she quickly washed and rinsed her body. As she shuffled around me so I could step into the spray of water, her hand slid down my side and over the curve of my ass. Just like that, I was ready to go again.

"I'll be out in a second," I rasped, stepping away from her.

She giggled as I paused, letting the water hit me directly in the face.

"You know, you'd do fine without me," she called over the noise as she dried off. "I don't want you to have to, but I know you would."

Sucking in a sharp breath as the water turned cool, I scrubbed and rinsed as fast as I could.

"Not happenin'," I said, turning the water off with more force than necessary. "Stop sayin' that shit."

"I have to be pragmatic," she replied, handing me a towel. She stepped into her underwear. "I can't afford to be otherwise."

"Just stop."

"I can't," she said flatly.

Running the towel over myself, I watched as she finished getting dressed.

"I can't be emotional about it," she said, turning to me as she put deodorant on. "If I let myself do that, I'll never be able to stop. I won't be able to make any decisions that have to be made."

"You don't have to make any decisions right now," I said.

"Yes, I do," she argued, leaning against the sink as I got dressed. "Even if I didn't have this ax hanging over my head—Olive deserves to have that security."

"You know she has it," I replied. "It's not like she'd go to strangers. Your family would take care of her."

"Yeah," she said, nodding. "But I want her with you, and I had to make sure that was clear. If not you—" she shrugged. "My parents are too old to start all over again, and I love Trix and Cam, but their boys are already half grown. So, Lily. Gray is young, and they'll probably have more. Olive would have siblings she could play with."

"You've really thought this through," I said, slicking my hair back from my face.

"It's impossible not to."

Crowding her against the sink, I rested my hands on each side of her hips.

"Nothin' is gonna happen to you."

"You can't know that."

"Yeah, I can."

"You're psychic now?"

"No," I shook my head slowly. "But I know that no God would take you from me now—not when I finally have you again."

"You believe in God?" she asked, raising her eyebrows in surprise.

"You don't?"

She opened her mouth and then shut it again. Finally, she spoke. "It's hard to believe after the things I've seen happen to good people."

"Opposite for me," I replied, smiling. "Hard to *not* believe when I see you sleepin' next to Olive, leavin' a spot empty so I can climb in with you." I gave her a quick kiss and stepped back. "We need to get goin'."

"I'll be right out," she said, turning toward the mirror as I opened the bathroom door. "I need to finish up."

"Don't forget the lipstick," I said knowingly, kissing the back of her neck as our eyes met in the mirror. "The red lipstick makes you look like one of those old school pin-ups."

"Get your head in the game," she teased, shoving at me.

My stomach was in knots as I went back into our room, stripping out of the dirty clothes I'd just put on. There were so many ways the day could go wrong. As I got dressed, every possible bad scenario ran through my mind on a loop.

Pulling my holster out of my go-bag, I slipped it over my shoulders, grimacing as it rubbed over my healing wound. We didn't even know if it would work. Without watching Warren's movements, we couldn't even be sure that he knew where the clubhouse was, much less Casper and Farrah's place. Sitting on the edge of the bed to pull on my socks, I paused, leaning forward to rest my elbows on my knees.

I'd trusted the club before, and I'd have to do it again. If Warren didn't make contact the way we planned, that just meant that we'd have more time to plan something better—something that didn't put Cecilia in the crossfire.

As I considered the possibility of just taking Cecilia and Olive to some random island in the Caribbean until her pop took care of Warren, a knock on the door startled me.

"Yeah?" I called out, going back to my socks.

"How you doin'?" Poet asked, poking his head in.

"This is bullshit, and I'm about to take Cec and run," I replied flatly.

Poet chuckled. "Yeah, I had a feelin' that's where you were at." He swung the door open and lifted his hand, shaking a bulletproof vest from side to side. "Your woman, Lu, told me to give this to you."

"They left?" I asked, taking the vest.

He nodded. "Should be all set up by now, I'd imagine."

"They better be," I replied, silently thanking Lu for having the presence of mind to pack a vest and the generosity of giving it to Cec instead of protecting herself.

"We got some of those, you know," Poet said, jerking his chin toward the vest as I dropped it on the bed.

"Not as good at that one," I replied, standing to slide my boots back on.

"You're probably right about that," he said thoughtfully. "That one's in better shape, for sure."

"You're stayin' here?" I asked.

"I'll be here," he said firmly. "Mack's already here. Leo's on his way back. A few others and a couple of older prospects on the gate. We'll keep an eye on things."

"Not sure if I'm pissed more people aren't stayin' with Olive, or glad they'll be there to watch Cecilia's back."

"Hell," Poet said, slapping me on the shoulder. "We'll also have the women here. Your mother-in-law is somethin' else with a shotgun."

"Farrah's not my mother-in-law."

Poet guffawed. "Soon enough." He turned and whistled as Cecilia came in the room behind him.

"Put your tongue back in your head, you old goat," CeeCee teased, slapping his chest with the back of her hand as she passed him.

"I'll let you two finish up," Poet said, grinning. "I don't see you—find me when you get back."

"Will do," I said.

As soon as he'd left the room, Cecilia pointed to the vest. "What's that?"

"This," I said, lifting it up, "is your newest accessory."

"Is that a bulletproof vest?" she asked, staring at it like it was going to bite her.

"Just a precaution," I replied, pulling open the Velcro on the side. I lifted it over her head.

"I thought they were heavier."

"The older ones are," I replied, closing the sides snugly around her. As soon as I was satisfied with the fit, I tapped against the front of it with my knuckles. "Okay?"

"It's bulky," she said, running her hands down the black fabric.

"You got a hoodie?" She nodded. "Put it on. Should hide it pretty well."

I grinned as she pulled a familiar gray hoodie from one of the bags. "Did you steal that from my house?" I asked.

"You wouldn't have even noticed it was gone," she grumbled. "You have, like fifteen of them."

"Hey, I like what I like," I said with a laugh. "Looks good on you."

"My boobs have disappeared," she said, looking down at herself. "Goodbye, new boobs."

I pulled on the neck of her hoodie, trying to peer down the front of it. "Nah, they're still in there somewhere."

"We're all set," Cam said from the open doorway. The light conversation had done little to relax us, but Cam's words erased any semblance of calm we'd been faking.

Cecilia turned and knelt down in front of the bags. As I watched, she took out her driver's license and slipped it inside the neck of her hoodie.

"You're drivin' the truck. We already unloaded CeeCee's car and unhooked the trailer, so you're all set," Cam said. I turned to face him. "The rest of us will be on our bikes."

"Ready as I'll ever be," Cecilia said as she got to her feet. "Where's Mom?"

"They're at the bar," he said. "Pretty sure she was changing Olive's diaper up there."

"That better be the last time she lays on that bar for any reason," I grumbled as we made our way out to the main room.

"What?" Cecilia joked halfheartedly. "You're worried about her doing body shots?"

"If she's anything like her mother—" Cam said, letting his words fade away insinuatingly.

"Shut it," Cec muttered, elbowing him in the side.

The next few minutes passed by faster than I would have liked. I watched as Cecilia held Olive against her chest, the baby's head resting against her cheek. She closed her eyes as she whispered to her, rocking from side to side. Then, in a split second, her expression changed, and she lifted her head. Determination lifted her chin and straightened her shoulders as she handed Olive back to Farrah and kissed her mom quickly on the cheek.

Without a word to me, she strode out the front door. If I hadn't turned back to Farrah in that exact moment, I would've missed the terror in her eyes as she watched her daughter leave. Within a heartbeat, her expression changed exactly the way Cecilia's had, and her chin tipped up. Even though I'd noticed the resemblance between the two women before, for some reason, witnessing this moment rocked me.

"I'll bring her home," I told Farrah, kissing the side of her head with affection that I hadn't felt in years. Leaning down further, I kissed Olive, too. "Be back soon, best friend."

When I got outside, Casper was waiting for me at the hood of the moving truck.

"You hold back about five minutes," he said. "Give us time to take separate routes and still casually meet up at our place before you."

"Got it," I said. "You put everything I need into the cab?"

"Everything," Casper confirmed. "Down to the brass knuckles and the grenade, you crazy motherfucker."

"I like to plan for any eventuality," I replied, glancing at Cecilia's pale face through the windshield.

"Just try not to fuck up my yard with that thing," Casper griped as he stalked toward his bike. He turned back and grinned. "Be real careful on those curves near the house, yeah? Don't take 'em too fast."

I jerked my head in agreement.

Casper's calm fed my own and I felt myself falling into a familiar zone as I opened the driver's side door and climbed into the truck's cab. Cecilia was still staring blankly out the windshield, and I gave her knee a squeeze as I bent down to pull my bag of supplies onto the seat between us. Opening it up, I matched the list in my head to the contents of the bag. Then I did it again as bikes fired up, and one by one, Aces left the safety of the compound.

I checked my watch.

Cecilia inhaled a long breath and let it out the same way, her hands fisted in her lap.

I started the truck and checked the gas gauge. Full.

I checked my watch again.

"Hey," I said, getting CeeCee's attention. She was grinding her teeth so hard that the tiny muscle in her cheek flexed when she turned to look at me.

I'd planned on saying something funny or dirty to soothe her nerves a little, but one look in her eyes, and I knew it wouldn't even be possible. Instead, I reached out and wrapped my hand around the back of her neck and tugged her toward me until I could reach her mouth with mine.

The kiss was hot and deep and desperate and filthy from the moment our lips made contact, and I sucked the feeling deep, letting it set fires under my skin and sharpen my focus.

I didn't let go of her neck as I pulled away from the kiss, keeping our faces only inches apart.

"Do exactly what we planned," I said, my voice gravelly. "No matter what happens."

She nodded.

"Give me the words, Cec," I insisted.

"I'll try," she whispered back. "We have to go. Now."

I closed my eyes in frustration and nodded as I let her go, the world tilting as I realized that, for the rest of my life, I was going to have a partner that didn't make promises she couldn't keep—even if it meant scaring the shit out of me.

Chapter 23
CECILIA

Taking a deep breath, I sat back in my seat, shifting a little as the vest I was wearing pressed uncomfortably against my waist. Its presence was more terrifying than comforting, because it reminded me of the large expanse of my body that it didn't cover. It also told me that Mark's team fully believed that what we were doing was going to work. I was about to be thrown into a situation that I felt fully unprepared for. I felt like a sacrificial lamb.

As we drove the familiar road between the club and my parents' house, I glanced at Mark's profile and got a feeling of déjà vu. How many times had we driven this particular stretch of road, racing to my house to be alone when I knew the house was empty?

"If I get in a wreck, your knees are gonna smash right into your face," Mark said, nodding at my feet on his dashboard.

"Then don't get in a wreck," I shot back, grinning as I wiggled my toes, the sunlight pouring through the trees around us speckling the skin and polish with rapidly changing shadows.

"It's not me I'm worried about," he said, reaching out to push gently on my thighs until I'd dropped my feet to the floorboard. "It's everyone else."

"You can't protect me from everything," I teased, turning in my seat to put my feet in his lap. "This better?"

"Not really," he said glancing at me with a small smile.

He turned back to the road and I sighed, leaning my head back against *the window so the sunlight warmed my face.*

"I'll do my best," Mark said quietly, wrapping his hand around one of my bare feet.

"Do your best at what?"

"Protecting you," he said with a squeeze.

"Give me a shot, first," I said with a laugh, digging my toes into his belly, making him squirm. "If you see things going south, that's when you can step in."

Mark laughed. "Fine," he grumbled jokingly. "Quit ticklin' me, I'm trying to drive here."

The memory was gone in an instant as soon as I felt the truck move from the smooth asphalt to the gravel of my parent's long driveway. Without conscious thought, I reached for him, my hand gripping his thigh.

"Showtime," he said, his eyes only leaving the road ahead of us to scan the surrounding trees. "Straight in the house, baby."

"Yeah," I said, trying to keep my expression relaxed.

We were only unloading my belongings into my parents' garage to be stored—nothing more, nothing less.

The men who'd ridden to meet us were already parked in front of my parents' house, and I watched in awe as they milled around, laughing and joking. Tommy made a rude gesture toward my brother Cam, and then laughed like a hyena. My Uncle Grease slapped the back of his head good-naturedly and said something that made Cam grin. My dad lifted his chin at us in welcome from his spot leaning casually against the porch rails.

Mark rolled down the window as we got close. "Should I back it in?" he called.

"Nah," my dad shook his head. "Grass is soggy as fuck, and you'd probably get stuck. We can carry shit an extra twenty feet."

"Hey, speak for yourself," Tommy complained. "I still think we shoulda brought one of those flatbeds that tilt—back up and pour her shit into the garage."

Cam laughed and nodded.

"This is the fucking Twilight Zone," I breathed.

"Seatbelt and scoot," Mark said as he rolled forward and parked in front of the garage.

I followed his order to the letter, knowing exactly what to do. Unbuckling my seatbelt, I scooted across the seat, pulling his bag onto my lap. As he stepped out of the truck, I set the bag to my right and scooted it into the driver's seat as I climbed down behind him.

"Be right back," I called to my dad.

"Hey," Tommy said. "Where you going, this is *your* shit."

"I have to pee," I shot back, never pausing as I strode toward the house.

My hands were shaking as I opened the front door and slid it closed behind me.

"Atta girl," Dragon said.

"Jesus Christ," I spat, my entire body jerking with surprise. "I wondered where you were."

"Wouldn't make sense for me to be here," he said from his place beside one of the windows facing the front of the house. "I'm the president, you know." He grinned and it completely transformed his face. "I'm not expected to help anyone move."

"Did you see anything?" I asked, glancing toward the window. "Are they out there?"

"Didn't see anythin', no," he replied, his eyes back on what was happening outside. "But instinct says they're close. Haven't been wrong yet."

I sat down on the floor and wrapped my arms around my knees. My dad had been very specific when he told me where to place myself once I was inside the house. My spot between the windows was impossible to see from outside no matter the angle. When I'd offered to hide in the bathroom, he'd shaken his head at me. Apparently, I needed to stay right where I was in case we had to leave in a rush.

Time passed so slowly that I started absentmindedly picking at my lips, unable to stop the urge. After what felt like an hour later, but must've only been a few minutes, I raised my eyes to the ceiling when I heard someone walking upstairs.

"Forrest," Dragon said without looking at me. "He's in Charlie's room."

"Why?" I asked automatically.

"Keepin' watch," Dragon replied, then paused. "The fuck?"

Sitting where I couldn't see what was happening was agony. My heart was beating so fast that it felt like I'd run a mile and the muscles of my shoulders were so tense, they were practically up around my ears.

"Someone's drivin' a fuckin' Hummer up the road," he said, his voice emotionless.

"They're not trying to sneak?" I asked in disbelief. I wasn't sure how much longer I could stay in position. I needed to see what was happening. My family was out there.

"Only one reason a man thinks he doesn't have to sneak," Dragon said grimly, pulling a handgun out of the back of his pants to methodically check the magazine. As he pressed it back into the grip, he looked at me. "He thinks he holds all the cards. Stay here."

He passed me, moving easily as he opened the front door and stepped out onto the front porch.

Crawling on my hands and knees, I made my way to the window, peeking my head up above the sill. I felt like an idiot. Like a kid playing hide-and-seek. But what I saw outside made everything inside me go cold.

Drake Warren was casually climbing out of the passenger seat with a small smile on his face as he paused. Behind him, someone was opening the back of the dark SUV. I held my breath as the person came into view, dragging a body.

I couldn't see the top half, but an uncomprehending moan escaped my throat as soon as I saw the lower half. Bloody, ripped to shred denim. One black motorcycle boot. One white sock stained almost completely red.

As the man dropped the body and stepped back, I covered my mouth with my hand to keep myself from screaming.

Leo's cut was almost completely ripped at the seam along his side.

"A trade," Drake said cheerfully.

"Fuck you," Dragon replied from the porch.

Drake smiled, making my skin crawl. He lifted his hand and pointed a pistol at Leo's prone body. He glanced around, and I knew without being able to see them that my dad and the boys had all drawn their own weapons.

"You're at a distinct disadvantage," my dad called out, his voice ringing with the high-class accent that he'd picked up in private school. I sucked in a sharp breath at the sound. I hadn't heard him speak like that in years—not since my last parent-teacher conference. My dad was called Casper for more reasons than I probably knew about, but the most well known was his ability to fit in anywhere.

"About that," Drake said with a shrug. With a slight nod of his head, men came from the trees. Ten that I could count, and my view was blocked on one side by the moving truck.

I looked at Leo. Was he breathing? I couldn't tell. If he was alive, he was in really bad shape. He hadn't shifted at all from where he'd fallen.

"We don't trade," my dad said in disgust.

"Perhaps it's not your decision," Drake countered. His eyes shifted to the left. "I'm growing impatient."

I knew he was looking at Dragon. I knew it, and my stomach twisted so hard that I almost gagged. He was making him choose. Me or Leo. Me, or his only living son.

I was barely aware of getting to my feet and crossing the room, gaining speed as I rounded the wall to the kitchen and headed for the door to the side of the house. I was outside in seconds, and I gulped as I saw the five men I hadn't counted on the other side of the truck. Without thinking, I strode forward, keeping the truck between me and the men I knew would never let me pass.

I heard the first curse as I rounded the back of the truck and came into view.

"I'll go," I said to Drake, holding my shoulders straight and lifting my chin as he stared at me.

I glanced down at Leo and had to swallow back the bile in my throat. What I'd seen from the window was a thousand times worse up close. His clothes were shredded, and from the short time he'd been laying in the gravel, little pools of blood had formed.

"That wasn't so hard, was it?" Drake said.

"Goddamn it, Cecilia," Mark roared behind me.

I couldn't look at him. I couldn't look at any of them. I couldn't let the fear on my face be the last memory they had of me.

Drake waved his hand for me to move forward.

"No," I said, holding my ground. My hands shook. "You come to me."

Drake laughed and stepped toward me, away from Leo. As soon as he was close, his hand snapped out and grabbed me by the hair.

"Thank you for making this easy," he said in my ear as he stepped in behind me. "I would have rather had you both, but once you're gone, it'll be easy to get little sister back. The courts put a lot of stock in blood relatives, you know."

I kept my eyes down and refused to react as he pulled me backward toward his SUV. *He'll never get Olive. Even if it all went to shit, Mark would make sure of that.*

As soon as we reached the back door, I put my hand into the kangaroo pocket of Mark's huge sweatshirt and prayed.

Apparently, I did believe in God.

The next few moments happened in slow motion as he reached for the door handle with the hand holding his gun. Planting my feet, I twisted my body toward Drake.

The surprise on his face when the pistol inside the pocket of my sweatshirt went off would be etched into my memory for the rest of my life, but it only lasted a split second as I bent at the waist and tore my head away from his hand.

I ran as gunfire exploded around me and I threw myself over Leo's prone body in the middle of the driveway, covering as much as I could.

God, it was loud. Men were running. And I watched detachedly as the door of the moving truck was slung upward and familiar men poured out the back of it, led by my cousin Will.

I couldn't see Mark. It was so chaotic and surreal that I had a hard time focusing my eyes on any one person. Mostly, it was just feet and the bottom of a row of motorcycles.

It went on for too long, though later, someone would tell me it was less than five minutes. Maybe my memory was off. Because just as I turned my head and saw the barrel of Forrest's rifle sticking through a hole in my little sister's window screen, something hit me so hard in the back that I was thrown forward, my head colliding with the back of Leo's.

CHAPTER 24

MARK

IF SOMEONE HAD asked me what the scariest moment in my life was, it would've been a tie. The first moment was when I realized that the men who'd been torturing me had just pulled up in front of Cecilia's house, where I knew her family was having a barbecue. The second was when Casper called to tell me she was hiding from a gunman in some house across town.

Neither of those compared to the moment when she stepped out from behind the truck and walked straight toward the man trying to kill her.

As I stared at her, laying on a pool table where the makeshift triage station had been set up, it took everything in me not to wring her neck.

"She needs to go to the hospital," I said as Forrest checked out Cecilia's back. "She shoulda never even come back here."

"I don't need a hospital," Cecilia said with a hiss. "Forrest has the good drugs—I can barely even feel my toes."

"You were fuckin' shot."

"It hit the vest," she argued.

"Vests just stop the bullet from tearin' through your insides," I ground out. "You were still hit with the impact of the bullet." I looked at Forrest. "Help me out here?"

"Sounds like you're doin' just fine on your own, Chief," he said in amusement, still pressing lightly on Cecilia's back.

"I'm fine."

"You—" I clenched my jaw shut as Forrest gave her a tap on the shoulder before helping her off the table.

"She's good," he told me. "Black and blue, but it was small caliber and far enough away—"

"See? I told you," she said tiredly. She looked at Forrest. "Whatever you gave me is *really* nice."

"Your woman's a lightweight," Forrest said to me before turning away to help the next person. "Don't worry—won't affect your breast milk. Same shit they give after a C-section," he said over his shoulder.

By the time the dust settled, every Ace and all of my team were still standing and none of Warren's were, but it hadn't given me any satisfaction until I'd been able to reach Cecilia.

"Is she okay?" Casper called as he raced toward us. "Is she breathin'?"

My hands shook as I rolled her off of Leo and searched her, looking for wounds. She was covered in blood, but as I slid my hands down her body, I realized that none of it was hers.

"She's out cold," I said roughly, putting my fingers to her carotid artery to check her pulse.

"Let me through," Forrest ordered, pushing past the Aces that had circled us.

"She's breathin'," I told Forrest as he dropped to his knees beside us. "Check him."

Forrest's nod was almost imperceptible as he turned to Leo. "I'm a doctor," he told Dragon, who was staring at his son helplessly, his hands outstretched but frozen, like he wasn't sure where it was safe to touch. "Help me turn him to his back."

All of my attention was on Cecilia as she started to stir, eventually opening her eyes. When she saw my face close to hers, she jerked and then moaned in pain.

"It's okay, baby," I said, brushing her hair back from her face. "Where

does it hurt?"

"My back," *she croaked, tears leaking from her eyes.*

"She bleeding?" *Lu asked as she ran toward us.* "I think she was hit."

"You saw it?" *Casper asked as he helped me roll Cecilia quickly to her side. I winced as she groaned in pain.*

"Saw the piece of shit aim for her," *she said, skidding to a stop on her knees beside me.* "I couldn't tell if I got off my shot before he did."

"Is that what that was?" *Cecilia asked breathlessly.* "Huh."

"I need to feed Olive," Cecilia said, cutting into the memory as she shuffled past me, handing me the sweatshirt she'd been wearing. It was covered in Leo's blood. "And then we need to get to the hospital."

I followed her back to the bedroom, where Charlie was laying with Olive on a blanket spread out on the floor, cooing and playing with the baby's feet.

"Hey," Charlie greeted, leaning up on her elbow. "You're okay?"

"I'm fine," Cecilia said, kneeling beside the girls. "Thanks for keeping an eye on her."

"No problem," Charlie replied, watching her sister closely. "Mom wanted to go to the hospital with Lily, so she said to hang with Olive on the floor until you came to get her." Charlie rolled her eyes. "I think she was worried I'd drop her or something. I changed her diaper, though, 'cause she was poopy. It was yellow, FYI."

Cecilia smiled and ran her head over Charlie's hair. "You did a good job, kid," she told her. "Once Olive's a little older, you can watch her for real. I'll even pay you."

"Sweet," Charlie said, grinning. Her expression slowly fell. "Is Leo okay?"

Cecilia didn't reply as she picked Olive up. She shifted her clothes a little and started nursing the baby before she looked back up at Charlie. "I'm not sure," she said softly. "He was in pretty bad shape, but he was breathing."

"What happened?" Charlie asked hoarsely.

Cecilia glanced at me helplessly.

"He wrecked his bike," I answered for her, sitting down on the edge of the bed. It wasn't exactly a lie—but it wasn't the whole truth, either. We'd found Leo's bike less than half a mile from the club's property, and Leo had definitely gone down with it, but we were all pretty sure that he hadn't been responsible for the crash.

"That's crazy," Charlie said in disbelief. "Leo rides every day, he wouldn't just lay his bike down like an idiot."

I held a smile back as I nodded. "We'll have to ask him how it happened once he's awake."

"Hopefully, he's okay," Charlie said, pushing herself up to sit cross-legged. "Gray already lost his mom. I mean, he has Lily now, and I don't think he even remembers, but still."

"I bet he'll be okay," Cec said, laying her hand on Charlie's knee. "He'd never leave Lily and Gray if he could help it."

Charlie looked at Cecilia curiously, and I imagined little hamster wheels spinning inside her head. I knew where the conversation was headed before she spoke.

"Why doesn't anyone like you?" she asked Cecilia, her words blunt but not unkind. "I thought it was because you liked Leo, but—" She gestured to me and shrugged. "It can't be that."

Cecilia huffed out an uncomfortable laugh. "You get right to the point, don't you?"

"Sorry," Charlie replied, chastised.

"No, it's fine," Cecilia said. She pulled her hand away from Charlie's knee and grimaced as she got more comfortable on the floor. "So, you know how our family was attacked before you were born?"

"Yeah," Charlie said, nodding. "Mom was pregnant with me."

"Right," Cecilia replied. "Well, I was a teenager, and I didn't deal with it very well."

"You weren't hurt though, right?"

"No," Cecilia said.

"Yes, she was," I said at the same time. I ignored how Cecilia glared at me. "She had a graze, right here on her shoulder."

"It barely bled," Cecilia said. "It was more like a burn, really."

"It scarred," I countered. "It's why she has that tattoo on her arm."

"That's not *why*." Cecilia widened her eyes at me in the universal sign to shut my mouth.

"It's there," I said stubbornly, looking at Charlie. "You just can't really see it anymore unless you're looking."

"This is all beside the point," Cecilia said stubbornly to Charlie. "After all that happened, I didn't react well. I was…mean. I was mean and hateful—that's why they don't like me."

"That's stupid," Charlie said flatly. "That all happened before I was even born."

"And after you were born, too," Cecilia corrected.

"Still," Charlie said, waving her hand in dismissal. "You've lived in California for-freaking-ever. They need to get over it."

"That's what I'm saying," I agreed, shooting Charlie a small smile. Leave it to a kid to get to the bottom of shit and tell it like it is.

"I think if you give enough reason for a person to dislike you, or distrust you, or whatever," Cecilia said gently to Charlie, "it's really hard to come back from that, no matter how long it's been."

"Bullshit," Charlie said firmly. She shook her head. "We're family."

Cecilia smiled at her little sister, inhaling shakily. "Fair enough," she said. "But remember what I said. It's hard to come back from that—so don't be an asshole."

"Too late," Charlie replied, rolling her eyes again. "I can't help it—it's in my genes." She stood up and stretched. "I'm going to go find Molly—we're all staying at her house tonight so the 'rents can be at the hospital with Leo. I bet she'd take Olive, too, if you asked."

"Thanks, toots," Cecilia replied. "I think I'll keep her with me, though. She's too little to be away from me that long."

As soon as Charlie left the room, Cecilia groaned and laid a now sleeping Olive back on the floor so she could fix her shirt.

"Fuck, my back hurts," she complained.

"I bet it does," I said unsympathetically. "What the fuck were you thinkin'?"

"Can we not do this now?" she pleaded. "You can yell at me for as long as you want later. I promise I'll just sit there and let you tear me a new one—but the day isn't over, and we need to go to the hospital."

"You need to lay down and rest," I argued.

"I need to be at the hospital," she said, getting to her feet. She took a step toward me and wrapped her arms around my shoulders. "I need to be there for my sister."

"You sure?" I asked, running my hands up the back of her thighs.

"I know she might not want me there," she said quietly. "But, if I don't go, then *I'm* making the decision not to support her. You know?"

"Yeah, I get it," I said with a sigh, wishing I didn't. She needed Lily to know that she was there—even if it went over like a lead balloon.

We stayed like that for a minute, each of us getting our bearings. It had been a hell of a day, and she was right. It wasn't over yet.

"You sure you don't want to rest for a little while?" I asked, gripping her hips. "They're gonna be up there all night."

"I'm sure," she said, bending a little to kiss me. It was closed mouthed, and simple, but she lingered there before pulling away. "I'm going to crash the minute I lay down. We need to go before the adrenalin wears off."

"Baby," I said as she stepped back, "I'll be surprised if you don't pass out on the way there."

"Maybe Forrest has some uppers," she joked, stripping out of her dirty pants and reaching for a clean pair. "I'll grab her bag. Can you put the car seat on the bed?"

"Sure," I said, going for the seat in the corner. "When did you bring this in?"

"My mom must've," she replied, crouching by the diaper bag with a small groan of pain. "She was probably going to take Olive with her before she decided to leave her with Charlie."

"Charlie's kinda young, don't you think?" I asked tentatively. It wasn't really my place to say anything, but I wasn't super comfortable leaving a newborn with Cecilia's kid sister.

"I was babysitting at her age," Cec replied. "But yeah, wouldn't be my first choice. Mom probably thought it would be okay, since there's always an adult here somewhere."

"Makes sense," I conceded as I lifted Olive from the floor.

"I'm glad she was able to go with Lily," Cecilia said as she dropped the bag on the bed and reached for Olive. "She must've been freaking out."

"Yeah," I agreed. "Leo didn't look good."

"I know," Cecilia said quietly.

"Cec—" I hesitated.

"I know," she said, her voice wobbling.

"His hand, baby," I continued gently anyway. "Not sure how many of those fingers they'll be able to save."

"I'm not thinking about it until we know for sure," she choked out, buckling the baby.

"He might not be able to sit a bike—"

"Later," she said, cutting me off. "We'll talk about it all later, okay?"

"Alright," I said, laying my hand on the back of her neck, threading my fingers through her hair. I gave a soft squeeze before letting her go.

I grabbed the car seat and followed Cecilia out to the main room of the club, which had pretty much cleared out by then. Forrest was cleaning up supplies and there were a few random guys milling around, but otherwise, things were quiet beyond the table that my team was seated around.

"We're headed to the hospital," I told them as I reached them. "Where's Eli?"

"He stayed behind," Siah replied, spinning his beer bottle around in his fingers. "To clean up."

"They let him?" I said in surprise. The Aces kept things in-house as much as they could, so it was surprising as hell if they were allowing him to see where the bodies were buried—literally.

"A few of those were ours," Ephraim said, stretching his arms above his head tiredly.

"Two were mine," Lu said in satisfaction. She looked at Cec. "Sorry I wasn't faster."

"What?" Cecilia replied in confusion.

"The man that shot you in the back," I gritted out, the words so disgusting that a new wave of fury raced down my spine.

"Shooting someone in the back is just poor sportsmanship," Wilson said, striding up to the group.

"Shit," I said, spinning toward him. "When'd you get here?"

"After all the fun parts," he said dryly. "I got a flight out right after I called you earlier. We need to talk."

"Can it wait until tomorrow?" I asked, glancing at Cecilia. "We need to head up to the hospital."

"Yes," he replied. "Or tonight after you get back."

"Not sure how late it'll be," I said.

"I'll wait."

"Thank you," Cecilia said, staring at Lu. "For what you did."

"Hey, like Wilson said," Lu joked kindly, "shooting someone in the back is poor sportsmanship. He deserved it."

With a nod, Cecilia looked at me expectantly.

"We'll see you guys later," I said, leading Cecilia away from the group.

"Where exactly did *you* hit him?" Siah asked Lu as we walked away, amusement lacing his voice.

"Shut up," she replied.

"I know where you were," Siah continued as we reached the front door. "At that angle, you had to be behind him—" His words cut off as we stepped outside into the cool night.

"I owe her a fruit basket or something," Cecilia mumbled as she hurried ahead of me, impatient. "Maybe a spa day."

"You are—" I shook my head, at a loss for words.

"Thankful," she said quietly, turning to look at me as she opened the truck door. "I'm thankful as hell."

"I love you," I said, grabbing her arm before she could climb inside.

"I love you, too," she said simply.

Chapter 25
CECILIA

I'D BEEN SO anxious to get to the hospital to see how Leo was and check on my sister that it should've felt like it took forever to get there—but it didn't. It was like I blinked and suddenly we were pulling into the parking lot. My stomach was in knots and guilt made my entire body feel heavy. Drake Warren had come for me in Eugene and somehow Leo, a man that I'd already betrayed in a variety of ways when we were kids, had born the brunt of his presence.

I hated the idea of walking up to a group of Aces, all of us knowing that everything that had happened was my fault. I wanted to curl up in bed and pull the covers over my head, to leave again, this time for good. I didn't want to face it.

Maybe I was punishing myself, because almost as much as I needed Lily to know that I cared, I also needed to take responsibility. I deserved to face everyone's anger.

Watching as Mark unlatched Olive's carrier and pulled it out of the car, I swallowed hard and straightened my shoulders. I refused to lose control of my emotions. If he had any idea how this was going to go, he would've never agreed to drive me to the hospital. I waited for him at the back of the truck and laced my fingers with his as he reached for me.

I'd forgotten how good it felt to have him at my back, sure in the knowledge that he wasn't going anywhere.

My hand tightened in his as I realized that feeling was back, almost as if it had never left. Even after everything we'd gone through in the past, I knew with absolute certainty that he wasn't going anywhere. I couldn't pinpoint when that had changed. Had it been when he'd stuck up for me to my mom, or later, when he'd crawled to me on the floor of Poet's beach house? Had it been something small that had tipped the scales or was it something bigger? I remembered his face, covered in greasepaint as he'd come into the closet where I was hiding, his eyes full of relief and confusion as they'd met mine. Had it been that moment when I'd begun to trust him again?

"Looks like everyone's outside," Mark commented as he led me to a lit-up area between the hospital and the parking lot.

"I wonder why," I said, taking in the crowd. My Uncle Grease was smoking a cigarette, his arm around Aunt Callie's shoulders. Will was standing close to Cam and Trix, talking with his hands. My dad stood with Dragon a little off to the side. Heather was sitting next to Mack on the edge of a cement wall, along with Rose, Tommy and Lily. A few other men and women that I didn't know as well filled out the area. Everyone grew quiet as we walked up.

"Jesus Christ," Rose muttered as she looked up and saw us.

I ignored her. I wasn't there for her. Not pausing, I made my way toward Lily.

"Hey," I said, searching her face. I'd been so concerned with getting to her, I hadn't planned on what I would actually say to her when I got there. I stood there, dumbly, taking in her tight mouth and terrified eyes.

"You came," she said, her voice flat.

"Of course I did," I said, reaching out to run my hand down her arm. "I knew you must be freaking out, and I—"

"I know it isn't fair," she said slowly. "I know it isn't your fault. But I can't deal with you right now."

I could've dealt with anger. I could've handled vindictive words and spite. I'd been braced and waiting for them. The unemotional way she dismissed me was a thousand times worse. It took everything inside me to hide how badly it hurt.

"You should go," Rose said from her place beside Mack.

I glanced toward her and saw Tommy's unsympathetic look and Heather's sympathetic one. With a nod, I took a stumbling step backward.

"You can't *deal* with her right now?" Mark said, his voice low and scary.

"Don't," I mumbled, tightening my fingers hard around his.

"What exactly can't you deal with?" he asked, ignoring me. "Your sister's concern for you? The fact that she showed up here, knowin' how you'd treat her, and she came anyway?"

"Mark," I hissed, staring at the ground, wishing it would swallow me.

"Maybe you can't *deal* with the fact that if she hadn't used her body to shield your man, you'd be preparin' for a funeral right now?" he said, his voice still low with fury.

"What?" Lily asked in confusion.

"Oh, nobody told you that, huh?" Mark said nastily. "Surprise, fuckin' surprise. Instead of runnin' away, like a fuckin' *sane* person would do—your sister ran into the middle of shit to protect Leo—and got shot in the back for it."

"Enough," I ground out, pulling at Mark's hand. "Let's just go."

"None of it would've even happened if she hadn't come running back to us for protection," Rose pointed out, coming forward.

"Don't get me started on you," Mark said, his body practically vibrating. "You and your man were at the clubhouse. You got no skin in this game—"

"This is my *family*," Rose argued.

"It's also Cecilia's family," Mark shot back. "And you've got a lot to say, for someone who'd be dead, too, if not for her."

"Fuck you," Rose spat.

"No, *fuck you*," Mark said as the group noticed what was happening and moved in to get control of the situation. "Cecilia saved your ass and you know it—standin' frozen until she pulled you behind that tree. Gettin' shot for her trouble *then*, too."

"She didn't get shot," Rose said. She looked at me. "You didn't get shot."

"For fuck's sake," Mark said to me. "You didn't tell *anyone*?"

"It was a graze," I said quietly, still pulling on his hand. "It doesn't matter. Let's go."

I didn't want to be there anymore. I wanted to go. I knew what he was trying to do, and I understood the purity behind it, but I wanted to escape. It felt like I was being peeled, layer by layer, and somehow, these people were seeing parts of me that weren't for public consumption. Somehow, Mark's words were twisting situations, turning what I'd done on instinct into some sort of heroism. It wasn't that. It had never been that. If I'd thought about what I was going to do, I would've saved myself first. Everyone knew that.

"You were shot that day?" my dad asked, disbelief threading through his words. "What?"

"I'm sorry, I didn't want to make things worse for you," I said to Lily, ignoring my dad. "We'll go."

"You were shot back then," she said, watching me closely. "And you never said anything?"

"Everyone was dealing with enough," I replied.

"God, CeeCee," she said, reaching up to pinch the bridge of her nose. "You saved Rose. We all knew you did, but—"

"I thought she was you," I blurted, the biggest secret of my life pouring out of my mouth like I had no control of it. "All I saw was her hair, and I just grabbed her. I thought it was you, okay? *So, just leave it.*"

"You didn't say anything because you thought she was me?" Lily asked dubiously.

"It was an accident," I ground out, taking a step backward. "I didn't mean to save her."

"You still did," she pointed out, throwing her arms out to the sides in disbelief. "Why wouldn't you tell anyone that you were hurt?"

"You were hurt worse," I said, trying to make her understand. "I didn't get to you."

"CeeCee," Lily said softly in understanding, her eyes filling with tears. "You couldn't have gotten to me. I wasn't anywhere near you."

I shook my head again. I didn't need to hear about it. I didn't even want to think about it.

"Gram saved me," she continued. "And Grandpa and Grandma Vera. They saved me. I had people to protect me."

"Doesn't matter," I said, swallowing hard.

"It does matter," she said, even softer. "Because you were the only one who could've gotten to Rose in time."

"I didn't do it on purpose," I said dismissively.

"Don't do that," Lily ordered, her tone firming.

"I didn't," I said emphatically. "It wasn't a conscious decision. If I would've thought about it, I would've saved my own ass first."

"Doesn't sound like it," she said. "Because you did the same thing today. You didn't *save your own ass* today."

"Leo was closer," I tried to explain. "I wasn't sure which way to go, and—"

"Bullshit," she said, coming at me. I held back a yelp as she wrapped her arms tightly around me, overlapping against my sore back. "You protected him when he couldn't protect himself," she whispered into my ear. "*Thank you, sissy.* You saved him for me."

Closing my eyes, I let go of Mark and held her against me, tucking my face into her shoulder. She smelled familiar, like family. Like *Lily*.

"I really didn't mean to," I whispered back, soaking up the feeling of my sister's hair against my face, her head resting against mine.

"It doesn't matter," she said, one of her hands lifting to smooth the hair down the back of my head. "You still did it."

We held each other quietly for a moment. It was the first time in years that I'd had any physical contact with my little sister that didn't feel forced. You don't realize how important that is, or at least I hadn't, not until it was gone.

"Well," I said, pulling back as I got myself under control. We had an audience, and as much as I liked the fact that she'd hugged me, their eyes felt like they were burning holes in my skin like tiny lasers.

"The doctors say he'll be okay," Lily said, stepping away slightly to give me the space I desperately needed. "As long as he doesn't get a really nasty infection. They have to do skin grafts, though, and try to fix his hand and wrist. They think he must have reached out to break his fall then the bike went down, and he slid pretty far, which is why he—" she got choked up and cleared her throat. "That's why the road rash is so bad. But thank God, most of it is superficial."

"They're pretty sure they can save most of his fingers," my dad said, putting his arm around my shoulder, completely unconcerned with my need for personal space. "Except the pinky. Gonna be a long road."

"Good," I said, uncomfortable with the shift in conversation and the sudden welcome into their closed circle, but nodding anyway. "That's good. I'm glad he's going to be okay."

"Brenna and Mom are up there," Lily said. "In case they have any news, but he's in surgery now, so we're all just waiting. Everyone forced me out here to get some fresh air."

"I know you want to wait with 'em, baby," Mark said, lifting Olive's carrier a little. "But you need to get off your feet and Olive doesn't need to spend the night in the hospital."

"Okay," I said, relieved that he'd given me an out. If Lily needed me, I'd be there absolutely, but Jesus, I needed a little space. I needed some quiet. A few moments to let the day sink in. A little time to cuddle Olive and assure myself that things were different now, that we were both okay and safe.

I desperately wanted to climb into bed with Mark and the baby and shut out the world for a few days.

"Woody said you were shot today," Rose said uncomfortably as she stepped forward. "Are you okay?"

"Just sore," I replied. "I was wearing a vest."

"Lucky," she murmured.

"This one likes to be prepared," I replied, tilting my head toward Mark. "We'll see you later." I turned to Lily. "Keep me updated?"

"Of course," she said, her lips tilting up on one side in a half-smile.

"Get some rest," my dad said, kissing my forehead. "I'll see ya in the morning and we're gonna talk."

I nodded. It was time to come clean with my parents about what I'd gone through in the aftermath of the shooting all those years ago.

I didn't meet anyone's eyes as Mark turned me around and led us away, so I was surprised at the pair of black boots that stood between me and the parking lot. I looked up to find Dragon standing in the middle of the sidewalk.

"They might not have known," he said, jerking his head toward Lily, "but I saw what you did today."

I nodded jerkily, the pain in his eyes making my stomach twist.

His hands came up and cupped each side of my head gently, almost reverently. "I owe ya, sweetheart."

"No, you don't," I choked out.

"It's a debt I'll never be able to repay," he said, ignoring my words. "You saved my boy."

"They might've left him alone," I argued reasonably. "He was already down."

"Guess we'll never know," he said, just as reasonably. "But the intention was there."

"I didn't think about it—" I replied, frustrated. Why was no one listening to me? I hadn't made some grand decision to save poor Leo.

Dragon leaned down so we were eye-to-eye. "Fact that ya did it without thinkin' doesn't make it less brave," he said seriously, tightening his grip. "It means that the core of ya, the part of ya that reacts on instinct, protects others before yourself. That ain't nothin' to brush off. I know men I've bled beside for years that can't say that."

"I'm glad he's going to be okay," I whispered back.

"I'm glad both of ya will," he whispered back. He leaned forward slowly and pressed his lips to my forehead, holding them there for a moment before letting me go. He looked at Mark. "Go put your woman to bed, Woody," he ordered. "She looks like she's about to fall over."

"I'm on it," Mark said.

I stumbled along beside him, trying to understand the weird shift that had happened. For years, I would've done anything to make people look at me the way they were now, but for some reason, now that I had it, it just felt wrong. Everything felt mixed up.

"Climb in," Mark said as he opened my door for me. "Get comfortable. If you fall asleep on the way, I'll carry you inside."

"There's no way I'll fall asleep," I replied, still trying to figure out what happened back there.

"We'll see," he said in amusement before shutting my door.

I waited while he put Olive back inside and climbed into the truck beside me. His hand came out to rest on my thigh as he backed out of the parking spot, and stayed there as we drove away from the hospital. Then, as if I'd finally run out of batteries, my eyes grew too heavy to keep open and I passed out.

★ ★ ★

"You scared the shit outta me yesterday," Mark said into my ear just as the sky outside started to lighten. I wasn't sure what had woken us up, but I'd felt the moment his breathing had changed. His hand slid up my torso until it rested at the base of my throat. "Why the fuck would you do that?"

"I don't know," I replied honestly, staring at Olive's sleeping face. "As soon as Drake started to fall, I just knew I had to move."

"We had it covered, Cec," he said in frustration. "You should've stayed in the house. What the fuck were you thinkin'?"

"I couldn't let him do that," I said softly.

"Who?" he asked, leaning up on his elbow to look at my face. "Warren?"

"No," I said, turning a little so we were face-to-face. "Dragon. I couldn't let him make the choice between me and Leo."

"Were you afraid he'd hand you over?" Mark asked, leaning forward, his eyebrows raised in surprise. "Baby, you know I'd never let that happen."

"No," I said again, shaking my head. My heart started pounding as I remembered the moment. "No, I was afraid he wouldn't."

Mark closed his eyes in understanding and let out a long breath. "Baby," he whispered.

"He's been through enough," I said. I swallowed, trying to dislodge the lump in my throat. "Plus, you know, it wouldn't have worked out for me, either. I'd never be able to show my face around here if that happened."

Mark scoffed. "You're full of shit," he said, opening his eyes to grin at me. "That shit didn't even cross your mind."

"Well, maybe not *then*," I conceded. "But I've thought about it since."

Mark laughed quietly. "You can't keep doin' shit like that," he said, his expression growing serious. "You've got responsibilities now. You know you're about to do somethin' that could get you hurt, take five seconds to think it over, yeah? Fuck, I about shit myself yesterday."

"You're kidding, right?" I said, wrinkling my nose at him. "From this point forward, the only thing you'll have to worry about is me twisting my ankle on the curb at the grocery store."

"Oh, yeah?" he said, his lips twitching.

I relaxed into the pillow we shared. "Yeah," I said with a sigh. "You know, my life was normal in San Diego. Nothing ever happened. I even paid my taxes."

"Well, holy shit," he said. "Better not tell Casper."

I laughed. "Poor Dad," I mused. "He's too intelligent for his own good. Someday all those back taxes are going to catch up to him."

"*I'm not payin' into some greedy politician's pocket,*" Mark said, mimicking my dad's voice.

"*Or the fuckin' lobbyists they pay off to get 'em elected,*" I mimicked, too.

Mark laid back down and used his chin to move the hair away from my neck, so he could kiss me there.

"You wanna stay here?" he asked quietly, pulling me snug against him.

"In Eugene?" I reached out to lay my hand lightly on Olive's chest. "Or in the clubhouse? Because I'd seriously like to get out of here."

"In Eugene," he clarified.

I thought about it before answering. I'd made a life in San Diego. I had friends there—not close ones, but friends all the same. I liked my neighbors and my condo. I knew the grocery store near my place like the back of my hand. Plus, there were a hundred beaches to go to. Restaurants with authentic food from all over the world. Sunshine all year round.

"Yeah," I said finally, thinking about the way my mom bounced Olive as she walked her around, showing her off. "Yeah, I'd like to stay."

"Okay, baby," he said simply.

"What about you?" I asked nervously. "You have a life down there, too. You own a house and your job is there."

"I go where you go, remember?" he said, kissing my neck again. "We'll figure it out."

"Seriously?" I tried to turn my head toward him, but he blocked it with his chin, keeping me in place.

"I can live anywhere," he said with a small shrug. "I'll sell the house and we can figure it out from there."

"What about your job?"

Mark was quiet for a while, long enough for my fingers to unconsciously start rubbing along the chapped skin of my lower lip.

"I can work from anywhere," he said finally, reaching up to grab my hand and slide his fingers between mine. "But I don't know. Not sure I wanna be gone for months at a time."

"You're gone for months at a time?" I asked, my stomach sinking. I'd just gotten him back, and that sounded like torture.

"Yeah," he whispered. "And I'm thinkin' that wouldn't work for either of us."

A quiet knock on the bedroom door interrupted our conversation, and Mark slid off the bed to answer it.

"What's up?" he asked, keeping his voice down.

"I apologize for the interruption," Wilson replied, his voice equally quiet. "I have a flight in a couple hours, and I'd like to speak to you before I leave."

"Alright," Mark said. "Let me get dressed."

The door closed again, and I rolled to my back to watch as Mark pulled on his clothes.

"He sounds—" I searched for the right word.

"Off," Mark supplied. "Yeah, I know." He came to me and kissed me, the soft peck turning naturally into a deep, satisfying tangle of lips and tongues. "I'll be back in a bit. Try to get some more sleep."

He left and I sighed, staring at the ceiling. There was no way in hell I'd be able to fall back asleep.

Ten minutes later, there was another knock on the door, and I knew who it was just by the sound of the knuckles hitting the wood. How many times had I heard that exact cadence? More times than I could count. I pulled on my clothes and took a deep breath as I opened the door.

"You were shot?" my mom said, staring at me in confusion, her face tear streaked. "Why the fuck wouldn't you tell me? I'm your *mother*."

"Come in," I said quietly, glancing at Olive as I moved back into the room.

My mom followed me inside with my dad right behind her. As soon as he'd closed the door, I sat on the edge of the bed, my hands clenched together in my lap.

"Things were really bad," I said, lifting my hand to stop my mom as she started to interrupt. "Things were really bad," I said again. "And I didn't want to make things worse for you."

"Bumblebee," my dad said, his voice full of censure. "It doesn't matter how tough shit is, you can always tell us anythin'."

"How did I miss it?" my mom said, still completely bewildered. "How did I not know?"

"I made sure you didn't," I replied. I swallowed hard. "It felt—" I searched for the right words. "inconsequential, compared to everything else."

"That's bullshit," my mom said. "Jesus, CeeCee. How bad was it?"

"It was just a scratch," I replied, reaching up to run my hand over the scar through my t-shirt. "I put a couple Band-Aids on it and it was fine."

My dad ran his hands down his face, pressing his fingers into his eye sockets in frustration or disappointment—maybe both. "We fucked up," he said, his voice strained.

"I didn't want you to know," I reminded him. "And I was old enough to hide it. I felt guilty that it was even there—it would've been a hundred times worse if someone had noticed I was hurt and made a big deal about it."

"Why in God's name would you feel guilty?" my mom said in confusion.

"Because I thought I'd saved Lily," I said, the words burning my throat. "I didn't realize I had Rose until we were behind the tree, and by then I couldn't move. I couldn't get to her."

My dad made an inarticulate sound and turned his back to us, breathing heavily.

"Lily was across the yard," my mom said, her voice barely above a whisper. "I couldn't get to her, either."

"I know."

We were quiet for a few moments, the room thrumming with emotion.

"Your grandparents took care of Lily," my dad said, breaking the silence. He turned to face us. "I used to feel guilty about that, too. Couldn't get to them. Couldn't get to her. Couldn't do a damn thing fast enough for it to matter."

"Cody," my mom breathed.

"Then I realized somethin.' Feelin' guilt, like I shoulda been the one to protect them, was disrespectful to the sacrifice that Gram and Slider and Vera made. 'Cause that's exactly what it was. A sacrifice."

I nodded, my nose beginning to sting.

"You saved your cousin," he said, holding my gaze. "You were in exactly the right place and you saved exactly the right person. Your uncle and aunt woulda lost two children that day if you hadn't done what you did."

"I didn't see it that way," I said, blinking back tears and spreading my hands out, palms up. "All I could see was Lily, struggling to make her way around the house, bumping into things and crying."

"That's all we saw, too," my mom said, her eyes welling up. "I'm so sorry, baby."

"It's okay," I replied hoarsely. It was odd, but that simple acknowledgement and apology seemed to soothe the resentment that I'd carried around silently for years. "None of us knew how to handle it."

"We were the parents," my dad said. "We shoulda done better."

I shrugged. "You did the best you could."

I'd begun to understand just how easy it would be to get the parenting thing wrong sometimes—especially when things got overwhelming. Olive didn't do anything but eat, sleep and poop, and I was still pretty sure that I was messing things up.

"Is that why you left?" my mom asked, the question dropping like an anvil in the center of the room. "Did you hate us?"

The lie was on the tip of my tongue, but as I looked between my parents, I knew that lying wouldn't be fair to any of us.

"Partly," I replied, making her wince with regret. "But that wasn't the only reason. I didn't like *myself*," I said honestly. "I didn't like who I'd become, and I couldn't seem to change anything when everyone here looked at me the same way no matter what I did."

"We saw the way you struggled," my dad said quietly. "We just had no clue how to help ya."

"Moving away was one of the best decisions I ever made," I replied, sending him a small smile. "I got to reinvent myself somewhere new, away from all the memories of the shooting and the aftermath and Mark."

"If you were trying to get away from Woody, San Diego was a surprising choice," my mom said, wiping her face as she huffed out a laugh.

"Yeah," I looked down at my hands and deliberately relaxed them. "I guess part of me was always waiting for him to come back. Knowing that we were in the same city made that seem possible, even if we never saw each other."

"C'mere," my dad said, gesturing with his hands.

I stood and stepped forward, and his arms gently encircled me, holding me against his chest.

"I'm so proud of you, Bumblebee," he said, whispering into my ear. "You know that? I'm so sorry for not bein' who you needed me to be back then, but I can't say I'm sorry about the woman you are now. You're a fuckin' force of nature, just like your mother."

"Love you, too, Dad," I replied, pressing my forehead against the cool leather of his cut as tears ran down my face. I'd waited longer than I cared to admit to hear him say he was proud of me and mean it. The surprising thing about it was that he'd said it like it had always been true.

"My turn," my mom said, worming her way between us. As she wrapped her arms around my shoulders and bumped my dad out of the way with her hip, I laughed. "I guess we're a family that hugs it out now. Like those fucking Hallmark movies that Callie watches."

"You know you watch them with her," I teased, relaxing against her.

"Lies," she countered, giving me a gentle squeeze. "I fucked up with you," she said with a sigh. "In most ways, you've always been our first. Cam came along fully formed, but you were different. You needed me in ways that he didn't, and I think I might have lost sight of that. I'm sorry, baby. More sorry than you'll ever know."

"Hey, at least with Charlie you have it all figured out," I joked, sniffling.

"Please," my mom replied, leaning back to meet my gaze. "We were so tired by the time she got here that the child is practically feral."

"You know she drops f-bombs like she's twenty-four?" I asked, grinning.

"If that's the worst of it, I'll count myself lucky," my mom mused, her eyes twinkling.

"Hey," my dad cooed as he moved around us. "Look who's awake. Hi, princess."

As my dad lifted Olive off the bed and smiled goofily at her, a sense of contentment settled deep into my bones.

Chapter 26

MARK

"I'M LEAVING," WILSON said the moment I reached the table where my team was seated.

"Yeah, you said that," I replied, accepting a hot cup of coffee from Forrest.

"Let me clarify," Wilson said. "I'm leaving the team."

"Say what?" Eli sputtered.

"I find myself with responsibilities that interfere with my ability to affectively continue as a member of this team," he said stiffly.

"Who'd you get pregnant?" Josiah asked, jokingly.

"No one," Wilson replied instantly.

"It has to be a woman," Lu mused, watching Wilson like a bug under a microscope. "It's always a woman." Her face morphed from concentration to surprise. "It's that militia girl."

"Her name is Kaley Campbell," Wilson said tightly.

"Why do you think you need to leave the team?" Forrest asked.

"I will not be able to focus on my responsibilities," Wilson replied uncomfortably. "I find that my attention is fixed elsewhere."

"She in trouble?" I asked, dropping into a seat. Well, fuck. I was wondering how I would tell the team that I was out, and now it was going to be a hell of a lot harder with Wilson gone, too.

"Currently, no," Wilson said. "However, history has shown that she will be again."

"And you're going to protect her," Ephraim said softly.

"Yes," Wilson said. It was said firmly, simply, with zero hesitation.

"I'm out, too," I said with a sigh, figuring I might as well get it out on the table now, while we were all in one place. "Same reason, mostly. I think Cecilia's hit her quota for trouble, but I gotta be honest—I'm done spending my time overseas takin' care of people I don't know now that I've got people here that need me."

"You sure?" Forrest asked.

"Not interested in spendin' months away," I replied. "I've been without her for long enough."

"Yeah, you have," Lu said, nodding. I looked at her in surprise. "What?" she said. "People around here talk."

"Fuck," Ephraim said, looking around the group in confusion. "You mean we're gonna have to break in two new members?"

"Three," Eli said quietly.

"Oh, for fuck's sake," Josiah spat. "What now?"

"The militia's got women and children trapped on that property," Eli said, crossing his arms over his chest.

"What, you're going to liberate them?" Josiah asked incredulously.

"I'm going to do something," Eli said. "Not sure how that'll play out yet." He looked at Wilson. "You need help, I'm there."

"Jesus," Ephraim muttered. "There's only four of us left?"

We all looked at each other.

"I'm out, too," Lu said, her words soft. She spread her hands out, palms up. "I don't have it in me to start again with a new team. I've got a shit ton saved up—I'll figure out something else."

Josiah leaned forward dramatically and smacked his head against the table in front of him.

"Goddamn it," Ephraim said with a sigh. He pointed to Forrest. "You're out, too. I can see it on your face."

"Wilson's gonna need the help," Forrest replied.

"He's a full-grown man," Josiah argued.

"And so are you," Forrest said calmly. "But you're the one who seems to be throwing the fit here."

"I'm not throwing a fit," he spit back. He leaned back in his chair and ran the fingers of both hands through his hair, slicking it backward. Turning, he and Ephraim looked at each other, and the nerves that had been making my stomach churn suddenly settled. Before he spoke, I knew what he would say.

"Fine," he muttered. "Me and Eph will stay, too."

"Don't feel obligated to offer your assistance," Wilson replied stiffly.

"Shut it," Ephraim replied. "Not like we can go off and make loads of money while you're all here, savin' poor women and children from the big bad wolves."

"Way to make us feel like assholes," Josiah grumbled.

I let out a relieved laugh, and the rest of the table joined me.

"You are assholes," Lu pointed out, still laughing.

"We'd still be saving people," Josiah argued defensively. "We'd just be getting paid for it."

"Uh huh," Lu teased.

"Just to be clear, we're all out?" Forrest asked as we quieted down. He looked at each person one-by-one. "Well, shit. Boss man's not gonna be happy."

"Fuck him," Wilson said crisply, surprising all of us into another burst of hysterical laughter.

We discussed logistics, where we planned on making our home base and the possibility of starting our own company on a much smaller scale than the one we'd been working for. Forrest and I had been in the business the longest and had plenty of contacts to get us started if that's the direction we wanted to go. I think, when it came down to it, we were all just burned out on seeing death and destruction playing out before us day after day. We all needed a break, even Ephraim and Josiah, who were a lot more hesitant to stop doing the job they loved.

By the time we went our separate ways, we'd agreed to a two-month break—enough time to relocate to Oregon and catch our collective breath before moving on to something new. Of course, that break would be dependent on what happened with Wilson's woman—if anything went down in that situation, we all agreed to cut our hiatus short.

I was grinning as I walked back to our room. Wilson was so rigid and technical in everything from the way he packed his go-bag to the way he spoke that I couldn't imagine what kind of woman he'd be attracted to. I didn't know what Kaley Campbell had done to gain Wilson's loyalty so quickly, but I was looking forward to meeting the woman.

"Hey," Cecilia greeted softly as I opened the door. She was sitting up in bed feeding Olive, her hair tangled and her face lined with pillow marks. "Everything okay?"

"Everything's good, baby," I said, toeing off my untied boots. I crawled in beside her and leaned my back against the headboard. "Told the team I'm out."

"Oh, yeah?" She looked at me and wrinkled her nose. "Were they mad?"

I chuckled. "Nope," I replied, reaching out to rub her shoulders. "They're all out, too."

"What?"

"That's what Wilson wanted to talk to me about," I said. "He came here to quit in person. Turns out, that woman he's been talking to is too distracting for him to do his job effectively—his words."

"Whoa," she said, her eyes wide. "Did not see that coming."

I laughed and explained all the decisions we'd made at our little round table. It felt good to have something settled, even if it was work. Hell, I had to admit, at least to myself, that it wasn't *just* work. The team had become a kind of family—and I was happy as hell that we'd continue as one, even if the circumstances had changed.

"They all agreed to live here?" she said doubtfully when I was done. "In Eugene?"

"Well, Lu's from Seattle," I said, leaning my head back and rolling it to the side so I could look at her. She was so gorgeous, even with her leftover makeup and hair flying in every direction imaginable. "She's happy to come back to the cooler weather and be a bit closer to familiar landmarks, and Forrest was never happy in southern California—too many people. He stayed there because it was close to headquarters and to the rest of the team—but he didn't like it. Eli's in. Ephraim and Josiah don't give a shit where they're livin'. I think they moved around a lot as kids, so that's what they're used to. And Wilson—" I shrugged.

"He's happy to be wherever the woman is," Cec said, a small smile playing around her lips.

"Pretty much," I said with a sigh. "And her name is Kaley Campbell," I said, mimicking Wilson's tone.

"Oh, excuse me," she teased back. She looked down at Olive. "It's over, isn't it?"

"Yeah, baby," I replied, brushing her hair back from her cheek. "It's over. The Aces still need to deal with the militia. There's some shit that needs to be handled that didn't have dick to do with Drake Warren, but you and Olive are safe."

"Are you sure?" she asked. The tentative hope in her eyes made me want to shoot someone, and I grit my teeth at the knowledge that I hadn't been the one to kill Drake Warren. That particular honor had gone to Forrest, who'd shot Warren from the upstairs window the minute Cecilia had pulled away from him. Cecilia's bullet had probably been enough to kill Warren eventually, but Forrest hadn't waited to find out.

"Your pop will make sure that the militia knows you're under Aces' protection," I said, nodding. "But I doubt you'll need it. That was

Warren's vendetta—not theirs."

"So," she said, letting out a relieved breath, "this is what normal life feels like. I'd almost forgotten."

"Well, I don't know about normal," I replied, glancing around the room. "You're living in a motorcycle clubhouse."

Cecilia elbowed me in the side. "You know what I mean."

"Yeah, I do," I said, leaning forward to kiss her. I pulled away, but not far. "We can start looking for a place today, if you want. Check the listings, get a feel for what you want."

"I already know what I want," she said, giving me a lopsided smile.

"Oh, yeah? What's that?"

"You're going to think I'm crazy," she mumbled, looking down in embarrassment.

"Why?" I hid a smile as she shifted uncomfortably. "Why am I going to think you're crazy?"

"The people next to my parents are selling their property," she said so fast that the words all mashed together. "I saw the sign as we drove past yesterday."

"You were payin' attention to for sale signs?" I asked in surprise.

"I was trying to keep myself calm," she replied defensively. "And I saw it and thought about how much I always loved that house and the orchard they have out back. Plus, there's a pond that we used to sneak over to swim in."

"Why would I think that's crazy?" I asked in amusement, everything inside me relaxing at the excited way she described the place.

"It's next to my parents'," she replied, drawing the words out as she looked at me expectantly.

"Oh, hell," I muttered, the full picture sinking in.

★ ★ ★

"YOU READY?" CASPER asked, his eyes crinkling as I slid on a helmet.

"You could enjoy this a bit less," I shot back. "I don't know why you won't let me take the truck."

"We're goin' in on bikes," he replied easily. "You forget how to ride?"

"You know I've got a bike in California," I bit out, looking at the bike I was using. It was a piece of shit, no way around it. The thing was a restoration project of Grease's and I seriously doubted its capabilities of getting me to the Free America Militia compound and back.

"Then this should do you fine," Casper said as Grease strode up to stand beside him, both of them looking the bike over.

"That's gonna be a fine piece of machinery," Grease said with a sigh.

"It's a piece of something," I muttered under my breath.

"What's that?" Grease asked. He was failing to hide the amusement in his expression.

"Is this some type of initiation or something?" I asked. "Because I've already dealt with this shit before when I was sixteen."

"Think of it as a refresher course," Grease replied.

"I don't need a fuckin' refresher course."

"We'll see," Casper mused, glancing at Grease with a grin. He reached up and scratched his cheek, flexing his hand as he dropped it. He hadn't said much when the highest ranking members of the Oregon Aces' chapter had made a quick trip to Sacramento, but I'd known what happened when he'd come back with hands so swollen they'd resembled boxing gloves. I hadn't been a part of that trip because I wasn't a member of the Aces, but I'd been filled in enough to know that the leak in their organization had been taken care of. If I'd needed proof, all I'd had to do was look at Casper's broken fingers to know that the man had gotten what was coming to him. If I knew the men that had raised me, he'd wished he was dead long before he actually was.

As Casper climbed on his bike and pulled on a pair of gloves, I grimaced. The thought of riding with hands that messed up sounded like torture, but Casper didn't even seem to notice it. The man was unnaturally calm.

A few minutes later, I followed the group of bikes off the Aces' forecourt headed south. Nearly the entire club was headed to the FAM compound in a show of force that would make any sane person shit themselves. Unfortunately, I wasn't sure how sane a bunch of skinhead doomsday preppers were.

Leo was still in the hospital, but from everything we'd heard, he was getting better. The skin grafts were doing well, and they'd only had to amputate his pinky and his ring finger at the top knuckle. He'd still be able to ride, which had been the biggest worry after we'd known he would live.

Cecilia and I hadn't been back to the hospital since that first night. I didn't have any reason to go, and though she knew she'd be welcome, she chose not to go, either. She still didn't feel comfortable with the situation, even if some of the Aces thought she'd been redeemed.

The idea that she'd needed to be redeemed still pissed me off, but I kept it to myself. I wasn't about to make things harder for her than I had to, and if that meant keeping my mouth shut—even to her—that's what I'd do. She was staying close to our room, only venturing out to eat or spend time with her parents, and I was anxious to get us out of the clubhouse and into something permanent.

I watched grimly as Eli passed me on Tommy's spare bike. Asshole. I knew there were other bikes that I could've ridden, but Grease and Casper seemed to be trying to make a point with the piece of shit that was currently shaking so hard it made my teeth rattle.

The ride was frigid as fuck, and by the time we made it to the large metal gate outside the militia compound, my hands, face and ass were all numb. I really hoped I wouldn't have to draw my weapon because I wasn't even sure I could.

"Blow the gate," Dragon ordered as the bikes idled.

I watched, impressed, as Tommy laid a charge and cleanly blew the lock off the gate with minimal damage to the actual gate.

I kept my head on a swivel as we rode up the paved driveway in a massive column three bikes wide, but nothing was moving. The place was silent, which was seriously surprising considering the amount of people that we expected to be on the property. As we reached a cluster of large buildings, the hairs on the back of my neck bristled, and I glanced to my left where Eli was scanning our surroundings, deep in concentration.

We called Josiah the architect, because he had the uncanny ability to look at a building and know with surprising accuracy where the entry points were, and approximate dimensions of the rooms inside. For whatever reason, he could read buildings like they were people. For this part of the mission, though, we'd needed someone else to get the lay of the land, someone who could take it all in—the landscape, the buildings, the vehicles, anything relevant—and like Wilson, Eli had a photographic memory.

We stopped in front of the largest building that seemed to be the center of everything just as five men came strolling out the front door, carrying shotguns. It was hard not to roll my eyes at their posturing. I was pretty sure that they didn't have anyone in the woods around us, but even if they did try some shit, there was no way any of the militia would make it out alive. Releasing the handlebars of the bike, I flexed my fingers as Dragon, Casper, and Grease finished what we'd come to do.

"What do you want?" the largest man asked. He was sporting a bald head that was too shiny to be shaved and a goatee that highlighted the jowls on each side of his face. The guy was massive. I couldn't help but think he'd be an easy fucking target.

"You know who we are," Dragon said calmly. "And we know what you've done."

"We haven't done shit," a scrawnier guy spat, making the fat man signal with his hand to quiet him.

"Man, we know you took our truck," Grease said in disgust. "Don't be a fuckin' moron."

The fat man looked across the sea of bikes.

"You here to collect?" he asked, trying and failing to hide his fear. I could practically smell the sour stench of nervous sweat. "I wasn't in charge then."

"Nah," Grease said. "Consider it paid in full."

"What?" the fat man replied in confusion. If anything, he seemed even more afraid. God, this was a waste of fucking time and all of us knew it. Without Warren at the helm, these men were a bunch of pussies that didn't even guard their gate.

I watched as Casper turned and pulled a game bag out of his saddlebags. He turned back toward the men, and with a flick of his wrist, emptied the bag.

One of the men on the porch started to wretch as Drake Warren's rotting head rolled a few feet over the dirt before stopping face up. It was almost poetic.

"This is what happens when you come after one of ours," Dragon said flatly. "In the future, you even hear our name whispered, you walk the other way."

"We can do that," the fat man said quickly, nodding his head.

"The baby and her mother are under my protection," Dragon said, as if the man hadn't even spoken.

"What?" Fat Man blustered.

"Under my protection," Dragon reiterated. He looked at each man, one by one, until they'd all nodded that they understood him.

And just like that, Cecilia's troubles were finally over.

As we started up the bikes again, the sound like the roar of a massive ocean wave, I looked up at the second story of the building and jerked as I noticed all the young faces peering out the windows.

"Eli," I said quietly.

"I see 'em," he replied. "Has to be at least twenty."

It went against everything in my gut to turn and ride away, but that was exactly what we did. We weren't there on a rescue mission, and even if we had been, we didn't have anywhere for those kids and their mothers to go. They'd have to wait, even if the thought of it made bile rise up the back of my throat.

"Soon," I murmured underneath the bandana covering the lower half of my face.

I had somewhere else to be.

Chapter 27

CECILIA

MARK WAS SURE that the Aces' trip south to deal with the militia would go off without a hitch, but I still sat up the entire night worrying. I was getting restless in the clubhouse, the constant flow of people in and out left me struggling for some peace and quiet, and that night wasn't any different. If anything, the place was even noisier with the guys gone because most of the women in my family were camped out, waiting for their fellas to return. I could hear their voices through the wall.

After nursing Olive and laying her back down to sleep, I carefully got off the bed and slipped my shoes on. Earlier in the night, I'd stayed in our room during dinner, assuming that I could go out to get some food after everyone was gone. Unfortunately, I didn't think any of them had left.

The sound of voices and laughter greeted me as I walked into the hallway, leaving the bedroom door cracked so I could hear Olive if she woke up. Smoothing down my hair, I strode forward confidently, then froze in the archway between the hall and the main room.

My mother was dancing on the bar next to Tommy's wife Heather, which wasn't super out of character for either of them, but it was a struggle not to laugh and announce my presence because Heather was trying to teach my mom some kind of move that even I hadn't seen before, and my mom was *not* getting it.

"I think you're doing it wrong," my mom said, shaking her head at

Heather.

"I'm not doing it wrong," Heather replied in exasperation. "I'm trying to show *you* how to do it. Look—" She swiveled her hips in some pattern that I couldn't really figure out, but was impressive. Heather had moves, even when she was sober.

"I could do that," Rose said, pointing.

"Don't," Mack said with a laugh, raising his beer to his lips. "I'm not watchin' you do it while I'm sittin' in the same room as your mother."

"I'll wait until we get home," Rose teased, laughing as he reached over and slapped her ass.

"Maybe shift onto the other foot?" Aunt Callie called to my mom, ignoring her daughter and Mack.

"Shifting isn't going to help," my mom argued, waving Aunt Callie off.

I watched as Aunt Callie's expression grew irritated, and I smiled as she got to her feet. I'd been watching the two of them my entire life—the way they played off of each other, supported each other without reservation, even if they knew the other one was wrong, and loved each other as much, if not more, than they loved their spouses—and I knew that Aunt Callie was about to school my mom.

"Like this," Aunt Callie said in exasperation, copying Heather's moves almost exactly.

"Oh, come on," Rose complained, covering her eyes as Lily whooped in encouragement.

"I don't think I should be seeing this," Molly said, her eyes widening. She was listing to the side a little and braced her elbow against the table. "You're like my *mother*."

My mom hooted. "Grease is gonna loooooove that," she said in glee.

"Get off the bar," Aunt Callie shot back, picking up her drink.

"You're gonna fall and break your hip, and I'm not wiping your ass for you when you do."

"Lies," my mom countered, hopping off the bar with the agility of someone far younger. Even watching her do it made *my* joints ache. She laughed. "You'd wipe my ass."

"Can we not talk about wiping asses?" Heather asked, climbing down much slower.

"Why?" my mom said, turning to look at Heather. "You have some problem with poop?"

Heather pressed her lips together firmly.

"Is it the smell?" my mom asked contemplatively. "Or the consistency? I mean, I'm regular, so—"

My hiding spot was blown as Heather raced past me toward the bathroom.

"Hey, what are you doing over there?" Molly asked. "Come sit down, we've got plenty of seats." She giggled.

I had to admit, it was impossible not to like Molly, especially when she'd been drinking.

"You guys are loud," I said as I moved toward them. "Does no one sleep around here?"

"I don't know what I did wrong," my mom said, throwing her arm around my shoulders as I reached her. "Cecilia goes to bed at nine and this one—" she pointed jokingly at Lily, swirling her finger in a circle. "Won't even have a beer with me."

"You know I have to be able to drive if Poet calls from the hospital," Lily said, rolling her eyes.

"She's a lightweight," my mom said in exasperation. "How did this happen?"

Aunt Callie laughed. "How did you end up with the good kids and I ended up with the delinquents? It makes zero sense."

"*Hey,*" Rose cried. "One of your delinquents is sitting right here."

"Speaking of kids—ours are fine, but we owe Amy a spa day for keeping them," Trix said as she came into the room with Brenna.

"Got a hang up from Dragon. They're less than an hour out," Brenna added.

"You got that from a hang up?" Molly asked in confusion.

"We have a system," Brenna replied with a smile.

"Oh," Molly breathed. "That's smart."

"We've been together a long time," Brenna said indulgently.

"Hell, I can tell what Cody needs by the way he walks," my mom said with a shrug.

"Don't," me and Lily said at the same time. Lily slapped her hands over her ears.

My mom laughed like a hyena.

"I don't get it," Molly said. As my mom's insinuation sunk in, she turned a horrified shade of red. "Oh."

"How're you doing?" Brenna asked me as my mom moved away, saying something to Aunt Callie.

"I'm okay," I said, shooting her a smile.

"Yeah?" she asked, tilting her head a little as she looked at me. "You sure?"

"I'm sure," I replied, growing a little uncomfortable with the scrutiny.

She jerked her head a little toward the bar and I followed her over. As we sat down on the old barstools, we turned to face the group.

"The minute we turn our backs to them, they'll think we're talking about something interesting," she said dryly. "If we face them, they won't even pay attention."

I laughed at the accuracy of her statement.

"I heard what you did for Leo," she said, and I groaned silently. I didn't want to talk about it or even think about it ever again.

"I'm glad he's going to be okay," I replied.

"You haven't been to the hospital," she said.

"I'm not your son's favorite person," I explained simply.

Brenna laughed, the sound low. "You have zero idea of the affect you have on people," she said. "It's a trip."

"I've got a pretty good idea," I replied. "I'm one conversation away from being on the outs again."

"You really think that?" she asked in surprise. "You do. Huh."

I didn't respond as I watched Heather join the group again, her face no longer pale and sweaty. She laughed at something Molly said and urged her to her feet. They danced across the room.

"How much do you know about when I came home?" Brenna asked. "I'm sure you've heard the story."

"You were the returning princess," I said, turning my head to look at her profile. Her hair was curly and wild, and she'd pulled it back into a high ponytail, making her look at least twenty years younger than she was.

"Not hardly," Brenna replied. "I came home with Trix, who Dragon hadn't even known existed, and I brought back a load of trouble with me. Trouble that got your dad shot."

"I know about that," I said.

"Well, you probably don't know that your Grandpa Slider pretty much told me that if I chose to leave the club's property, I was on my own against anyone that held a grudge against the club," she said quietly. "And that I wouldn't be allowed to take Trix with me."

"What?" I said, jerking in surprise. I couldn't even contemplate that kind of threat. "He did what?"

"Oh, yeah," she said with a huff. "Pop sided with him, too. With the club. God, I felt betrayed."

"With good reason," I blurted.

"It took a while," she said, her eyes unfocused. "But I got it."

"I don't," I replied.

"I'd already taken off once and betrayed Dragon in the process," she said, looking at me. "They were saving me from myself, even if it didn't look that way at the time."

She seemed sure, so I didn't argue. It still sounded supremely fucked up to me. I'd kill anyone that tried to take Olive from me, and that included my dad. I couldn't even imagine my dad putting me in that position, though. I'd always considered his loyalty to me absolute—he may not always like me, but he'd never go against me.

"Leo's a lot like my pop," she said as we watched the shenanigans happening in the center of the room. "He's loyal to the extreme, but he also has very stubborn ideas about how things should go."

"Yeah."

"He doesn't hate you, CeeCee," she said quietly.

"He doesn't like me, either."

"He loves you," she said, and I scrunched up my face in horror, making her scoff. "Not like that, idiot. He's in love with your sister to the point of obsession. But you're family. You've always been family, and you'll always be family."

"I don't know about that."

"If he didn't consider you family, he wouldn't give a fuck what you did, or who you decided to be with," she pointed out. "He remembers how it was after Woody left you, and he's not going to forgive him for it—or agree with you going back to him."

"It's not his place to forgive, and I don't need his permission."

"I know," she said. "Give him some time. He'll see how the two of you are together and soften. He probably already has—which is why you should go see him."

"I don't mean to be rude," I replied, my lips twitching as my mom started dropping into a crouch and shaking her booty, "but I've got about all I can handle already. Leo's feelings are pretty low on my priority list."

"That's fair," she said, reaching out to pat my arm. "But you saved his life and you should give him the opportunity to thank you."

"I didn't save him," I said, my voice rising.

I was strung tight. Mark still wasn't back, and I was starting to worry. I'd been cooped up in the clubhouse longer than I wanted to think about. My hormones were still out of control. And even though people were being nice to me, I still didn't feel comfortable around any of them, knowing that, at any moment, I could say the wrong thing and suddenly be persona non-grata.

I didn't trust them, and it made every conversation I had become like some sort of minefield that I had to pick my way through. I finally snapped.

"It was my fault that Drake Warren was even there. I'm the reason Leo was run off the road. I'm the reason that he's in the hospital. So, stop saying that I saved him. I'm the one who got him hurt." By that point I was shouting, and the clubhouse grew silent around me as someone shut off the music.

"I'm the reason your dad was shot," Brenna said, yelling back at me. It startled me so much that I slid off the stool to my feet and backed up a step. The room was silent for a beat.

"I'm the reason my parents died," Aunt Callie said. "Your grandparents."

"I knew the man that was responsible for the shooting that killed our family," Trix said quietly. "The guys tried to keep it a secret, but I know."

"I almost got my children killed when I got into the car with a man I knew wasn't *right* and my son bore the scars of that for years," my mom said, her eyes pained as she watched me. "My daughter was shot, and *I didn't even notice.*"

"I kept it a secret when I knew my best friend was being hurt," Hawk said, pushing her blue hair away from her face. "And he died before I ever stood up for him."

"Not your fault," Aunt Callie said, shaking her head.

"I left my dad behind, knowing that the moment I did—he was dead," Molly said, all signs of drunkenness gone. "I still left."

"Shit, I dated a guy that betrayed the club, and when I was finally shot of him, he hired skinheads to torture and kill us," Rose spat, looking at Mack. "And because of that, Kara almost lost her dad."

"I made you do that," Mack said quietly. "You didn't have a choice."

"I had a choice," Rose replied guiltily.

Everything was silent as I took in the different guilty and regret-filled expressions in the room.

"Don't look at me. I'm an angel," Lily muttered, lightening the mood slightly. "I need a drink." She got up and headed toward the end of the bar.

"Bottom line," Rose said, looking at me. "All of us have been through some shit—and most of us know that we were at least partly responsible. You're not the only one, or even the most tragic. So stop lurking around the clubhouse and hiding in your room. The only person blaming you, is you."

"That's not true—"

Rose lifted her hand and made a flicking motion that irritated the shit out of me. "Emotions were high," she said in dismissal.

"Maybe if you weren't such a bitch all the time, I wouldn't have to hide out," I said flatly, surprising myself. I'd been so careful with my words since we'd come to Eugene. I should've known I'd blow it eventually.

Aunt Callie started to laugh. "Pot," she said to me, then swung her arm toward Rose with a flourish. "Meet Kettle."

Almost everyone laughed at that.

"Boys are home," Lily said from behind the bar. "I can hear them."

"Why do you still have bionic hearing?" I asked, spinning toward her. "Your eyesight is back, your hearing should go back to normal."

"I'm just more observant," she shot back, wiggling her head as she took a drink of her water. "And Olive's fine, by the way. I haven't heard her, even after your little shouting match with Brenna. Brave of you."

I looked over to see Brenna striding toward the front door. "It was an accident," I admitted.

"They're right, you know," Lily said. "All of us have done things we weren't proud of, or felt responsible for shit that happened. You don't hold the record on that."

"Fine," I mumbled. "I get it."

"I mean, you *were* still an asshole to me when we were younger. Remember when you threw that pen at my face?"

"When Leo was over?"

"Yeah," she said, rolling her eyes.

"I got into so much shit for that," I said. I thought back to that moment. I *had* been an asshole. I'd also been a stupid kid and so desperate for Lily to get better that I'd thought that if I could make her angry or startle her badly enough, her eyesight would instantly come back. She'd been so scared that she went blind, it made sense that the opposite could happen, right? My stomach burned at the memory. Explaining my motivation seemed pointless, I'd still been a jerk.

"Hey, baby," Mark said, finding me as the men funneled into the room. "Why are you still awake?"

"It's loud as hell here," I said, leaning into him as he wrapped his arms around my waist.

"You ready for bed now?" he asked.

"Sure."

"I'll see you tomorrow," Lily said, shooing me. "I'm going to get a couple hours of sleep before I head back to the hospital, but I'll see you at some point."

"He's really okay?" I asked, almost embarrassed to ask.

"He's going to be okay," she said, smiling softly as she reached out to squeeze my hand. "Just a few more scars to add to his collection."

I knew it was a massive understatement, but I was thankful for her reassurance anyway. I'd never wanted anything bad to happen to Leo, but it would've been so much worse now, when he held my baby sister's happiness in his hands. I smiled before turning to kiss Mark hello.

"How'd it go?" I asked as he towed us toward our room.

"Woulda felt better if the rest of the team was there to get a look at things," he said. "But it went fine."

"How long is Eli staying?" The rest of his team had headed out that morning to take care of things in San Diego, and I knew Eli was anxious to do the same. I was finding that Mark's friends weren't the most patient people when they had a plan in motion.

"He's leavin' tomorrow," he said with a sigh, stripping as we reached the doorway. He was down to nothing but his jeans in less than a minute. I checked on Olive, who was still completely passed out, before watching him slide the denim down his hips.

"When are you going to go?" I asked tentatively. I wasn't looking forward to being apart, even for as long as it took him to pack his things and put his house up for sale. There wasn't any question that Olive and I would stay in Eugene, though. I'd dragged her on enough road trips for a while, and we'd already agreed that Mark would go alone.

"Don't wanna think about that tonight," he said softly, reaching out to help me pull my shirt off. "Alright?"

"Fine with me," I said, raising my arms.

"You're so beautiful," he breathed. "Fuck, sorry my hands are so cold."

"Fine with me," I said again, smiling.

Mark laughed quietly. "Thought about you all day," he said as he finished pulling off my clothes. He knelt at my feet to take off my socks and help me step out of my pants and underwear. "Just like this."

"You thought about me naked?" I asked dubiously.

"I always think about you naked," he replied, running his hands up the backs of my thighs. "Its my favorite way to think about you."

"What was I doing while I was naked?" I asked teasingly.

"This," he said seriously. "Just this." He sighed and laid his forehead against the small pooch beneath my belly button that had refused to disappear, even though I'd lost all the baby weight. My body was never going to be the same, but I found that it didn't bother me that much.

"Well, that's not very imaginative," I said, running my hand through his hair.

"Doesn't need to be," he replied. "This is my happy place. Right here."

"I could probably make you happier," I mused, giggling as he tipped his head back and looked at me.

"Still too soon," he said. "I looked online."

I huffed out a laugh. "I don't know," I said, kneeling down with him, grateful for the quilt we'd left on the floor for Olive to lay on. "I'm feeling pretty good."

"Yeah?"

"Yeah." I leaned up and kissed the center of his throat. "Do you have any condoms?"

"Yep," he said instantly. "I got lube, too."

"Lube?" I sputtered, my eyes widening. "I wasn't offering you back door action."

Mark started laughing. It was the kind of laughter that was so hard and fast that it didn't even make any noise. His body shook with it.

"What?" I asked in confusion, laughing a little, too.

"I didn't get it for that," he wheezed. "I read that it might help, you know, when you get back in the saddle."

"What?" I asked, still staring at him.

"Breastfeeding," he said breathlessly. "And you know, the hormone shit."

"The hormone shit?" At this point, I knew what he was trying to say, but I got a small sliver of satisfaction watching him try to explain.

"You might be dryer than normal," he finally said in exasperation, clearing his throat uncomfortably. "And things might still be, you know, tender. So, lube. It's supposed to help."

My lips twitched.

"You knew that," he said flatly.

"It is seriously sweet that you actually searched the internet to see how to have sex with me," I said, fighting a smile. "Who said chivalry is dead?"

"You're an asshole," he said, grinning. "You know that?"

"I've heard that, yeah," I said.

Mark shook his head, his hands sliding up my back until they reached my head. Leaning forward, he kissed me, his lips pulling at mine. Knowing that we were actually going to have sex, well thought out and carefully planned by him, sex, made my hands shake. It had been so long.

"Hold that thought," he said, twisting to reach for his bag. A second later, he pulled out a small, wrinkled paper bag. "Condoms," he said, pulling out a box and handing it to me. "I'll get the lube ready."

I nodded and started tearing at the cardboard. I was nervous, and the situation wasn't helping. I shivered. Without his hands on me, I was acutely aware of the cool air around us and my lack of clothing.

"Hey," he said, gently pulling the box from my fingers. "Hey, no rush."

"I just thought—"

"When have I ever fucked you without playin' first?" he asked, raising one eyebrow. "Come here."

My nerves vanished as he pulled me against his chest, his hands sliding down my back until they gripped my ass. Lifting me a little, he tipped his head down to mine and kissed me slow and deep. It was languid and a little bit filthy, and I whimpered as he bit my bottom lip just hard enough to sting.

"Lay down," he said, his voice low.

I wasn't sure how long he explored my body, running his lips over my shoulders and down my arms, sliding his hands from the tips of my toes to the juncture of my thighs. I lost count of the number of love bites he left on my ribs and the bottom of my breasts and the insides of my legs. But, when he finally slid his long body up and my knees fell open to welcome him, I'd lost any reservation whatsoever.

I sucked in a quick breath as the cool lubricant landed on my skin, the sensation seriously erotic as he used his fingers to warm it, sliding it over my skin and finally pressing one, and then two fingers inside of me.

"Okay?" he asked, his nose touching mine.

"Yeah." Closing my eyes, I tipped my head back and relished the feeling. It had been years since anyone had been inside me, and nothing had even come close to the way Mark's hands felt on my body. He'd been the ruler against which everyone else had measured and come up short.

"I'll go slow," he said as he positioned his cock at my entrance. "Tell me if it hurts."

I nodded, unable to speak past the lump in my throat.

Sex had never been emotional for me, not even when Mark and I had been together before. It had been at times fun and passionate and angry, but I'd never had the urge to cry at the beauty of it. That changed as he slowly rocked, pressing a little further with each stroke, until he was fully seated inside me.

"Jesus," he said, pausing and dropping his head to my shoulder.

"You okay?"

"I'm okay," I replied, ignoring the slight twinge inside as my body adjusted.

"I love you," he said as he began to move again in slow, steady strokes.

I wrapped my legs around his waist and smoothed my hands over his hot skin, memorizing every ripple of muscle and bone. He didn't speed up or slow down, keeping that steady, even pace until he'd come.

It was exactly what I'd needed.

Quicker than I would've liked, he reached down to secure the condom and pulled out so gently that I sighed.

"You didn't come," he said, dropping the condom before leaning down on his elbow, the other hand reaching down between my legs. "Let's fix that."

It didn't take long before I was seeing stars.

★ ★ ★

"Come on," my mom said, waving her hand in a circular motion. "Let's go, let's go."

"I am," I griped, making sure my breast pads were in place. "My boobs are leaking."

"You're stalling," she argued.

"No, I'm not," I replied, stomping toward her. "I don't want the front of my shirt all sticky with breast milk."

I glared at a man staring at me. "Breast milk," I said succinctly as we passed.

"Stop terrorizing people," Mark said as he hefted Olive's car seat a little higher.

"He was staring."

"Who cares?" my mom replied, leading me down a long hallway.

I was honest enough with myself to admit that I wasn't exactly in the best mood. After spending the last half of the night wrapped up in Mark's arms, having more orgasms than I could count, my mom had woken all of us—including Olive—by pounding on the bedroom door. I wasn't sure why I'd agreed to go with her to the hospital, but I was seriously regretting the decision as we stopped outside a halfway open door.

"I'll keep Olive out here," my mom said, taking the car seat from Mark. "They're worried about infection in there, so no kids under fourteen."

"What kind of infection could a newborn spread?" I asked dubiously.

"Who knows?" she said with a shrug. "It's not my rule."

"Come on," Mark said, laying his hand on my lower back to lead me inside the room. "Knock, knock," he called. There was a curtain closed around the bed so we couldn't really see anything, but I could hear the TV playing low.

"Come on in," my sister's voice answered.

I braced myself as I pulled the curtain back, but what I saw wasn't as bad as I'd been envisioning. Lily sat next to Leo on the bed, not touching beyond their entwined fingers.

"Hey," Leo said gruffly, turning his head toward us.

He looked like a mummy. That was my first thought. His entire body not covered by the sheet was wrapped in white gauze. The only patches of skin visible were his throat, face, and the arm closest to Lily. I couldn't stop myself from looking down at the hand I knew was mangled, but it was wrapped in so much bandaging that it looked like a little club of fabric.

"How you feelin'?" Mark asked as we moved further into the room.

"High as a kite," Leo said with a small smile. "Ready to go home."

"You're not ready to go home," Lily countered.

"I'm ready," he said again.

They bickered like an old married couple. The sight soothed me somehow.

"Hospitals aren't my favorite place to be, either," Mark said in commiseration. "I like to hold my own dick when I piss."

"Amen," Leo said with a laugh. "They're at least letting me do that now." He looked at me. "How you doin'?"

"Me?" I asked in confusion. "I'm fine."

"Heard you were shot," Leo said, watching me. I looked at Lily. "She wasn't the one who told me," Leo said in amusement.

"I'm fine," I said again. "I was wearing a vest."

"She's still black and blue," Mark said, countering my words.

"It's a bruise," I muttered. "A freaking bruise."

Leo laughed. "Still can't handle people worryin' about you, huh?"

"There's nothing to worry about," I replied. "I'm fine. Everything is fine."

"I'm glad," he said.

"Me, too."

"I won't thank you for what you did," he said, his tone practically daring me to interrupt. "And I won't tell you that I remember when I felt you lay on top of me and cover my head with your arms."

I stopped breathing.

"I won't tell you that I was so out of it that, at first, I didn't realize what was happening, but I was scared as fuck once I figured it out, and the only thing that gave me any comfort was knowin' you were right there with me."

My nose stung.

"I also won't tell you that you didn't have to do that. That I would've gladly taken a bullet if it meant you got to go home to that sweet baby of yours."

I refused to blink as my eyes filled with tears.

"I won't tell you any of that because I know that you'll find some way to dismiss it, and I'm not in the mood," he said. He cleared his throat. "I will say that I'm glad your sister's got you back now and I hope you guys are stayin' local so I don't have to pay for tickets to San Diego every coupla months."

"We're stayin'," Mark said when I couldn't reply. "Cec has been eyeballin' that property down the road from Casper and Farrah's."

"I love that place," Lily said excitedly. "We used to sneak over to their pond to swim in the summer."

"Don't tell Mom I used to take you with me," I replied, finally able to speak past the tightness in my throat.

"I can hear you, dumbass," my mom said from the hallway.

"You have any idea what you wanna do with that massive shop?" Leo asked Mark.

"I've only seen pictures," Mark said, stepping over to a chair and pulling me onto his lap as he sat down. "Is it as big as it looks?"

"The thing is massive," Leo replied. "Used to keep horses, I think."

"Ooh, horses," I said dreamily.

"You gonna shovel shit?" Mark asked me. I wrinkled my nose. "That's what I thought."

"You could get goats," Lily said leaning forward a little. "Goats are so cute, and it's good for kids to have an animal." She looked sideways at Leo.

"I said we could discuss a dog once we move into a bigger place," he replied dryly.

"You can get a dog," Mark said to me.

"Thanks for the permission," I replied sarcastically.

Lily laughed at us.

The conversation went on like that for a while. Easy and simple as we talked about the house we were interested in. Leo and Lily were also looking for a place, but not seriously, not yet. Their ideas were mostly daydreams, but I liked listening to them explain what they wanted. The things that were important to them when it came to their home said a lot about them as a couple, and it was a little like a peek into their lives. It was comfortable in a way that I hadn't felt around my sister in a very long time.

By the time we left, I felt centered in a way that I also hadn't felt in a very long time.

"Glad you came?" my mom asked as we walked toward the exit of the hospital.

Mark coughed like he was choking and I stared at him in bewilderment.

"Jesus Christ," my mom complained, handing Mark the car seat. "Boys never grow up. They just get bigger."

Mark snickered.

"Are you serious right now?" I asked him, stopping in the middle of the walkway.

"I'm just happy," he said defensively, grinning at me. "Are you glad you came?"

"To the hospital?" I shot back in exasperation. "Yes. Last night? Not as much if you're going to act like a teenage boy the next day."

My mom cackled as I hurried toward her.

"You fell in love with me when I was a teenage boy," Mark reminded me as he slung his free arm over my shoulder. "Can't complain now."

"I thought you'd grow up," I joked back, smiling. His good mood was infectious and I couldn't keep up the attitude I'd been throwing his way.

"I did," he said, kissing the side of my head, "but some things never change."

I leaned into him and watched as my mom flipped off a car as it drove through the crosswalk.

"Thank God," I said, wrapping my arm around his waist. "I love you."

"Love you, too, baby."

Epilogue
CECILIA

"Do you remember when she threw up in that potted plant?" Trix asked, lounging back in a small, plastic pool that had seen better days. "She tried to say it was food poisoning."

"How many times did she try to blame it on a hangover?" Rose asked.

"More times than she should've," Molly said in exasperation. "Who tries to convince people they *are* drinking to excess when they're pregnant?"

"You realize this is my baby shower, right?" Heather said, throwing her arms up in the air. I grinned at her as she waddled toward us, her round belly highlighted by the bikini she was wearing. "I'm the guest of honor. Stop giving me shit. You know I was trying to figure out a way to tell Tommy before I told any of you."

"Normal people don't wait to tell their partner until they're too big to hide it," Trix said with a laugh.

"Only Tommy would be dense enough not to figure it out when his wife is puking five times a day and doesn't have a period," Rose joked.

"Only you would wear a thong bikini when you're pregnant," Lily said, shaking her head as Heather walked over to the table covered with party favor-sized sunblock and personal fans. Lily misted herself with a spray bottle of water and rubbed her own bare, rounded belly.

"You can borrow it if you want," Heather said easily.

"My boobs would never fit," Lily replied. "By the time I give birth, they're going to be the size of watermelons."

"Enjoy them while they last," I said, glancing down at my own string bikini. My boobs were still larger than normal, especially around the time Olive needed to eat, but they were nowhere near as big as when I'd been pregnant, or right after Olive was born.

"It takes all shapes and sizes," my mom called out from the towel where she was sunbathing. "This was really the best idea for a baby shower, you know? Just booze and sunshine and cake and presents. Every party should be like this."

"Every party *is* like this," my Aunt Callie countered. "Except for the cake and presents."

"I agree," Lily said to my mom. She pointed at me. "You and Rose need to take notes for mine."

"I love that you guys are so impressed by my poor party planning skills," Heather's sister Mel replied. "Maybe I should start my own company."

"Babies and Booze," my mom said.

"Drink and Deliver," Rose said.

"Ain't no party like a drunk baby party," I said with a chuckle.

"You guys are horrible," Molly said, fighting a smile. "Seriously."

"Don't worry," Rose replied. "The girls are in the house, so we're not setting a bad example."

"As if *this* conversation is what's going to set them on a bad path," Brenna joked dryly.

"Speaking of going down the wrong path," Mel said, looking around the group. "Who wants a drink?"

"Margarita," my mom called out waving her hand.

"Me, too, please," Molly added.

"Me three," Trix said.

Everyone called out their orders, but when Rose spoke, the entire group went silent.

"Do you have some bottled water?" Rose said nonchalantly.

Heather stopped rubbing sunblock on her leg. "You want water?"

"Why aren't you getting a margarita?" Molly asked suspiciously.

Trix splashed water at Rose with her foot. "You too good for tequila now?"

I looked over at my sister, who was wearing a huge, cheesy grin, then at Aunt Callie, who was fighting a smile.

"I only *joke* about drinking while pregnant," Rose said finally, her expression so happy that it took my breath away.

"Oh, my god!" Molly yelled, scrambling out of her lawn chair to rush toward Rose. "You're pregnant!"

I watched as everyone surrounded Rose, chattering excitedly as they asked her how far along she was and how she'd been feeling. I was on good terms with my cousin again, and I normally would've been right there with them, squealing and hugging and joining the merriment, but nausea kept me in my seat.

"Anything to drink?" Mel asked as she made her way to the back door.

"Just water, please," I said, giving her a smile.

Her expression grew knowing and she sent me a wink. "I'll church it up a bit with some ice and a glass—make sure to wince when you take the first drink." She jerked her head at the group of women. "They all know I buy shitty vodka."

I met my mom's eyes across the yard and she looked at me searchingly. She glanced down at my belly and back up to my face again.

I shrugged, unable to hide my grin.

Her mouth dropped open in shock.

Yeah, I hadn't been expecting it, either. I couldn't wait to tell Mark.

That year was what the Aces would later call *the baby boom*.

Acknowledgements

To the bloggers and readers who have made it possible for me to make a living doing something I love so much. I see you. I'll never stop being grateful and thanking you for your support.

To Mom and Dad – It's been a year, hasn't it? Geez Louise. Thank you for the endless cups of coffee, the long chats, the babysitting, and for just being you. You're the foundation beneath my feet and I couldn't do life without you.

To my kiddos – I know that parents aren't supposed to be best friends with their kids, but you're definitely my best friends. There's no one else I'd rather be stuck in the house with for months. You three are the coolest, smartest, kindest and funniest kids I know and I'll never forget how lucky I am to be your mom.

Sister – thanks for being a listening ear and the order to my chaos. We're two sides of the same coin, better together than we'd ever be apart.

Nikki – We did it again! I can never fully explain how much your input and opinion means to me, but I hope you know. I don't ever want to write without you at the other end of the phone, kicking my ass and telling me where I've veered off track.

1775 – Thank you for the laughs. The late night messages. The unwavering support through all life's ups and downs. We got this.

Toni – Peas and Carrots, dude. Always.

Letitia – I hope you know how awesome you are. I can be stressed as hell, rushing, and ask you for help at the last minute and all I have to do is give you a broad outline, and you bring the cover of my books to life quickly and beautifully every time. It's a joy to work with you.

Michelle, Pam and Beatrice – Thank you a million times for stepping into my online shoes and carrying the Aces reader group while I couldn't, posting discussions and games, and generally being ridiculously awesome. Your help is so invaluable and I'm so thankful that this book world brought you into my life.

Amber and Melissa – thank you for being my first readers every time I finish a book—as soon as I'm done editing you guys dive right in and give me feedback before anyone else, which gives me the confidence to actually put these books out into the world.